DRAGON'S RING

DRAGON'S RING

DAVE FREER

DRAGON'S RING

This is a work of fiction. All the characters and events portrayed in this book are fictional, and any resemblance to real people or incidents is purely coincidental.

A Baen Books Original

Baen Publishing Enterprises
P.O. Box 1403
Riverdale, NY 10471
www.baen.com

ISBN 13: 978-1-4391-3319-4

Cover art by Bob Eggleton

First printing, October 2009

Distributed by Simon & Schuster
1230 Avenue of the Americas
New York, NY 10020

Library of Congress Cataloging-in-Publication Data

Freer, Dave.
  Dragon's ring / Dave Freer.
      p. cm.
  ISBN-13: 978-1-4391-3319-4 (hc)
  ISBN-10: 1-4391-3319-0
  1. Magic—Fiction. I. Title.
  PR9369.3.F695D73 2009
  813'.54—dc22

                                                    2009017405

10 9 8 7 6 5 4 3 2 1

Pages by Joy Freeman (www.pagesbyjoy.com)
Printed in the United States of America

This one is for my sons, Paddy and James,
the two finest lads in my universe.
I hope it may give you even one thousandth
as much pride and joy as you have given to me.

══ Acknowledgements ══

This book owes its existence to my agent Mike Kabongo, and to editor extraordinaire Toni Weisskopf at Baen Books. My thanks to Artist Bob Eggleton for giving me a great cover, and to Jennie Faries and Carol Russo for fixing the last minute glitch with the name, which I appreciate ever so much.

My first readers: thank you, my friends, for putting up with erratic grammar and worse spelling and helping me chop the story out from the raw state, for seeing its potential in the rough, and for the constructive shredding. It's the cutter who turns the gemstone from a mere rock into a jewel.

And finally, thanks to my wife Barbara, who somehow copes with a husband whose head is often in another world entirely, and still does more for my writing than anyone else.

Characters

Actaeon   Centaur exile.

Belet   A king among the creatures of smokeless flame.

Brennarn   Dragon, ruler of Cark.

Breshy/Dvalinn   The leading artificer of the dvergar.

Díleas   Black and white sheepdog.

Finn/Fionn   Black dragon. (The word means "fair.")

Gywndar   Alv prince of Yenfar.

Groblek   Lord of the mountains. Possibly a mountain.

Haborym   A duke among the creatures of smokeless flame.

Hallgerd   Meb's stepmother.

Hrodenynbrys   Merrow and magical musician.

Hrolf   Meb's older step-brother, skipper of the fishing vessel.

Ixion   A centaur head of a phalanx.

Jakarin   Dragon who had lost her hoard. Friend of Myrcupa.

Justin   Scribe, petty thief, informer.

Keri   Innkeeper's daughter, Justin's lover.

Margetha   Chieftainess of the Merrow.

Meb/Anghared/ Scrap   Human magic worker.

Mikka   Meb's younger stepbrother. A fisherman.

Myrcupa   Dragon, nasty piece of work.

Leilin   Loftafar woman, seamstress.

Lyr   All sprites are called Lyr.

Motsognir   Elderly king of the dvergar.

Ragath   Alvar duke of Starsey.

Rennalinn   An alvar lord from Maygn Isle.

Tessara   Female dragon, much involved in the dragon sisterhood.

Vorlian   Dragon overlord of Starsey. A large powerful dragon.

Zuamar   Dragon, old, rich and powerful. Ruler of Yenfar.

═ Prologue ═

THE DRAGON FLEW ABOVE THE RAGE OF THE ELEMENTS. ABOVE THE tumultuous maelstrom of ocean swirling into the void. Above the sheet lightnings and vortexes of dark energies released as the tower fell, with the vast granite masonry shattering into swirling dust.

A fierce delight filled his dragonish heart as he looked down on it.

The narrow—and, to Fionn's strange vision—coruscating band of twisted and constrained elsewhere that was one of the seven anchors of the place of dragons, stretched. Torrents of energy, shimmering fountains of it, across all the spectra, crackled and shrieked away into parallel planes. Great gouts of paramatter appeared briefly to interact with here-matter, before reaching an implosive null-state, destroying more and more of the magical foundation of the guardian tower.

The tower fell at last, into the endless void . . . and the threads of constrained elsewhere parted.

The dragon, his work done, fled.

Even a dragon could be destroyed by that cataclysm he'd caused. Pieces of here and elsewhere roiled in the backlash wave, a tsunami of water and debris that bore all before it.

Nothing could live through that wave.

Except . . . something did.

Something small, soft and terribly fragile, which was torn from a desperate mother's arms. A mother somewhere on the other side of elsewhere.

1

The dragon, winging his way south, was not aware of it, in all the chaos he had caused.

This was beyond the babe's understanding too. She only knew that she was suddenly cold, wet and frightened. But the sea would not hold her, nor could the wild surge warm and caress her. She screamed, demanded that it be changed. She did not understand how or what was happening. But she wanted it to stop, NOW.

And it did. Her kind could not drown. The wave cast her up on the broken shell shingle. She wanted warmth, and she wanted a breast. For comfort, as much as anything. So she called for it.

"It's alive!"

"Leave it. It's no mortal child, Hallgerd. Let the sea take it back to where it belongs."

"It's a baby, Wulfstan. I know a human baby when I see one," said Hallgerd, picking up the girl-child up. It burrowed into her arms, nuzzling. She knew right then that she'd never give it up, no matter what the headman said. It filled the hole her own lost child left in her heart.

"It's ill luck to cheat the sea of its meat," he said, crossly.

"The sea spat it out," said Hallgerd, unbuttoning her blouse.

Wulfstan spat too, onto the wet shingle. "Nothing good will come of it, mark my words."

=== Chapter 1 ===

A FEW YARDS IN FRONT OF MEB, THE GREEN HEADLAND DROPPED away to the sea far below the fractured basalt of the cliff. The wind carried the shriek and mew of the gray-backed gulls swooping out from their cliff-nests. That should have been a warning to her.

But Meb was too busy. Dreaming, and lost in her dream.

When the boats came in on the morrow's tide, she'd be working too hard to dream. Along with every other woman in the fishing hamlet, she'd be gilling and gutting fish, as fast as her hands could work. A person had to concentrate when they had a razor-sharp knife in their hand. She still had the scar from learning that lesson. Today . . . well, today the East wind had kept everyone home, with not as much as a coble out on the bay. A cold mist clung to the water out there, as it did when the wind was in this quarter, hiding reefs and landmarks, muffling the warning sounds of surf.

She sighed. There had to be more to life than fish-guts. She turned the focus of her attention inward again, not sure what had disturbed her. In her mind, she rode a dragon across the sky of Tasmarin. His scales gleamed obsidian . . .

Being precise by nature she tried to get the details of the dragon right, but it evaded her. Of course, there was no such thing as a black dragon, but the basic shape was the same for all dragons. Their overlord, the dragon Lord Zuamar, flew seldom, but if only he would appear and take a turn over the bay, and land on the fang-rocks across the inlet.

3

She looked out across the sea, her gaze drifting unseeing across the black ship clawing its way inwards across the bay. Another, and then another, followed it, sliding out of the cloaking sea-mist, long oars raking herringbone patterns on the still water. Meb was not truly aware of their presence. They were not what she was looking for.

And then, to her delight, she saw the dragon spin down from heaven in a tasseled and spiky spiral of shimmer of sable, flaring its wings to land on the rocks across the water from the ships.

Suddenly her mind registered the shrieking gulls . . . and the ships. Her first thought was that the fleet must be in early—the gulls were flying off to feast on the scraps. And here she was idling on the cliff-top! She stood up hastily, wiping her hands on her patched skirts.

But . . . but they hadn't gone to sea today!

A second, incredulous look told her that this was something far worse than being late for the gutting. The gulls might be fooled into believing that all ships were fishing-boats, but Meb wasn't. She knew a galley from a fat-bottomed fishing smack, no matter what her adopted family said about her.

A bare second's hesitation and she lifted her skirts and began to sprint back, frantically screaming "raiders!"

The broken basalt of the cliff curved high above the bay. From time to time pieces fell off, down into the hungry waves that ate at its foot. Running along its edge Meb was gasping for breath already. If she'd stopped to think for a moment, she'd have realized that she couldn't both run and yell, but she wasn't thinking, right then. Still doing her best to sprint, she cut as close to the curve of the rotting cliff-top as she dared. She had to get to the village before them.

Too late, Meb realized that she'd dared too much.

A curl of white-hot steam drifted away from Fionn's mouth. His talons dug into the sea-etched basalt. He twitched, sending a shimmering shiver through his ebony scales. He'd always been a bit wary about the vast surge of salt water. It was even more relentless than dragons.

You had to see the funny side of it, he thought, grinning wryly to himself. He was aware that the force lines of everything from water to earth had been badly twisted and torn here by some adept's bungling magics. That was not surprising. Magic workers usually used magic, without understanding how—or what—they were doing, simply following a rote. He was used to having to adjust objects and tweak forces after their bungling. But it was the first time he'd actually been a part of the crude tangle. Well, the balances out here near the edge of the world were unstable anyway. There was a seasonal flux, something you got so close to the edge of existence, where matter had been twisted and abused. Still: Yenfar was one of the largest and most stable of the islands. He had not expected it here.

Fionn blinked his huge scarlet eyes, adjusting his vision to the entire spectrum of energies, not just the visible spectra, but all of them. Now he saw the world as a swirling soup of complex patterns, not merely as reflections of light. And the weave here was indeed twisted, dented and torn. Water, sky and earth energies swirled well away from the true shape of their physical being. Chaos and misery! He sighed. A planomancer's work was never done. He'd rather be sitting in the shade, drinking cool wine, with a platter of crispy fried whitebait and baby squid on the side—which was exactly what he had been doing before the summonsing—than wrestling with this mess. He chuckled. Ah well. It had got him out of paying for the earlier bottles of wine and platters of food rather neatly. Saved him a bit of trouble.

It was odd, though. The summonsing had felt like human magic. But there were no human magicians in Tasmarin.

Dragonkind had hunted down and killed all of them.

Falling takes a long, long time, thought Meb. It was either that, or time itself that stretched. The first idea was somehow easier to deal with. Like the scream that came from her mouth, falling to her death seemed to be happening to someone else. Even if she survived the fall, the sea would kill her. The villagers knew perfectly well that it killed men, let alone women. Women didn't even go out on the fishing boats, never mind into the sea. The blue water was full of sharks, rays, whales and merrows. She'd never actually seen one of the merpeople. She had, somehow, a time for regret and to try and imagine what a half-fish half-man really looked like before she hit the water.

It was a lot harder than she'd thought it would be.

Fionn shifted his weight uneasily. There it was again. Just as he'd worked out what would need re-alignment, something plucked and twisted at the water energy lines, changing them. The cliff on the far side of the bay was re-aligning itself, cascading in a shower of rocks and turf into the foam-edged blue. That could not account for this tweak, however. It was more like a great, clumsy hand pulling fatelines, with no care for what it did to water or earth or even fire. He frowned.

Humans!

Fionn paid more attention to humankind—the lice, as the others put it—than most dragons in Tasmarin did. They were an unusual interest for a dragon. But then, he was an unusual dragon. Unique on this plane, possibly the last of his kind on any plane, anywhere.

That didn't mean that he interfered with human affairs, any more than other dragons who merely taxed them.

It would have been a great deal too much like hard work, for a start.

He paid no attention to the raider-galleys whose keels were crunching onto the shingle. Instead, he reached a long-taloned forepaw into his front-pouch and hauled out a wad of folded parchment. He looked around and grimaced. These rocks were not a good spot. Nowhere flat to lay out the diagrams. In truth he didn't really need them, but he loved the detail and intricacy of them. They helped him decide. He spread his wings, unfolding the joints, extending them. It was a lousy place to launch from, but it was either fly from here or swim. The water looked cold, and might get at the charts. There was much labor in the drawing of them, and didn't feel like doing it again. The way things were finally falling apart on this plane of existence, he didn't think that he'd have enough time to, before the end.

He'd done enough work to get it into this dire state.

He launched. A trailing tip of his vast wings just touched the water. It was, indeed, cold.

Meb found that the water was not only hard, but also icy. The sudden shock of the cold broke the odd unreality of her falling trance. She was going to die! DIE!

Eyes wide open, all she could see was trailing bubbles and blue. She thrashed wildly, panic overwhelming thought.

Her head broke through into the air. She gasped for breath, frantically flailing at the water to stay afloat.

A wave hit her in the face, tumbling her.

And then strong, web-fingered hands seized her, dragging her under.

She fought them with all her remaining strength as they hauled her down into the watery darkness.

She was so busy struggling that she took a while to realize that she could breathe. And hear.

"Will you stop all this thrashing about, woman!" said someone irritably. "'tis hard enough swimming with you, without that."

Part of Meb was unwilling to let go of her panic. *This was the sea. You died in the sea.* Another part of her, the odd rational bit that poked fun at the rest of her, that also dreamed dreams that rose along way above fish-guts, said: *Don't be afraid. Be terrified. And breathe deeply.*

As usual, the ordinary village Meb listened to the inner voice, after a while. She was stiff with fear, but at least she could breathe . . . And cough. It was amazing that there still was any sea left out there. She seemed to have swallowed most of it. And now she was dead.

The rational part of her mind said: *so why are you still breathing?*

"Sit here. There's a bit of a shelf," said the voice. "I'll need to make a light so that we can inspect the damage."

The "shelf" was narrow and rough with barnacles. The current plucked at her as she sat on it. But at least she was half above water, on something solid. She tried to dig her fingers into the very rock. The place reeked of drying sea-life: seaweed, dead crabs and a hint of fish.

Then she saw a greenish-white spark glowing in the darkness. It grew into a globe of light of the same color, held in a webbed hand. The hand had rather more fingers than was normal. It was also blue and scaly, like the rest of the merrow it was attached to. He smiled at her. His smile revealed white teeth. They weren't square and blunt like human teeth. No, his teeth were pointed and sharp. He held the light up, looking her over thoughtfully.

"Well, you don't appear to be bleeding too much," he said, sounding a little regretful. "Any other injuries besides those that I can see?"

She stared at him. At his tasseled fins and the toothy smile.

"Shark got your tongue, maybe?" he said, sardonically. "I asked you a question, human wench. Are you all right?"

She coughed.

"I'll take that as a yes, shall I?" said the merrow.

"What are you doing to me?" asked Meb, weakly. She started to shiver.

"Ah. Now that'd be a question," said the merrow, with yet another nasty toothy grin. "Saving you from drowning would be my guess. What do you think?"

"I mean, why did you bring me here? Where is this?" she tried to keep the thin edge of hysteria out of her voice. As with stopping shivering, she failed.

The merrow seemed amused. "Well, it was a question of staying where you were, or going elsewhere. You don't seem to be much of a swimmer, wench. You'd need to be doing much better than the floundering and flapping you were busy with, to not be dashed into the cliff. And there were a powerful number of large rocks falling down, too."

His insouciant humor helped to quell her panic, anyway. "We fisher-people don't swim," she said defensively. "If we fall overboard, we would rather drown quickly. Anyway, women never go into the sea." Which was only partially true. The sea had spat her out originally, if Mamma Hallgerd was to be believed.

He seemed to find this hilarious. "I can tow you back out there and you can get on with drowning, if you like. Or maybe I can take you down, down, to merrow lands, to dance among the fish, or even to be sucked away into one of the great cracks in the ocean floor? There are maelstroms down there that not even I can cope with, places where the very water streams away into the nothingness. I'd hate to stop you doing what you think you were supposed to do."

"No! No, thank you very much," she said hastily. "I really don't want to drown. It's just . . . Where am I? I have to warn the village. There are raiders coming!"

He shook his head. "To think of not even knowing where you are. Why, 'tis obvious. You're under the cliff. There are some caves here. It's to be hoped we can get out again after all the rock you brought down with you. It was a careless thing to do."

Caves? Trapped? With this creature . . . with teeth like that? "Why did you bring me here?" she asked, suspiciously. "Why didn't you take me away from the cliff if you wanted to save me?"

The merrow snorted. "It's grateful that you are! Were you wanting to go to those boats in the bay instead?"

The rational part of mind had to admit that he was right. But it didn't stop her being cold, and very scared. Obviously she looked it, because the merrow relented a little. "There is a current under here. It has to go somewhere. The cliffs are riddled with these tunnels. I could have you out to those boats in the bay in no time, I daresay."

Taking her courage in both hands she looked at the creature in the way Hallgerd said made her look like a shameless hussy . . . but it did seem to get her what she wanted sometimes. "Will you rather take me to the beach?" she begged. "Please? Please, please? I must warn my people."

He seemed to find her look-of-helpless-appeal amusing. "They don't look much like you," he said, showing no sign of agreeing to help.

It was true enough. The fisher-people who had taken her in were straight-haired and blond. Her hair was dark and naturally curly. But . . . they were all she'd known. All she could remember. And even if they laughed at her, and teased her because she was different, they were her people. "Please?"

He scratched his chin with a webbed hand. "Ach. I suppose I could. For a price."

Meb gasped. He . . . She got ready to fend him off. The boys in the village had taught her that much. Even if she didn't look attractive, and she knew they didn't think so, the boys were keen. It wasn't her face they were interested in.

He laughed loudly enough to make the tunnel echo at her reaction. "You've a high opinion of yourself, wench. I'll admit you're bluer than you were when I brought you in, and it is somewhat of an improvement, but you're not a pretty sight. Not to me anyway."

Innate honesty forced her to say, "But I have nothing else. Please."

"Well, then you've got nothing," he said with a nasty grin. "I'll be going then."

"But . . . you can't just leave me here!" she protested.

"And why not?" he asked, pausing. "You're alive, thanks to me. And not a strand of hair's profit I'll have out of that."

Hair. She remembered now. Drowned bodies washed up . . .

without a hair on their heads. It was said that the mermen treasured human hair, used it to string sea jewels on. But it was supposed to be the worst of bad luck to let them have it. You were sure to drown.

The inner voice said *and if you don't give it to him, you're sure to drown.*

"I'll give you my hair," she said. There was a lot of it anyway. When it was loose she could nearly sit on it.

He scratched his chin. "It's not very straight."

She suddenly recognized the look in his eye. He'd said that it wasn't lust. Then it must be desire . . . to bargain. To think of this creature being just like the pack-pedlars! "That just means that it's longer," she said stretching out a piece.

"True," he said nodding. "We have a deal then." By the speed that he agreed she knew that she'd offered too much, too soon. He abruptly produced a bronze knife. She started back and nearly fell off the rock-shelf. He laughed. "You want me to pull your hair out instead? Now, if you be wanting me to take you to the beach without the raiders seeing you, you'll have to raise the price. Say the dress too." With a sinuous flick he pushed himself up out of the water, onto the shelf, and found a place to balance his light on the rock wall. "Hold still, will you, unless you'd be wanting to be parting with more skin than hair."

She did her best not to shiver. But it felt pretty close to having her hair pulled out anyway. He tucked the bundle of wet plaits into a pouch at his waist and put the knife away. "Now do we have a deal on the dress?"

"I suppose so," she said, crossly. "But not my drawers. Or my breast-band." Everyone in the village had seen her in that little anyway.

He flapped his fish-tail. "I've not much use for drawers," he said conversationally. "Off with it, then."

Meb bit her lip. What if he'd lied? You heard stories about mer-women . . . sailors' tales. A merrow would not be that different.

After a moment's panic, the voice inside her now coarsely shaven head said, *he's bigger than you and he has a knife. Why should he bother to trick you into taking it off?*

So she did.

He took it, rolled it up and tucked into another pouch. "I've not much use for it," he said cheerfully, "But I thought it'd be fitting punishment for thinking such things of me." And he disappeared into the water, with hardly a splash.

For a moment Meb stared at the water in horror. And then she started to swear. The lying, cheating bastard. At least he'd left her his light.

Then the merrow's head popped back out of the water, just has she was getting to her third breath and her foster-brothers' more choice vocabulary. The merrow looked impressed. "You've got a fine tongue on you, for a girl!" he said, clapping. "Now, it's as I thought," He reached for his light. "The way is still clear. Come." He grabbed her arm and pulled her into the current.

There was a reason that the villagers and their boats kept away from the cliff that sheltered the bay from the South wind: the current. The waves broke over the sandbar at the bay-mouth, and the water had to go out somewhere. The current sucked boats that came too close onto the rocks. Plainly it ran through these caves. But the merrow obviously was more than a match for the current. He pulled her along through it almost effortlessly.

"Last bit." He said. "You'll have to hold your breath again."

They went down. When she thought her lungs would burst, Meb saw the blessed gleam of sunlight through the water. And then they popped out into the open air again. They were in the middle of the still patch of weedy water where the cliff, the shingle and the sea intersected. The place was called "the perilous pool" and it wasn't even any good for throwing a line into. Village children were forbidden to play here. Meb knew why, now. The current still sucked at her feet.

The merrow was, however, as good as his word. He pushed her across to a slab of rock on the edge of the pool. "Up and off with you," he said cheerfully, swatting her across the behind.

She gasped—but grabbed at the leathery kelp fronds and hauled herself upwards, scraping her bare knees on the pink edged key-hole limpets. She was out! She scrambled higher up onto the rock, and then onto the crunching pebbles and broken shell of the beach. It was only then that she looked back, feeling she ought to wave, acknowledge he had been fair at least. And he had saved her.

The merrow had vanished back into the depths as if he had never been there.

Meb ran. Well, she did her best to run. The fear and cold water had sapped her strength. She could see smoke ahead. The

common-sense part of her mind said that she was running the
wrong way. That didn't stop her though, even if the shingle-beach
was long, and very awkward to try and run on.

The village was tucked in behind an overgrown dune that gave
it some shelter from the East wind. The seaward slope was a mass
of fish-drying racks, hung with salt-crusted, yellowed, flayed cod.
Meb panted her way up it. Nearing the top of the dune the sensible
part of her mind finally got the upper hand: *running down into
a fight*, it said to her, *a woman in her in underthings, unarmed,
is not the cleverest thing she'd ever done, and she'd done a lot of
stupid things before*. So she grabbed a fish-rack pole. It wasn't
much to soothe the inner voice, but it was something.

Meb crested the dune—and realized that she was too late. Far
too late.

All the little reed-thatched crofts were burning. So were the
boats, hauled up onto the little second curve of shingle on the
edge of the estuary. And the raiders, in their black cloaks and
steel mail shirts were the only people she could see, stalking
among the burning crofts.

It hadn't been a big village. A hundred or so people—when
the boats were in. It hadn't taken at least twice that number of
armed men long to over-run it. Looking down, Meb saw that some
of them hadn't managed to flee, either. That was old Hallgerd's
body sprawled down there, in front of Meb's croft. She couldn't
mistake that dress.

Meb sat down, dropping her pole. And then lay down and
sobbed. The old woman had been a terrible scold, but she was
also the nearest thing to a mother that Meb had ever had. Meb
had expected a real telling off for slipping away to the cliff-top
to idle this afternoon. She'd been faintly dreading it.

Now she would have welcomed it.

The raiders weren't searching for people to seaward. A few
quested like dogs through the gorse slopes behind the village.
The rest seemed to be kicking about the village. Looking up at
the skyline, looking inland.

Looking at the watching dragon.

So this is why the winged creature had come here. To oversee
his pack of sea-wolves. To destroy her home, her life.

Sitting there among the fish-racks, looking down at the destruction of her life, Meb did the unthinkable. Dragonkind ruled here

in Tasmarin, with an absolute power. Always had, and always would. Under them other creatures lived and died at their will. Someone had once said that humans were nothing more than kine to the Dragon Lords. Before this happened that had seemed like the natural order of things. Not something to be thought about, let alone defied. Now she raised her small fist and shook it at the sunset silhouetted dragon. A cold flame of bitter rage burned in her heart.

"We are more than just your cattle," she said grimly, in voice far older than her seventeen years. "I'm going to destroy you."

It was a ridiculous, futile gesture, and she knew it.

══ Chapter 2 ══

THE LYR PRESIDING OVER THE GROVE HAD NO IDEA WHERE THE celebrants had got the idea that the rites they performed should be done naked. Like so many of the things humans did it was something they had decided would please the lady of the trees—possibly because it would please them. The bodies of animal life had very little to interest her, except as fertilizer. They smelled vile—like the animals they were. They came, secretively, to the gatherings deep in the forest. At first the Lyr had struggled to grasp why they came. She had killed some of those who had infringed on her sleeping groves. That had made them respectful and yet more ardent. She had watched some of them rutting in the forest. There was some of the same heat about them when they came to worship. Their overlords had heard about it, and forbidden the gatherings. For those who came that seemed to make it more attractive.

It had not taken the Lyr long to realize that that these foolish worshipers would do anything she ordered them to, in her service. The reward she gave . . . well, it was in their heads really. The Lyr gave them meaningless ritual, sacrifice and sex. It seemed faintly ridiculous to the Lyr. But like the alvar, these humans were somehow besotted with the Lyr. It was a simple thing to encourage, and very useful.

For centuries now, in groves across the islands, the Lyr had allowed humans to recruit themselves by their own stupidity. They were more practical than slaves. A slave had to be bought and fed.

These fed themselves, and gave their utmost to the tasks the Lyr set. Gave their heart and soul, they said—whatever that was.

Right now the high priest of Yenfar grovelled, his little bare buttocks quivering. "Lady of the Trees. She wasn't there. Yes, some of the villagers fled. But the talismans you gave us led us to the sea. I swear it. And the dragon, Lady. We were afraid for our lives. The slavers wanted to flee immediately . . . We only stopped them with difficulty." He pointed to his bruised face. "Will you punish them, Lady?"

"Wait."

He remained on his hands and knees. Shivering. It may have been at her anger. Or it could have been the cold. They died, sometimes, if the Lyr forgot them.

She talked to the trees. The trees talked to other trees. It was not fast communication—vegetative life lacked that nasty animal quickness. But it was sure. It was an unlikely alliance, between the Lyr and the creatures of smokeless flame, but the energy beings had access to magics that the Lyr could not use. They also shared a common goal, at least up to a point. And, unlike animals, the beings of energy did not devour plants. The fire-beings were unable to pass over on the soil of Yenfar, and thus the worshippers of the Lyr had a role to play. The Lyr knew they were normally actually quite effective.

It took time, but she got word back from her contact, Haborym: The human with the gifts still lived.

She went back to the high priest. "Find out where the people of this village went. Search among them."

═ Chapter 3 ═

THE GOLD OF HIS HOARD GLEAMED DULLY IN THE RED LIGHT OF the dragon's lair. He did, of course, remain between it and the others. He might tolerate, and indeed, conspire with lower life-forms, but there was a limit. Other creatures might *want* gold. Dragons *needed* it. Dragons were not builders. The lair had once been mere caverns. Some dragons had had slaves in to improve them before they moved in. This had cost them dear, and had not happened here. There were no secret passages or hidden doors. Just rock. The caverns—with exception of smoothing by passage of hard bodies over generations—were as they had always been. Not a place which something other than a dragon would have found comfortable. A dragon would have found it pleasant, because of that hoard. Having them meet here, in his lair, this close to his gold was a gesture of faith. Almost unheard of faith. He wished that the sprite had not insisted on this place, as even talking to them here made him uncomfortable. But Lyr the sprite was a very necessary part of his plans. The tree-woman made no allowances for emotions. She didn't understand them in the same way that the warm-blooded species did—although the sprites could feel hate.

"Let us call this meeting to order," said Lord Rennalinn. The alvar lord looked as uncomfortable to be here as the dragon was to have him. Alvar did not like caverns. And they liked to delude themselves that they, not the dragons of Tasmarin, were the greatest power in the plane. "We need explanations. How dared you attack a fellow Lord's demesne in force?"

17

Haborym, an almost-face in the dancing flames, replied. "Our auguries suggested that we would have the best chance of success."

"We knew that you would not consent," said the Lyr coolly. She always spoke like that. It was not a royal "we." All the sprites were part of the same tree.

The flames danced as Haborym spoke again, his voice warm and persuasive as usual. "We thought it best to present you with a *de facto* situation. We've known that our final component is somewhere in Zuamar's demesne for several moons. What have we done? Sat and argued. Zuamar is not aware of the intrusion. The raiders are not aware that they were sent thence by us. Even if they are caught, they cannot betray us."

"It's not right," grumbled Rennalinn. "It's not done that way. It's not the tradition."

"Actually," said the centaur Actaeon, from the far corner—without stopping his narcissistic posing in the standing mirror there, "it is traditional, Lord Rennalinn. This business of respect for another's demesne is a new thing. Historically, territory belonged to he who could hold it."

Rennalin scowled. "Yes, but we've moved on from the war years. Civilization, Lord Actaeon . . ."

"May I remind you, alv, that we are trying to prevent the collapse of that," interrupted Lyr.

"And sometimes we have to go outside the rules of civilized conduct to do so," said Haborym.

The dragon snorted. But quietly. He needed those two. True, Rennalinn was powerful and wealthy on his island. But alvar conspirators were ten a penny. Merrow and dvergar mages could be compelled—and virtually every one of their kind had some skill. But one had to remember that all the sprites were effectively one creature. Alienate one and you alienated them all. And the untrustable creatures of smokeless flame . . . well, Duke Haborym had orders from on high, or the fire-being would not be here. They were more hierarchal than creatures of flesh and blood. Even their names followed a certain rigid tradition—based apparently on some arcane joke on humankind! The dragon did not share their sense of humor, but well . . . Anger their Emperor, and that would be the end of their collaboration. He needed one of each of the intelligent species, a representative from each of the ancient planes, if his plan were to work. Besides, he rather agreed with the sprite and fire-being. Rennalinn's petty insistence on protocols, meaningless outside the traditions and rituals of alvardom, made reaching decisions like plowing through mud. A dragon flew above that. He was accustomed to making up his own mind, and doing whatever needed to be done himself. This need for consensus was un-dragonish.

"My good fellows, we are here to prevent a catastrophe. A catastrophe that will destroy our world. Yes, preventing it requires that we take actions that are frowned on by our various kind. It will take courage, and taking risks and breaking rules, because we pursue a high purpose. All we need is a human magic-worker. Lord Rennalinn, you know that we have caught and put to the test seventeen so far. Every one proved a fraud or of such minor power as to be useless for this task. We know that the one we need exists. By divination we have pinpointed it. We cannot afford to wait indefinitely. Since the loss of the South-Eastern tower, we've found serious cracks in the Western, South-Eastern and Northern towers. Dragon and alvar have bent their skills to the attempt to repair them. We have failed. And there have been sudden and cataclysmic infalls—sinkholes in the very reality of Tasmarin. Are we going to sit and argue and worry about breaking a few rules to save our world? I say no. We only need one human . . ."

"There are a few other things," said the centaur—too valuable a conspirator, if a hopelessly vain one—to be incinerated for stopping a dragon in full oratorial flow. "The treasures."

"Those can be easily obtained," said the Demon.

"Perhaps we need to do that then," said the centaur. Like all of his kind he was a historian. Centaurs recorded everything in the endless stories of their oral tradition. Almost certainly he would recite all of this, even though his kind had foresworn contact with other species. They had withdrawn onto the high grasslands of their islands, and kept themselves to themselves. They had a very high opinion of their culture and their histories.

They also had the best and most complete record of the magical creation of this place, the refuge of dragons. Vorlian knew that he would need that, as much as he needed a centaur. Besides . . . treasures. No one had mentioned those before. And treasure often equalled gold. He was a dragon. He needed gold as other beings needed . . . air. The fire-being and sprite did not of course, but the other species could not do without air for very long. Humans tended to think dragons wanted gold for mere greed. There was that too, of course. It was beautiful. But at least there was real need behind their greed. "Tell us," he said suspiciously, "about these 'treasures.' And why no one saw fit to mention them before. It is apparent several of you knew of them."

"Because they really are not an issue," said the fire-being. "They're mere symbols of the power of each species—given into the keeping of another species' treasure as a gesture of faith." Was that a hint of snicker in the fire-being's voice?

"So where are they?" asked Vorlian, allowing his displeasure to show in his tone.

"We have the alvar treasure. And that of centaurs," said Haborym. "The former was given to to us, as there was no human to hold it."

Vorlian wondered about the "given" part.

"We have the treasure of the humans," said the sprite.

The centaur nodded. "And we hold the treasure of the sprites. The dvergar hold the dragons'. The dragons have the treasure of the creatures of smokeless flame, the merrows have the dvergar treasure, the alvar that of the merrows."

"Are they . . . gold?" asked Vorlian.

Several of the conspirators had the temerity to laugh. "Only the dragon one," said the centaur. "They are symbols. The harp of the alvar is silver, the staff of the sprites is, naturally, wooden. The diadem of the merrows is a thing of pearls and dried sea-wrack."

"Of course," said Haborym, "the leather bag we had from the centaurs may be full of gold."

The centaur snorted. "You know full well that it is not! Any more than the copper cauldron of humans is full of gold."

"But I believe that the last holder did make jam in the pot," said the fire-being. "Humans are not fit custodians."

"The iron hammer of the dvergar should hardly be kept in the salt sea either then," said the centaur. "The flame of the people of smokeless flame you have seen often, Vorlian. It burns in your conclave. A globe of the eternal fire."

He'd seen it. Every dragon had. Never thought twice about what it was doing there, or what it might be. It was just a globe of flame on a plinth at the entry, that had always been there. It should be easy to go and take . . . "So, should we not be gathering these items?"

The fire-being's flames shrugged. "Why? The dvergar and merrows can be compelled to give what they hold up to us. You know how it works, dragon. The weaker species cannot resist."

The centaur twitched. It really didn't like Haborym. The centaur disliked having its expertise challenged too. "Not really. There is a balance of compulsion between the species. But it is in our favor in this instance. In fact the only issue is the merrow treasure."

"Surely we have one of the leading nobles of alvar in our midst?" said Lyr.

Rennalinn looked excessively uncomfortable. "I am not on the best of terms with Lord Gywndar of Yenfar."

"Yenfar?" said the dragon. That was the dragon Zuamar's demesne . . . where those two had just raided in their search for a human mage.

═ Chapter 4 ═

FIONN THE DRAGON LOOKED DOWN ACROSS THE BAY. ACROSS THE burning crofts. It was a lucky thing for most of the villagers that there'd been a thunderous rockfall on the cliff that had drawn their attention to the sea. If that hadn't happened he might just have had to bestir himself, with all the consequences that that might have had. It was none of his business, after all, but he did come from an earlier time, when life had been more precious.

The bulk of the fishermen, and their women and children, had fled, scattering into the gorse. There were always one or two who were damned if they'd leave, and they'd paid the price. But what had been oddest was the dance of energies around the village. Someone had been using magic. Using it liberally too, in a place that should barely have boasted a midwife, let alone a spell-worker of great power, if vast ineptitude. Magic had its price, and the village could certainly not have afforded it. Odd. It was also a place that was truly not worth a tenth of the cost of that raid. Even if they'd taken alive every man, woman and child to sell, outfitting and equipping at least a hundred and twenty men would cost far more than the profits could be. Human slaves were cheap, after all. There was a strong magical compulsion on those raiders. There'd have to be. Raiding this deep into Zuamar's territories was a risky pastime, as Fionn had reason to know. The old dragon was lazy, but this was still his territory.

Magic and money had been spent on wiping out this fishing hamlet. Why? And why had someone else expended magic on making it a good place to live? To a planomancer such as he, the energies of the place were as twisted as any he'd seen. Fionn puzzled on it, briefly. It was not his business, although he had made a habit of interfering in things that weren't his affairs . . . It would be fascinating to find out, but he had a lot to do in a fairly short time, if he was going to finally destroy Tasmarin. He'd done the little adjustments necessary for the energy flow in this area. A matter of aligning some rocks and destroying a small dam on the stream.

He'd spent enough hours here. He stretched his wings to fly, and kicked off up into the twilight, riding the last thermals of the dying day, using his magics to multiply their effect. He flew up, up into the thinner air. Far below Tasmarin's endless lacework of sea and islands stretched out to the sunset. When he got high enough he could see the other dragons flying up, distant shapes against the purple of night-fall.

It was something of a conceit having the seat of the conclave in the sky, far above the world below. Fionn rather liked it.

It also meant that it was a place no lesser life-form could ever reach. Even if they had the magic to assist the flight and infall, none but a dragon could manage the airlessness.

Fionn always thought that particular aspect of the conceit something of a delusion. But then, he smiled to himself, dragons were prone to delusions. He could think of several mechanical means, let alone magical ones, of achieving the trick.

As moons went, this one was an unimpressive thing, and it took a fair amount of bending of the laws of physics to keep it up here, so close that the great rock was almost in the atmosphere of Tasmarin.

It was not a very stable arrangement. But then, neither was the plane of dragons that was this world. The plane that dragonkind had carved out for themselves had all the permanency and stability of a hen's egg balanced on the small end, on a sow's back. A drunken sow, at that. Fionn felt that it was fitting that the conclave should be held in a place equally frail.

The guardian towers were all visible from up here. Six great bastions on the edges of the world . . .

Fionn smiled wickedly to himself. There had been seven for many years. Soon there'd be five. And after that the fall would be fast.

He spiraled in to land at the gates of the conclave. He'd bet that they didn't even remember that it had been he who, all those long years ago, had arranged for air to breathe up here. Dragons could cope without it, but it did limit conversation to pointing and hitting. That was fine if you were the biggest dragon with the longest and the most powerful tail, but Fionn wasn't. Talk opened far more opportunities for making size a slightly less relevant factor in winning arguments. Not that talk counted for too much. Among dragons, size was really what counted most.

Fionn furled his wings and walked in through the portal. The great cave was full this evening. Dragons were normally solitary creatures. They mated and parted. Young dragons were hatched and reared by the mother. And she didn't keep the young past learning to speak and fly. It had created the isolation that had made the all-powerful dragons victims to other species that did organize. They maintained they did not need others . . . but the conclave gave them something that they'd lacked hitherto: a place to brag. And that had, to some extent, socialized them. Fionn grinned at them all, long sharp teeth showing, which of course was normal for dragons. With the amount of hot air being produced here tonight, he needn't have bothered with providing an atmosphere. He sauntered slowly through the vast, dragon-crowded cavern. More than one dragon drew their wings aside, as if fearing contamination. Fionn thought that that was pretty funny too, all things considered. He found himself a position near one of the magma vents and sat down to listen. He had very keen ears—keener than the others realized, and he had discovered that if he was patient enough all the news and all the rumors in this place would eventually come to him.

Listening in: It was the usual soup of plots and counterplots. Of petty fights and shifting alliances. Of ineffectual plans to do something about the destroyed guardian-tower. They'd been at that one for the last seventeen years, and were still no further on. They weren't much good at admitting that they lacked the skill. Of course, there was also a steady discussion, and the usual dissent, over what should be done about the slow dissolution of Tasmarin. The latest break-up, it would appear, had caused the dragon Jakarin's lair to collapse into the sea . . . along with the better part of her hoard. Fionn found that almost as funny as if he'd done it himself.

He did laugh a little immoderately. Enough to pause the heated conversation taking place some yards away, and turn several arctic eyes onto him.

"And what, if I may ask, is so funny?" demanded a large vermilion dragon. Myrcupa, if he recalled the name correctly. One of the self-appointed guardians of the guardian towers. A self-important tailvent if there ever was one. Even in this select company of like-minded dragons he was exceptional. Called himself a High Lord!

"You are," said Fionn, cheerfully. "And she is." He pointed a wing at Jakarin.

The vermillion dragon was not amused. "Your manners are as offensive as your misshapen body, runt," snarled Myrcupa, pushing the incandescent Jakarin back, and pushing his extensive chest forward instead. "Jakarin has just suffered a terrible loss."

"Tch. That's too bad," said Fionn in mock sympathy, grinning.

"Bad? BAD! Is that all you can say, worm?" demanded Myrcupa, thrusting his flared nostrils into Fionn's face.

Fionn wrinkled his nose. "Bad seems a good description. Nearly as bad as your breath, in fact. Been eating carrion again?" asked Fionn, waving a languid wing-edge in front of his face, and winking at the shocked onlookers.

"Carrion!?" shrieked Myrcupa.

"Well, it's not surprising really. It's all you can catch with a body that's nearly as flabby as your wits," said Fionn loftily. "Now, I can recommend a course of swimming. It'll help you and that fathead to lose some lard. And maybe you can save some of her hoard in time for molt. I'd shift shape into something more suited for swimming, mind you. Maybe a well-larded whale. It could only improve you."

Jakarin and Myrcupa's tails twitched almost in unison. Odd. The thought had never struck Fionn before, but they looked remarkably like cats about to pounce. Direct insult and straight derision was something they'd probably not had to deal with for many years. They were both very large. And very stupid. As far as Fionn could see the two traits seemed to go together far too often. It was a natural progression, really. When you were that powerful, you didn't have to think. And to imply that they'd shift shape to something less lordly than their dragonish forms was the vilest insult to most of dragonkind. Dragon was, after all, the ultimate form! Heh. Any moment now these two idiots would start a fight right here. That would solve a few problems for everyone.

And then, just when it was all going splendidly . . .

"Jakarin. Myrcupa." The dragon Vorlian pushed forward. He was bigger than both of them. And there was no fat on him. "Cease. You know our law as well as anyone. He is baiting you to that end."

Briefly, Fionn allowed himself to scowl. What call had Vorlian to interfere? Without him, the problem of a dragon without a hoard could have been avoided. Vorlian was big enough to be safe from likes of these two, away from here. Looking at the idiot Jakarin, she was close to molt. She'd have to get enough gold before then, and that meant trouble for the smaller, younger dragons. Better if she'd been dealt with here and now. *And* it would have gotten Jakarin's charming friend away from the guardian-towers. Not that he'd be in any position to stop what Fionn had planned for them. Even dragons couldn't resist those forces.

Jakarin and Myrcupa, thus paused, realized just where they'd been heading.

The self-named High Lord narrowed his slit-eyes and peered angrily at Fionn. "I won't forget this. And you won't always be in the conclave, runt."

"Indeed," said Fionn. "And my hoard is out there, somewhere, too. If you look hard you might find it and me, before Jakarin molts."

"Bah. Your hoard!" snorted the now-hoardless Jakarin. "You wouldn't have two bits of gold to rub together."

Fionn grinned. "Actually, I have a hoard far bigger than any other dragon. I've been collecting for a long time. A long, long time. All you've got to do is find it. Here." He tossed a coin at the startled Jakarin. "A start for your new hoard. A small thing, but of great age. It's a ducat from lost Earth."

The dragon caught it. No dragon could resist gold, no matter what. They needed it, come molt, and they could never have enough. No dragon gave it away. Not ever. Not even one coin. Fionn's action shocked the surrounding dragons nearly as much as it did the catcher.

"Of course, if you still want to fight, you can step outside the conclave," said Fionn, cheerily.

"Right," said Myrcupa firmly, turning immediately. "I'll see you there. Come, Jakarin." Together the two stumped towards the entry, and went out.

The large Vorlian looked at Fionn, who was sitting watching them leave. "Are you going?" he asked, eventually.

Fionn regarded him with some amusement. A chief, or a king of dragons, was a ridiculous concept. But Vorlian would have been one among the alvar or the humans, had he been born among them. "And why should I go out there?" asked Fionn, in mock puzzlement. "I don't want to fight. Would *I* fight here in the conclave?" he said, loudly and sanctimoniously.

This was too much even for Vorlian. "But you said . . ."

"I said if they wanted to fight they could go outside. They obviously do."

"But they wanted to fight you!" Vorlian shook his huge head in exasperation.

Fionn spread his wings against the vents, enjoying the warmth. And laughed. "Ah well. You know what they say: 'You can't always have quite what you want.' I don't want to fight, and I'm not there. They'll have to make do with each other."

Many of those present considered laughter beneath their dignity. Some of them lowered that dignity.

Fionn knew himself to be reasonably safe. Even a dragon couldn't remain in the thin bare traces of air out there for too long. Dragons had been designed to survive all the conditions that the planes of existence could throw at them. But vacuum was strictly something they could only cope with merely passing through. Myrcupa and Jakarin had slim choices. Come in again, or fly off down to the thicker air. If they thought to wait lower down where they could breathe, the spill of dragons leaving from the conclave flying hither and yon to their lairs would see the two of them doing a fair amount of exercise before morning. They'd be lucky to have breath to fly, let alone fight. If they came in again . . . he doubted that they'd be as good at keeping their tempers twice, even with Vorlian's intervention. And given the events of the evening, the other dragons, as little as some might like Fionn, would have no choice but to act. They could act. Dragon could kill dragon. Fionn had no such luxury. It was awkward that he could not simply directly eliminate his dragonish problems, but those were the constraints he worked within.

One of the joys of being the dragon of no fixed abode was that

Jakarin and Myrcupa couldn't go and wait around his lair for him. And Fionn never told anyone where he planned on going next.

As it happened, it was a place called Tarport on the island of Yenfar, in the dragon Zuamar's demesne, where he had some unfinished business.

═ Chapter 5 ═

MEB LAY ON TOP OF THE DUNE, SHIVERING AGAIN. NIGHT HAD
fallen, and in the moonlight the raiders could be seen moving down
to their war-craft. It was going to be interesting to see how they
got over the bar at the mouth of the bay, thought Meb, vengefully.
Unfortunately it looked as if they were just readying their vessels,
waiting for the tide. The raider ships probably didn't have the draft
of the fishing-boats, anyway. They'd skim over the bar.

Soon they were out on the bay, waiting for the tide, safe from
any revenge attacks, with the village's boats lying burned on the
shingle. Occasional sparks blew from the sullen embers of the
crofts of the village. Otherwise there was darkness and desolation
in what had been her home. Steeling herself, Meb edged her way
down the bank. She had to make sure poor Hallgerd was dead,
as little as she wanted to go down there.

She established that fact quickly enough. Her stepmother was
dead and stiff already, her old dress dark-stained with blood
even in the moonlight. Gently closing Hallgerd's eyes, Meb pulled
Hallgerd's dress down again.

Meb's tears were swallowed down into an acid hatred that burned
in her belly. No one would have dared to raid on Lord Zuamar's
territory without his permission . . . or without a larger dragon
dealing with the local dragon overlord. No one! And Zuamar
was one of the greatest of dragons. Yenfar's people were proud
of their dread lord, be he ever so greedy with his taxes. He was
bigger and more dangerous than the dragons of other islands.

31

She ground her teeth. Somehow, Zuamar would pay for this. He was supposed to defend them! She knew in her heart of hearts that this was as futile as hating the sea. But that didn't stop her hatred. It ran right then, as deep as the heavens were wide.

After what seemed like an eternity, Meb got up off her knees from next to Hallgerd. When she stood up, she was a much older woman than the girl who had knelt down there in village street. Standing up, Meb was stiff, sore, hungry and cold, miserable to the core . . . and she had absolutely no idea what to do next. She tried to put it all aside, to be logical, to think. It didn't work very well. Her teeth were chattering with cold . . . so finding some warmth—even if it was just from the embers of her home, she thought bitterly, was probably the most important. Her other dress was burned. As was the blanket she would have slept under. She really needed some clothes. And then some food and shelter, but clothes came first. Then she'd have to bury Hallgerd. Alone, if no one else came back to help.

She tried again to think about clothes, warmth, without letting the horror of it all overwhelm her. It was a pity that she'd washed her other dress the day before. Otherwise it might still have been drying on the flag bushes behind the houses. Maybe there might be other clothes there? Would the raiders have bothered with fisher-folk's washing?

She made her way back towards them. The straggly bushes everyone used to hang out their washing on grew along the bottom edge of the dune she'd just come down.

Near them, she tripped over another lump that shouldn't have been there. In the moonlight she saw that it was Leofric's son, Alemric. He was also dead. She swallowed and backed away. He'd been the leader among those who had felt that she had an ugly face but an interesting body. She'd really hated the boy. Been scared of him. But she hadn't wanted him dead. She left as hastily as she could.

The flag bushes did yield one thing. A boy's tunic. Old and threadbare, but at least somewhat warmer than her salty skin. She struggled into it. It was fairly tight—it must have belonged to one of the village's younger boys. But it helped with the night-wind. The only other clothes she'd seen were on dead people, and full of their blood. She didn't think she could cope with that. Not yet anyway.

She made her way back towards the burned croft, sidestepping Alemric's body. Instead she kicked his trousers. Meb carefully avoided even thinking about why he wasn't wearing them. Instead, she gritted her teeth and pulled them on. Boy's clothes on a girl might be indecent. But it wasn't half as indecent as her underthings. At least they kept the cold wind off her skin.

She found a place next to the remains of the croft that was out of the wind. Near—but not too near the body of Hallgerd. Somehow she fell asleep. She didn't mean to. But the gamut of emotion and stress, to say nothing of running and nearly drowning, took her to a deep and dreamless place. It was sometime before dawn when she woke again, cold to the bones.

And hungry. Starving.

It seemed really heartless, but she had to get some food. She could root around in the ashes, perhaps, but what would be left after the fire? Well. There was always fish. Salt fish was too salty to eat for pleasure. It was salted hard, so that when the wagoners came at the beginning of autumn, it could be packed like boards into their wagons, for transportation and sale inland. It would keep through the winter, and—if you had a day to soak it—and changed the water a few times, it could be made into something edible. If she chose one of the newer-caught fish that hadn't gone hard yet, she could eat it. All the kids in the village did it from time to time, despite scoldings and beatings. The newest fish were closest to the top of the slope, and Meb made her way up there again.

The cod was like soft wood in texture, heavily laden with fishiness and salt. She had no knife to cut it with, which would have made things easier. However, it was still food. It did nothing much for the ache in her heart, but helped the ache in her belly.

After eating she needed water, badly.

She made her way back down to the village water-supply. The estuary water was salt to brackish, but someone had built a small dam on a spring up the hill. A pipe ran from there to splash into a big clay bowl outside Wulfstan's croft, before it trickled away down to the estuary. The village headman had had the best place for his croft. Close to his boat, and close to the fresh water. His wife and daughters had very little distance to carry their water-crocks.

When she got there she found that someone had broken the

bowl. And no water was coming out of the pipe. Meb, having eaten too much salt with her fish, was thirsty, really desperately thirsty. There was no help for it but to follow the pipe. It was made out of rolled bark and cord, and was forever rotting and breaking . . . or being stood on by something obstinate enough to break the arch of sticks that guarded it. Sighing, Meb set out to walk along it. If she could fix it, that would at least be something positive. But the rolls of spare bark would have burned with Wulfstan's croft. Weary, and thirsty, Meb started walking, following the arch of sticks up the hill. She knew that she would be able to hear the water gurgling in the bark pipe when it was intact. That sound would tell her when she'd passed the break, if the water from it didn't wet her feet. She looked forward to finding it . . . she could at least drink then.

The sky was paling as she walked. It was a full mile and half to the dam.

Her walk took her all the way to the dam wall, or what was left of it. The stream trickled through the broken earth and off down its original course. It would enter the little estuary too high up to be of any use to the village. Up where it was too shallow and too muddy to bring boats in.

It wasn't as if there was just a hole in the dam wall. There was just no more wall. It had been knocked to smithereens. And in the dawn light Meb could see dragon prints in the mud.

Meb was too thirsty not to drink the spring-water. But she was choked with anger and tears too. The dragon had left nothing undone when it came to destroying the village. And she couldn't see why. They paid their taxes, like everyone else. They were left with precious little copper, and the dragon got the gold. That was the way it was, and had always been.

Once she'd drunk, Meb wondered what to do. She'd imagined being able to make some kind of temporary repair. Now, with the sun beginning to burn down already, she knew that that was impossible. The dam had raised the level of the stream enough for it flow twenty yards or so down an earth ditch to the pipe. Without the dam, the water was confined to this gully. She had brought nothing with her to carry water in. By the time she'd walked back down to the village, she'd be thirsty again. And she was really too tired and miserable to think clearly or properly. For a while, as the sun rose higher, she just sat. Sat and stared at the water that had been the lifeblood of the fishing village. Eventually, she stood up. She walked uphill to the spring itself and drank. She might as well drink enough before starting to walk back down again.

As she reached the top of the little ridge that had separated her village from the stream's natural flow, she saw them. There were people moving around in the village! Up on the dune among the fish-racks too. For a moment she thought that it was the raiders back again . . . but it could also be the other villagers. She'd only seen two dead bodies. Surely some of the others must have got away? There were no ships—except the burned ones, pulled up on the shore.

She walked back trying to do two things at once . . . see who it was, and keep a low profile, in case she needed to get away.

By the time she was halfway back she was very sure that it was just the villagers who had survived the raid. Some were digging through the ruins of their houses. Others were gathering fish off the racks. Piling them up on what looked like some sailcloth. That was odd.

She walked a little faster.

She arrived hot and out of breath, and inevitably, thirsty. The first person she saw was Wulfstan. The headman was staring moodily at the charred ribs of his boat. He'd loved that boat more than his wife, which, if you'd met Alfrida, was quite understandable. "What's happening?" she asked.

Wulfstan looked at her with some puzzlement. "Who are you, boy? Get to work. We want the fish ready for loading by the time Serbon gets back here with a wagon. Not that it'll be worth as much as if it were properly dry, but we can't just leave it here."

She blinked. Realized it was the boys clothes and haircut. "It's me. Meb," she explained. That she wasn't his favorite person, was something that was belatedly coming back to Meb. Hallgerd had apparently insisted on keeping her, the foundling baby that she'd picked up on the beach, after the great storm. Wulfstan had always said, on every occasion that he had fought with her stepmother—and there were many—that ill-fortune would come of cheating the sea of its prey.

He looked at her incredulously, and then rounded savagely on her. "So. You've done it finally. Brought your evil luck down on all of us. And on poor Hallgerd too. And all the while you've been off behaving like a hoyden somewhere, to come back in some lad's clothes. What kind of decent woman dresses like a boy? So you cut your hair off. Who did you think you'd fool?"

She'd certainly fooled him, initially. "But I . . ."

"Be quiet," he thundered, building himself up into a weak man's rage. "If I want you to speak I'll ask you to. There'd be no place in my village for you, if there still was a village! Get out of my sight, you little trollop." He advanced, swaying on his feet, swinging a piece of burned timber he'd snatched up. "Go and don't come back."

"But where . . . ?"

"Run before I beat you. Go back to the sea that should have kept you." Plainly he'd—somehow—been drinking. And equally plainly he was taking out his fury about his lost boat on her. She was a lot softer target than yesterday's raiders had been. Huh. He should have fought them, not her. He was getting very close. Meb's nerve broke, and she turned and ran. Not too far, but far enough for Wulfstan to give up the chase.

She sat there, in among the gorse, thirsty again, hurt and angry. And half fearful that it might be true. Had the raiders come to destroy the village because the sea had been cheated nearly seventeen years back? And then the logical part of her mind turned to the dragon. Watching over the destruction of the village and its vessels. Destroying their dam. Hating it was a relief. It meant that she didn't have to carry the blame. She'd just stay here for a bit until Wulfstan calmed down, or, more likely, until the drink made him fall over and vomit.

Even if she wasn't to blame, it didn't stop her feeling vastly sorry for herself. She'd tried to help them! Tried her best. Meb sniffled. She was tired enough to cry herself to sleep in a patch of sun between the low prickly bushes.

She didn't realize just how tired she'd been, obviously, because when she woke again, hungry and thirsty, the sun had already slipped so low that she was in deep shade from the ridge. She got up hastily. Now they'd call her lazy for not helping. She ran hurriedly back to the village.

Only—when she got there, there was no one in it.

She walked between the burned-out shells of houses, calling warily. Had the raiders returned again and she'd slept through the attack?

Then she saw a face peeking around the shell of his cottage. Not a particularly welcome face under normal circumstances, but right now, any familiar face was a relief. "Roff. Where is everyone?" she asked the net-maker.

The net-man looked suspiciously at her. "Who are you, boy, and what do you want?" His hands were black and he had a wooden spade with him.

"I just want to find everyone. Mikka and Hrolf. Where has everyone gone?" she asked humbly.

"Tarport, boy. This place is history. It's finished. Lord Zuamar himself let them wipe us out. Our boats are ash. Our water, he destroyed himself. Some of the women saw him do it. Our homes are burned. Nothing left for us here. Now get away with you, snooping around our sorrow."

Gone! Gone to Tarport, the big harbor some miles up the coast . . . Well, it made a kind of sense. With their boats burned, there was no way the village could feed itself. In Tarport there was always a call for crewmen, at worst. And after the attack, she wouldn't mind being inside a bigger settlement herself.

"Well, what are you waiting for?" demanded Roff. "Get along with you, boy. Your friends have gone. Go."

He plainly didn't recognize her. Good. He'd repeatedly tried to lure her into that smelly croft of his. He presumably had something hidden there he wanted to dig up. Village rumor had always made him out to be rich, but mean.

Meb simply turned away and began walking, almost blindly. It was a good nineteen miles to Tarport. She'd never get there before sundown. And she was both hungry and thirsty.

She walked along the rutted track the carters used to fetch the salted fish, wishing that she'd first gone to wherever they'd buried Hallgerd. The fishwife had been as shrewish as could be, and a hard task-master. But she'd taken Meb in, given her a home and food, and in her way, loved her.

The ruts were deep enough to follow even in the growing gloom of twilight. And walking was at least doing something. Behind her was the ruined remains of her home. Her whole life. It seemed that she'd lost what family she had. At least Hallgerd's two sons might be in Tarport. Might be. Roff had not said anything about them. She crossed a stream just before total darkness fell, and was able to slake her thirst. By then she wished that she'd kept the half-dried fish.

At length, walking on, following the ruts in the light of the risen moon, she spotted lamp-light through a chink in a shutter. It was a snug little farmhouse. Meb wondered if she dared to go and beg for shelter. But they'd probably set their dogs on her at this time of night. There was a hay rick, however. That had to be better—and warmer—than out here. Tired, hungry, scared, and very much alone, Meb burrowed into it. It was prickly, ticklish—and out of the night-breeze. At least it wasn't raining. It was coming on for the time of year when the cold autumn rains could endure for a week at a time. By then she would need to have a roof over her head at night.

═ Chapter 6 ═

THE PLACE HISSED WITH SMOKES AND STEAM. ENTIRELY TOO MUCH steam as far as those who called it their home away from home were concerned. They were creatures of energy, not flesh. The steam in the fumarole would have cooked flesh. Most flesh anyway. Not dragon-flesh, which was a source of some grievance among them. They found the steam cool, and worse, wet. Sulfurous smokes were preferred . . . but they had known from the first that this was a hardship-posting—with great rewards, it was true.

"They failed," said the one who, when not among creatures who were patterns of energy, was sometimes called Haborym. He went by numerous names. He even, with difficulty and for a short period of time, assumed the appearance of flesh. The illusion was hard to maintain, and not a true shape-shifting. It was worth it, however, for dealing with other species.

His master, one who was great enough to keep contact with their master across the twisted dimensions of time and space, simply sat there and waited, staring at him with a vermilion heat. Waiting until Haborym felt he had to add something more. "I destroyed them of course. As soon as the sprite was not there."

"You have set in motion the recruitment of more?"

"King. We recruit constantly. You know that. The amazing thing is that the others have not found the signs of it. I destroyed those merely in case the accursed sprite used her powers later. She was suspicious that I could find a hundred and twenty armed men so close and at such speed."

39

The demon lord spat, a plume of flaming incandescent matter. "A pity. Why did they fail?"

"Because we mis-guessed the human's power. We'd given the hunters a simple talisman that would have glowed when they found her. But the idea was to round up all the women and take them away. Something alerted the village to the raiders, presumably her. And they were badly mazed by the place. Seeing things that frightened them. A dragon. I presume that she has some skill with illusions. I had to leave all of that to the sprite, and you know how they are about getting too close to conflict. Yet they love others to use it. To kill. I would have sent in a pack-peddlar or something. But she wanted blood spilt. Her worshipers went back there and found one of the villagers. They put him to the knife and lash until he talked, and confirmed that she'd not been seen after the raid. But the people of the village went to Tarport. One of them claimed that he'd seen her."

"Fss." His superior hissed in irritation. "It had to be Yenfar that this human turned up on. Well, subtlety was always been our strength. I assume you have now been able to over-ride the sprite as her plan failed?"

"Yes," said Haborym, glad to have something positive to report. "I have dispatched seven of my very best men from Cark. We are hampered by my not being able to go there."

The demon lord sat and fulminated. But now Haborym had nothing to add, so he simply waited. Eventually, the demon lord spoke. "It would seem that the right answer may be to remove that which blocks us from the place, because I feel that your humans will fail. However, you will have to exert your charm on the sprite. Persuade her that it is her idea to go and remove the treasure from the place where the alvar have kept it. As long as it is not returned to the merrows. It is to be assumed that the magic that keeps us from the place is bound to that object, not the place. They were less trusting of us in those days, the alvar."

The flames that were Haborym nodded, in the fashion of his kind. "I will do this, Lord. But she will not act herself. I know her."

"Point her at a thief or two." The demon lord laughed and so did Haborym. "And get a simulacrum fashioned. One that will at least stand cursory examination. That way we may be able to avoid trouble with the alvar until it is too late."

═ Chapter 7 ═

IT WAS AMAZING, MEB THOUGHT, HOW A COUPLE OF APPLES AND a few handfuls of late blackberries could change the way you looked at things. She'd woken before dawn, and beat a hasty retreat from a sniffing, but tail-wagging dog. She hadn't been able to resist the apples in the orchard next to what was becoming a country lane. She still felt guilty about them. They had just been windfalls, but still. One didn't steal, even if the common sense part of her mind said that the pigs could spare a couple of bruised windfalls. But now she was wearing stolen clothes, and eating stolen fruit. Hallgerd would have said that she was on her way to perdition.

Thinking about her made Meb's eyes misty with sadness and half-realized tears. She didn't even notice that, as she crested the hill, Tarport had come into view.

It was, by Meb's standards, a vast metropolis, and very frightening. Hallgerd had always been full of horrific tales of what happened to nice girls on the streets of that sinful city. Of course the details had been rather vague, possibly because Hallgerd hadn't had much of an imagination, and she'd only been there a few times herself. But girls definitely came to tragic ends if they went there alone, without a male escort.

When Meb looked up, it was there. The great city. Even from a mile away she could smell it—a mixture of fish, smoke, tar from the tar-pits a few miles inland and other less pleasant smells from thousands of people, a handful of dvergar, and an occasional

visiting alvar come to oversee the work of their underlings. She
didn't have much of a choice but to enter it alone.

A little further on her coastal track joined the main pike from
the tar-pits, and from the farmlands inland and from the more
populous South Coast. Fresh wares, inclined to spoil, came in
by cart, rather than by the canal that ran next to the road. Meb
was thirsty, but she didn't want to drink that canal-water! It was
dirty green and smelled of rot. Small bubbling tufts of suspicious-
looking emerald drifted in it.

Eight-horse drays loaded with stinking barrels—material to
calk and seal ships across the seas of Tasmarin—trundled along
slowly. Carts and even a carriage with some alvar lord in it made
their way among the walkers and donkey trains.

No one seemed to notice a girl in boy's clothes, with bare feet
and hair that had been roughly cropped by a merrow knife. It didn't
stop Meb looking very warily at the people around her. Anyone
of them could be the vehicle of her horrific fate, after all.

Being alone took some of the magic out of the place. Despite
the smells, the idea of strange places had always fascinated her.
Now, in a large part, she was simply too scared to marvel at
wonders like buildings that were three whole stories high. And
made of brick too!

In the jostling crowd at the open city gate she did feel ghostly
fingers in her pocket, but as she had nothing to steal, these vanished. The men always said that in Tarport you kept your money
in your fist, and your fist in your pocket, and even that didn't
always work.

Meb had not thought much beyond walking to Tarport. Now
that she was here, alone, in the thronging streets, it occurred to
her that she had absolutely no idea how to begin looking for the
other villagers, let alone her step-brothers. Well, said the sensible
voice in her head, if the boys were anywhere, it would be down
at the docks. But, in between the houses, she seemed to have
lost her sense of direction. Finally, after wandering—for a second time—past a tantalizing smelling bakery, she steeled herself
and asked a porter with a load of cloth-bales. He looked a little
puzzled. "Back the way you've just come, sonny. Most of the boats
are out, though. Yellowtail are running off Headly point. They
were taking everybody who could haul a line this morning."

"Thank you, sir." Just in time she stopped herself curtseying, and managed to turn it into a bob of a bow. Yellowtail! The boats could be gone a week, with smacks ferrying the catches in as the men worked, hauling bright spoons of polished white-metal for the big fish. Still, what else could she do but to go and look?

The fishing harbor was indeed mostly deserted. Across on the other side of the bay most of the berths were full, with lines of porters carrying cargoes onto bigger vessels. Here on this side there was just one boat, hauled up on the slip, with the three men working on replacing some planking on the bow, looking as sour as green fruit. She walked over to them.

"What do you want here, boy?" asked a fellow with a tar-bucket and line-scars on his hands. "Come to prig stuff, eh?"

"No, please Sir, I'm looking for my brothers. Mikka and Hrolf Gundarson. From Cliff Cove," said Meb, humbly.

The fisherman shrugged. "They'll be at sea. Every fisherman and every man Jack and the gutter-sweepings of the town are out after the yellowtail. The fish have come in strong after the easterly. That's where we'd be, if it wasn't for these stove-in planks."

Meb's heart fell. What was she going to do now? The apples of this morning seemed a very long time back. "Please Sir, do you have any work for me, then?" she asked. Maybe at least they'd feed her. And they were fishermen. More familiar than the townspeople.

The fisherman pointed with a tar-brush at a grey haired man with an adze, a plank and a look of extreme irritation on his face. "Ask the old man. But now's not a good time."

And, indeed, the man shook his head. "You're too small. We're not some cargo-lugger that likes pretty boys on board. Try over on the cargo quay."

The one with the tar-brush grinned. "You want a spot of my tar to seal your butt first, boy? You'll need it with that lot."

Blushing furiously, Meb beat a retreat. She didn't have much in the way of breasts. Hallgerd had said that they'd come with children, if not before. But with her small build, short hair and breeches, she obviously passed for a boy—with the jokes aimed at boys. So . . . what did she do now?

In the short term, the answer was: she didn't know. She settled on mooching around the town, hoping to spot some of the village people—besides Wulfstan. She looked for possible places to find work. She even tried the baker and a fruit stall.

Neither had any need for a ragged little boy in fisherman's breeches. There were quite enough around town, as they made plain with hard words and, in the case of the fruit-stall owner, a hard blow on the ear for a ragged boy that was not quick enough to dodge. The market, with barrows of everything from bolts of bright cloth, that she longed to touch, to mountains of late fruit, to stalls hung with dried squid, and others loaded with ewe's-milk cheeses, was a wonderful place indeed—except that it made her even hungrier. The stall-owners also made it very plain that they didn't think that she looked like a customer. So she left and wandered back toward the docks, walking along the canal, watching the horses pull the heavy barges loaded with everything from coal to fleeces.

For quite a while she watched a couple of women—who didn't look much older than herself, but were dressed in what Hallgerd would have described as a "wanton" fashion. Their faces were very painted, and their hair was loose—a shocking thing too. But then maybe the same standards didn't apply in the big city. They didn't seem to be selling any goods. It was only when a sailor came up, talked briefly to the women and walked off with one of them that Meb realized that they were displaying their wares, all right. And Hallgerd's assessment would have been right. Women working in the market stalls or carrying their shopping home all had their hair done up, mostly in braids or twisted and pinned to the tops of their heads.

Ruefully, Meb felt her own head, looked at her "borrowed" breeches. She'd only taken them to cover her undress and to protect her from the cold. She'd really meant to give them back. But it did close that possible avenue. She realized just how hungry and scared she must be to even think that way. The odd practical voice inside her head said that for women enduring a fate worse than death, at least they didn't appear to be starving. The practical voice horrified her village morality sometimes.

Meb began to wonder if she could make her way back to the windfall apples and the hay-rick.

The Gate-horn signaled that she'd left it too late, however. And the sky, which had been growing ever more heavy and dark, decided to add rain to her woes. It came cold and thin, blowing in gusts chased by a bitter wind. The last stall-holders began folding up their awnings and packing their barrows. They turfed their scraps into the gutters and onto the cobbles, and then, collars up, pushed the barrows away down the streets and alleys. Meb had hung around the market area for just this reason. There had to be some scraps she could eat?

Too late she realized that she wasn't the only one waiting for them to leave. Half a dozen feral-looking boys had beaten her to it. And they weren't keen on sharing either. They surrounded her. "Get out of here," said the largest of the ragged urchins. "This is our turf, see. Get away before we fix you good."

Meb backed away. At least two of them were bigger than she was. She had no desire to be "fixed good." But she had to find some food, and some shelter. The wind that brought the autumn rains came all the way from winter. She went hunting a drier spot. The alley seemed tempting, overhung by buildings, it must be nearly dry, even if it stank of urine.

She walked into it, without thinking much about the comments the men made about keeping out of the alleys in town. It was indeed nearly dry under the eaves.

In the darkness somebody grabbed her from behind. Wrapped their arms around her, and held her. And someone else hit her over the head as she tried to scream. Her shoulder had taken part of the blow as she tried to pull free, but it was still painful and left her feeling stunned and weak.

She was vaguely aware of someone feeling in her breeches pockets. And lifting her shirt and feeling her bare skinny stomach. The voice seemed to come from some great distance off. "Damn. No money belt either. I were sure he were a runner. Pretty boy like that, usually works for them."

"Fool kid to come down here," said a second voice. "Shall we toss him in the canal?"

"Nah," said the first voice, dismissively. "Who's going to care if he got a rapper on the bone-box? Skinny street brats a-plenty out here. Come on. We might as well go to the alley just past the Green Lantern. There's bound to be drunk or two come in for a leak."

"Usually not much gelt on them by the time they get there," grumbled the second voice. "And it's wetter than here." But he was moving away. Or was that her consciousness?

Meb blurred upward out of the painful darkness to be sick. There wasn't much more than bile in her stomach, but she threw it up anyway. She was cold, she was damp. The eaves above her dripped steadily, splashing to join the trickle in the middle of the noisome alley. Her head hurt. How her head hurt! With an effort she sat up properly, leaning against the wall. What was she doing here?

Slowly it came back to her. They'd tried to rob her. Succeeded— except that she had had nothing to steal. Scared, her eyes probed the darkness. Other than a vague lighter patch she could see nothing. Hear nothing either . . . except . . . squeak . . . skitter . . .

Desperately Meb got to her feet. Not rats! She couldn't stay here with rats, no matter how awful she felt. With one hand on the half-rotten bricks of the wall, she staggered out into the rain.

There was little enough light here either. Slivers of a warm yellow glow leaking into the rainy air from the shuttered windows was all—except for a green lantern hanging from the eave of a building a little further down the canal-path.

The sight of it brought up an alarm signal in her mind. The ones who'd attacked her had said something about that. She started to walk in the opposite direction. But a group of men, swaying and laughing came around the corner from that side. So Meb turned hastily and walked back toward the Green Lantern, walking in the rain, rather than too close to the shelter of the buildings, until she was well past it.

Because she walked there she spotted the drunk. He was asleep—in the rain—on the little stair to the water-level, just beyond the Green Lantern's front door. If he hadn't been wearing something bright yellow she might still have not seen him.

He snored peacefully. And looking down, Meb saw that his hand rested on a pouch. It bulged.

She walked on. The revelers turned into the door of the Green Lantern and were soon noisily making merry inside.

The voice inside said: "If you didn't go back he'd be robbed by someone else." The Meb brought up by Hallgerd's strict principles said: "It's theft." The practical voice inside her head argued that he'd probably die of cold sleeping in the rain anyway. If she felt that way about it she could leave him something.

Biting her lip, she turned back. Her head still throbbed. Her shoulder—which had taken part of the blow, was just plain sore.

She crept down those stairs as quietly as she could. The Green

Lantern provided enough light for her to see that what had caught her eye was a cloak—actually a motley of bright yellow and crimson. A traveling gleeman! Guilt plucked at her again. The gleemen and their 'prentice-boys had come to the village now and again. Wulfstan said they stole. But they always provided welcome news and laughter in exchange.

She nearly crept back up the stairs then. But her eyes hadn't deceived her—it was a pouch, protruding from under the edge of his cloak. It bulged. And right now she didn't care if he was a prince, if that bulge was bread and cheese or gold coins she was going to take it, or some of it . . . actually, bread and cheese might be better for her conscience.

Tentatively, slowly, she reached out a hand to the pouch.

As her fingers closed on it, it all went horribly wrong. A talon-like hand locked onto her wrist. The shut eyes snapped wide open, and the jester laughed evilly. She screamed as he pulled her towards him. She kicked out as hard as she could, and somehow she twisted free. Staggering, she tripped on the narrow stair . . . lost her balance, and fell.

Into the canal.

She screamed again, kicked and swallowed water. Went down. Somehow came up again.

And then her victim jumped into the water too.

He grabbed her by the collar, rather as if she was a kitten, and hauled her towards the steps, swimming strongly. He pulled her up onto them, and then picked her up over his shoulder, as if she weighed less than a bag of feathers. She coughed, spluttered and rid herself of a fair amount of water. None too gently he put her down onto the hard stone. Meb managed to get as far as her hands and knees, still coughing.

"Now what in hell did you do a silly thing like that for?" asked her victim-rescuer, looking down at her. "You poor clumsy little scrap of humanity." He was grinning as he said it. "Now I'm all wet and your screams will likely have frightened my targets off. They'd never believe I was asleep again."

Meb managed sit up. "S . . . sorry," she sniffed, between shivers. To her shame she started to cry.

It seemed to take the gleeman aback too. "Now, now. It's not that bad. I'm not for turning you in. You've had a wetting, and a lesson. You'll be better at it next time."

"There's not going to *be* a next time. You should have let me drown," said Meb miserably, knowing she sounded like an ungrateful, sulky brat, but unable to stop herself. She sat and shivered, the tears running down her face.

She heard the sound of a cork being drawn. "Here, scrap," he said in a tone that held both amusement and sympathy. "Drink some of this and take heart." He pushed a small metal bottle at her.

She waved it off weakly. "No. I don't want it."

He took her by the bristles of hair that the merrow had left her. Tilted her head back, and put the bottle to her lips. "I wasn't asking if you wanted it. I was telling you to drink it, little scrap."

Thus constrained, Meb did. It was like drinking honeyed fire. It went down, but started her coughing again. The gleeman gave her what he obviously considered a gentle pat on the back. "Let it work. It'll put heart into you. You're obviously fairly new to this sort of trade." She caught the flash of grin. "Or you'd have learned to swim *and* chosen a warmer night."

His firewater—or perhaps it was the honey in it—did seem to have helped. She wiped her eyes and nose with a wet shirt-sleeve. "Never did it before. I just . . . I was so hungry and cold and I saw your pouch . . . I'm sorry."

He grinned again. "Nothing in it but a few old rags. Learn. If you can see a fat pouch, belike someone wants you to see it. It was a bait, but I wasn't planning to catch a little fish like you."

"Are you a thief-taker then?" she asked warily. Even in little Cliff Cove she'd heard of them.

He looked shocked. "Me? Now what sort of thing is that to say to fellow who plucked you from the mucky water of the canal, scrap? No, I'm more like a taker from thieves."

"What do you mean?" she asked, curiously.

He looked up, cocking his head to listen. "Patrol coming. Come, we best be away from here. I'll explain. Methinks we need a fire to dry you out, youth."

She followed him up the stairs, and saw that he was heading for the alley next to the Green Lantern. Grabbed his cloak. "There are muggers waiting up there. I heard them . . . after they hit me, earlier."

The gleeman laughed, took her hand from his cloak and hauled her toward the alley. "You've had quite a night of it, young scrap.

I know. I was waiting for them to come to me, when you decided to come for swimming lessons."

Meb looked at him in astonishment.

He took her by the sleeve, pulled her into the alley. "The patrol are just around the corner. Come on. Your two 'friends' have gone now. Let's get you some fire and ourselves a little something to pay for supper and bed. You look in need of them. It's that or getting you home to your mother."

"My mother is dead and my home has been burned to the ground," said Meb, dully. "I haven't got anywhere to go. I'd be very grateful for some food and a dry place to sleep. That's why I tried to steal from you. I didn't know what else to do."

He snorted. "So this is the first time you've ever stolen anything?" he said, his tone full of unbelief.

"A couple of windfall apples," said Meb, guiltily. "The dragon destroyed our village and our dam, and I had no food."

"Ah. A hardened criminal you are!" he said admiringly. "I could tell. So a dragon destroyed your home . . ." He paused. "A little fishing village, no doubt. Hmm. Let's get you a bit of recompense from the dragon."

She gaped at him. "From Lord Zuamar?"

"Could it have been another dragon?" asked the gleeman rhetorically. "This is his island after all. And it suits me. I like stealing from thieves. It's most entertaining. But if I can't take from small thieves, I'll take from a big one. And get you a fire to warm you properly, at the same time."

Meb's inner voice had to admit that she could see the pure joy of mugging muggers who had attacked her. With that in mind, and no certainty of what he planned to do next, but glad to let someone else do the planning, she let him lead her along several alleys and out into Tarport's central square. The scavenging boys had long gone, having disappeared rather like the barrows had earlier. "A fine sight," he said, pointing to a two-story building across the square. It was lit by a series of lamps, each in its neat little sconce.

"Yes," agreed Meb, impressed. "What is it?"

"Zuamar's tax hall. Let's burn it down."

═ Chapter 8 ═

MEB LOOKED AT THE GLEEMAN IN HORROR. HE COULDN'T BE serious. "You can't set fire to a building!" she said, shocked.

He looked quizzically down at her. "But it won't burn unless I set fire to it, Scrap. And getting into it unless it's burning is too much like hard work. Besides, the fire will warm you up nicely. You've started shivering again."

Meb shut her mouth by force of will. It had fallen open involuntarily at the gleeman's crazy idea. She took a deep breath and shook her head. "You can't set fire to buildings," she said firmly. "People will get burned and hurt."

He raised an eyebrow at her. "But there is no one in the tax hall at night. They only extort during daylight hours. So no one gets burned. In fact, even the tax-men will be grateful. They'll get a few days holiday while Zuamar organizes another place for them to work."

Meb had sworn vengeance against dragonkind—no matter how ludicrous the idea. But a lifetime's ingrained deference came pounding at the doors of her conscience. "You should call him 'Lord,'" she said firmly.

The jester snorted. "Why? He's no lord of mine. I'm no one's vassal. A lord has a duty to give his a vassal a living, and my pouch is empty tonight. A lord has a duty to protect his vassals, and your home is ash."

Deep inside, Meb knew that this was dangerous talk. But she found that it did make a peculiar kind of sense. A very appealing kind of sense. The very idea that there should be some form of duty imposed on lords, just as there were taxes imposed on the lesser people! The logical part of her mind said, "*I bet the lords will just love that idea . . . and anyone who comes up with it.*" But she nodded all the same. "We can't, though. Fires spread. It's not right that others should be hurt," she said sanctimoniously, hating herself for saying it, but knowing that she must do so.

The jester laughed. "You're a *good* little scrap aren't you? No wonder you make such a dismal thief. Look, it's raining. The tax-hall stands well away from other buildings. I'll probably have the merry devil of a time getting it to burn, let alone anything else. Anyway, all you have to do is yell 'fire, fire!' which is exactly what a public spirited young fellow like you would do anyway. Then we help to put it out. Good citizens!" he said loftily. "We just charge a little tax money for our services! It is our money, after all, eh? You get dry, and we go off and find a nice inn for a spot of supper and a couple of warm beds, eh. Besides, it's an ugly building. Burning it down would be a public service," he said in a tone just as sanctimonious as hers had been earlier.

She found that she had to laugh a little. Uneasily, but still she was laughing. "You're sure that there is nobody in it? You're sure that it won't spread?"

"Sure as death," he said cheerfully, flicking his cloak over to hide the bold motley. It was a drab grey on the inside. "Now, you stay here. As soon as you see the flames, you sing out. Yell 'fire' at the top of those fine lungs of yours. Then let a few people arrive, before you come and join me. I'll be with the bucket carriers."

Meb waited back in the shadows, as the jester walked across to the building. The logical part of her mind said: "Run. NOW." But it was outweighed by a horrified fascination. He couldn't really mean to set the building on fire, could he? It was made of brick and surely bricks didn't burn? She saw him walk up to next to one of the urn-like lamps. It went out abruptly. Next thing she saw someone moving up on the roof cornices. There was just a dark, spidery, rain-hazed figure, but she'd swear there was an urn with him. A little later he climbed back down.

There was a sudden gush of flames from the little alcove where the lamp had been. The flames ran hungrily up the wall, following a gleaming trail of lamp-oil. Next moment the flames were at the roof.

"Fire!" yelled Meb. What else could she do? Just let it burn? "Fire!" She yelled again.

Shutters began opening across the square. Smoke and flames were rushing out of the tax hall roof by now. People with buckets began pouring out into the street. Joining in was the easiest thing, armed with someone's spare bucket, Meb found herself with those filling at the square's central fountain. "We need to get inside," bawled the gleeman, pushing against the door. "Help me here, all of you!" Several watchmen, their quarterstaves forgotten, joined him, and the doors gave way. "Buckets!" yelled a watchman. "Bring buckets, boys."

Meb was among those who responded. And there in the smoke and darkness was a cheerful gleeman's voice. "Come on," he said, taking her by the elbow. "It's not even burning in here, but there is plenty of smoke. Let's break down a door or two. Make a little confusion for everyone."

He suited action to his words and a wooden door cracked open. He was certainly very strong. And, it seemed, quite able to see in the dark. "Nothing here, except a lot of paper. Frightfully flammable stuff." And a flame licked at it.

"Time to go," he said. "Tch! Don't use that bucket on something I've just lit, Scrap!"

He kicked another door. By the time she got through there, a kist was burning merrily. And the gleeman was pouring a handful of coins into his pockets and then a second handful into hers. "Right," he said, cheerfully. "Time we got out of here. That lot'll be a fine mess of melted gold in with the silver coin. Take them a while to figure out what's missing, if they ever do. And it sounds as if the guard and the fire-watch are getting here. It's definitely time we left."

She followed him, coughing. He was yelling, "Everybody out! The roof's coming down," which was a chorus the others took up loudly.

And somehow, in the smoke and darkness, Meb took a wrong turn.

She ran down a passage . . . and realized that he wasn't ahead of her any more. There was just a closed door. She tried kicking it, as he had. All it did was hurt her toes. And now there were flames behind her too. Even the clangor of yells predominated by "Out, out!" were more distant.

Desperately she went back to the door, about to kick it again. They'd broken when the gleeman kicked them! In the firelight she could see a handle. She tried that and the door swung open. There was a flight of stairs beyond it and she raced up them. This led onto another corridor. Looking back she saw that flames were burning up the stairwell. There was no way back down there. The air was hot and smoke-filled. She could not hear voices any longer. Just the hungry cackle of flames. She wished desperately for the sound of one voice, any voice. But Meb, poor, tired, confused Meb, wasn't ready to give up yet. There was another door. She must find a way down or at least get to a window. This door—a large one, with a bright-polished handle, was locked. But there was a bench—narrow, plain, sturdy and well-worn, in the corridor. Meb picked it up.

She wasn't very big, but a girl from a small fishing village had to be strong. There were always loads to carry, work to be done. She backed off, going as close to flames as she dared and then charged the door with her bench-ram.

It didn't break. But she rammed it again . . . and then again. This time the wood cracked and let her crawl into some high panjandrum's sanctum . . . with shuttered windows. She wrenched them open. Cool, blessedly wet night air rushed in.

She peered out of the window. It seemed a fairly long way down. "Tch," said a voice behind her. "You can't even manage to burn down a public building well, Scrap? No training in arson, either. You've had a sadly neglected upbringing, youth."

Meb turned to find the gleeman standing in the doorway looking at her, his hands on his hips, his toothy grin white in the firelight. "Can we get out that way?" she asked. "It's a long way down."

"Alas, no," he said with a shrug. "With the front doors open and the roof burning this place is an excellent chimney. We'll have to leave by the window that you so wisely found your way to. Let's see. Those drapes should make a fine rope, if you mislike the jump. Never jump onto cobbles in the dark. They make for poor landing places." He ripped the drapes off their hooks as he spoke. "The bench will do nicely," he said. "Bring it to the window."

Meb did. He looped the now-knotted drapes around it, and pointed at the window. "Out you go. Slide down it like a rope. Drop when you get to the end. And head for the alley across from the fountain."

Meb had never slid down a rope in her life—but boys did that on the boats—so at least she'd seen it done. She took her courage in both hands and went over the sill. It was a lot more difficult than it sounded. But the fire was behind him, and he'd come back to find her. She had to do it. It wasn't that far down . . .

Sitting, rubbing the seat of her breeches, she knew that rope-sliding would be the next thing that he would say she needed to learn.

"What were you doing in there?" someone asked, helping her up. "That's the chief inspector's room!"

"We were trying to put the fire out. We got stuck on the second floor. We had to break in there to escape the flames." She thought fast. Better to sound like a real firefighter. "Mairi's going to kill me. I left her bucket in there . . ."

"She'll probably be glad to have you back in one piece, you young tearaway," said the man, laughing.

Meb had been watching anxiously for the gleeman. He didn't appear. She'd have to go back for him! He had come back for her. Could the smoke have overwhelmed him? She got up, and headed back toward the burning building.

"I thought I said the alley across from the fountain," said a voice behind her.

"I thought you were still inside," she said gaping.

"I found a side door. I'm good at that," he said quietly. "I thought if they were going to look for anyone, it shouldn't be the two of us. Head for the alley."

She did, and he arrived moments later. "Time to go," he said. "Unless you want to serve in the bucket chain. They're getting organized, and the rain seems to be coming down harder. Unfortunately. I've never liked tax halls."

He led her through several alleys and out into a broad street, then off down a side road, to an inn. Standing outside under the hanging lantern he looked speculatively at her. "Hmm. You're smoky smelling, and your clothes and your face are sure giveaways, blackened like that. Are you dry again?"

"Er. Yes." She was, fairly. The heat had been enough to frizzle the hair on her hands, which, now that she looked at them, were black. Her face probably looked much the same.

"Good. Time to get you wet again, then," he said, evilly. He somehow seemed to have escaped the worst of the smoke and ash. "There's a well around the back. Come. Over the fence rather than in the front door. The front door is not for the likes of us, anyway. The only time I see the front door of an inn is when I'm being thrown out of it." He led her to the gate at the side of the building and said, "Well, up and over then."

It was a good bit taller than she was. But he seemed to expect her to climb it. So Meb tried. And failed. After the day she'd had her muscles felt like jelly. Even the walk back through the streets had seemed a long, long way.

The gleeman shook his head. "Not like that."

"I'm sorry. I'm just so tired. I can't," she said weakly, hating herself.

"Ach. You poor little scrap of humanity. Here. Have a boost." And he made a stirrup of his hands, and lifted her, so that she had her waist over the top. With a scrabble Meb tumbled headlong into the small yard.

He came over the top as easily as a lizard.

"Good." he said quietly. "No dog."

The idea hadn't even occurred to her. She really wasn't very good at this, the inner person admitted, but she was so tired . . .

He hauled up a bucket of water from the well, and they washed hands and faces. The water was cold—and it wasn't going to do anything for her clothes. But the gleeman seemed to have thought of that too. He slipped into the barn and returned as she was still scrubbing. "Here," he said, handing her a bundle from the pack he'd retrieved from a hayloft. "I've . . . um . . . outgrown them a little. Fling those clothes of yours in the manure pile, and toss a bit of straw over them. I'm going to open a back way in for us. I think we'll have been here quietly, all evening."

Meb was relieved when he went so that she could change, anyway. But her very tired mind did ask her if she knew quite what she was getting herself into. And that was no reference to the red and yellow jester's knee-breeches and the loose tunic-top he'd given her. There was even a cloak, too. It was good cloth, if rather worn. She scrambled into them hastily. And there were boots . . . she'd never had real shoes. They fitted surprisingly well, even if they did feel odd.

"Ah. Well, you'll pass as a jester 'prentice," said her new-found mentor, coming back so quietly that she hadn't heard him. "Got rid of those clothes yet?"

"No . . . but there's good wear in them yet. They just need a wash," she said.

"Tch," he clicked his tongue. "People will maybe be looking for a fisher-boy. Those are too recognizable. And too smoky by half. Give." She handed them over to him. He shook the bundle, and shook his head. "You even forgot to take the money out of the pockets, Scrap."

She blinked. "Sorry. Very tired."

He patted her shoulder sympathetically. "Food and sleep then. We'll need to make an early start tomorrow. We want to be a long way gone when Zuamar starts looking at his tax hall."

"We?"

He grinned. "It would seem that you're probably the worst possible choice for an apprentice rogue. Therefore I've decided to take you on."

She blinked. Gaped at him. "But . . . my step-brothers. I've got to wait for them. They're off at sea. They won't be back for days."

"Best place for them to be," said the gleeman. "I suspect that there is going to be a fair amount of trouble tomorrow. Some people are going to remember you jumping out of the chief tax-inspector's window."

"How will they ever know we did it?" asked Meb, fearfully.

He made a face. "Trust me. They will know someone did. And the bigger the thief, the nastier they get about being robbed, even if it is nothing but some small change you took from their pockets. Come on. There's a back window unlatched. You'll have to keep quiet. Someone is asleep in the room."

On her own Meb would never have dared to go into a room via the window, let alone past two sleeping people, snoring together in bass and alto harmony. She stumbled over some garments abandoned on the floor, but the jester caught her arm before she fell into the bed with the snorers. They navigated through the room to a dimly-lit interior passage, and slipped into the tap-room, to a table in a back corner.

A slatternly, tired-looking woman came to the jester's wave. "We'll have another drink," he said. "And maybe a plate of stew, eh, Scrap?"

"Have you got money to pay for it?" the waitress asked suspiciously.

The gleeman shook his head sorrowfully. "Where's charity these days? Here." He held out a small silver coin. "The boy's had the flux for half the evening. I suppose he'd better just have food. Or maybe a half of ale. He's not used to drinking yet."

The coin improved her expression. "I'll bring you the tail end of the squab pie that we had for our dinner. If the lad's got the flux already, I wouldn't eat the stew. Some parts of it died a bit too long ago."

The noise, the warmth and length of her day were finally telling on Meb. She rested her tired head in her hands, elbows on the rough wooden table, her head spinning gently.

"He looks all in, poor mite," said the woman. "Too young for your sort of life, gleeman."

"We all have to start somewhere," said the gleeman. "Now, let's get some food into him, before he falls asleep at the table."

The squab pie was excellent. Succulent, flecked with tarragon and set in crisp pastry. Even struggling to focus and stay awake, Meb knew that it was finer food than she'd ever had in her life, even without hunger adding sauce. Meb did find it a little odd that there should be no fish in it, but maybe other people did sometimes have meals without fish.

It didn't stop her falling asleep on the table.

Fionn looked at the sleeper across the table from him, her head resting on her arms, with her rough-cut hair a few finger widths from a puddle of spilled beer. He smiled crookedly. Well. Here was a pretty coil he'd got himself into. Somehow he'd have to teach her to leave fewer traces. She probably didn't know what she was doing. Actually, make it that she certainly didn't know what she was doing. When Zuamar came to look at his tax-hall, he would smell magic and dragon fire all over the place.

Fionn had long since given up on any belief in luck . . . or in fate. A planomancer such as he knew that everything revolved around energy. Sometimes you manipulated the energies of the world, and sometimes . . . they manipulated you. Given the way that she was tweaking flow-lines it was not surprising that she'd come to him. In short order Fionn knew that he would have been looking for her. She could very easily ruin his design, even destroy both him and it. It was most amusing that she'd come to the one dragon who really didn't want to find a human with magical skills. To the one who wouldn't either kill her or use her. Still, keeping her would allow him to fix the damage as she caused it and, of course, to thwart the designs of others. That would be sweet. And amusing. As funny as plucking a handful of tail-scales from Zuamar, just as burning his tax-hall had been. Besides, the place really had been a drain on the water-energies of the city. Of course there were other ways that he could have fixed that, but this had been more entertaining.

═ Chapter 9 ═

WARMTH. RICH FOOD. MORE ALCOHOL THAN SHE WAS USED TO . . .
Meb should have slept like the dead. Perhaps it was being in a
much softer bed than the thin straw pallet she was used to. This
one had, by the smell, old feathers in it. It sagged under her and
seemed to threaten to swallow her. It was warm. Too warm. She
drifted in and out of sleep and strange shadowy half-nightmare
dreams—which were eerily real. Flames, hot, angry and devour-
ing. The spiky dark shape of the dragon etched against the pallid moon. And lines in colors she had no words for. Lines that
drifted and wove through everything, in some vast kaleidoscope
pattern, that spread out and out and out, shaping waves, edging
the very stones of great buildings, a tower that hung over the
endless void . . . And then the flames again, flames and a dragon.
She woke, sweating.

Finn stood by the window, silhouetted by the moonlight. She
saw the flash of white teeth in the dark face. "Ah. A bit warm
here under the thatch," he said, fiddling with the window.

It was always confusing in the dark. She could almost have
sworn that he was partially closing it.

Meb was unsure how she'd got here. A vague memory of being
let upstairs, and a fear that she'd been undressed . . . but no, she
was still in the clothes the gleeman had provided. No wonder
she was hot! She undid a button. Pushed the cloak aside, and
lapsed back into sleep.

✧   ✧   ✧

Fionn stood watching, unblinking. Eventually, when her breathing had slipped back into the regular cadences of sleep, he walked back from the window, and took a small flask from his bag. He poured some of the liquid into his hand. It was a shame to waste it, but she'd been on the verge of setting fire to the place. He traced lines of water-force around her bed, quietly, and as gently as possible picking up the foot of the bed to re-align it. She did not wake.

After a while Fionn crossed to the window and stepped out onto the sill.

Meb stirred slightly as the spiky shadow of his wings passed briefly over her face. But she did not wake, as the dragon rose into the night with the swift and powerful beating of his wide wings.

Soon he was up where the air grew thin.

Others were already leaving the conclave, and Fionn skimmed low over the broken lunar surface, almost as if having got this far, he was leaving again. It was an effort of will and magic to reach this place, the air being far too thin for flying. It was easier, soon, to land and walk among the scattered rocks—something beyond the dignity of most of Fionn's peers. That suited him. Mostly he was hidden in the shadows. He came, at length, to a massive crater, and climbed down the rimwall, carefully avoiding certain holds, to enter a fissure near its base. It was dark on the way in here, but Fionn had no need of visible light. He rounded three corners, stepping on certain rocks only. The hoard that lay there was vast, lit up by a warm glowing orb on a high rock shelf. Fionn looked happily at the gold-pile. He had some coins from Zuamar's tax hall to add to it. He was, after all, a dragon. The model on which others were created.

Fionn knew a great deal more about gold than most dragons. He knew for instance how the magical conductivity of it was what underlay much of the magic of Tasmarin. How that had been used in the creation. Dragons, dvergar and humans . . . they undermined the very fabric of the place, which was quite amusing. Its foundation was the finest tracery of dragon-gold, but they probably had not understood that. Gold could be spun out so thin that it could not be seen. But it could easily be broken.

Zuamar had used the space and respect granted to the old, the rich, the large and strong within the conclave to find a time and opportunity to have a word with his island-neighbor, Vorlian. They could not talk outside the conclave as that would have meant entering the territory of the other—a difficult and dangerous process.

Vorlian was afforded similar space of course. He was rich, large and strong, even if, by Zuamar's standards, he was not old. The maneuvering was subtle, but, in its way, obvious. Zuamar seldom visited the conclave. It was most likely that he'd come here just for this purpose.

Their bows were a measured performance. So carefully measured Vorlian, judging his own, as to be precise mirrors of the other. "My good Zuamar. And how does the night find you?" asked Vorlian, carefully urbane.

"Angry, Vorlian," said the older dragon.

Vorlian wished he had less of an idea why. Or knew just how this had come back to him. "Ah."

"It's these humans . . . and I think some of the other lesser species. Things fall apart, and they're growing restive."

Vorlian hoped that his relief did not show. "I think we've been preoccupied with the situation, Zuamar. Allowed them to get above themselves." Actually, he thought most of dragonkind had diverted their attention from the true crisis to the petty pursuit of vendettas and ensuring that they got their respect and dues from those within their demesnes. But if that was what Zuamar wanted to hear about raiders attacking his island . . .

The older dragon nodded his vast head. "We need some kind of alliance against the pernicious lice. You are too young to remember the dark times before Tasmarin, Vorlian. They pitted dragon against dragon to serve their ends. The alvar and centaur-kind are supposed to be our allies. But they too were a part of it. And it's happening again. I've had a human raid on one of my villages. I went there this afternoon to inspect." The dragon snorted sulphurously. "I can smell magic, Vorlian."

It was an ability some dragons had. Vorlian for one. Magic left traces. "What kind, Zuamar?"

The Lord of Yenfar stared at him through slitted eyes. "Odd kinds. More than one kind. But one thing has raised my fears and my fury enough to come to seek you out."

Vorlian smiled attentively. "And what was that, and how may I help?"

"There was a dragon there. A dragon on my land. By the prints it was a smaller than average one. I cannot believe that such would dare to trespass. I suspect compulsion. I want that dragon found and I want those who dared compel it, destroyed."

Vorlian took a deep breath, absorbing the information. Had Haborym and the sprite found a dragon to serve their purposes? Were they playing him false? "My Lord," he said carefully, "there are—in these times of upheaval—dragonkind that have been left destitute. Some may have been . . . desperate enough for gold to participate in these activities, without compulsion. It is not easy to compel . . ."

Zuamar snorted a cloud of pungent steam. "Vorlian. That sort of story is well and good for the younger ones. We've done our best to make sure the lesser species believe it. But you are not that stupid and neither am I. We were created impervious to most spells. At best we can be stunned by certain combinations of magic. Otherwise only our own magic works on us . . . except compulsion. How would the First have sent us about their errands otherwise?"

Vorlian was shocked. The First were seldom mentioned. And talk of dragonkind running errands . . . the subject was completely taboo. Many of the younger ones, those born here, would not know of it all. "We don't talk of such things!"

"Forgetting the First is a mistake, Vorlian," said Zuamar. "You can be certain that centaurs and some of the others do not. Here in Tasmarin we are the masters. But we need to remember that it was not always so. Changes are coming. It may not always be this way. We do not want to return to servitude. We need to deal with any that dare to interfere."

Vorlian found himself in much sympathy with that point of view. "I will investigate."

Zuamar hissed between his teeth. They were large, needlelike teeth. "So will I. I gather like minds, Vorlian. If we find those who consort with the lesser races, we must act swiftly and harshly. It will be dragon against dragon again. Are you with me, Vorlian?"

"If it comes to that, yes," said Vorlian with calm assurance. The older dragon should remember something besides the servitude and the First. Who actually knew what they'd been, anyway? Zuamar needed to remember that dragons were masters of many things: war, the elements, and deceit. He served a higher purpose. And he was sure that he was not compelled to do so. "You could check on a dragon called Jakarin. She lost her hoard recently. I had heard a rumor that she was looking for any sources of gold." Vorlian's mind turned briefly to the smaller dragon of the encounter a few days back . . . Fionn. Dismissed him. He was sharp-tongued. Too clever for his own good. But there was something about him that made Vorlian wary about accusing him. It might just get back to him.

.

Fionn spiraled his way in a slow sinistral curve down towards Yenfar and Tarport again. The rain had set in, in earnest now, blanketing the place in cloud. But Fionn could find any place. That was an aspect of his ability, aided by the fact that he saw deep into energy spectra, and Tarport glowed, even through the rain. Soon he landed on the roof-tree of the inn, and changed once more into the form of Finn the traveling Gleeman. He slipped—almost really slipped, back down the roof and into the attic-room. He hadn't slept, but, well, he was refreshed. Fionn resolved that one day he'd find out why gold affected dragonkind like that. He suspected that it was a catalyst of some sort. They needed it, particularly for molting and breeding.

The scrap of human-kind was asleep now, sheltered and safe within the wall of dragon-tears. Fionn erased their mark as best he could. Magic would leave a trace for the very skilled, of course. It always did. Fionn lit a candle. There was no one to see how he did so, so he did not bother with his normal fakery. It had taken him years to master not reducing the candle to a pool of tallow with that breath.

He touched her cheek, and she stirred. Burrowed down into the bed. She looked fragile and very innocent . . . well, if he left her here, she'd be broken soon enough, and they'd use that innocence. "Up you get, Scrap. It's time we were away."

She sat up. Yawned. "But it is not even light."

"All the better reason to be away, before it is. We have some distance to travel today."

She didn't argue, just got up, and followed him. He liked that in a human. They were inclined to be complicated early in the morning. Far too full of questions. As usual Fionn had carefully scouted a way out . . . which he had to modify a bit. She wasn't able to transform her body. But when all else failed there was always the front door. It was so unlikely that people always assumed you'd taken a harder way out.

= Chapter 10 =

THE SONS OF CHIRON STOOD AROUND THE SACRED POOL LIKE statues, perfectly placed and ordered. Not a tail moved, nor nostril flared, as they focussed their will on the pool. The peat-stained water was very dark and very still. That stillness was a rare thing up here where the winds were born. Yet the faintest ripple would destroy the working that they had struggled so to achieve. This was an ancient place, steeped in magics. The future that they sought to explore was always an uncertain country.

There was not a hint of a breeze but the water shivered. Gradually it stilled. Images began to form in the water. Images of chaos and death. And twined through the shifting possibilities, over and over, a black dragon. But one area of water remained clouded. There were hints of reds and yellows. But the colors shifted and moved like oil on water, defying their will, refusing to resolve into a shape. And then briefly, a vista, a vast panorama, looking out across the autumnal hills and across the wild oceans to the purple mountains . . . two humans. One short, one tall, in grey cloaks with their backs to the centaurs. And the black dragon was there supporting the scene on his outspread wings . . . The vision flickered rapidly to a snow-capped mountain, a stone 'beehive,' and, as it did that, the patch of water it had appeared in vanished in a sharp curl of steam. Like tossing a stone into the pool that had created ripples, spreading and distorting.

The ripples reached the edge and bounced back. And in the fading last visionary moments they saw Actaeon's face. The price

67

of his vanity was a high one, they knew. The emptiness, so far from the high plateaux and endless song of wind and grasses, must be hard to bear.

═ Chapter 11 ═

THE STREET WAS DARK AND STILL. THE SOFT RAIN FELL, AND THE cloud blanketed any hint of pre-dawn that might be lurking. Since the gleeman had snuffed the candle and left it in the hall, Meb had followed him more by sound and feel than anything else. She was terrified that she'd lose him. So terrified she'd taken a hold of his cloak-edge. She was sure that no real 'prentice boy would have done that. They were all big and brave and generally bad. But it was very comforting, and her new master had not complained. She was still very much in frightened awe of him. She could hardly believe what they'd done the night before . . . .

"The gates will still be locked," she pointed out. But he would know that.

"True," he replied cheerfully. "But we have work to do."

"What? I mean . . . not burning anything down is it?" she asked suddenly wary.

That amused him, by the snort of laughter. "Perhaps later. Right now we turn our cloaks around and visit a cart-shed. How are you with carts, Scrap?"

It seemed she had a new name. Well, "Meb" was a sure giveaway of her sex. "I don't know how to drive a cart," admitted Meb. Being a cart-driver was a high ambition for a boy from a fishing village. For a girl like her it was just not to be thought of.

"It's fine," said her new master. "You won't be driving. You'll be jumping down and picking up the buckets."

"Buckets?"

"A town this size needs to dispose of its nightsoil somehow, Scrap," he explained. "Or it would have poisoned itself even more completely by now. Now, you just stay here until I call you. This is not the kind of trick you are ready to learn just yet."

So Meb found herself standing alone under a dripping eave. After a while she began to wonder if he'd gone off and left her there. She couldn't blame him, and whatever he was going to do next would be terrifying, but being deserted here was just as terrifying.

She didn't even hear him come back. He could move very silently. "This way. Here, take hold of my cloak again."

He led her on, through a creaking gate and to a chink of light. It proved to be coming from a crack in the door of a barn. It must have been a very strong light, Meb realized, as it had to fight its way past the stench that also came out of the crack. Tarport-town stank. This made that reek seem like perfume. The jester pulled the door open to reveal an elderly two-wheeled cart, with high sides. "Nightsoil cart," said the jester unnecessarily.

Meb had never met one before. But the cart could be identified by its smell. "Do . . . do we have to travel inside that?"

"Fortunately not! Help me hitch the donkey up. Then there is a smock over there next to the wall. Change into that. Save your kit."

Donkeys were unpleasant, uncooperative, and frightening too, Meb discovered. Well, they were to her. The donkey seemed to be afraid of her master, if not of her. Still, at least Finn knew what they were supposed to be doing. And he chased her off to change while he adjusted the harness. She had been wondering how she was going to do that. The answer was: very quickly, behind the cart. "Come hold the donkey's head while I change," he said, when she'd barely done. So she did. She was allowed to sit on the seat next to him, as the cart trundled out of the yard. There was just enough light to see now. It made her feel very grand indeed sitting on the seat of a cart, even a noisome one like this. But as she soon discovered that she didn't get to sit for long. The donkey knew its route, and Meb was soon leaping down to pick up the buckets of filth and tip them over the high sides into the tar-lined bin of the cart. She soon became aware that gutting fish was not the worst job on earth after all.

They even went past the remains of Lord Zuamar's tax hall.

The square was over-run with soldiers. The Lord Zuamar's officials were grubbing around the ashes and masonry like frantic ants. "Where do you think you're going?" demanded a captain as the donkey plodded into the square, ignoring his soldiery as only a donkey can.

"Here to collect the nightsoil, general," said Finn, bobbing his head. "'tis my job." He sounded like a half-wit, suddenly.

The officer rolled his eyes . . . and held his nose. "So I can smell. Go away."

"I can't do that. 'Tis my job. Junior clerk Mr. Panjar will have my guts for garters," said Finn, stubbornly edging the donkey forward.

"Go away before I send your guts back to him without the rest of you," said the officer.

"You'll give me a chitty to say I was here?" said Finn, looking helplessly at him. "I can't go otherwise. 'Tis my job, see."

"Oh lord. Yes." The man scrawled on a piece of paper and held it out. Finn prodded Meb in the ribs. She was nearly frozen with terror. "Fetch it, boy."

So she did.

"Now get yourself and your donkey and the cart out of here!" said the officer.

They did, although the donkey did not like a change in the route at all.

They were soon back on its familiar route, and Meb was heaving buckets. Finn had relieved her of the note. He must be able to read and write, Meb realized, to her surprise. He had, it would seem, a quill and ink with him in that pouch.

They worked on. The cart plainly only worked the better part of town, and the donkey's cart was soon trundling along, near brim-full, to the city gate.

The guards were checking every vehicle and person out of the city. It was apparent they weren't too sure just what they were searching for. But they were turning a fair number of ordinary people back.

"What have you got there?" asked the guard.

Finn stood up and scooped a bucket full. "All the treasure we looted from the tax hall," he said, waving it under the guard's nose. "Do you want some?"

"None of your lip or I'll run you in," said the guard.

Finn was not impressed. "You bugger off or I'll give you this lot up your snout." He held out the piece of paper. "Here. From Captain Flesch. We've got a permission to go and dump our load. Unless you want to search it. Stick your spears through it in case we've got thieves on the cart. Maybe have a feel for the gold in the bottom, eh?"

The guard peered at the bit of paper. "Get along with you. And don't give me any more trouble," he said with an attempt to show that he was really in control of the situation.

So they got. Meb could scarcely believe it, as the donkey plodded slowly out of the gates and onto the main pike next to the canal. The water still looked filthy. But she itched to jump into it and wash and wash. The donkey knew where it was going and soon they branched off the pike road and onto a track to a sandy field near the sea. There were two men there with wooden shovels, resting next to a tree. They got up when they saw the cart. "You took your time," said the taller one. "Thought you'd never get here. We'll have that silver now, jester."

Finn jumped down. So did Meb, with relief. She'd got used to the smell, just not the idea. Finn reached up and tossed a bundle from the seat to her. "Off you go to the sea, Scrap. Get yourself washed off. You stink."

It was true that lofting the buckets, she'd had the worse job. And even seawater looked good after that. She was still scared of it, but . . . ankle deep should be safe enough. And it let her change in a little privacy. So she ran over the low dune and onto the beach. Finn seemed on friendly enough terms with the men.

She pulled the smock off and washed, rubbing her hands and forearms with the coarse sand, keeping a weather eye out for Finn, or anyone else. She had her new breeches and tunic-top on, and was sitting pulling the boots on before he finally appeared.

Unselfconsciously, he stripped off, washed, dressed. Meb tried as best as she could not to stare. Or blush. Or behave as a boy would not. But he didn't seem too observant, to her relief. They took the stained and mucky smocks back to the night-soil men, busy emptying the cart, seemingly oblivious to the smell.

Soon they were making their way cross country, away from Tarport. Finn led them to a rutted lane, overhung with hedgerows. He seemed very wary. "When I tell you to get into the bushes, do it."

"Why?"

"Because Zuamar plainly hasn't heard about his tax hall. Someone will take word to his eyrie, eventually, little as they may want to. And he's a bit sharper than those dozy guards."

Sure enough, a little later Finn said "Bushes" sharply, and even though she was busy obeying, he hoicked her sideways into the hedge. She hadn't even been aware that there was a gap there, but there was enough space for them to hide. The autumn sunlight was cut by a sudden shadow. Meb was deathly afraid. Wished herself invisible. The shadow passed along with the ponderous wings of the great dragon.

"He's going to be really mad, soon," said Finn. "How do you feel about running, Scrap? Every bit of distance counts, and there is running water just up the hill."

Meb hoped it was clean water. She could use a drink and, indeed, some breakfast. She had a feeling that it might be a while before she ate, though.

Fionn had worried that she might just have given them away with the power of those magics of hers. It was plain that the child had no idea just what she was doing, let alone what surges of power she was putting out. Although it had undoubtedly been with her since birth, in humans this sort of thing usually began to flower at puberty. She would probably go on developing for several more years. Her little village had no idea how lucky it had been. And how lucky it had been not to be destroyed. That 'not here' of hers that she'd pulled down on them must have looked like someone had cut a hole in the fabric of reality. He'd been hard-pressed to weave an illusion above it, and afraid that Zuamar would notice the working. Some dragons were more sensitive than others at range. All of them were aware of it from close at hand.

Zuamar would be getting a reek of it in his big nostrils now, thought Fionn, sniggering. And they'd cast a powerful illusion over themselves in leaving the town. More than a few would remember the nightsoil men. But they'd remember them as nightsoil men. Too obvious to suspect. And while those big nostrils of Zuamar would be smelling for human and dragon magic, the smell of shit would help to hide it.

Fionn could have left the town as he'd come. But there was

this human girl-child. He wondered just where she'd come from. She was human, all right . . . but the dragons of Tasmarin had hunted down far smaller traces of magic than that. Magic ability was heritable, and he'd thought that there wasn't much left in the gene-pool. Perhaps she was a throwback . . . but she felt as if she came from elsewhere. Whatever she was, he would have to train her somehow, or she'd create enough trouble to enmesh even him.

Anyway, she was almost falling over from exhaustion. Panting like an angry centaur. They'd have to take shelter where she could believe it was safe, soon. Otherwise powers of water, earth and sky alone knew what she would do next. Well, he'd avoided the dvergar for some years, after last time. They'd probably got over it by now.

Meb was gasping for breath, and her feet seemed to have lost touch with her eyes. They kept tripping over things that she knew she'd seen. And the gleeman just seemed tireless in his long easy strides. Maybe she'd just fall over. Lord Zuamar could catch her.

Then she heard, or rather felt, the dragon's roar of rage. At least . . . she must have heard it. They were nearly a league from Tarport, she was sure. But it seemed to echo in her skull. She swayed, and her tired feet managed to trip her, and send her sprawling and slithering on hands and knees into the stream. The gleeman hauled her upright by the scruff of her tunic. "He's loud and he's angry," he said, grinning. "Come on. Pull your boots off, and walk in the water. Couple of hundred yards more. Can you do it?"

"Ye . . . es," she panted. Really what she wanted to do was to lie down and then drink. Her spit was dry and sticky and clung to her lips. She was sweating like it was the midsummer ship-haul for careening—yet her feet were in agony. The stream-water was numbingly cold. "I . . . icy."

"It comes down off the mountains," said Finn, pointing. She could just see the distant tops of the purple-blue mountains of the interior. It was a place of fear and strangeness to the fishermen, a mysterious place where the alvar had their palaces and, somewhere on the highest peaks, Lord Zuamar had his eyrie.

Somehow she kept walking through the pebbly shallows after

Fionn. A fish darted from her feet, and she nearly fell over. They came to a series of small waterfalls. Finn did not let her touch the dry rocks on either side but made her scramble up through the slippery splash. And then they came to a long narrow pool between huge boulders—boulders the size of two houses each. A far larger waterfall poured splashily into the far side, maybe thirty yards away, but the ripples from it were lost in the mirror smoothness of the water. The pool fell away from the clear yellow and brown pebbled shallows into the blue-grey depths. Her heart fell. It looked deep, and she already knew that it would be bitterly cold. She was relieved when he held his hand up for her to stop. He whistled.

She hadn't seen it until it moved. The furry head dropped under water with a plop and a set of rings on the still water. A dark shape swirled away.

"Otr," said the Jester.

"Otter?" She'd heard of those, and had seen sea-otters.

"No. Otr. He's a tricky one. One the oldest. He'll have gone to talk with the rest."

Meb looked back toward the town they'd left that morning. Finn caught the glance.

"Zuamar's rising. You feel it, do you, Scrap?"

She did. She could feel the rage. And she wanted to run and hide. He put a steadying hand on her shoulder. "You are safest in the water. Anyway, with luck we'll have a hiding place."

Fionn knew that he was taking a chance. He'd stretched their traveling as much as he could . . . and she'd showed that the working did not affect her. He'd seen her response to Zuamar's fountain of rage. She'd clutched her ears. Fionn knew that it wasn't actual sound that she was aware of. The principle of reciprocity applied well with magical forces. If you could feel the other, the other could probably feel you. The water would help. Water force would dissipate her sendings, scatter them down the stream. But it was time to call a favor due. The dvergar owed him. Of course no one liked being reminded of that.

═ Chapter 12 ═

THE FURRY, SLEEK HEAD POKED ITSELF UP OUT OF THE WATER. "What do you want, Fionn Troublemaker?" asked the otter. He sounded, Meb thought, both suspicious and resigned.

"Is that any way to greet an old friend?" said Finn, grinning.

"Means you're in trouble again," said the creature wrinkling its whiskers. "The human with you? Breshy will have to bring a boat."

The otter submerged again, this time a fraction more slowly, with barely a ripple.

"What . . . ?" Meb stared.

"They're water-dvergar," explained Finn. "Black water dvergar. Shape shifters. They have chancy tempers so you want to be cautious with them. But they're all right if they take to you."

Meb knew of shape-shifters. There were wolves that could take the form of men, and other terrifying things whispered about in fire-side stories. "W . . . won't they kill us?"

Finn laughed. "Their food might. They like to eat frogs."

"Frogs," said a gruff voice, "are good for you."

Meb looked up. The speaker was paddling a coracle made of skin and withy along the pool. Fierce dark eyes peered back at her out of a mane of black hair. There was almost more hair than person . . . but the person was small and stocky, half her height if about the same weight. "I can only take one of you. You'll have to swim, Fionn."

"You can come back for my new apprentice," said the jester, walking through the shallows to the small boat, and getting into it. "You stay put, Scrap. Exactly where you are, and don't touch the shore."

77

So Meb stood. Her feet were numb now, anyway.

The black dverg turned the little boat and stirred it back up the pool to an overhanging wall of one of the huge boulders. Then . . . he vanished. Meb shivered superstitiously, and not just from the cold. Next thing he was back, without Finn. Cautiously . . . nervous, but not knowing where to run to, Meb got into the small round boat. The dverg never actually took his paddle out of the water, he just flicked and turned the handle, sending them wriggling upstream. Meb wondered if it—and the disappearance—were magic; maybe there was a huge fish on the end of the paddle-shaft. Maybe it wasn't a shaft, but its fin-spine. Now, in the overhang shadow, Meb saw a low lip, maybe three hand-spans above the water level—a dark opening below it.

"Get your head down," said the gravel-voiced Breshy.

So Meb ducked. Breshy tossed the paddle into the boat, grabbed the lip and pushed the coracle down into the water so a little slopped over the edge—and the boat went under the edge. Next the dverg dropped down into the bottom of the boat, gave a quick shove on the roof . . . and they popped back up again. In darkness. All Meb could see was the tiny slit of light where they'd come under the rock, which they moved swiftly and silently away from. The coracle bumped against something. A strong hand hauled her out of the craft, up onto cold rock.

"Give us some light, will you," said Finn.

"Ach. In a moment. I seem to have a fish on my paddle blade," said the dverg.

So the jester made a flame himself. He must have had flint and a steel, because there was a spark and a flare of a fire. He lit a wick—one of a bunch in a clay bowl. The black-haired dverg was wrestling with a fish.

"A nice salmon," said Finn. "A change from frogs."

"Give us a hand," said Breshy, beaming, square teeth showing in the bearded face. "Pull the boat close to the quay. The current will suck it away to the mill otherwise. What a bit of luck! I must have hit it with the paddle."

So Finn and Meb pulled the coracle up—the dverg was not letting go of the fish. "Otr will be green with envy," said the dwarf, cheerfully. "Follow me."

So they did, along the rock-cut passage next to the water, past the slow turning waterwheel and down another passage. More of the simple lanterns lit the way down. "Where are we going?" whispered Meb.

"Under the stream. They mine and work gravels from it. Living directly under the water keeps them safe from dragons."

Meb could—right now—see the value of that. But . . . this was Lord Zuamar's land. He protected it . . . or was supposed to. "Er . . . why?"

The gleeman chuckled. "They mine gold. Dragons are uncanny about finding it. The black dvergar don't like parting with it. Not without payment."

A few days ago that would have seemed very wrong. Then Lord Zuamar was their overlord, entitled to take whatever he saw fit to take. Now Meb saw their point. The passage curved yet again, and now the sounds of hammering metal—almost lost in the splashing of the waterwheel earlier, came echoing loudly. The passage opened into a cave, in which a forge-fire burned and several more of the small hairy dvergar were working. They looked up as Breshy bounded in with his fish.

"Look!" he said, triumphantly.

It was plain that it was a welcome sight. "How did you get that!" demanded one of the bellows-men.

"I think it was one of his tricks," said Breshy, jerking his head at Finn. "But a good one this time."

"Better than frogs," said Finn, with a sly grin.

The dverg was not used to being teased, and the comment simply went over his head. "Frogs are good eating, but it's a change," he said, seriously. "Otr has caught everything that isn't a small trout by now. It's not the biggest of streams."

Up to then Meb had not been too sure if the frogs had been a complicated joke that she wasn't party to. Now she realized it hadn't been. Maybe . . . eating frogs was normal, away from a fishing village? She didn't think that she wanted to find out, even though, right now, she felt as if she might just fall over.

Someone must have noticed because they did catch her before she actually hit the flagged floor, or landed in the gutters that took water back to the pumps.

They all gathered in a large rock-chamber with ornate metal lamps, a cheerful fire and rather a low stone table with equally low benches around it. Dvergar carried in steaming platters and dumped them on the table. "They're not long on manners," said Finn, "come and sit or you'll get none."

Meb, driven by the smells of cooked food, had her feet under the table and herself in front of a trencher so fast she even beat Finn and some of the little black haired folk.

The dvergar made a meal look like a battle-zone, with knives stabbing this and hacking that, and spearing the other, and little strong hands grabbing to pile on the trenchers. As there was no blood spurting and she was very hungry, Meb took a deep breath and joined in the carnage. She thought that what she'd snatched were the drumsticks off very small birds at first.

They tasted like slightly fishy chicken. The salmon was much nicer. The dark mead that was circulating in jugs was even nicer. "Don't drink too much of it," said Finn, "or you'll start believing you are a poet. That's small-beer in the tall jug."

So she stuck to that. It was at least familiar, unlike some of the food.

Now that the initial rush was over, the dvergar slowed to a more reasonable pace of eating and drinking, laughing and talking.

Meb drank that in as much as the small beer. She was warm, dry, full of food and surrounded by good cheer. And she'd got to meet real mining dvergar!

Much later, next to the banked furnace, Fionn sat with Motsognir. The others had long gone to join his little human in dreamland. But there was gold here, enough to stimulate Fionn. And the old dvergar lord claimed he was past the age of needing much rest. "If I sleep . . . I may not wake again, dragon. So what really brings you here?"

"Oh, the usual. Trying to destroy the world. Stealing a bit of gold. Indulging in good food and practical jokes. Occasionally setting things to rights. Causing fires."

The dvergar gave a wintery smile. "You don't like us to take you too seriously, do you?"

"No. It would weaken me," said Fionn.

Motsognir's shoulders shook slightly. He was old but still carried the heavy muscle of a lifetime—a long lifetime—of metal-work. Finn was not too sure how old he actually was. But it was possible that he was old enough to remember too much. The dverg had changed his name over the years, several times. As far as Fionn knew he was the only creature who called the old king by his true name. But it was one of the skills given to the planomancer. Fionn had to know true names.

"Possibly," said Motsognir, his tone dry, "But only in that your foes might realize what they faced."

Fionn nodded. "Exactly. Better to have them just a little surprised."

Motsognir laughed again. "Dragonish cunning. But I have dvergar cunning, which is reputedly also deep and dark. So, spare asking me to believe in a chance passing. Save that for the younger ones. Why are you here?"

"I needed to hide the little human. She's a worker of wild magics."

The old dwarf-lord raised his eyebrows. "A human. I thought her kind were extinct."

"She will be if they find her. Or after they have finished using her she will be. She's a damned nuisance to me in my line of work, but she thwarts some of the designs of others."

Motsognir shook his head slowly. "Much as I do enjoy thwarting the designs of your fellows, sooner or later they'd find her here. We're cunning artificers, not great magicians or warriors. This is a place of hiding, not an impregnable fortress."

"I know. And I would not ask that of you," said Fionn.

The old dvergar king looked at him intently for a few heatbeats, and then asked: "So what do you want . . . besides temporary respite? You're up to something, Fionn. But so far you have always dealt fairly with us. Come to our aid a time or two. Usually passed it off as a nasty joke. But you didn't come here by accident. There are plenty of other dvergar. There are other hiding places. And you are good at finding them."

"And you are entirely too clever," said Fionn, allowing a wisp of steam to escape his nostrils.

The dverg's dark eyes twinkled. "Yes. I have that reputation. Which I also try to avoid having talked about. So . . . stop evading the subject and answer me. You want us to make something, don't you?"

Fionn nodded. "For her. Dvergar are better at binding power into objects than most of the other species. She needs a way of hiding herself. Or at least of hiding her magic. She has the power to do it, just not the skill."

"And we have the skill but not the power. So you want something that will harness her own powers?"

"Yes. It doesn't have to be anything particularly wonderful. I wouldn't ask for one of the masters like yourself. Just get one of the younglings to hammer out something. An amulet she can believe in or something."

The dvergar king put his hand to his beard, hiding his mouth. "I see. You wouldn't have any particular artificer in mind, would you?"

"What about young Breshy? He needs the practice. He could get his brothers to give him a hand."

The dvergar gave a little snort of laughter. "Oh yes. Fionn, you know all of the true names. Why do you call him that, instead of Dvalinn? Yes. Very well, I will ask. He was pleased with the fish."

"She did that. It left me with a mess to put right."

"There is a price of course," said Motsognir, looking at Fionn from under half-lidded eyes.

Fionn shrugged. "There always is. Tell me, so we can get on with the bargaining. And it's not the Brisinghamen I am asking for. So don't even suggest that for a price."

The black dvergar laughed. "And she's not exactly Freya either. Why is she pretending to be a boy?"

"I am not too sure yet. Of course, for a girl on her own, that's sometimes a good idea. If that is what she wants, so be it. I'll find out why, eventually," said Fionn, waiting. Sooner or later the other side would offer.

Motsognir waited too, silent. He could play this game just as well as the dragon. Then suddenly . . . he changed his mind. "Ach. We'll do it for nothing, Fionn."

"Now why do I feel I would be better off paying a price for it?" asked Fionn sardonically. "You want me in your debt, Motsognir?"

"You're honorable enough about paying debts, for one of drag-onkind," said Motsognir. "But no. Actually, I think we want *her* in our debt."

It was Fionn's turn to look thoughtful. "Honesty compels me to tell you that there are many dragons who will be less than pleased with you for doing this. They'll want to know where she got a dvergar artifact."

Motsognir waved his thick hand dismissively. "A mere bauble made by one of my children. Why should they fuss?"

Both of them knew he was lying. But perhaps it was best that way.

✧   ✧   ✧

Meb awoke, somehow aware that she was being watched.

It was the fish-catcher, Breshy. He was just sitting there, looking at her.

A quick glance showed that Finn was nowhere about.

"What do you want?" she asked, nervously.

"Well," he said thoughtfully, "The occasional fish would be good. Do you want to come and choose the stone?"

Now Meb was thoroughly confused. "Stone?"

He nodded. "The old one told me to make you something. Well, me and my brothers. But I am the shaper. He said you need something to help you with hiding. A seeming-charm. Nothing of great power," he said apologetically. "Just something to cloud a watcher's eyes a little. Motsognir says you wish to be taken for a man, not a woman. This will help."

Meb gaped at the dvergar. "How did you know?"

He shrugged. "How does one know what metals are in an ore? You are. Dvergar do not see things as you humans do. We work metals. You work with living things. A fish now and again would be welcome. And it would not upset the balance of things too much," he said, humbly.

Meb had no idea what he was talking about. Well, besides about the fish. "I hope you get lots of fish!"

"Oh no, not lots. Just one once in a while would be good. Come. We need to work while the mist is on the water."

"Why?" It sounded magical.

"It hides the smoke from the forges better. There are charcoal burners in the forest anyway. That accounts for the smell of smoke to most passers-by."

"Oh," He'd led her down a passage, to a series of ridged sorting boards, with water and a mixture of gravel playing over them. The place was full of the rhythmic thump-thump of a pump of some sort. The fishing boats had all had pumps to clear the bilges, but this one seemed to work by itself. Several of the dvergar were stooped over the ridged boards, picking at them. Breshy walked her over to a tub, sitting in a corner. It was full of pebbles. Some were translucent, and a few as clear as city-glass. They came in a variety of colors. "Pick a stone."

Meb looked at the barrel. "Uh. What kind of stone?"

"The old one thought it best that I make you a necklace of some sort. So I wouldn't make it too heavy."

Meb felt her heart beat like a trip hammer. The practical Meb in her head said: *It's a trick.* The other part said nothing. Just yearned. But she knew it was just so wrong. "You mean . . . jewelry. Like rich people wear. I . . . am too ordinary." She'd seen some necklaces and a few of the women in the village had had copper and even brass bracelets. Most wore amulets of shells strung on pieces of gut. Like most of the fisherbrats she'd collected shells and tried to make them too. But real jewelry . . . with silver or gold? That was too expensive to even have dreamed of, let alone something made by the dvergar. Their work was legendary for its beauty and craftsmanship.

"Ach. It'll be something to bind the spell to," said the dverg, easily. "Go on. Pick a stone."

So Meb picked through the half-barrel. They were a number of lovely colors. Deep red, azure, amber, clear. Very pretty, really. But . . . she was Meb. A girl from a poor fishing village. So she picked the smallest and dullest little stone. It felt . . . like her. Oh, she had wanted something beautiful, maybe even precious. But this little black knobbly rock was so small and dull in this barrel. Just an ordinary river pebble.

She handed it to Breshy, suddenly aware that all the others had stopped working and were watching. "Can I have this one?"

The dverg's eyes twinkled. "I did say you could have any one." The tone was somehow satisfied. Good! That meant that she'd been right to take something small and uninteresting.

"It will become what you need it to be," he said, turning it in his hands.

It looked like a golden dragon biting its own tail. It was perfection . . . yet it was the eyes that fascinated her. They moved and changed color . . . Meb stared at them fascinated but fearful.

Breshy saw how she stared. "The eyes are your stone. I didn't cut it in two, just polished it and put it into the head. You can see a little of it through the eyes. Opals are fragile and the head will protect it. There is a thin film of our crystal on it to protect it too. It is mostly hidden," he said, apologetically. "But the virtue is all there. Hidden or not. And that too is a symbol."

Meb wasn't actually sure what an opal was. So she asked.

"A wondrous stone," said Finn. "An opal has the virtues of all the other gems in its colors. And this one is more. It is a wood-opal, where the stone has replaced the wood of some long buried tree. They have powers of wood, water—because they are part water and part stone. And changing with the light and angle. Powerful symbols for powerful magics."

"And a dragon to watch over it all. Dragons are sky symbols. And gold binds them." The dverg seemed to find that terribly funny.

Meb could not help touching it. The tiny links moved like a serpent, golden and sinuous against her skin. The eyes seemed to look at her, into her. She wanted it, as she had never wanted anything else. "It is too valuable for me," she said resolutely.

"You can't refuse a dvergar gift," said Finn, smiling at her. "Even if they will often turn and bite you. Say thank you, and put it on."

Meb looked at it. Bit her lip. Shook her head. "It's . . . it's too precious. I might lose it or break it or . . ."

Breshy laughed. "It'll not come off, once it is on, unless you take it off. And please, our treasures do not break. And it will focus your will. Help you to . . . hide what you do not want seen."

"You mean it is magical?" That was even more frightening, more precious.

Breshy nodded. "We've put what virtue we can into it. It will help you become what you wish to be. To do what you wish to do."

"But someone will steal it . . . I . . . I can't." She wanted it, desperately.

"Many's the dragon would eat you for it," said Fionn.

"If they saw it," agreed Breshy. "But it's not easily seen. Put it on."

So she did. It was delicately made, but she could feel the weight of it.

"Clever," said Fionn. "Look in the mirror."

She had to reach up and touch it, when she did. She could feel it, the links were there! Solid and sinuous. Definitely there! But she couldn't see it.

"Explain it to her," said Finn.

Breshy shrugged. "While it lies against your breast it cannot be seen. It will lend you its virtue, to hide what you do not wish seen, to show what you wish shown, to do what you wish to do . . . but you must lend it yours."

Meb was not sure she had any virtue, unless it was what Hallgerd said she should be careful about men for. But now that she had the dragon pendant on, she knew that she would not part with it willingly. She thought that she now understood, just a little, suddenly, why dragons loved their gold so fiercely.

"Thank you," she said, her voice cracking slightly. "I . . . I hope you catch a fish . . . just as often as you need to."

"That's clever," said the dverg. "It makes it mine to use, but not to abuse."

"And mine to fix," said Finn. "Ah well. My work is never done. Come. We need to start practicing our routines, Scrap. And you want to be seen doing them. Remember that!"

So they went back to tossing balls. Meb tried as hard as she could, but she just could not see how he kept them all in the air, let alone caught them behind his back. As for how he made them disappear . . . it had to be a trick. But it looked like magic.

Finn was a hard taskmaster, she'd learned. She had to throw those balls perfectly and exactly in time with his tapping toes. He made it look very, very easy, but Meb was quick-witted enough to realize that in part, it was just the result of endless practice. He had quite a repertoire—juggling, tumbling, even balancing things on a stick on his chin—and she felt fairly useless. She couldn't even do cartwheels, let alone acrobatic somersaults. Still, she applied herself to the juggling with a will. She wanted to be good enough to go on being his 'prentice, for as long as possible. She dropped the balls a lot, while trying. She was aware that the dvergar were watching, surreptitiously. She was also aware that they betrayed themselves with helpless laughter when she failed. They seemed to almost like watching that more. Practical-Meb the inner voice said that the important thing was that they watched, not why they watched. So . . . even as she got better, Meb would fumble a ball every now and again. The practical voice in her head was right, as usual. The watchers loved it.

Meb was not too sure how long they stayed. It was always lamplight, not night or day. And the meals were . . . irregular. Frogs' legs were quite nice, provided she pretended they came off something else—like a very small chicken. Finn spent some time teaching her, and some time . . . just not anywhere around. About his mysterious business. Well, she'd always thought gleemen just traveled around doing tricks, telling stories and moving on. But it would seem that there was more to it. She'd come in and found him muttering over a complicated looking set of charts, once. The part of Meb that was practical and down-to earth said that it was none of her business. The other part wished that staring at writing long enough could make her able to read. Sometimes the squiggles almost seemed to be trying to reform themselves into words for her.

When he disappeared she worked on her juggling. She'd been awake for an hour or two, she guessed, doing so when he came in to the cavern, suddenly, moving as silently as only he could. He startled her into dropping all six balls. She was very proud to be up to six. She hoped that he had noticed.

If he did, he didn't say so. Instead he said: "It's time we were off. The road is calling. There's mischief to be done, trouble to be made."

She nodded. But . . . this was safe. Warm in the teeth of autumn. And . . . and the dvergar had been nice to her! Her face must have showed her feelings. Finn smiled wryly. "Chin up, Scrap. The trick is not to wear out your welcome. It's time we were on the road again. The hue and cry will have died down a bit. Zuamar will be hunting further afield. We need to get out there and stir him up again."

Meb had almost forgotten that she'd sworn terrible vengeance from between the fish racks. Life—her life—had moved on. Grown immeasurably more complicated and odder than even her daydreams had ever made it out to be. She touched the dragon-pendant. It was comforting. "Yes. I suppose we must."

He seemed to understand that too. "There'll be more folk to meet, offend and befriend, Scrap."

It was on the tip of her tongue to tell him that her name was not "Scrap." It was Meb and she was afraid of all of that. But the inner voice said: *shut up,* so she didn't tell him that she was a girl and really couldn't be his apprentice. Instead she gathered up all the balls.

═ Chapter 13 ═

VORLIAN HAD ACTED WITH GREAT CIRCUMSPECTION, CALLING them together only some days later. It was probable that Zuamar had talked to other dragons. It was possible that he'd talked to Vorlian merely as a feint, or a warning. He was one of the old ones and they were as cunning as only a dragon that had survived to that age could be.

"It would seem," he said coolly to the sprite and demon friend, "that you underrated Zuamar. He's been hunting high and low... for your dragonish conspirator. Who is he?"

Even the sprite, who normally looked just faintly supercilious, looked confused. "If we had one we would hardly have come to you," said Lyr.

That had the ring of truth and logic to it. Of course anything a demon was involved in made treachery likely, but they needed him. Dragons prepared to work with the lesser... other species were rare. Did this mean that another dragon was involved... perhaps in a separate plot? Given dragonish nature, you could not discount the possibility.

"Anyway. Zuamar is searching both the land and ocean for your pirates. He's convinced that a dragon was involved. I hope I've sent him off on a false lead. But we need to act with circumspection in Yenfar. It's only a single little human girl-child, and she almost certainly doesn't know what she is capable of, or, if she does, has no idea how to control it. She's hardly a danger. Can we not arrange a quiet kidnaping without bloody mayhem?

89

Humans disappear all the time. They will think that she's run off, probably."

"Her village is deserted. We followed the trail to Tarport," admitted Haborym.

"Carefully," said the sprite. "We have some human agents. Religious ones."

"Tarport," said Lord Rennalinn. "There have been some strange rumors out of there. Some of my bondsmen sailed from the place. But their ship was searched from stem to stern. And the dragon Zuamar himself came and sniffed between the decks, apparently."

Vorlian started. "He knows what is afoot!"

Rennalinn shook his head. "No. Someone set fire to and looted his tax hall."

The very idea shocked Vorlian almost as much as the idea that Zuamar could have found—and killed—the human mage they needed. Of course she would have to be killed. Dragonkind would settle for no less—the old ones like Zuamar still remembered that human mages had abused them and used them in their conflicts. But they planned to kill only after her work was done. But to dare to steal gold—because they would have stolen gold, what else, from a fellow dragon? Tarport would be lucky if it escaped incineration.

"Zuamar is an impediment. We need to remove him," said the centaur—as if a dragon was a mere human or dverg. To Vorlian's surprise the others nodded.

"But a dragon in his own demesne is not easy to deal with," said Rennalinn.

"I disapprove," said Vorlian. "But I believe that he's looking for a dragon called Jakarin that recently lost her hoard. I . . . er, cast suspicion on her. It is possible they may fight. Jakarin is fat bodied and witted, but . . ."

"Zuamar is one of the great old ones," said Haborym. "Not likely to be killed by a conflict with this dragon. But it might distract him."

Vorlian was struck, once again, by just how well informed the fire-being was about dragonkind. They didn't know everything, but they certainly had studied dragons. Vorlian wondered why? Well, perhaps it was natural. Dragons ruled Tasmarin, after all.

"Nonetheless I think we need to act with some caution about that merrow 'treasure' held by the alvar lordling of Yenfar."

"We have secured the services of a very skilled thief and provided him with a simulacrum of the merrow treasure. It will defy even the most expert detection. Prince Gywndar is away too. A hunting trip, I believe," said the fire-being.

Once again they were moving too far and too fast. And knew too much.

A little later, after some further discussion the conspirators went their various ways. Vorlian found a reason to delay and have a private word with Lord Rennalinn. "A word, alv, before you go. It concerns our relationship."

Rennalinn seemed flattered. "Of course, Lord Vorlian. We—as the ruling classes of Tasmarin—must have matters to discuss."

Vorlian smiled. Some of the alvar did delude themselves that rule of Tasmarin was shared. He said nothing however, just waited until the others had left.

"Now, Lord Vorlian," said Rennalinn—putting himself in dire danger by sauntering toward the dragon and his hoard, "what can I do for you?"

"I want to know about the magical compulsion of the other species," said Vorlian, restraining himself.

Rennalinn blinked. Looked faintly guilty. "It is possible, Lord Vorlian. But not to dragons, of course. They cannot be compelled."

"Zuamar said that that was most distinctly not true. Dragons can be compelled, and were. He said that this was how they were forced to act by the human mages before the creation of Tasmarin. And by the First before that."

"Ah. By humans. But not by the First. We alvar are directly descended from them. And human mages are now extinct. Besides," said Rennalinn with a hasty and rather false little laugh, perhaps suddenly grasping that Vorlian's tone was far from friendly, "you'd know straight away if anyone even tried, my Lord."

"And you are sure that this ability was confined to humans?" said Vorlian.

"Absolutely certain. That was why the dragons eliminated them."

"I have to point out that we have good evidence they're not extinct. Or without power."

"Don't worry, Lord Vorlian," said Rennalinn. "The balance of power among all the species is such that human magic works poorly on us. Or the creatures of smokeless flame."

Vorlian found that relatively uncomforting.

✧   ✧   ✧

Lyr watched. Communication among her kind was not instantaneous, but, as long as there were growing things around, she could pass word and receive information through the vast delicate chemical net that the sprites controlled. One of the reasons that the sprites disliked this world so much was the endless islands. The sea, of course, had plants too, from the great kelps to the things that floated and could not be seen. But they fell at least in part under the magic of the merrows, with whom the sprites had an old enmity.

She did not like the meeting place the fire-being had insisted on. The cave was above the tree-line. There was little that grew up here beside lichens, and she hated the place as a result. But she understood the demon's reasoning. It made Vorlian so uncomfortable that he could barely think. Because all sprites were one, Lyr knew that this was not the only dragon they'd got to that point, but the others were less able and more difficult to push in this direction. She listened. So, he was suspicious. But at least he had asked the alvar-fool.

═ Chapter 14 ═

IT HAD TAKEN HRODENYNBRYS A LONG TIME TO SWIM BACK TO the halls of his people. The merrow had time to think. He was, according to most of his kind, too inclined to do that anyway. A merrow's place was to revel in the wild water and the storm, to hunt great fish, whales or giant Kraken, and, naturally, to keep up the traditional pastime of caging the souls of drowned sailors. Hrodenynbrys was not entirely sure that that was worthwhile, or that successful. One couldn't ever get them all. He was fond enough of wild water and the hunt. But . . . it might be that they hunted bigger game, and in a wilder ocean, this time.

Perhaps he shouldn't have let her go. But he had her hair. He smiled at that. Humans really didn't understand the value of hair.

He swam on, to a place where the gap between the cliffs funneled the currents into a tumbling churn of angry, ship-eating surf. That wasn't how merrows saw it, of course. They saw a huge whirlpool sucking vast amounts of bubbles down as an entertainment and opportunity.

Firstly, it made a good wild ride. And secondly, the bubbles could be trapped in the fine meshwork that channeled them upward along into the sea-home. It was dvergar work and amazingly fine and cunning. The water rushed out and the bubbles remained. Hrodenynbrys swam steadily along the snaking seaweed-hung pipes into the vast sunken caldera that was Merrow-home.

Here, far beneath the waves, the light was muted, blue. The

impossibly tall fragile-seeming towers swayed slowly. Shoals of fish drifted between them. No merrow would hunt here, nor did they allow other predators to do so. 'Brys allowed himself a moment of joy and pride. Merrow-home made alvar castles look like clumsy, earthy things. Once, long ago, there'd been better relations between alv and merrow, and some had even come here. But 'Brys had other things on his mind now. Hair for a start. Magic for seconds. Both hope and fear.

He swam past the soul cages and into the halls of Margetha. Merrow-kind had always resisted formal hierarchy. It would take a very odd merrow to admit that he was inferior to another. Still: there were times when they needed disputes settled, and the like. What little leadership they had, she provided. The chieftainess Margetha dispensed justice, decision and abuse with a skill that gave her respect from merrow-kind.

"Look at the bit of flotsam that just drifted in," she said from where she lounged on her judging chair of delicate corals—with sponges for comfort. "Hrodenynbrys. I thought a dogfish had eaten you. Pity I was wrong, to be sure."

She really did like him.

"Ah, I'd like to say that I couldn't stay away, but that'd be stretching the truth," he said easily. Merrows were fairly solitary, but it was good to have words with his own kind now and again.

"And you'd have given the dogfish indigestion. So: to what do I owe this momentous privilege?" she said, lazily. Hrodenynbrys was not fooled. She was intensely curious.

"Well, I thought you might have a passing interest in knowing that great things were on the swim. Strange tides are moving," he said in a passable imitation of a sententious courtier.

"And there I was thinking that you'd come to tell me that the dogfish didn't like the taste. So: what news is this? More important than a dogfish's sudden discrimination?"

"In a manner of speaking, yes," said Hrodenynbrys. "I was summonsed."

She scowled. "It's something that happens."

"Ah, but not recently by a human mage."

With a sinuous flick Margetha was out of her chair, all pretense of lethargy gone, green eyes narrow, intent. "You're sure, Hrodenynbrys?"

"Sure as death. That's why I bothered to come and tell you."

"Where?" she asked.

"Ah, that's more interesting still. On the coast of Yenfar."

"What?" They both knew the significance of that place.

Hrodenynbrys nodded. "And it was no little 'if you happen to be passing come closer' spell either. A working of great power. I must have been fifty miles away. I left my second best trident in a skip-jack," he said regretfully.

"Whisht! It's come to this at last," said Margetha, biting a webbed finger.

"I was thinking the same," said Hrodenynbrys. "Maybe those sprite-folk knew more than we thought they did, when they came seeking a bargain."

"They're not to be trusted," said Margetha, grimly. "It's to be wished that you could have got a bit of cloth or something of hers."

"Oh I have that, and better than that. I've got the hair off her head, given in free exchange, yet," said the merrow, hauling it out of his pouch.

She laughed incredulously. "Hrodenynbrys, how is it for some-one so ugly you're so beautiful?

"Ah, 'tis my natural charm," he said grinning like a shark. "And I am clever too."

═ Chapter 15 ═

IT HAD TAKEN RELATIVELY LITTLE EFFORT FOR ZUAMAR TO FIND
the dragon Jakarin. She had not found a new lair. Instead she
clung to the cliff top on what remained of her island. It was a
bare shard of broken rock, balancing above the hungry waves.
The hole in the fabric of Tasmarin had healed up, but there was
not enough of an island left to be really habitable. Lord Zuamar
wondered if Vorlian could possibly be misinformed. She was
in gold-grief by the looks of her. On the other hand her loose
scales indicated that she was coming up to molt. Dragons always
needed gold. But in molt . . . well, they had to eat some of it. If
she had none, and some human made an offer . . . Dragons had
been trapped like that before.

She hissed angrily at him, eyes wide and angry, teeth exposed.
"This is mine, mine. GO."

"I hear you've been consorting with humans," said Zuamar.

She did not answer. She simply attacked. Launched straight
off the cliff edge at him, spewing a clumsy ill-directed fountain
of flame.

It was so unexpected it almost succeeded. Zuamar folded
his wings and dropped like a stone, the ferocious heat of her
flame hot on his tail. He turned the maneuver—which left him
dangerously exposed from above—a dragon never willingly gave
up height advantage—into a steep banking turn. She followed,
clumsy in her haste, revealing her youth and anger in doing so,
instead of gaining height. His wings were bigger than hers, even

97

if she had youth on her side. She tried to flame him again . . . but either she had less breath or flame than she thought she had, for it came nowhere near him.

He beat his way up into the sky, tendrils feeling for the advantage on the thermal above the sunbaked rocks of her island. She was doing no more than to try to follow him by sheer wing-power. Had she never dueled with another dragon of similar size? Zuamar knew that the answer would be "probably not." Once, before Tasmarin, dragon had fought dragon, often. They'd been SENT to fight—aside from anything else. Zuamar was the veteran of a dozen such duels, and many more minor skirmishes. Nowadays . . . picking on something your own size was not a particularly clever thing to do, and there was seldom a reason to do so. He turned his head to give her a burst of flame . . . but she'd lost ground. She was out of range. Zuamar knew his range precisely, and would not waste dragonfire. Besides, if he could get above and behind her . . . He gained more height. Too late she worked out what a precarious position she was getting herself into. He dove. Frantically, with what was plainly every ounce of her strength, she managed to veer away from a direct impact. But his talons tore one of the webs on her wing, and his blast of flame seared her delicate wind-tendrils. He banked and used the momentum to regain some of his lost height.

She began . . . to flee.

Zuamar simply continued to climb. She was struggling to fly, losing height, trying to reach that piteous island of hers. A worthless strategy, as she had no cave to retreat into! He dove again. This time she failed to evade his talons. In a spiraling wash of crimson fire—mostly his, they fought. She fought with the desperation of one who knows that there is but one possible end to it all. He—largely out of reach of her claws—ripped through her scales and wing-webbing, tearing great gouges into her muscles. Dragon blood spewed as they fell towards the broken and shattered stone of her old eyrie. At the last minute, Zuamar tore himself clear.

She could not halt her fall. Dragon scale, skin and bone were tough beyond all other forms of living flesh, but not harder than the new-splintered rocks.

Lord Zuamar roared his triumph to the sky. And then, as was ancient tradition, he sank down onto her carcass and began to feast.

He felt . . . younger and stronger afterwards. They might claim that here, on a plane of Dragons, that dragon should not devour dragon, but he was larger than most of them. And those that he was not larger than, would not raise a single claw against him.

He quested about for her hoard. It was—rather like her attempts to fight—pathetic. Barely a dozen bits of gold. Several rings, a bracelet, and the rest in coins. One of those caught his attention. It was something he had not seen for many years. A ducat. He wondered how such a treasure had come into the hands of the fat-witted Jakarin. Well, he couldn't ask her now.

— Chapter 16 —

IT WAS GOOD TO BE OUT IN THE SUNLIGHT AGAIN, MEB REALIZED. The leaves were turning and changing the land into a vast canvas in shades of reds, ochres and yellows. The countryside so far from the sea was strange and unfamiliar. There were no gulls, and the breeze carried a thousand smells that were not salt or rotting seaweed or fish. Decay, yes. A wet-leafy, mushroomy smell, which, to her surprise, she discovered went along with huge numbers of mushrooms. She'd never had much to do with them before. It was rapidly apparent that Finn had.

Mushrooms, it appeared, were something that came out in the woods and fields after the rain. The trees were still dripping. That didn't stop her master bounding around under them, pushing over little hummocks of wet leaves and chortling with glee when he found a good mushroom. She did her best to join in. Her efforts were hampered by not having the slightest idea what she was doing. He was not impressed by the red and white spotted ones. "Hallucinogenic. Throw them away." Her next effort was, if anything, worse. "Good grief, Scrap. Do you not know anything about mushrooms? In the name of the First don't touch your mouth, nose or eyes. Here, rub them thoroughly on that moss. There is a bit of a trickle over there by the sounds of it. You need to wash those hands of yours. And rub under your fingernails with that moss too."

"I'm sorry," she said humbly. "Mushrooms don't grow much in the cove. And no one picks them. I thought those were the same as the ones you had."

"Ink caps. You had deadly destroying angels. Look at them carefully. Remember them. Notice details. Anyway, I think we have enough for a feed. Now we'll need a fire."

That was something they were unlikely to get in the wet woods. But it seemed that she had underestimated Finn's ability to find semi-dry wood, and to make it burn. He also seemed to have the most amazing assortment of useful things about him, and in that pack of his, including a little piece of fat bacon and a small iron skillet. And he had very tough hands and a mouth that seemed impervious to heat. He could eat sizzling bacon fat fried mushrooms with his fingers, straight from the pan into his mouth. Meb had to spike them on a knife-point and then blow on them. They were, however, worth running around the damp forest for.

When the last mushroom and scrap of bacon had been devoured, Finn looked regretfully at the pan. "Well, it's a change from frogs and fish. I've been told it's an unnatural taste for one of my kind, but wild mushrooms are one of my weaknesses. One of many," he said with a grin. "And now, looking at that sky, unless you have a fancy for a soaking, we'd better move along."

He cleaned the pan roughly with some leaves, kicked out the fire, and they set off again. A mile or two down the road they came to a large rock that someone had crudely chipped an arrow onto, with what Meb imagined was the name of the next settlement and of course, the distance. She could read some numbers. She was very proud of the skill.

Finn clicked his tongue, looking at it. "We'll have to move that. Come on, Scrap. Push and shove time."

Meb looked at the boulder. There was no way they'd budge it! But he was already putting his shoulder to it so she scampered to join him, and pushed.

She nearly fell on her face because it moved . . . it came free of the earth with a ripping crack, and rolled onto the track.

"Phew!" Finn blew on his hands. "Now. Let's see . . . Over there."

Between them they rolled the rock about five yards down the hill. It took all their strength . . . but it moved. The arrow now pointed at the hillside, though a generous tangle of bramble.

"A job well done," said Finn with some satisfaction. "No respect, these people. That stone was put there for another purpose and didn't like being a signpost. Things are better balanced now. Come on, let's go. We're still racing the rain."

They walked on. Meb wondered just what local people would make of the rock's movements. It seemed a lot of hard work for a practical joke . . . to the extent that she wondered if it was.

It was starting to rain when they reached a hamlet, complete with a local inn. "Time for us to sing for our supper, Scrap," said Finn.

Meb hoped that she didn't really have to sing. Somehow she thought sea-chanties would not get them much supper, and she didn't know anything else. The locals looked pleased enough to see the gleeman, though. They were hauled into the tap room, which was a long step down from the inn in Tarport. This one had old straw on a dirt floor, and a few rough-hewn benches. And beer. Meb realized that she was going to have to get used to that. So she set about doing so. It wasn't that she'd never tasted the stuff before. Just not much of it. People said you got used to it.

Fionn was expecting another quiet night of some mediocre brew, ordinary food and providing a little entertainment in exchange for the same. Of course he knew that humans got hopelessly drunk and disorderly. They often did. Dragons had multiple and complex livers for dealing with toxins. It took some very special spells bound to gold to have much effect on him. He'd almost forgotten that Scrap wasn't his kind when he'd seen the mushrooms. She was too observant for her own good, let alone his. He could—and did—eat mushrooms that would have killed her. She was trying hard to fit in. He'd been careful enough to keep her to actual hard practical work which took concentration, not daydreaming. He was fairly sure she had no idea what that imagination of hers could do, given the right cues and stimulus. So juggling had seemed a good thing to teach her. Of course, because she wanted to please, and wanted to do it well, she was bending the rules of causality a bit. Nothing that would cause more than a few misshapen trees, un-seasonal sunlight or strangely human faces on occasional root vegetables. Nothing to worry about.

Until she'd added beer into it.

They'd started much as usual. A bit of juggling. A bit of patter. A tumble or two. A break for beer and a few coins. Small coins here at a rural inn, but enough for food and shelter.

Fionn cursed himself for a fool. He should have seen to it that food came before beer, and that the human brat kept to drinking a minimum of the beer.

In part it had been his fault, he admitted. The craft of the dvergar-made wares was legendary, and of Dvalinn and his brothers more so. It was their reason for keeping themselves to themselves, and their names a secret. They also had the reputation of taking people literally. It would make her what she wanted to be. He'd meant in appearance. They, it seemed, hadn't. Of course it *would* work as he'd intended, but possibly not when her inhibitions were awash with beer.

Now, in a barn a good mile from the inn the human was sleeping it off.

It was a pity she hadn't gone straight to that stage!

It was relatively unlikely anyone magically skilled had been about to notice her pyrotechnics. But the marks of it would remain.

She inspected the scratches on her hand and arms. And felt her face. "What . . . what happened?"

"The scratches, I think," said Fionn with some satisfaction, "come from when you attempted to juggle with the cat. In all fairness, I don't think you knew it was a cat at that stage. But you deserved what you got. That was before you threw up on the innkeeper's wife. You deserved what you got there too. You'll have a very fine black eye."

She blushed to the roots of her hair. "She deserved it too. I am sorry, master. Must I go?" There was just a hint of a sob in the statement. Repressed. This one did not cry easily.

Finn laughed. "No. But we'll not be back here for a while. Firstly, I think the innkeeper would be after us with a besom, and secondly, we'd never be able to put up another show like that. You've set quite a standard for other traveling gleemen to follow."

What he did not say was "and left traces of powerful human magic all over an inn that never did any worse than serve watered beer." Instead he said: "Most of what we do, Scrap, is trickery. I need to teach you to do more of it, and not quite so spectacularly. We like to pass through without people noticing much. Not them remembering us in every detail for many years."

"I am sorry, master. I remember everything the gleeman did

the twice he came to our village," she said, humbly. "I didn't know you weren't supposed to."

She would remember, of course. She must have a very precise imagination and memory to allow her powers to work. And as she saw more . . . it was going to become worse. She'd recreated some of the tricks she'd seen the night before. Only . . . they hadn't been tricks. He knew of course how to palm a coin and pretend to pull it out of a local's ear. Meb had made it lodge in the fellow's ear. He'd been lucky it hadn't been inside his skull, and it had been lucky that he'd been near as drunk as the scrap of humanity. Finn knew how to make a coin disappear. He would have made the same one reappear, not a silver thaler. That's what had started the fight . . . She was no better at dealing with that than she had been with being propositioned by the innkeeper's wife.

Meb was inwardly crawling with shame . . . in between feeling really like throwing up and dealing with a dull headache. Gleemen drank beer. And she was a failure at it. A failure. The inner voice said *Well, he hasn't chased you away. And he could have left you there. This isn't the inn.* Wherever it was, she had to get up and get out in a hurry, because anything that was still in her, needed out. At a staggering run she bolted out into the rain.

When she got back shivering and empty, he had a fire going— something that would probably horrify the owner of the barn—and a small pannikin broiling. He poured some out liquid out of it into a metal mug. "Get that down yourself."

"I don't think it'll stay down," she said, warily.

"Well, let it have a passing acquaintance with you," the gleeman said cheerfully. "And next time learn to spill most of the beer they buy you onto the rushes on the floor. That's the advantage of a dirt floor, with straw or rushes. They help the sound and bad light will let you get away with it. The fleas will be grateful and you won't have such a head on you in the morning."

"Not to mention not doing such silly things," said Meb shame-faced, remembering some of it.

He snorted. "I wouldn't dream of mentioning it. Doing them, that's another matter. You'll learn, Scrap, that's exactly what we do. Silly things. But usually we know we're doing them. Sometimes we even tell people what we're doing. They don't believe us."

She hung her head in embarrassment. "Sorry, master." The stuff

in the mug hadn't come up. Actually, it was making her feel better than she had earlier, though that wasn't hard.

He gave her a lopsided smile. "And now you're making me feel
bad about it. I'm usually the one to cause trouble, Scrap. Most
of the time on purpose, but sometimes just because trouble likes
me. I'm just not used someone else doing it."

"It really wasn't on purpose," said Meb. "Or at least I am
sure I'd remember if it was. I was just . . . trying to be a good
apprentice."

He snorted with laughter. "At this rate you'll be a master before
you know it."

She was taken aback by that idea. She didn't want to be a
master. She wanted to be his apprentice. "Oh no. I have far too
much to learn."

"That's true," said Finn. "And your first lesson for today is that
you should never stay around for the deeds to catch up with you.
It means early starts. A lot of no breakfasts."

She shuddered. "I don't feel much like it this morning."

"I'll avoid talking about it then, until you've walked it out," he
said, getting up and smothering his fire. "Get your cloak around
you, Scrap. It's going to be wet."

It was. And a long time before lunch. They walked—mostly
uphill—towards the mountains. It got colder. And the rain was
replaced by drifts of mist around the ridges. Even while walking
Meb was cold. The gleeman-cloak shed a lot of the rain. But wet
crept in around the neck. She was very glad indeed when he led
them off the trail and to a shallow cave in the woods. He seemed
to know the country very well. Meb supposed one had to learn
it. But how had he known there would be a cave there, hidden
in a piece of wildwood? You couldn't see it from the muddy track
they'd been following.

"Chilly tonight," said Finn. "But we'll get a good fire going.
Even the alvar won't be out in this."

That seemed to please him.

"Where are we going?" asked Meb. The whole world was a
strange place to her, but she was beginning to feel that she should
learn all about it.

"Tonight, here. Tomorrow elsewhere. Collect some deadwood.
I'll get a fire going," said Finn.

Collecting deadwood had to be easier than lighting a fire in this, Meb reflected to herself as, tired and hungry, she trudged through the trees. Still, he could have given her an answer. The inner voice said *but he probably doesn't know the answer.* Meb was in no mood to let mere common sense and logic stand in the way of feeling aggrieved. She found a large dead fork, piled it with what she'd got so far, and walked back dragging it, picking up a few pieces as she went. It was all dead . . . but wet.

He did have a fire going. And he'd chopped a pile of bracken—wet bracken—and laid it out to dry near the flames. "Not a bad haul," he said looking at her load. "I'll get some more. I'm going to see if I can find us some dinner. You stay and tend the fire."

Meb wondered what—besides possibly some more mushrooms, he could hope to find in the wet, wild woods. By now even frogs' legs sounded tempting. But she would be glad to sit and tend the fire. She was exhausted. It was a hot enough little fire to dry the wood she had available to put onto it. She just had to keep feeding it while everything dried out.

Unfortunately, that meant staying awake. She would have walked, pinched herself or done something to make sure that she didn't sleep . . . if she'd realized that just closing her eyes for an instant would have her away to the land of dreams, where she was still living in a cold fishing cottage.

It was that cold that woke her. The evening was closing in, and the little fire was down to a few smouldering embers. Her sudden panic left Meb wide awake and even colder—with an icy sick feeling in her belly. If she'd failed at this simple task he'd surely be furious. And rightly so. They'd need a fire tonight . . . and where was he? Darkness was closing in. Had he fallen and broken a leg? Had he gone off and left her here, because she was too much trouble? Hastily she piled splinters and sticks on the embers. Blew carefully. One or two smoked. Nothing else happened. She frantically felt about for more tinder, ripping the bark off the sticks to expose the dry stuff. Forcing herself to try and be calm. Pushing the embers together. Blowing again. Desperately wanting a flame . . .

It blossomed into a conflagration that singed her eyebrows and made her fall back as half the wood and the bracken caught fire too.

Meb scrambled back and broke a green branch and started beating it out.

"You never do anything by halves," said Finn admiringly. Well, with what could be admiration. He put the string of neatly cleaned small animals he carried onto a limb and helped put out the fire.

"I'm sorry. I didn't mean to . . ." said Meb.

"Really?" he seemed faintly amused.

"I fell asleep," admitted Meb. "I was just trying to get the fire going again."

"And you really wanted it to burn. You're wearing a dvergar treasure, Scrap. What did the cunning little devils tell you it would do?"

"They said that it would help me . . ." she caught herself in time.

"No. Typical of the tricksy little fellows. 'It will help you become what you need to be.' And right then you needed it to help you get the fire going. Or you thought you needed fire, badly."

"Oh." She fumbled for the necklace.

"What are you doing?" he asked.

"I have to take it off."

He put a restraining hand on hers. "You'd do better to learn to use it properly. Besides, what would you do with it if you did take it off?"

"Uh. Throw it away."

"Besides the fact that the dvergar could be quite upset about that—their gifts are not lightly given—it wouldn't stay lost. That's the way of their treasures. And the next finder might do a lot worse. Kill themselves or others. If it fell into a dragon's hands . . ."

"I could give it to you," Meb offered.

He laughed. "No, you can't. Now give me a hand with our dinner. I have some salve for you to put on your hands and face. Lucky for you they're not burned too badly."

It was a very soothing ointment that he provided. She was not too sure just what the small animals that they ate were, but even when she was told that they were squirrels, well, any food was good right now. And food in the stomach had a calming influence on her mind. That was still in some turmoil, but it was sleepy full-belly turmoil. Wrapped in her cloak, with some more bracken Finn had cut under her, sheltered from the wind and warmed by the fire, sleep came all too easily.

✧   ✧   ✧

It didn't come easily to Fionn. Curse the black-hearted black-haired little mischief makers . . . Only, it was possible that they hadn't meant it as mischief. They'd liked her. Or if they had meant it as mischief, it almost certainly hadn't been in that way. It was also possible that they simply hadn't guessed just how powerful . . . and uncontrolled, she really was.

He wanted to fly back up to the conclave tonight. The moon was overhead . . . but he was wary about leaving the scrap. For a start she might have attracted unwelcome attention with her fire-flare. And for seconds, she might die of cold without him. He had tampered a little with local airflow, keeping the cave a bit warmer. But they were late in the year and high in altitude for humans to sleep rough without more shelter than a cloak. All dragons should be given a human to raise, he thought ruefully. It'd teach them to value the strengths they had.

There would be limits to that power of hers, even focussed and amplified by dvergar magics. That was the balance of all things. It had been so structured by the First who understood the need for it. Thus alvar magics were potent against humans, and merrow spells in turn effective on alvar. The sprites were effective against the centaur-folk, and the dvergar against the sprites and so on . . . each with more or less mastery of the different types of energy. Of course the dvergar, cunning little fellows, had done their best to give her a talisman that would expand that. Earth, wood, water, air—always a weakness of humans, and the bound and unbound, and of course metal and fire in the making, and light in shifts of color in the opal. All of that would affect forces and energies not normally easy for humans to access.

If only the dvergar been prepared to travel more, they could have been as good a set of mischief makers as he was. As it was, they did quite well at getting others to do it for them.

He sighed. Just what was he going to do with her? She was a serious impediment to his speed and ease of movement. . . . But there were those who wanted any trace of human magic dead and buried. That could not be permitted.

Then there were at least three groups trying to renew the old compact of the species and rebuild Tasmarin. The sprites and the creatures of smokeless flame were part and parcel of all of them, for reasons he could guess at. Even without his interference the place was going to fall apart eventually because of the time differentials in the different planes that pieces of the refuge of the dragons had been taken from. Renewal would have a serious effect on his own plans and tasks—to say nothing of the damage it could do. They needed her alive—at least until they had achieved their end. It would all need re-doing soon enough, but they wouldn't know that, or care, for that matter.

Basically, he was left with keeping her alive, and keeping her away from those who would use her. Well, his next move should put nice lumps of diamond in the mill of the latter. Anyway, the presence of so much sea-magic high inland had a terrible effect on the energies of the place.

He had to change that, and moreover, get himself (easy) and her (hard) away from the consequences of his actions. He thought about it deep into the night, occasionally dozing, occasionally tossing another piece of rock into the fire. While she slept she wasn't going to know that he was burning rocks, not their supply of wood. If you knew the right ways of releasing energy from it, rock had a lot more fire-fuel in it than wood.

By morning he'd evolved a plan. Not a great plan, and not one without flaws. But it was the best he could think of right now.

They'd just walk in and take it. That, he knew from experience, would work.

It was getting away that would be problematic.

═ Chapter 17 ═

THE SKY WAS STILL LEADEN, BUT AT LEAST IT WASN'T RAINING when they started off the next morning. She also didn't feel as terrible as she had on the previous day, so in general Meb found the world a better place. Her master had even come up with some stale rye bread for breakfast. He plainly didn't think much of it, but to Meb, it was a familiar sort of food for a morning. If it hadn't been for a lurking feeling that she was a disaster looking for a place to happen, she'd have said it was the best experience a poor girl from a fishing village could ever dream of. She had to be grateful to that merrow for taking her hair . . . and turning her into an imitation boy and thus into the gleeman's apprentice. She had a lot to thank him for, besides being grateful for him saving her from drowning.

"Where are we going today, master?" she asked, fully expecting "elsewhere" or some such answer.

"Alba."

She gaped. Wanted to skip with excitement. Alba! That, to a girl who had dreamed of going as far as Tarport, was the other side of the world. The citadel of the alvar was a place of legend to the fisherfolk. Nobody had ever been that far! Why, it was leagues away, in the mountains.

Which, looking around her, might be where they were now, if the cloud would lift. They walked on, Meb with a new spring in her step. Inevitably it came on to rain—but it was a brief shower, and after it was over the clouds did break up a little, giving her glimpses of steep slopes and distant peaks. And then they rounded a spur and came out of the trees onto an open—and windy—point of gray rocks and grass clipped by grazing sheep.

Yenfar stretched out below them, the sun breaking through the clouds and picking out bright patches. Forests adorned in autumnal shades, still-green patchwork fields, and the distant, sparkling sea. Looking across the water there were hints of purple mountains beyond that again.

"Aye. It is beautiful," said Finn, taking a seat on a boulder, as Meb stared, trying to drink in the bigness of it with her eyes. "It's a pity it is not stable."

"What do you mean, master?" She looked again, wondering if it would disappear.

"It's a mishmash of magical places, stuck together with magic. It's beginning to tear itself apart."

"Now?" she looked at her feet. Across the landscape.

"Not just yet."

"Then we should fix it," she said resolutely.

Her master got to his feet. "Not me. Come on, we've a few hours walk ahead of us."

The track they were on joined another track, a larger, muddier one. That joined up with a third . . . which was paved. It pleased Meb. It was very splendid, even if there were now other people on the road too. She'd enjoyed their solitude.

Her master seemed taken up with studying the sharp granite ridges and the cuttings that had been made through them to level and straighten the road, so she thought she'd juggle, practicing as they walked.

"Don't," said Finn. "Just work on being a quiet unobtrusive boy, walking along the road. Make an effort to think of yourself as looking like one. The kind of person no one would look twice at. Really want it and try to look like it."

She put the balls away. "Yes, master." She was quick enough on the uptake to understand: he wanted her to use the dvergar magic to appear innocuous. He was up to something. It frightened her a little. But at the same time . . . she trusted him. He'd led her into trouble but had also got her out of it. And it had been at some risk and effort to himself. The ordinary Meb, the one that had been raised by Hallgerd to be a good girl, said she ought at the very least to run away, or better, tell someone in authority. The inner voice just laughed at her. So she worked on being a simple country boy. It seemed to work. The sharp-eyed alvar guards at the checkpoint scarcely gave her—or him—a second glance. They did seem to be taking an extreme interest in the travelers coming up the road.

Finn led her on towards the vast sculpted gateway to the white citadel. It stood on edge of a lake, looking across the still water to the mountain beyond. Tall, slim towers soared above the wall. What struck Meb was the endless carving on the translucent white stone of the gate-towers. There were patterns—flowers and leaves—below and a long hunting scene frieze carved there above.

"It's so beautiful!"

"Yes. So daft as well. The walls are carved too. And the whole place is made of alabaster. Very white. Quite soft. It's a good thing it's in the middle of the island, just about under Zuamar's eyrie, or someone would have taught them the advantages of using harder stone, and making less handholds."

Meb was rather taken aback at his lack of interest in the romance of the city. She still thought it was quite the most beautiful place she'd ever seen. That was, she admitted, not a very long list of places. But it left Cove village and Tarport in the shade. Perhaps the gleeman had seen many such places. He'd traveled. "What do we do now? Find an inn? I promise I won't drink any beer," she said, virtuously—and meaning it. She still hadn't forgotten how she'd felt on the morning after her first serious exploration of beer, let alone what she'd done under its influence.

Finn snorted. "I wish. We'll get a pass ahead, that'll allow us into the city for the day. Don't lose it. There are no inns inside for the likes of us. This is an alvar city and they'll see that you don't forget it."

It was even more beautiful inside the walls than outside them, with the wide paved streets set with tall, slim poplars . . . and the only people afoot were visitors like them, and men in simple uniforms whose principal task was to clean up after the fine horses of the alvar. There was—of course—a market-place, and that was were they, and most of the other visitors headed. There were alvar goods on sale, and—essential for alvar customers—fresh food.

"They're hunters. The mountains can't sustain the pressure of the population of a city this size. So they have to ship in food," explained Finn. "Of course it would make more sense to spread out, or to live in the lowlands, or to grow crops. But they're big on tradition. We've come to buy clothes or a few lengths of cloth to get some really fancy clothes made up for us. It depends on what they have."

Meb didn't think that she'd actually ever had clothes bought for her before. It had always been hand-me downs or, at best, sewed from the cheapest cloth that Hallgerd had been able to buy from the pack-peddlers. She looked eagerly at the stalls. They were full of the stuff of dreams for anyone who had ever yearned for finery. Silks, satins, gold-threaded brocade, fine lace, pretty carved mother of pearl buttons, ribbons. And that was in the part of the market that catered to male customers. To someone who had only ever seen one piece of silk close up, to whom clothes had been made from flax or wool . . . it was nearly overwhelming. Finn seemed at ease and familiar with it, telling her the names of materials she did not recognize . . . and spending money. More than a fisherman might earn in twenty years, with a level of casualness that awed her. It didn't seem to make a huge impression on the stall-holders, so Meb came to realize that it was probably quite normal for them.

They finally left with all their parcels and their passes, which they had to hand in at the gate a few minutes later, and followed other shoppers down a rutted track which branched off from the paved road about half a mile from the gate. It led away from the pretty valley—into another valley—which was rather full of small houses and looked like a mixture between the Cove village and Tarport. Narrow, muddy alleys squirmed their way between crowded houses.

They made their way down one of them to something that was little more than a hovel—a far cry from the alvar beauty of the white city.

The gleeman knocked. Eventually a woman answered. She smiled radiantly when she saw him. Hugged him. Meb knew a moment of jealously. She was—especially considering the very run-down house, a pretty woman. "Come in," she said, "It's cold and miserable out there."

Meb decided that she preferred the weather outdoors. Really. But as Finn went in, she had little choice.

Inside, the house was considerably more prepossessing. It had, which Meb found very strange, bright globe lights and a skylight directly above the huge table—a table piled high with linens. "It must be a good three years since I was last here," said Finn, grinning.

"Nearer to five," said a second woman who was sitting and stitching. "I didn't think you'd ever come back after that."

"And who is the young man?" asked the first woman, still holding on to Finn. Meb smiled determinedly. "I am his apprentice," she said as gruffly as she could.

Finn did not either confirm it or deny it. Instead he said: "The scrap of humanity is a good juggler. I want clothes appropriate for an alvar lordling's fool."

"You'll need a wig for him then. Girls are in fashion. But fortunately, so is juggling."

"Well, Scrap," said the gleeman, raising an eyebrow. "Do you think you could manage to be a little alv girl? You'll need to wear a dress, I imagine." Meb nodded, open-mouthed, wondering if she should explain. But Finn had already turned back to the two women. "And you can tell me just what has got the alvar so stirred up?"

"There is a rumor," said slightly younger one, still holding on to Finn. "That some thief plans to rob them."

Finn laughed until he had to sit down.

The two women were seamstresses. They were craftswomen of note, Meb realized, watching how they set tiny precise stitches at a speed that was almost supernatural. In fact, watching them work, Meb had to believe they were using magic. Their comments on the fabric that Finn had bought were not flattering. "You should have come to us first. Who on earth is going to wear that violet?"

"Me," said Finn, cheerfully. "I'll be suitably pale and blond."

Leilin—the woman who had met them at the door—and who was making every excuse to touch Finn, snorted. "You'll stand out like a candle in a coal-scuttle."

Finn nodded. "That was the idea, m'dear. But I rely on your clever fingers and needlework to make it look as if I am rich and wanting to be noticed."

"And your . . . apprentice?"

"Oh, definitely noticed. I expect at least one offer to buy the beautiful young thing from me. So that I can turn it down with suitable disdain, Scrap. I'm sure you will make a very pretty young juggler girl, in quite startling motley. But we're going to need to get out of the outfits very quickly. So there will be no sewing anyone in."

Leilin grimaced. "This is going to hurt Prince Gywndar? Badly?"

"He will lose face, considerable face," said Finn. "Indeed, I suspect there'll be some calls for his head."

"Good," said the older sister, showing a vixen-smile. "We will lend some of our glamor. That's what you want isn't it, Finn?"

He nodded. "Of course, your exquisite company and stitchery as well."

They both laughed. "You're a liar, and a rogue."

He bowed. "I do my best."

"A wig and powder and a bit of cornflower on the nose and ears will go a long way before we even start. You apprentice is slight enough, just a bit on the short side."

They became very professional about it, measuring and cutting. It was still going to take a few days of work to complete, they informed him. It wasn't just a simple task. As well as that, one of them slipped out to buy a wig. They made Meb practice walking. They said that she was a quick study at being a young woman. "Glamor works best when you work with it."

Meb could make no sense of it. Glamor? "What do you mean?" Glamor was something the alvar had and used.

"Show her," said Finn, from where he'd made himself comfortable in the best chair. "She's less likely to drop the balls if she sees it now."

The two women looked at each other. Shrugged in unison. "Walk towards the mirror," Leilin said. "Walk as much like a woman as you can. Move your hips."

Meb did as she was told, doing her best not to be irritated and pleased at the same time. The dvergar necklace had helped to disguise her, and it was satisfying to fool these two, but . . . she walked toward the mirror. And saw how her face grew longer, with higher cheekbones, and her eyebrows developed a delicate arch. And her ears . . . She stopped. Shook her head.

The seamstresses laughed. "Glamor."

"Um. Thank you. That's magic, right?"

They both tittered. "Of a kind, yes."

"They're good at it," said Finn, lazily.

It had been startling. But what Meb did not say was that what she had seen in the mirror was even more startling. The two seamstresses—so ordinarily human looking—had been something quite different reflected in the mirror. It hadn't been her own ears she'd been startled by.

Later, when the sewing women had gone to sleep she quietly asked Finn. "They're alvar, aren't they? Why do they live in this horrible place instead of in the white city?"

He nodded. "Yes, little Scrap. Your education continues. But you must understand. There never were—or at least not for many years—just all 'alvar' any more than all humans are alike and belong to one group. The sprites and fire-beings are different, of course. The sprites are effectively one creature with many bodies, and the creatures of smokeless flame have a very powerful hierarchy that tolerates no dissent. But that was not true of the alvar. The alvar, broadly speaking, were divided into Loftalvar and Dokkalvar, Huldralvar, and Stromalvar. And of course several smaller factions, each with their own little kings and lords. The Stromalvar were always closest to the humans, and, with the Loftalvar, ascendant and dominant before Tasmarin."

He paused. "You must remember that the formation of Tasmarin was the work of a lot of malcontents. Inevitably though, quite a lot of ordinary folk who just happened to be living in the areas that were taken, also ended up here. The alvar got pride of power and place here, under the dragons, once they had killed the human mage Arawn. Only that was not—obviously—the Loftalvar. The Stromalvar took on the role of Loftalvar, took on their style of dwelling—although always by water—and did their best to out-high-alvar their image of the Loftalvar." Finn smiled wickedly. "That went down really well with the few Loftalvar that happened to be drawn in. And of course with the Huldralvar. They fitted in better than the Loftalvar did. But still . . . a good half of those living in this rat-warren are alvar. They're ashamed. They use their glamor to hide what they are. And they do not like or cooperate with the present rulers. Leilin and her sister are of Loftalvar blood."

"How do you know all this, master?"

He shrugged. "I've been around. And I tell stories, and listen to them, as well as juggle and do tricks and make people laugh."

"That's not all, is it?" she asked.

"Well, all that you need to think about now, Scrap," he said, wryly. "I forget that education in small fishing villages tend to be about how to gill and gut fish."

It seemed a slight on the village and Meb was still feeling slightly touchy. "Oh, we learn about the weather and the sea too. And I met a merrow once. Lands-people don't."

He looked at her with narrowed eyes, and a small smile. "Now that is interesting. They're sharp, are merrows. You have to watch them carefully. They're honest enough, but . . ."

She nodded. "They've got sharp teeth too. And they can be sort of . . . nasty-nice."

"They collect the souls of drowned sailors. And love storms," said Finn, his tone neutral.

Meb shuddered. "He didn't seem evil."

For once Finn's customary smile disappeared. His face was grim. "Not all that seems evil is. Not all of those who destroy and wreck all that is good are evil. It's not something quick or easy to recognize."

She nodded, halted by his seriousness. "But . . . how do you know what's right? What to do?"

He shrugged and grinned. "I suppose we just have to guess and muddle through."

Meb nodded, because he was her master. But deep inside she disagreed with him. You could feel "nasty," sometimes. But, true enough, since the dragon had overseen the destruction of her home, she'd realized that it wasn't always the obvious that felt that way.

═ Chapter 18 ═

"WHAT MUST BE DONE, MUST BE DONE, 'BRYS," SAID MARGETHA. "And it is fitting that it should be you doing it. It's an honor, as well as a fair reward for being far too clever for your own good."

"Virtue is its own reward," said Hrodenynbrys wryly. "I should have guessed." In actuality, he was quite pleased, even if the whole idea of a merrow going on land, let alone on land and out of sight of the sea, was an odd one. It had been done before, of course. Just not recently.

"Yes, indeed," said Margetha sourly. "Next time you find a human mage, try to make it one with straighter hair."

"Fussy! I'm the one who'll have to deal with the workings you do on it. She seemed a relatively simple fisher-lass, even if she had a fine tongue on her. She could swear a demon out of the fire-pit, that one."

"Good. Should make her easier to deal with," said Margetha, tying the net-knot.

Hrodenynbrys looked at her work. The net of hair was hardly visible, it was so fine. A sprat would be able to tear it . . . except that the spells and the very nature of it would make it hold what it was intended to hold. Compared to the simple charms on the cages this was high magic—which was why Margetha had to do it. "I've got me doubts. She's a strong minded lass for all that."

"We'll bind her soul, 'Brys. She will have no choice," said the chieftainess grimly.

"We could follow her. We have a part of her." And the part

remained bound to the whole, no matter what the distance, Hrodenynbrys knew.

"And then? Ask her nicely to get the Angmarad back for us?" Margetha said sarcastically.

'Brys shrugged his fins. "Human magic is a dangerous thing, we've learned. Why not do a scrying at least? It would at least tell me where to go. Where the nearest water is."

She rolled her eyes. "Very well. A strand I can spare."

The scrying surprised both of them.

"That's both easier and more difficult than I had expected," said 'Brys.

Margetha showed her teeth. "And it means that you have no time to waste."

"You need to finish that," He pointed at the soul net.

"And you need to collect your cape. I will be ready for you, and of course will have a calling bracelet for you. Go."

"I've never been that fond of fresh water . . ."

"Go! I have work to do," she said crossly.

So Hrodenynbrys went. He swam to his home, collected the red cape—it was actually made of dyed seal-fur—and his next best trident. The cape was something all of his kind had, but rarely used.

By the time he got back to the palace she had the soul-net ready for him, as well as a plaited loop of hair which had the threaded seed-pearls and ear-bones of giant cod on it. It pulled towards the source of the hair . . . In case he did not know where to go.

— Chapter 19 —

WITH HIS CHARGE AS SAFE AS POSSIBLE, AND WITH WHAT SAFE-guards he could contrive on the house to hide her, Fionn was able to slip out. There was considerable work to be done, preparing things. Firstly that abomination of a straight road had to be prepared to be set at rights. That involved some magic, some brute force and some careful balancing. Then he was overdue some time with his gold, not to mention spreading his long ears for rumors and information in the Conclave.

One piece of news did surprise him. He need no longer worry about the idea of Jakarin ambushing him. It appeared that a lack of gold at molt was not going to be a problem for that dragon any more. The conclave was full of the story. A fight to the death between Jakarin and Zuamar. A grim and desperate struggle . . . if a one sided fight. Jakarin had had little more than a large mouth to defend herself with, and that had proved inadequate against the speed, strength and the experienced cunning of the older dragon.

Fear stirred in the conclave. Yes, smaller, younger dragons fought. Some died, although it was rare. But the great old ones had not battled, not for centuries anyway. Everyone knew Jakarin had lost her hoard. Everyone assumed she had tried theft on Zuamar. Mostly, they believed that she'd deserved what she got.

But Zuamar had sought her out afterwards. And her friend Myrcupa swore that she'd been nowhere near the older dragon's territory.

Of course, he would say that.

But there was a lot of talk of the old times. Times when dragon fought dragon. When dragon was sent to fight dragon.

Zuamar himself had not come in. But he was reported to have been seen flying over the ocean. Flying a slow, questing search pattern.

Other dragons had been seen with him from time to time. And he was not confining himself to the sky over his demesnes.

It was a time of changes, and changes made for great uneasiness.

— Chapter 20 —

MEB WOKE IN THE PALE HOURS OF DAWN. SLEEPING AS SHE HAD been, in the big sewing room, light came in through the high skylight. Besides it was not quite as quiet as a house could be at that time of day. They moved like ghosts, but Leilin and her sister still couldn't pack quietly. Meb watched for a while before saying anything. She couldn't see Finn anywhere . . . .

"What are you doing?" she asked warily.

"Ah. The 'prentice wakes," said Leilin, with just a hint of sarcasm. Meb suspected that the alvar woman didn't entirely believe that she was Finn's apprentice. "We're leaving for a while."

"Maybe forever," said her sister. "The sort of trouble that Finn brings along with him is something that we'd rather avoid. He'll be gone and then people will come looking for him. Somebody might have seen him arrive here. So by the time they come searching we'd like to be a good long way away."

"Where is he?" asked Meb, slightly nervous. She still wondered if the jester would somehow just disappear.

The two looked at each other. "About his usual mysterious business I would think," said Leilin. "It doesn't pay to inquire too closely into what he gets up to. He tends to vanish when you do. He didn't spend the night with me, however."

"He's up to mischief somewhere," said her sister. "He'll be back. He always comes back, eventually."

"Mind you, it can take him a few years at times," said Leilin.

Just at that point Finn stepped in through the doorway. "You're

123

running late," he said. Plainly their departure was no surprise to him.

Leilin waved airily at Meb. "We were trying not to wake the sleeper."

Finn found that rather funny. "Time that the scrap was up, fed and watered anyway. And definitely time you two were away. You will take my advice, and take the bridle path going across to Mount Jindar?"

Leilin grimaced, nodded. "It's muddy, but I assume you have your reasons."

"Put it this way, I don't think anyone will be following it for a week or two, if ever again," said the gleeman. "And Jindar's a stable area. Firmly grounded, and correctly aligned."

It didn't make a great deal of sense to Meb. But then she didn't quite understand at least three quarters of what Finn said. She wondered whether all traveling gleemen were just as mysterious. But surely that was unlikely? People would have realized they were up to something by now. *Or would they? They never stayed anywhere very long, or even came back that often,* her inner voice wondered beginning to dream a great conspiracy of gleemen . . .

"Snap out of it, dreamy-head," said Finn, "and help the girls pack. It's likely this area will be a hornet's nest of searching guards by tomorrow."

So Meb did her best to help, and went along with them to help carry their belongings to the livery stable. They did not seem too unhappy to be leaving.

Meb asked.

"I'd like to stay and see the mess," said Leilin with a nasty smile. "But he's been very generous with someone's silver. And I can't say that I'll be sorry to see the back of this place. That was our lake."

"And may be again, Leilin," said her sister. "Good luck, child. Take care of Finn."

That made Leilin laugh. "You'll have your work cut out for you."

Somehow Meb hadn't thought of it as her having to take care of Finn. She was, by the standards of her fishing village, a grown woman, only unmarried because . . . well, she didn't look particularly womanly, or pretty. Her darker skin and wiggly auburn hair hadn't helped. And she'd had no kind of dowry at all. But she'd resisted growing up. Resisted being responsible. The idea of being responsible for someone like Finn seemed even more bizarre. Yes, he did strange and unpredictable things. But he seemed so casually capable of taking care of himself. "I'll do my best," she said, doubtfully.

"All we can ever do," said Leilin. "And farewell, Finn. Until next time."

He nodded. "There may be one. You never know."

They went back to the house of the seamstresses, ate and then packed up their belongings, with Finn's gaudy outfit and her dress being carefully folded before being put into a simple, anonymous canvas bag, of the kind that peddlers often used for their wares. Finn had another two of these—much larger ones—but he did not explain what was inside them.

A little later they made their way away from the tucked away grubby slum, and back down to the beautiful straight paved road to the white gate-house of the delicate and elegant city by the lake. They collected their passes . . . as he took them Finn dropped one of the bags, seemingly accidentally. The side ripped open, and a delicately made cage rolled out and opened. The small, brightly colored birds inside the cage seemed so shaken up that they nearly didn't take advantage of the opportunity. Then they, one after the other, fluttered out. None of them went too far in the first few seconds. "My birds! Boy, catch my birds. Help me catch my birds!"

A frantic, clumsy chase followed. Finn showed himself to be singularly inept at catching the little fluttering creatures, even losing his grip on the one a helpful guard shooed into his face, but he did get most of the other people who had come to visit the marketplace distracted into trying too, and had all the attention of the guards. They failed at catching any of the birds, and eventually a dismal-looking Finn had to watch them fly off, before he and Meb continued into the city.

Meb had been around the gleeman for long enough to realize that that had been no accident, and that he'd been up to something. But they were already safely inside the city, so it had not been to evade the guard. She tried to puzzle it out. "What were you doing, master?" she finally asked, when they were comfortably out of earshot of anyone.

"I was returning their passes," said Finn cheerfully. "Now, as far as their numbers are concerned, when they close the gates this evening, we will already have left. It's a pity that we won't have."

They walked to where you could see the palaces sloping down to the limpid azure water. Here they quietly left the second large bag under a bush. Finn had found a perfect place for them to hide and change—a large colonnaded building full of artwork. At least, Meb was sure that some of it was artwork. The place was entirely deserted.

Finn surveyed the strange sculptures on their plinths. "An appreciation of the finer things in life is something that everyone likes to pretend they have. Or at least everyone who likes to pretend they are important likes to pretend they have."

Meb found herself wrinkling her forehead at this: "They like to pretend to pretend?"

"Something like that. It doesn't work very well."

"I think I also pretend too much sometimes," admitted Meb. "I like to imagine things. I used to do it a lot back in Cliff Cove," She looked around. "I got it wrong a lot."

"Imagination and pretense have their uses and places," said Finn. "Like now, when we need to pretend to be what we're not. I need water to affect my disguise. You slip in behind those pictures and change. Roll up your clothes up and bring them along. Meet me back here. I'll need to give you a hand with a bit of make-up."

So Meb did. She'd tried the clothes on for several fittings, but now they felt different. She wished she could see herself in the outfit—lilac and canary. They were beautiful colors on their own . . . but together? She was just a fisher-brat, but surely not? She had five crimson tasseled balls to juggle with too.

"The girls did you proud with the glamor that they put on that dress, Scrap," said a tall alvar with a raised crest of red hair, wearing a lilac coat with canary knee-breeches and lilac hose, who was leaning languidly against the wall.

Meb nearly ran . . . and then recognized the suit and the voice. "Master?"

"Who else would wear such a charming outfit, Scrap? A fright helped your pallor, but I'll add to it with some makeup. And I need to sort out your ears and nose."

It was his voice . . . but he was so tall and slim and supercilious-looking it made her suspect that he too had used a magical glamor.

A little later they sauntered slowly down a broad boulevard into the part of the city that was off limits to visitors: heading towards the royal palace. Most of the alvar rode, of course. But there were enough others taking the evening air—it was a pleasant evening, one of those autumn evenings which ought to be in summer, when a layer of cloud had sealed the warmth of the day in—for the two of them not to be unusual. Well, they were, of course. But Meb noticed several other alvar in similarly odd clothes.

In the distance, a great horn sounded. Finn held a canary-yellow handkerchief indolently in front of his nose. "It's the cabbage they eat in these parts."

"What?" Meb looked around.

"It's either that or they have closed the gates," said Finn. "Their little town is all secure from riff-raff like us now." He grinned. "Shall we go? I think a bit of juggling is called for, Scrap. You leave the talking to me. Actually, pretend to be dumb. Pull your tongue in and point at your mouth and make some gargling noises if anyone tries to ask you anything. You have an unconvincing accent."

Besides that, thought Meb, she had no idea just what to say. This was all too strange. She felt like a piece of driftwood in a wild sea, caught in a storm so big that she was only vaguely aware of the greatness of it, and was merely feeling the effects of individual waves. It was almost swamping her with new experiences, not to mention doing things that her village-bred morality insisted were wrong. And yet . . . defiantly, she didn't care. She was going to do them anyway.

The palace, it appeared, was not a house as other houses were. People came and went, it seemed, almost casually. The great doors were thrown open and gentle music tinkled somewhere inside. And while Finn was taller and somewhat more outré in his dress than others, he was merely an exceptional eccentric among many. The grandees looked like some vast field full of butterflies, thought Meb, as they walked into a great salon. Finn behaved as if he owned the place . . . and it bored him. Meb was glad to be able to start juggling, and to focus her concentration on the tasseled balls, instead of gaping.

"What a magnificent accouterment!" said an alvar in a tall cockaded hat. He was dressed all in black, which made Meb want

Dave Freer

to ask who had died. He had a small fluffy white dog . . . carried on a black satin cushion by a servitor. "Sell her to me, do, Lord? Can you sing, girl?" He sounded as if he'd burned his mouth eating.

Meb took some pleasure in gargling at him. Why, she was becoming as bad as her master!

"I am afraid not. She bites. And she is dumb," said Finn, in an accent indistinguishable from the black-and-white alvar's. "But she does tricks that help to relieve the ennui."

They moved on.

They walked through the enormous high-vaulted hall, where a trio of musicians played stoically above the noise, and went out of a small far door. "Leads to the jakes," said Finn. "But there used to be a door here . . . Ah, just behind that planter. It'll be locked, but I can deal with that."

He did, with a wiggle and a sharp cracking of wood. They stepped through into the passage beyond, closing the broken door behind them. The passage was a narrow one, and obviously not intended for the butterflies out there. The only servant they met looked puzzled to see them there. Puzzled, but respectful. Certainly not about to raise a hue and cry, or even to ask what they were doing here. Meb decided it must be the angle of Finn's nose. It was enough to make her want to apologize for being alive.

They walked out of the narrow passage and back into more plausible areas for a noble alvar to be in—into a large gallery in which many portraits hung. "The rogues' gallery," said Finn, with some amusement. "Look there, Scrap. That is the current master of this pile. Prince Gywndar."

Meb looked up at the cold alvar face. "He looks like he had some bad fish for breakfast," she said, seriously.

That made Finn laugh, as he led her off down a different passage. It was still the kind of passage that you might find nobles in—if they were the sort of noble that actually worked in the royal establishment. It was high and well lit, but simply utilitarian. It led down. Down, down into the depths of the palace. To a place that was important enough to be guarded.

"Halt!" said one of the guards.

Finn looked down the length of his nose. Meb just kept on juggling, changing to a cascade, because they were standing still.

"What is your purpose here, my lord?" asked the taller of the two guards, both of whom still stood, watchfully, in front of the locked door.

"I've come to rob the royal treasury," said Finn, with a yawn. "What does it look like, sirrah?"

The guard blinked. "Er. No disrespect intended, my lord. But you need special permission to go into the treasury."

Finn drew a large key from a pocket. "Having the key would seem reasonable permission to me. Do you know who I am?"

One of the guards stood hastily aside. But the other was made of sterner stuff. "I am sorry, my lord, I don't."

"Well," said Finn, frostily, stepping forward and putting the key into the lock. "You'd better see that you do something about that." He waved his free hand at the guard who had stood aside. "March him off to see Commander Pencival, and ask him to explain who the new high magician is."

"Er. We can't leave the place unguarded, sir," said the first guard.

Finn nodded. "True. Very well. I should not be long. And I'll need someone to carry certain treasures up to my chambers in the east tower. He can accompany me, and talk to the Commander." He jiggled the key slightly and the heavy metal-barred and studded door swung open. "Come, little one," he said to Meb. "Let us go and loot the royal treasury," he said, with a toothy smile at the guards.

"We didn't know, m'lord," said the one who had been doubtful at first. "No one ever tells us ordinary soldiers anything."

"Ah," said Finn, as he closed the door behind him. "You can't say I didn't. And most of it was the absolute truth too. I even had a chamber in the east tower, once. Unfortunately, people usually hear what they want to hear. Come on, Scrap. It's not every day you get to loot an ancient alvar treasure house. And I missed an important bit last time, because it wasn't in here. But it is this time. I made sure. Now we just have to find it."

"What are we looking for, master?" asked Meb.

"Bit of dry seaweed and a few little pearls, and there might be a dried starfish together with some other things you might find on the beach, if I remember right. Value means different things to different folk, I guess. In the meantime there are too many rubies in this place. Take some with you. And there is far too little gold for a good treasury. I don't share the alvar taste in sliver."

Meb was not too sure what a ruby was—besides red, so it

was a good thing that he showed her what he was talking about. There were a lot of them. Dry bladderwrack, on the other hand, she had seen plenty of cast up on the strand. So maybe it was easier for her to spot it in the narwhal ivory casket than it had been for him. There were pearls, yes, but they were small, and set in little bits of carved narwhal and walrus ivory, spiked into the dried seaweed and a few starfish, and the whole thing was spiked together with fishbones... An odd treasure!

"You'd better carry it then," he said sniffing and grinning. "You're more used to the smell of fishy things than I am."

The bladderwrack was so old and dry it could hardly have smelled. But, if he wanted her to take it...

"Put it in the bag for the juggling balls," he said. "And don't let go of it. There are going to be some folk who will be very glad to see it again." He was busy pouring a handful of gemstones into the front of his bulgy knee-breeches. "It's to be hoped I don't leak gems past the buckles."

Meb ended up with several jeweled rings on her fingers, and jewels in her pockets. She refused all the necklaces. "I have one, master."

So... he was a thief, then. She had known it... but had never really acknowledged it before. And now, so was she.

Finn took a pair of rather ugly but very ornate ear-rings, which had some small bells on them, as well as dazzlingly faceted, fiery stones.

"Go first, then drop these. I'm going to have to deal with the two guards," said Finn, casually.

The guards were armed. He was not. And... well, it seemed unfair. She'd resolved to leave fishing village morality behind, but... "Can't we just bluff our way out again?"

"We could," said Finn. "But then the guards would be hanged. This way they can tell their officers how they fought like the very heroes and were only laid low magically."

Somehow that lifted the feeling of oppression that admitting that he was a thief—and that she was too, had put onto her. She skipped along to the door and, trusting him completely, opened it and went out. She actually juggled with the ear-rings... until she realized that wasn't going to work. They didn't realize that those weren't her props. So she dropped them. And one of them bent down to pick the noisy bauble up, while the other laughed.

And Finn stepped out, no longer the languid dandy, but something more like a striking adder, hands moving so fast he almost seemed to blur. They were armed alvar wearing mail-coats and metal helms . . .

And falling.

Meb had been in enough rough-and-tumble fisher-brat fights to know that it wasn't that easy. Or it shouldn't be. She'd been ready to try and help . . . and secretly expected to lose. Maybe. Her master seemed so good at everything, but an element of doubt had crept into her mind about fighting armed alvar. They were great and terrible in war.

Finn grinned. "Neatly done, Scrap. I think we'll leave the door open. A little surprise for Prince Gywndar. I can just see him standing there and enjoying the sight."

So could Meb. Clear as anything she could see the alvar prince with his look of dyspepsia disappearing into rage as he stared at the door. She was still full of adrenaline from the sheer audacity of it all and the sudden violence.

The shout of outrage from the Prince echoed down the passage.

Finn's look of surprise was closer to the one Meb had imagined on the Prince's face. But Finn charged straight at him. After a moment's hesitation the prince turned and fled, as nimble as only an alvar could be.

"That's torn it," said Finn. "Come on, Scrap. We need to run now ourselves. Try to stay with me. And don't imagine any more disasters."

But seconds later they had one. The Prince had a group of four soldiers with him, coming at a run. Finn yelled triumphantly. "Got him! Seize that alv! He's an imposter using a glamor to pretend that he's Prince Gywndar! It's a trap!"

Such was the conviction in his shout as he ran toward the alvar—who all had swords drawn—that they did pause for a moment. Gywndar fell over one of them. He went flying, and landed in a sprawl between Finn and his soldiers. Before he could get up Finn was onto him. He had him by the scruff of the neck, holding him between himself and the soldiers. "Prince Gywndar is hunting in Mortdale. Everyone knows that! It's fifteen leagues away over the mountain."

The Prince struggled. "Unhand me! He's an assassin! I am your prince! Kill him!"

Finn slapped him hard enough to rock his head back. "Don't be ridiculous. If I was an assassin and you were the prince I would have killed you. I am unarmed, as you can all see." He thrust the stunned Prince at a soldier. "Quick, take him with you! We need the guard-commander. And we need to call a general alert! There may be more of these miscreants in the palace. There was a trap back there with swordsmen. We barely escaped with our lives! Come on, run! Protect us!"

And the soldiers did, half dragging the prince along between two of them. And somehow Meb and Finn were lagging just behind the soldiery . . . and then they sidestepped into a passage. Finn closed a heavy door behind them, dropped the bar, and they ran on.

They ran. And ran. The next few minutes of Meb's life—which had gone from predictable to chaotic ever since she'd seen the black dragon over the bay—were an extreme of chaos. They seemed to run from one group to the next, each escape getting narrower, but they were getting higher. Finn seemed to be trying to get somewhere, besides just away.

They found the place he'd been trying to reach. It was a small, locked room, at the end of a narrow passage. The pursuit was close, and Finn fiddled with his key. It seemed to fit a great many doors. Meb had always thought that keys fitted specific doors—she just wished this one worked faster. At last the door swung open and Finn pulled her in behind him. The floor was painted in an ornate pattern, with small candles set around it at various cardinal points, and little mirrors shining on tiny glass globes.

"Aha!" said Finn. "How convenient. Traditionalists. Well, let's show them that the night is traditionally dark. Alvar see well in the dark, but not as well as I do. And it should release sufficient energy. Balance things up nicely. It's going to go dark in a few moments, Scrap. Very dark, and the cloud has hidden the moon. You can cling onto my coat again. It'll crumple it, but I don't mind. Lilac really isn't my color, after all."

Meb had noticed the pale, glowing globes that lit the palace. But like so many other things their mechanism was beyond her understanding. Light, as she knew it, came from tallow dips, or fish-oil lamps, or candles, or fire or the moon. Mysterious alvar devices were not something she understood. Just accepted.

Finn walked around the room, roughly brushing away patterns, pushing candles together . . . They grew very bright, and then very suddenly went out. His deep chuckle was loud and . . . almost not human in the darkness.

To Fionn, the absence of visible light really was no impediment. He could see heat, magnetism, and the lines of force from earth, air, water, just to start with. He could also see his young charge. He had to laugh. He'd brought this on himself, hadn't he? The dvergar treasure she had on her neck was bad enough, and he had made her carry a load of water-magic too. He'd thought it wise to avoid direct contact with the treasure himself, considering the protections on it . . . he hadn't thought of the consequences of having her take on even more of a magical load. With the alvar being river-folk and her being a summonser to start with . . . Ha. What a mess. And now they had to move out, because the cascade of overloaded force-lines was about to get re-aligned.

"Take hold of my coat, Scrap," he said. He wondered if she had any idea what her true name was. Possibly not. Of course he knew. It was written into the very fibre of her being. To Fionn she might as well have had it tattooed on her forehead.

It was not a name to be taken lightly.

There was something very reassuring about the firm grip she had on his coat even if she could see nothing at all. She could certainly hear enough! The palace had been disturbed with shouted orders and yells before. Now added to that were sounds of panic and screaming. They walked down the passage, turned right—the way they'd come, turned right again . . . and Finn said: "Time to sit down, Scrap. Let's hope this place is well built."

They sat. It was not quite what she would have chosen to do, but she was glad of the rest. And her master seemed to know what he was doing. Which was more than she did. Her plans went as far as "run, because they really all want to kill us."

And then it seemed that the earth wanted to kill them too. Because the world shook under her. She was glad to be sitting down. She was also very afraid and clung to Finn.

"It's all right, Scrap. Just a little realignment of natural force lines." He sounded pleased. Satisfied. "And to make it even better, their pipes have burst. The lake does not like being constrained."

Neither, by the sounds of it, did the people of the white city like what had happened. There had been a lot of shouting in the palace. Now there was yelling, lots of screaming and, by the sounds of it, panic in the entire city. He couldn't have caused a minor earthquake, could he? Surely not. He was just a gleeman . . . and a thief . . . and seemed to know a lot.

"You can stop clinging to me, Scrap. I doubt if there will be any more. The noise is mostly panic. It wasn't a big one. Broken windows and the like, and quite a bit of good flooring flooded, that's all. The real damage is on the road, which is empty at night. They have a curfew . . . Come, we must get out while confusion reigns. Back to the museum and we can change into more comfortable clothes."

He led her off again, and while water washed over their shoes once, that was the most serious problem they had. They had to wait until some people passed—and just let others run past them. Soon they were outside the palace, in the walled gardens, but the wall provided little obstacle to Finn, and he hauled her up it easily. The streets were full of milling alvar. Meb and Finn were just some more of the same. Order was being shaped out of chaos by the yelling and by soldiery spilling out of the palace, but it was not quickly enough to stop the two of them walking peacefully to the museum. It was just as dark inside there, after Finn had let them in with his "fits anything key," but he knew his way, or could see a great deal better in the dark than she could. Soon she was reunited with her familiar breeches, cotte, cloak and boots.

"Don't forget to transfer the things you have in your pockets. Or to bring with you the bag with the Angmarad in it. It's been a lot of fun, but I think it might be harder if we had to do it again too soon," said Finn from the darkness.

═ Chapter 21 ═

FIONN HAD ALWAYS BEEN ADEPT AT USING A MIXTURE OF MAGIC, trickery, brute force and mechanical means to do his work. And his glib tongue of course, although he tried to avoid levering rocks around with that.

The road from the white city was as much of a problem as the vast collection of rubies—and the magical energy associated with them—that its treasury had accumulated. Of course all things are interlinked, something the First had been aware of. The road ran too straight, carried too many people with the energies they trafficked, quite unintentionally. They'd cut through several granite spurs and altered the course of the river to achieve that. Fionn had discovered, quite by accident many centuries ago, how to make magically activated detonators. It was simply a case of having too much power pass through any one point at any time, and he had several options here. The area was overdue for an earthquake . . . in fact, the longer it took before it happened the worse it would be—he could see the plates and tense-bound energies waiting for the slippage.

He'd laid his explosives carefully, wedging them into cracks, and laying them behind piles of precarious rock. Of course the spurs and the river had been his first choice. But any place where his explosions would cause some deep, low frequency vibration would work. That was partially the result of the explosions . . . and partially the rockfalls. The vibration caused the planes of rock to start their slippage and release their stored energy, which, compared to his puny explosives was a giant compared to an ant.

✧   ✧   ✧

Leagues away across the wide and island-studded ocean, Myrcupa, self-styled high lord and defender of the tower, had been sulkily staring at the great edifice that had been magically constructed long ages back to guard the strand of here and elsewhere that held the plane of Tasmarin. He was thinking of quitting this thankless task and seeing if he could ambush Zuamar of Yenfar. Yet he felt compelled to stay.

The death of his sycophant had hurt him. When the tower at Morscarg had fallen, seventeen years back, the talk had been that some nihilist had somehow managed to sabotage and destroy the foundation.

Dragons are nothing if not patient. He'd guarded this one faithfully in shifts since. But . . . well, the Tower had repelled any life-form—including its guardians. That was what it was supposed to do, Myrcupa knew. But he had felt—a little resentfully, that it might have given its defenders some . . . well, respect. Not that it was alive . . . Knowing it was illogical had not stopped him feeling that way.

He was supremely unaware of an earthquake many leagues away.

But he did see a crack in the vast masonry, one of several they were monitoring, suddenly grow and spread and run with a long, thunderous tumult up the wall.

He still could not reach it to do anything about it.

But although he took to the wing and searched, there was no-one visible attacking it, despite a strong scent of magic. It smelled . . . human.

Myrcupa despised humans.

The centaurs had always been the cusp between animal nature and civilization. Over the long history of their kind they'd swayed between the two. They believed that at last they'd reached some kind of balance, here on the high plains. Here philosophy and the noble arts of poetry and the sagas, the wild music and great dance had risen above the old scourges of conflict and war. Yes, the sheer, high cliffs of Thessalia, Laconia and Lapithidia limited the extent of the high tableland which they lived on. It had meant an end to the great migrations. But on the other hand it kept the Children of Chiron to themselves too. For centuries they had had limited contact with the other species. The plane of centaurs had always been one of poorly defined boundaries, in which conflict with humans, alvar and even the sprites had been a prominent part. Those years had honed the centaurs for combat. A man-horse could out-maneuver any horse-man. And they had become, perforce, great archers.

But the arts of war had been relegated to yesteryear, here. Until now. The dark glass of the seeing pool had caused old sabers to be sharpened and polished, and spare arrows—war arrows, with heavy heads for penetrating armor—to be made and fletched. Now the dust from great phalanxes of centaurs drilling and training hung over the high plains. The Children of Chiron had never been at home at sea. But they had been slowly accumulating transports. And the magical arts and defenses were being practiced. The time was coming. If... when ... the black dragon brought down the next tower, or even before that, the fatelines all led to war.

Or extinction.

Ixion paced the looping trail that looked down on Lapithidia's only port, a good half a mile below. He looked down on the ships moving slowly toward the harbor. His companion Hylonome scanned the skies.

"Dragon," she said pointing.

He would have seen it too, as it was closing in on two vessels out beyond the Lapith point.

"It's green," he said, "Not that that will help the sailors."

They were too far off to see the crews—doubtless leaping into the water. But they could see the sails catch fire.

"It begins," said Hylonome in a heavy voice.

Ixion said nothing. From here they could not to do anything to help either.

The stream that flowed down from the mountains had offered Hrodenynbrys little respite from having to get out and walk next to it. Land was just so awkward. He couldn't merely swim over obstacles. He had to go around them. And slipping out of the water made merrows terribly vulnerable. He was very glad to reach the lake. Merrows had been this far before, of course. But the Angmarad had not been given into the keeping of alvar at a whim. The spells of warding set on it would, the merrow knew, protect it, and prevent him from getting any closer. The alvar had been their usual thorough selves about it, Hrodenynbrys had to admit, sourly. They'd protected it against the magics of all the species, calling in help, where need be. Well, all species except alvar, and humans of course.

It had seemed a fine gesture at the time. And merrow and alvar had been on good terms.

It was supposed to be a temporary measure.

Hrodenynbrys had barely slipped into the quiet waters of the lake, where the reflected lights of their 'burg gleamed, before they went out, and the earthquake began.

The water stirred and roiled and shook like a wild live thing.

It was nearly enough to frighten 'Brys witless—and enough to send him swimming as fast as he could for deeper water.

In time the water was still again. It was all stirred up, belching methane bubbles, and other smelly and nasty things best left in the still depths. But calmer.

Hrodenynbrys looked at the following charm he carried. If he went now . . . in the darkness? Would that be best?

He wanted to stay in the water. He really did not want to go out in the dark and shaken chaos that would be happening over there. He could hear the yelling across the water.

But duty called. The Angmarad needed the sea, and the sea desperately needed the Angmarad. And when would they find the hair of another human mage?

So he began swimming, slowly, toward the city, admittedly at a pace that would have made a crippled flatfish seem like a harpooned marlin. Just how was he going to get to it?

═ Chapter 22 ═

"AND NOW, MASTER?" SAID MEB. PITCH TORCHES AND CANDLES WERE showering a sprinkling of points of light through the city.

"Now we head for the lake. To where I stashed the other large bag. We'll need to do a little engineering in the dark."

Meg wondered just what he planned to build. She found out soon enough.

"It's a coracle. Willow laths and an outer skin. It'll leak, but it will get us across the lake."

"Not . . . not this lake, Master." Even she had heard about it.

"They're getting organized behind us, Scrap. By first light there'll be a hue and cry like nothing this island has ever seen. We need to be a good long way away by then. Preferably hidden under a big rock."

"But master . . . the Nichor. He lives in the lake. He'll pull us in if we as much as touch it," said Meb nervously.

"Ah. That's the last lath in place. Help me to get it on my back, Scrap. The Nichor . . . well, it's his lake. But we'll toss him a ruby or two. There really is no other way out. Trust me."

She did. But she was deathly afraid, as they slipped out on the dark, quiet water. Sitting still—it was a tiny cockle-shell of a boat, with only a hand's width or two of freeboard while they got further and further out onto the water, with the pinpricks of flame-light in the city behind them receding slowly.

"Why don't they fix their light-magic?" asked Meb, desperate not to think of the green-toothed worm-beast that everyone knew haunted this famous lake.

"It may take them some months," said Finn. "It's part alvar magic, part dvergar contrivance, and part dragon-magic. They've burned their bridges rather badly with the dvergar. You noticed that there was little gold in that treasury?"

"Uh. Yes."

"Well, the alvar will hold that they prefer silver, and that it's a purer color—a matter of opinion. But the truth is the dragon takes the gold, and the alvar see that he gets it. Of course your old Loftalvar think that treachery. But the Huldralvar and Stromalvar made bargains with dragonkind. So now, as you know, your Prince, the one I swatted about the ear, calls himself Prince of Yenfar. The dvergar say he is nothing more than a tax-collector. But then the alvar can deal quite effectively with dvergar and their magic. There's no love lost, now."

Meb said nothing . . . because she was too afraid. It was overcast, but the sky was still lighter than either the water or the shore. And now part of that light was blotted out. A tangle of dark . . . it must be hair, was rising behind them. It must be hair, because set below it were definitely eyes. Huge eyes that glowed with a pale inner light, their glow illuminating a green face and a slit of a nose . . . and the mouth. An open mouth full of snaggled teeth. Long, clawed hands with seven spidery fingers were reaching for Finn.

Her mouth was too dry . . . "Nichor," she managed to croak in a tiny voice, pointing.

Finn turned the coracle. "How right you are. Go away, Shellycoat. We're not your meat." He tossed a stone at it, presumably a ruby.

It didn't seem to be planning to listen, or be interested in rubies.

He flung the paddle at it like a spear. The Nichor hissed like a fire that had just had water spilled onto it. The paddle didn't deter it, though.

"Take that bit of sea-weed and pearl out of the bag," said Finn, quietly.

She did so with shaking hands. She pulled back her hand to throw, but Finn reached forward and stopped her. "Just put it on your head."

"Whisht," said a voice in the darkness. "And just what have we here? Be off with you, Shellycoat, or I'll be putting my trident just exactly where you'd least like to have it put."

"Your work, Scrap?" asked Finn, sounding surprised.

"Work?" Meb was puzzled. The nearest she'd come to work lately was a bit of juggling.

"Calling a merrow to us," said Finn, quietly. "What is it doing here in fresh water otherwise?"

"I could just be looking for something that was taken from us," answered the voice. "It's to be hoped you can swim, because the Shellycoat's gone all stupid on us. They seem to get like that when they're really big. It's going to attack your little boat."

"I am about to splash you," said Finn, quietly to Meb. "I'm telling you just so you don't get a surprise and upset us or jump overboard. As soon as I do, you tell the Shellycoat to get gone. Firmly."

By now, Meb's nerves and wits were jelly. Even knowing that it was coming—the water that hit her in the face was an icy shock. She really didn't mean to start swearing. But she did. With every word garnered from her step-brothers' vocabulary she told the Nichor to leave them alone. She'd die defiant anyway.

The Nichor nearly swamped the coracle . . . the wave rocked it and slopped water over the edge. The creature dived with all the haste it could muster.

There was a silence. And then Finn began to laugh. "Do you know how anatomically difficult it is going to be for the creature to obey you?" he asked.

"It's a fine tongue you have in your head," said the other voice from the water, reminding Meb that they were not out of trouble, yet.

But the voice sounded amused and, if anything, impressed. "Well, what are you doing out on the water on a night like this?"

"Much what you're doing, I suspect," said Finn. "Trying not to get eaten, Hrodenynbrys."

"It's a good ambition, I'm thinking," said the voice. "And how did you know who I was?"

From the chilly lake water Hrodenynbrys considered his options. It would take him only a moment to tip the coracle. On the other hand . . . the fact that other human knew his name, and didn't seen in the least perturbed to find him here, was worrying in itself. And she was now wearing the Angmarad. The force of it—when water touched the poor long-dry stems—had been like a tidal bore. She might just use it on him, if she fell in. She didn't do too well in water, as he remembered. And he liked the attitude of the lass. She had fine tongue on her. Swear a fire-being out of the hot place, let alone a Shellycoat back down into the depths.

The intrinsic problem was that he was supposed to bespell her to fetch the Angmarad . . . not for her to take the power of it and give it into fresh captivity. Well, merrows were gamblers by nature. That meant knowing when to bluff and when not to bet too. "Before I give you a tow to the shore, as you are short a paddle now, I'd still like to be knowing how you knew my name?"

"Ach," said the man, easily. "Your fame goes before you. Really."

There was something almost familiar about the speaker. Enough to make Hrodenynbrys wary, and glad that he hadn't merely tipped the coracle over. "If I was to believe that, I'd have to be human, or something equally daft. Have you a bit of rope? It'd make pulling you easier."

It was still hard work. But gave him time to think. That had been the biggest Shellycoat 'Brys had ever seen . . . and what had happened over in the alvar city? Who was this human with her . . . he fenced as well with words as a merrow. And more relevant: why had she got the Angmarad . . . and what was he, Hrodenynbrys, going to do about it?

By the time he got to the shore, 'Brys had decided that he'd better play it the way Margetha intended, even if it went against his better judgement. He pulled on the cape—which allowed him to change into human form. There was some confusion about that, in human circles. It was something merrows were keen to see continued.

"I think I might have some trousers to lend you," said the man, as he stepped ashore. "It seems a fair exchange for the ride."

Hrodenynbrys had forgotten humans felt like that about nudity. Merrows seldom went on land these days. No wonder those women gathering berries had run away from him in such surprise. "I forgot," he said. "I have them here in my bag." It was good hunting misdirection. He pulled out the throw-net, so cunningly made and bespelled, its fringe weighted with coins from shipwrecks, and he flung it with a smooth, perfect cast.

And that was the last thing that went well.

As he threw, she—who had been carefully not looking at him—stepped closer to her companion. Instead of catching the one fish he had two. Considering the magic expended on every knot of that net it should have ensnared any human, and also made her his to command. It should have bound her as still as stone, beyond anyone but him freeing her. He'd reckoned that he could retreat into the water if the man gave him any trouble that a trident couldn't fend off. After all he just wanted the Angmarad off her head, and he'd be away so fast that they'd think he was a sea-pike.

Margetha's spell-work—or that of the human mage, or the effects of the Angmarad on her head—failed completely, in a series of little sparkly explosions as the two of them tore free. Hrodenynbrys held his trident at the ready and retreated back into the icy lake.

"Soul-net," said the man. "Well, well, what do you merrows think you're playing at? I was all set to give your bauble to you to carry back to the sea for me. But now I've changed my mind. Scrap, tell him to get his trouserless butt out of the lake. I've got work for him to do."

"Me, master?" she asked, her fright showing in her voice . . . but not her posture.

The tall man chuckled. "No, me master, you Scrap. You're wearing the spirit of the waters on your head, so you tell him what to do. And if he doesn't listen you can send him off to do to the Shellycoat what you have the creature trying to do to itself. It must have a crick in its spine by now. Tell him to get out and to take that coracle into the lake and sink it. Too deep for Zuamar to see from the air, and then to get back here, and give you that cape of his."

So she did . . . 'Brys found himself compelled to do as she ordered, and to wonder firstly, just what sort of a mess he was in this time, and secondly just what the man had meant, and how he knew so much. Hrodenynbrys had a feeling that he'd gone grailing for flat-fish and stuck his trident through his own foot instead of a fat flounder.

But he had little choice but to do as he was told, and then to return, and put on the spare clothes . . . and to part with his cape of red sealskin.

He was trapped in this awful form without it.

But on the other hand, he had to stay close to the Angmarad, even if it meant that all he could to do was to—somehow—pass word on to his fellow merrows as to where it was.

✧   ✧   ✧

Meb was unsure about what was going on. Unsure what that
bit of spiderweb and sparks had been about. All she knew was
that it had made Finn angry. She hadn't really seen him angry
before, she realized. He was furious with the merrow . . . who
seemed both frightened and desperate. Well . . . the merrow had
saved her life, once. She was pretty sure it was the same one.

"Right," said Finn. "Thanks to Mr. Clever Merrow there's a sign
here, etched indelibly into these stones, that merrow-magic and
a few other flavors of enchantments were used here. And not
ones that we wanted to advertise. The alvar will get to searching the lake shore eventually. Or Zuamar may to do it for them.
You damned fool, merrow. You've as likely as not started a war
between your kind and the alvar, not to mention dragons. Was
that what you had in mind?"

The merrow stammered something . . . about the "Angmarad"
and need and duty.

Finn snorted. "You've more balls than brains. But that is typical
of merrows. Come on. Let's move out. Walk in the water. Yes,
your feet are going to get wet, both of you. Live with it."

So they walked. Across the water, the chaos of pinpricks of firelight had resolved itself into orderly moving lines of torches.

"They're searching," said Finn, a little reluctant admiration in his
voice. "One thing you have to grant the alvar. They organize better
than humans. And the merrows," added as an afterthought.

The merrow snorted. "Organizing is for those who can't to do
it alone."

"Well, then you ought to learn," said Finn.

Meb's feet were completely numb when they came to a spit of
rock that spiked out into the water, with a low cliff facing them.
"This is as good a place as any. Right, up we climb."

It was not particularly difficult even with feet like lumps of
wood. Meb scrambled to the top, easily enough. The merrow
found it a lot more of a challenge. "Could I not go around?" he
asked after the second try.

"No. Use your feet. Don't try and just pull yourself up."

The effort it took him would have had Meb over the white
walls of the alvar city. "It's a little different to swimming," he
said, panting.

"And there's worse to come," said Finn. "I'm going to wear

those fin-feet of yours down to stubs running." At least, by his tone, her master appeared to have recovered his sense of humor, somewhat.

Finn led them along the ridge. In the dark it was a scary half-climb, half-scramble. Eventually they came to a narrow neck and something of a way down. Meb did not know how Finn saw where to go, but he did. Then they were off and into the pinewoods, walking.

And walking.

And walking. Meb was barely able to stagger when he finally let them stop at a small overhang, where water dripped down one edge. The sky was beginning to pale above the spiky, dark trees.

And if Meb thought she was tired, the poor merrow simply fell over when they stopped.

"Hmm. He won't be used to this sort of thing," said Finn. "Right. Let's get a fire going and a bit of food into us. We'll need it before the chase is done."

Chapter 23

LYR WAS AT ONE WITH THE GROVE OF ASPENS ON THE SLOPES
above the alvar city. She'd come in response to a message from her
worshipers that the human they sought was in the slum outside
the city, that they were just trying to locate her precisely. This
sort of thing was why her kind had made an alliance with the
flame-creatures. The sprite-gestalt did not deal well with humans or
their values. She understood theft. Just not how to make humans
do it. She tended toward a different style of attack—but it was a
large, fortified city.

When the earth shook, it uprooted some trees. Shook her from
her bed. The sprites were more attuned to growing things than
the rock, but she felt the wave of force that reverberated along
the white road.

She had not expected Haborym's gang of renegades to strike yet.
But surely only moving the treasure of the water-people could cause
such a thing? Haborym had suspected the treasure to be hedged
in enchantments. Well, they knew that the alvar had protected
against the fire-beings. But the alvar always had an arrangement
with the sprites. They believed they had a special bond.

If they wished to believe that, the tree-people would not gain-
say them.

She watched with cool green eyes. She disliked the fire they
kindled, but it did look as if the merrow treasure had been successfully stolen, if not successfully replaced. Well, the latter didn't
matter to her. Haborym was far better at sneaking and deception

in his shallow sort of way. The sprites were not fooled. But now she could hand the hunt for the female human magic-conduit over to him.

She would check first, of course. Her kind were thorough.

At first light the patrols of alvar were pouring out of the white city like ants. Some—it would appear—had been dispatched last night to blockade the roads. Now more were marching or riding post haste in various directions. The theft had certainly disturbed them . . . well, that and the earthquake that it must have been the cause of. She hoped the thieves had got away with it. It would be much more difficult to do it twice, she thought.

She made her way down from the aspens to the checkpoint on the shattered road below. A part of the ridge had fallen across it, and a few travelers were being turned back already. The alvar were allowing foot-patrols to pick their way across the landslip. Horsemen were looking for another route. That was the problem with good roads, the sprite reflected. They'd become reliant on them. She could go wherever the trees grew. Her natural affinity was to the tall, slim birches or aspens. Others had different affinities. But not here. The others were lost and far away.

The alvar were all so susceptible. She smiled in the way that she knew would have the guards mesmerized. "And what has happened here?" she asked.

The alv guard bowed respectfully. "Lady of the forests, there has been a robbery. A terrible theft. It appears that the thieves took advantage of this disaster to loot the noble Prince Gywndar's treasure. That's humans for you. Always take advantage of someone else's misfortunes."

"It is to be hoped that you can catch them," she said, turning away.

"Oh, we will. If we have to scour every inch of Yenfar . . . The prince has sent word to the dragon Zuamar too," said the guard. "I hope you're happy for winter here, Lady. The road is not going to be passible for months, and once the snow comes . . ."

The dragon was as unwelcome news as the other had been good. Dragons were very sensitive to fire-beings, and not susceptible to the beauty of sprites. Actually, they had been known to set them alight.

Was nothing ever straightforward? That was why the sprites liked to avoid dealing with the other species. The disorganized creatures had their own desires which ran counter to the only right way. She sent word to her sisters. The news would pass from tree to tree all the way to the coast. There a Lyr would be obliged to take to a boat. The sisterhood disliked that. Firstly, boats were made of killed wood. And secondly the motion made sprites feel unwell. It was one of the reasons the sprites disliked the salt-sea. But Haborym would get the news and come to Yenfar, and capture the human. And the sprites could have their reward.

She did not think the fire-being understood what they were asking for as the price of their help. That was a good thing. Of course the creatures of smokeless flame were trying to deceive and cheat too. But that was expected of them.

Lyr was not worried by the damage to the road. She could, and would prefer to, move through the forests, and to be away before the snows fell, if she was not too late already.

Zuamar turned across the great bay, making the first of a series of turns that would take him back to his eyrie. In his fury at the loss of some of his gold, he had been forced off his mountain, away from his hoard and the contemplation of the beauty of it, and out onto the wing. Into conflict and conquest. It had, overall, been a good thing, he decided. Yes, there was talk of the end of the world. There always was, and always had been. He'd paid that little black wyrm no particular attention then, and had no intention of changing that. But the situation had become stratified, stuck in the pattern and balance they'd all assumed in the early days when there had been a need for that stability.

By the very nature of the places that Tasmarin had taken to be a part of itself, it was a world principally of seas and islands. The places at which the planes of existence had linked had often been either mountains, or wild coastlines. It had been something to do with the energy configuration of those places, he believed. There were islands beyond counting. In his flights he had become aware that while the dragons had taken roost on the great islands, with the size of the island being more or less proportionate to the size of the dragon, there were many islands out there. The alvar and the humans had generally clustered for protection under their dragon (to protect them from others), since anything without a protector was fair game. Yet . . . there were still a lot more islands out there. And as time had passed and dragons had done less raiding, more and more of the kine were living on those smaller islands . . . with no overlords. Yes, younger dragons had carved out holdings for themselves on some of them. The islands were technically subject to the nearest dragon-lord. They were relatively small and poor, these places. Yet, there were many of them. There was a profit there. And a danger. It was time they were thinned out. He had enjoyed starting that work.

Zuamar was somewhat surprised to see an alvar and his horse at his lower gate. He was, of course, instinctively suspicious as to why anyone would come this close. But the alvar was waiting in the open, a respectful distance from the cave. He had kindled a small fire . . . less respectful perhaps, but an indication that he'd been there a while. There was a doorbell of sorts, there. A messenger. Perhaps they'd caught some of the miscreants. That would be pleasing.

The alvar bowed low. "Lord Zuamar. My prince sends word that he has need of your aid."

That was not what he wanted to hear.

The alvar messenger continued. "The royal treasury of our great city has been robbed. Much treasure was taken, including a magical relic we had custody of. We are searching for raiders."

Zuamar's eyes narrowed. There was a pattern here. He just had to see what it was. Robbery and raiding were still commonplace things. But thieves did not raid the rich and powerful. They did not attack the tax halls of dragons. They avoided the treasure halls of princes. The weak and defenseless were the target . . . although to gain greater wealth the richer were more lucrative.

He was one of greatest of dragons. Yenfar one of the largest and most wealth-generating of islands, only rivaled, really, by the smaller fertile islands around the great sunken caldera to the South—but those had never been popular with the alvar. They loved the high mountains. Thus Prince Gywndar was one of the most powerful of princes among the alvar.

Only a very avaricious, brave thief . . . or possibly, a powerful foe would dare to raid here.

Or was someone tweaking their beards on purpose?

— Chapter 24 —

ON A COLD MOUNTAINSIDE, ENTIRELY TOO CLOSE TO THE ALABASTER
city of the alvar and the lair of Zuamar, Fionn stared out from the
ridge he'd gone up to, to scout from, and contemplated his next
moves. Left to himself he would have transformed into a more useful shape for running, or even flying, and kept right on going. But
the presence of the other two was an impediment. He was really
not too sure what the merrow's game was. On deeper thought, he
was sure that Scrap hadn't summonsed the merrow—he was less
sure about the Nichor. He could, in all truth, simply be there by
chance. The merrows had come as close as they could, any number
of times, he believed . . . No, he couldn't believe! The soul-net proved
the merrow was here, seeking the scrap of humanity in his care.
He'd expected the sprites, demondim and alvar . . . and definitely
the dragons . . . and possibly the centaur-folk. The horse-people
got up his nose and itched a bit. He knew them least well. The
dvergar . . . well, they had declared themselves solidly on her side.
He still was not entirely sure why. That was a thing of great power
that they'd made for her. There was usually a price to dvergar gifts,
but they were clever about it.

Events had come to a head entirely too fast back there. The alvar
would all be seeking a human mage after her little accident with
that princeling of theirs. Seeking her, if possible, more intently
than they sought the merrows' precious treasure. He had a difficult balancing act here . . . He'd intended the alvar to think it
was one of their own who had stolen the Angmarad. That would

have had Prince Gywndar furious and angry—but unaware that the thing was back where it belonged. There were enough bitter factions and petty princelings to have made it possible that some other alvar had taken it for spite, merely to prove Gywndar an unworthy custodian.

But now . . . well, there was human . . . and, when they found the trail on the far side of the lake, dragon and merrow mage-sign. Fionn chewed his lip. He had planned to quietly secure the rest and ensure that they could be—as best as possible—used when he finished his work. The hell-flame he had already. And that gave him the alvar and the centaurs' treasure in trade with the creatures of smokeless fire. They prized and feared their ancient glowing ball of strange energy. A trade of the Angmarad would have given him the dvergar treasure. The merrows returned that faithfully to the land each year anyway . . . and he was really not sure the artificers had not just made another. They were inclined to do that.

Still, complications or not, he'd had a lot of entertainment out of it. Who would have thought shepherding a human around could be quite so fraught with disaster? Generally speaking, Fionn liked disasters. Chaos was his metier, after all. And right now, from here he could not see the pursuit. That didn't mean that they weren't coming. He walked back to the little camp. The merrow and his little Scrap were examining their feet. Hmm. He should have thought of that. Dragon-hide—even changed—was still a lot tougher than human skin, or merrow skin.

It put limits on how far and fast they could run today. Fionn tasted the air . . . looked at the shifting clouds with a slight brownish tinge to them, and then grinned to himself. It was not a safe refuge, but the three of them might get out of it alive, if they were lucky. Merrows loved to gamble, and so did he. Scrap would just have to go along with them. He didn't expect the untoward degree of cooperation he was getting from her to last indefinately, if he was any judge of human character—and he should be. He'd spent a lot of time with them. He liked humans, and not just roasted.

The place they were about to seek shelter was populated by one of those who prefered their humans raw, but would eat them cooked. Fionn wasn't too sure how he'd feel about merrows. Groblek had a sense of humour. Maybe he'd think they tasted funny.

"We'll eat and rest," he said, looking at their feet. "I don't suppose you have anything sensible to put on those feet of yours, merrow?"

He shook his head. "My feet are tougher than human feet . . ."

Fionn looked at the cut he was attempting to clean. "But you've never walked more than a mile on them. Well . . . I'll have to see what I can do. We need to climb toward the snowline. It's going to be colder up there, and rocky underfoot."

"Where are we going?"

"The house of dreams and shadows."

"Is it hard to get to?" asked the scrap tiredly.

"Yes," admitted Fionn. "But it is not going there that's the problem. It's leaving again."

He let them sleep while he stitched. Cobbling was not his trade, but he'd learned a little about a lot of things over the years.

— Chapter 25 —

ZUAMAR SETTLED ON THE WALL OF THE ROYAL PALACE. IT CRACKED under his vast bulk, dropping pieces of alabaster carving that had survived the earthquake. Prince Gywndar arrived moments later. This was plainly no time for his usual folly of a slight delay to show his importance. It was always just a small delay, as Zuamar had eradicated the probability of longer ones some generations of alvar rulers earlier, by flaming a tower when he was kept waiting.

"We have recovered some of the loot," Gywndar said grimly, "but some of the theives remain at large. We need your help, Lord Zuamar, to track them down."

Zuamar began to spread his huge wings. "I have other matters to deal—"

"One of them is a human mage," interrupted Gywndar.

Zuamar let his wings fall. "What! You must be mistaken."

"No, Lord Zuamar. I have had my best magic workers there. They say there is little doubt that it is not one of the other intelligent species. The miscreants we've caught were human."

Zuamar snorted. "We were very careful to destroy every last trace of magical skill in the blood of humankind. I do not believe this. I must go to the place myself."

Gywndar looked at the bulk of his overlord. "My Lord Zuamar . . . it is a narrow passage and down where the palace is dug into the rock. But . . . I myself was a victim of this sorcery. It is possible that the taint of it still clings to me."

155

"What happened to you?" asked Zuamar. Really, this fool would probably consider a flash of burning magnesium to be magic.

"I was transported, magically, instantly, some fifteen leagues."

Zuamar blinked. That, if it had happened, was powerful magic indeed. "Come closer," he said.

And yes, it was there. The scent of something he had not smelled for centuries.

He nearly cremated the prince in his roar of rage. Just in time he turned his incandescent fury to belch up into the sky. He was angry, yes, that a human mage should be here on this island of his. But he was still angrier at himself. There had been a hint of the same scent of magic in his tax-hall. At the time the fact that there'd been dragonfire there had been enough to stop him thinking about it. Now . . . Now that linked the two incidents. Maybe even the third one.

"Come back here!" commanded Zuamar. The cowering alvar princeling returned from the colonnade he'd run to. It would not have saved him. "I want to know all about it. Every last detail."

The alvar prince nodded earnestly and began to tell the dragon just what they'd established thus far. In alvar fashion they were very efficient at piecing it together. There were still some large and inexplicable gaps in the story. "You found the merrow treasure, but not the thieves?"

"We found some thieves, my Lord Zuamar. A large and well armed band. They fought. The survivor confessed under torture that they had come to steal the merrow treasure." He paused. "But the human mage was not among them. In fact there was no sign of the two I had encountered."

"And one assumes that the survivor could not tell you why they had left the treasure, and why the mage summonsed you?"

"He died . . . we have no skills at necromancy."

It was a fire-being skill, and not a safe practice, Zuamar knew. He still briefly considered flying the body to one of them. But they were so steeped in devious behavior as to make dragonkind look straight-forward . . . anything he got out of them would be tainted; and besides, it was not a matter that he was keen to inform them of. "So two of them are still at large. Or at least two of them. One assumes, with your usual efficiency you have made some attempt to block the trails?"

The Prince nodded. "We've been both helped and hindered by

the earthquake. The white road is impassable in several places. We sent guards out on horseback within an hour to seal off the main trails. We have patrols sweeping the lesser trails. It is unlikely that they could have escaped by natural means. We've sent messengers to close the ports. Unless they used magic to leave, they're still on the island."

"This is not something we can tolerate," said Zuamar.

"Yes, the theft must be—"

"Not theft, you fool," snarled Zuamar. "The existence of a human mage. It must be found and destroyed. If need be we will hunt down and kill every human on this island."

"But . . . my Lord. We need them. They produce—"

"Need them, Prince?" asked Zuamar, dangerously.

"They . . . they grow much of our food. And they provide a large part of your tax base," said Gywndar, his voice quavering a little.

The latter, it was true, gave Zuamar pause. "They're like lice. They can breed up again. But for now we will hunt for the miscreant. Before we make an example of some of them."

"Yes, My lord Zuamar." Prince Gywndar nodded respectfully.

A panting alvar messenger arrived. Bowed. Zuamar was amazed at the temerity of the fellow. So, by his expression, was the prince. "Why are you interrupting us?" he asked, in a tone that indicated that the answer had better be an extremely good one.

The alvar bowed again, nervously. "The . . . the teams you had out scouring the area for any sign of human magery . . . they've found something."

"Ah. Where?" asked Gywndar, mollified.

"On the far side of the lake, Prince," said the messenger.

Zuamar spread his wings. "I will go."

Gywndar nodded. "I will send my troops. I never thought of the lake . . . it has a guardian."

Zuamar knew that. He wondered if it still did. Or how this arrogant fool had imagined such a thing could resist a summonsing mage? He said nothing. Instead he spread his mighty wings and surged away from the wall. He used the thermals to gain some height to take him across the lake. It was already late afternoon, and even in the teeth of winter, the city was a good place for warmer air. From up here he could see a small knot of alvar on the shore and a few scouring the slope beyond. He flew across the limpid azure waters, looking for the drifting corpse of the lake's inhabitant. He didn't find it, but what he did find when he reached the far side shocked him more.

There had been very powerful magic used there. The traces of it were etched onto the rocks themselves.

And, taking the scents and flavor of it, for the first time in many years, Zuamar was afraid. He did not speak to the wary alvar on the scene. The Prince's magicians would work it out soon enough. He lumbered with difficulty into flight. His first thought was the conclave. His second was to hunt down the miscreants first. Hunt them at range, with cleansing fire. He began to circle, in order to gain height and to scan the ground below. He could guide the alvar to close with them. And when they were distracted, burn the lot of them.

There was dragon, merrow, and human and possibly even something dvergar about that scent.

Zuamar could still remember when he not been the mightiest of dragons, but just a lowly messenger.

He'd burn every last one before he went back to that.

═ Chapter 26 ═

FIONN HAD SEEN ZUAMAR FLYING HIGH ACROSS THE MOUNTAINSIDE, and known that the chase was finally on. A dragon, naturally, knew just what a dragon could see, and how to avoid being spotted from the air. Fortunately, most dragons could not see as far into the infrared as he could, or they would have had a worse problem. If it had not been laid into the very fibre of his being by the First that he should not kill dragons, Fionn would have cheerfully taken to the air then, and dealt with Zuamar.

Fionn knew there'd be alvar on horseback and hounds tracking and harrying them soon. Still... it was barely a couple of hours to sundown... The advantage of an aerial spotter would be lost then. And Fionn had dealt with hounds and horsemen before. Horses, alas, were much more sensitive than humans. You wouldn't get them coming within five ells of a dragon, no matter what shape it assumed. Dogs were braver... or more foolish. They still didn't like coming too close. Fionn grinned. He couldn't blame them for that. Fionn had often wished to try riding a horse, but that wasn't going to happen. A donkey cart was his limitation, so far.

He roused his charges. "Up, sleepyheads. We have a mountain to climb, and they're after us."

That salve of Finn's had done wonders for her feet, Meb thought. Now if only it could do something for her muscles. She ached. And very soon she realized that it wasn't over yet. At first it

159

was just the far off sound of the hounds giving chase. Then the sound of hunting horns, and occasional glimpses of a dragon in flight far above the trees. Meb was truly grateful for those trees ... only the three of them were going upwards, and the trees were definitely smaller and more scattered up here. The sun was lowering, about to spear itself redly on the smaller peaks to the west. And now the yip of the hounds running, let alone the sound of them giving tongue when they found the scent, came echoing up the valley.

"Will ... will they stop for dark?" she panted.

"I doubt it," said Finn. "But he should." He gestured skyward. "It's an effort to keep flying. There is much magic in the flight of dragons, but that's because they're too heavy to fly without it. It still takes some physical effort. And the hunt is strung out. They'll not take us easily."

"How ... far to this shelter?"

"Ach. There are doorways everywhere. But Groblek likes rock and snow. And we need moonrise. Onwards, Scrap!"

Somehow, she drove her body onward. Onward and upwards. At this time of the year darkness came very quickly. Nearly as quickly as the hunters were coming.

Onward. Onward.

She was stumbling, holding onto his cloak again. The merrow was holding onto her in turn. Below them a forest was abruptly on fire.

"He's still flying!" said Finn. "The alvar won't be pleased about their woods."

The red glow reflected on the clouds helped her to see a little.

She could hear the dogs panting now. Looking back she saw a glint of armor in the moonlight—tinted red by the burning forest. "Up there," yelled someone. Meb looked in desperate hope for the refuge Finn had said was close.

For a moment she thought she saw it. Rough steps leading to an odd beehive of stone. But when she turned to focus on it ... it was just an illusion of shifting shadows and moonlight. There was nothing there but black rocks and a few patches of snow ...

"Aha!" grunted Finn. An arrow buzzed past them. The dogs were baying now, baying for the blood they could finally see.

"Up the stairs!" said Finn. "Don't look, just follow your feet. Quickly. Groblek is going to be tetchy enough without the dogs."

Finn seemed happy enough climbing the illusionary steps. So Meb followed him, holding onto the edge of his cloak. She'd swear she was not even on the mountainside. And the dogs were . . . below her. She nearly fell off the stairway. They were above the dogs. Walking on stairs she could only glimpse as she turned her head. They were tangible underfoot though. And, illusion or not, she was scared of those big lean dogs. She was just so tired. It was easier not to think. Just step up. Up and up into the cloud, to the door of the beehive-castle. It must be on a high ridge or something. It looked as if it was perched on the cloud, in the moonlight.

The door Finn knocked at was a huge, heavy one, made of roughly rived oak. It didn't look as smart as the planed and polished doors of the rich merchant's houses of Tarport, let alone the palace at Albar. Meb began to feel slightly more hopeful. Perhaps this was the servants' entrance. But why was it so big?

The reason became painfully obvious as soon as the door swung open. If Finn had not grabbed her shoulder she would have run back to the dogs. The person inside needed all the height that the door afforded him. Finn was tall, the door-opener was at least twice his height, and maybe three times the width. The broad face was rimmed with a thick fringe of wild hair, and a beard that curled down to meet another layer of curly fur that spilled out of the top of a rough leather jerkin. He did not look pleased to see them. His mouth was set in a hard line. There was no warmth in the deep-set brown eyes that stared out at them from under his heavy brow. He did not move or say anything. Only his wide nostrils twitched.

Finn bowed extravagantly. "Ah, Groblek. So glad to find you at home. May we come in?"

The hairy giant did not move. He merely raised an eyebrow. "I didn't think you'd have the gall to come back here." His voice was so deep that Meb expected it to shake the stones of the archway loose.

Finn smiled, his sharp face wicked in the moonlight. "Now, Groblek, you know me. I have an infinite amount of gall. And I could hardly be passing your charming abode without stopping in to see how you're doing."

The corner of Groblek's mouth twitched upward. "Whoever is chasing you must be very close," he said with grim pleasure.

Finn shrugged. "A large number of very angry alvar and their dogs do appear to be chasing us. There was somewhat of a misunderstanding, it seems."

Groblek raised both of his eyebrows. "You'd think that they would know better than to bring their dogs up here," he growled. He turned sideways so that he no longer blocked the entire doorway. "You'd better come in. I'll go out and have a word with them."

He ushered them in and stumped out. Meb noticed that he had—for his vast bulk—small feet. Hairy feet, rather like every other uncovered bit of him that she could see besides his face.

The door swung shut ponderously. It was not latched, but the sheer size and weight would have made it a challenge for her to budge, let alone open.

Now that they were out of the wind, and had stopped running, Meb simply wanted to collapse, possibly into sleep before she actually hit the ground. However, something about Finn's posture said that they were not out of danger yet. He'd seen her through all sorts of problems, so far beyond her small fishing village background that the best that she had been able to do was to follow blindly. But the difficult part of Meb, the part that had always come up with the daydreams and the practical solutions, had been telling her for some time now that it really didn't like being a leaf in this whirlwind. It felt that she must stand on her own feet fairly soon. It also wanted to know just who the traveling gleeman really was? What was he actually doing? And why had he decided to take her along with him? Meb told the inner voice to shut up. She was barely coping with what was happening, let alone wondering about why. The voice niggled that it might just make coping easier. Meb wasn't too sure about that. What she was sure about was that she could smell food. Her stomach informed her that it had been a long time since she had last eaten.

She looked around, taking stock of their surroundings. The place was lit by a branch of candles each as thick as her thigh. The walls were constructed of huge slabs of roughly shaped stone, chinked with moss. It was obviously little more than an antechamber to this Groblek's strange castle, or, more accurately for his size, house. She tugged at Finn's cloak, which she realized she was still holding on to. "Who is he?" she asked.

"Ah. The hard questions first," said Finn smiling. "It all depends on who you ask. I think he may be different things to different people. To some of them he is a giant."

He was gigantic, she had to admit. Yet . . . not as big as she had somehow thought giants would be.

"To others he's the Migoi, the Kang Admi, the Ts'emekwes. In yet another place they think that he is a mountain, or possibly a mountain-troll. Or Bergtana, the disappearer, who captures innocents who wander out on to his mountains."

"So . . . what is he?"

"Probably all of those. And a few other things in places beyond our ken. He's not helpful. But he does have a sense of humor. Make him laugh. . . ."

There was a huge, thunderous, rolling roar outside.

Finn grinned. "I imagine that's several dogs and huntsmen who won't come up here again. Not unless a dragon's hot on their heels and then I am less than sure that they wouldn't be better off with the dragon."

"Will he kill us?" asked the merrow.

Finn thought about it. "Probably not. But the question you should ask is will he let us go?"

"Well? Will he?" asked the merrow.

The door swung open. Groblek appeared, blocking out the moonlight, rubbing his enormous hands together. "Cold out," he rumbled. "Come through. It's not often I get guests at the front door. I normally have to find them out on the mountainside. Except him, of course," he gestured with a big thumb at Finn. "What persaudes a human, and stranger still, a merrow, to associate with him? He's a liar, and a rogue, and thief," he said in an amiable rumble, as they followed him through another door, into a large room, where a fire burned, and the smell of baking was still stronger.

"I am seldom a liar," said Finn. "And in my case, theft is more a question of perspective. I'll admit to the rogue."

"Very generous of you," said Groblek. "But I was talking to them. So you shut up. You're entirely too glib with that tongue of yours."

Meb realized that she'd been relying on Finn to talk them out of this difficulty too. And now he wasn't going to be able to. Well, Groblek hadn't been pleased by the dogs or alvar. "We were

running away from the alvar and their dogs. Finn said we could
find shelter up here," she said in a small voice.

"He did, did he?" said Groblek, thoughtfully. "And so, what
did he tell you about me, little human? Don't lie. I have no liking for liars."

Meb knew she was a very poor liar, and anyway she had no
idea what to lie about. "He said you were a giant. Or a mountain
or a troll. And some other things I didn't understand. He said
to make you laugh."

Groblek's lip twitched. "He knows a great deal. Too much for
it to be honestly acquired knowledge. So: make me laugh. I'm
waiting."

"Um. Can I juggle?"

"I don't know. Can you?"

She nodded. "Yes. Finn taught me. I . . . I want to be his
apprentice."

Groblek smiled, showing enormous square teeth. "Very good.
You almost made me laugh then. Well, show me. And then your
merrow friend can see if he can do as well. Or is he not a juggler?"

"Er. I don't know. I . . . don't think so," admitted Meb, wishing
that she was less tired, fumbling in her sling-bag for balls . . . and
only finding rubies. They were a little small for her purposes.

"Well, merrow? Do you? Or what other way can you come up
with to amuse me?"

"I don't juggle, Lord of the Mountains," answered the merrow.

The mobile eyebrows twitched. Meb decided they might have a
life of their own. "I haven't been called that for a while," Groblek
said, mildly. "So what do you do, besides swim and chase fish?
Merrows are not something that I see here too often."

"I play the pibgyrn," said the merrow, looking distinctly uncomfortable. "But it's not a thing I do in public."

"Too bad. I don't have any supper for those who fail to enter-
tain."

"And there isn't any other food in the place, or a way out of
here without him," said Finn.

Groblek fixed him with a chilly stare. "I thought I told you
not to talk?"

"Consider it unsaid."

The gigantic Groblek shook a finger at him. "And that trick won't work to get you out of here this time."

Meb realized, looking around, that she couldn't see the door they'd come in through. The place was shadowy. When she turned her head there were things she almost seemed to see, just out of the corner of her eye. There were vast, shadowy vistas there. She screwed up her eyes and blinked. The room was bigger than it could possibly be. She'd seen it from the outside.

Groblek noticed her staring. "It is much more complicated than it looks," he said smiling a little. "Mountains are. There are distances folded into them."

Meb's inner person had one of those moments of epiphany—this place was what mountains *were*. Not what they looked like. This was the spirit of the mountains. And Groblek was somehow part of it as well as living in it. He looked big and solid and quite . . . ordinary, in a giantish way. But she suspected that he wasn't, any more than steps into the air, or this room that had subtly changed and hidden the door was. A part of Meb was very afraid, at dealing with things so far beyond her little village. And another part of her was fiercely delighted to find that her dreams were true. That the world was really infinitely bigger than that narrow window onto it that she'd had. That part of her took control, took a deep breath and said: "I need something to juggle with. And this is a very wonderful place."

Groblek nodded. "Yes. Not many realize that straight off. I normally juggle boulders myself, but they might be a little large for you. Hmm." He scratched his head. "Ah." He reached out. His hand went . . . somewhere else. Meb could see his arm, shimmering and at a strange angle, fading away. He drew it back and brought out a handful of snow. Then he squeezed it down to a round hard ball just bigger than her fist. "How many do you want?"

"Um. Six?" she said. That was the best she'd ever done, really. But she had a feeling this needed her very best.

"You have done this for many years?" he asked, reaching into the strangeness, bringing back more snow, and shaping it.

"Uh, n . . . no." admitted Meb. "I started a few weeks ago."

The mobile eyebrows showed his surprise, but he said nothing. Meb was very doubtful about the snowballs . . . it had rarely snowed at sea level and her memory of the soft flakes had been that they melted quite quickly and were, well, relatively soft.

These snowballs weren't. They were surprisingly heavy and hard. She gave them a few experimental tosses to get the feel and weight . . . and realized that they were all slightly different. Terrible to juggle with. But she wanted to succeed. She'd do Finn proud. She began her throws, going for a simple sequence first, and then increasing the number of balls she had aerialised. And realizing to her horror that they were really cold. Finger-numbingly cold. There was nothing that she could do about it but to ignore the pain and toss them higher. To divorce herself from worrying about them slipping or her losing grip, and pretend that she was somehow outside herself watching the gleeman throwing his brightly colored balls in increasingly complex patterns . . . And suddenly she realized that the ball she'd just flung up in air was not snow. It was the brightly colored ball in her mind's eye. It was startling enough to make her totally lose concentration and for the balls to come thudding down around her as she gaped at it. Then she realized what was happening and tried to catch and toss the remaining balls, and slipped on one of the balls on the floor, nearly fell on her face . . . tossed the next ball up, slipped again and landed hard on the seat of her trousers. She sat there, and the rest of balls landed neatly in her hands amid the thunder.

It wasn't thunder. It was laughter. "Oh, very clever," said Groblek, "you misled me very well."

Blushing to the roots of her hair, Meb bowed her head. Finn helped her up.

"I think the pupil just outdid the master," he said. "And yes, Groblek. I had to say that."

"I'll let it pass. Although she may have caused snowstorms and avalanches across twenty worlds. You need to be careful with magics here, human-child." He seemed just at that moment vast and old, but the next he was just a giant in a leather jerkin with a great deal of wild hair again. "You've earned a bite or two of supper. I don't get to laugh often enough. Now, merrow, will you or won't you play for us?"

"I don't play in public," muttered the merrow.

"Ah, but this is hardly public," said Finn.

"That is the final word from you," said Groblek to Finn, in such a way that she knew this time he really meant it. "But it's true enough. Consider this the wide open spaces. An alpine meadow."

And briefly, it was. But the moon that shone down on them was bigger than any moon Meb had ever seen, and there was a second moon, low in the sky. The she-bear feasting on the berries there plainly saw them and took fright. She lumbered away into the darkness.

"It'll be tricks of shadow that you're playing on me," said the merrow. "But very well. On your own head be it then." He dug into his shoulder-pouch and produced an instrument—a chanter with a horn mouth-piece and on the other end a curved horn bell—cut so that the end formed a mouth of ferocious teeth. It was polished, carved and beautiful. The merrow blew a few notes, and then began to play. Meb found her feet tapping almost immediately. He was good, better than any musician she'd ever heard.

Actually, she soon realized, he was better than just very good. The sound, haunting and compelling, was moving her . . . physically. She was swaying in time to the music. Then, with those sharp merrow eyes shining wildly, he changed tune. Now, it was fast and staccato . . . Meb knew the tune. It was one that the sailors danced to. And now it was one that they all danced to, with varying levels of grace. The giant's dance made the floor shake and sounded like thunder, although there was a certain enormous delicacy and precision about the way he crashed his feet down. But it was a thunder far too close for comfort!

The merrow lowered his horn mouthpiece from his lips. "Have you had enough?" he asked, defiantly. "I can play all night if you be willing."

Groblek panted . . . and laughed. "I deserved that. And I enjoyed it too, little fish-man. You play well. But the mountains need a rest from the snow and the thunder you've caused between the two of you. Now, we will dine."

"And not on us, with luck," said Finn.

"I hardly ever eat guests who make me laugh," said Groblek.

Meb was not sure if he was joking or not.

Fionn had watched very carefully when Groblek had reached through the dimensions to give her snowballs. Looking at it again, he felt that he was just on the brink of understanding what Groblek was doing. Groblek was reaching outside of Tasmarin. In fact, Fionn was sure that he was reaching outside of the entire cycle of worlds that had been drawn from to make Tasmarin. Fionn had known the others existed, but it was just this ring that he was responsible for. Tasmarin still needed to be destroyed because it was damaging the rest, upsetting their polarities. It was also a trap which prevented him from seeing to his work in the wider cycle. He was stuck here and that would spell disaster for them all. Besides that, he found it intensely frustrating to be trapped here, knowing work needed doing badly out there. It ran counter to his purpose not to do it.

He had tried to get Groblek to explain it to him last time. But the giant was not someone you could force to do anything he did not want to do. In times before Tasmarin's building, back when Fionn had still roamed the fractal planes of existence, fixing imbalances across the ring which had been his responsibility, he had seen traces of the giant, from time to time. Huge bare footprints in deep snow. Footprints that came from nowhere and led to nowhere. Then, when he'd been trapped here the first time, he'd been foolish enough to contest Groblek physically. Fionn had learned: you cannot fight a mountain. You can only work with its natural bent, and try to out-think it.

=== Chapter 27 ===

AS FORTUNE WOULD HAVE IT, HABORYM WAS AS CLOSE TO YENFAR as he dared to go, without the slow leeching of his life-energies affecting him enough to kill. The rocky caves of the little islet a few miles off the coast were much used by smugglers, and Haborym did a great deal of business with them. Even here, he could feel the effect of the magical wards . . . and then, abruptly he could not.

"I need your ship," he said to the smuggler-captain he'd been discussing the price of a shipment of untaxed tar with, moments before. "Now. I must go to Yenfar."

The captain looked at him in puzzlement, possibly because he'd dealt with Haborym for some years, and this was the closest his business associate had ever come to the island. "But the cargo is still on board. It'll take us a couple of hours to shift it, Beng."

"Beng" was the name Haborym used when he assumed the illusory image of a human. It pleased him. He considered briefly. He could cross the ocean on his own. Not being a thing of mere flesh, he could drift above it, but his kind had an uneasy relationship with water. Instead he concentrated his will on the hapless captain. He did not care if the stinking tar-barrels were on board. He quite enjoyed the smell. A few minutes later the smuggling galley was nosing out to sea, heading for the coast of the larger landmass, her frightened crew pulling hard, driven by their still more frightened captain.

It was near moon-set when Haborym left them at a small beach

hemmed with cliff. He did not need to find his way through the
network of caves they used. He drifted up the steep rock walls
instead. So: here he was—at last able to hunt their prey here in
this, the one place on Tasmarin that had been denied to his kind.
It was sweet. But first he had work to do. Lesser species might
call it murder. But it was what augury required. Blood. Blood
of her kind. He drifted on, coming soon enough to the walls of
the town his smugglers hailed from. This was Yenfar: they were
unprotected against the smokeless flame.

It did not take him long to find what he was looking for. She
was getting old for the flesh-trade, which was probably why she
was still out at this time. He performed the rite with practiced
skill. It would fill the locals with horror. The results of the augury
filled him with horror, although the deed did not.

She wasn't on this island. And neither was the merrow treasure.

Haborym knew fear. He knew how the strict hierarchy of his
kind apportioned blame. He looked at the blood and filth and
the patterns of invoked power, and knew his own end would be
worse, if the human mage was dead. He hissed with rage and
fear. Couldn't the sprites do anything right?

After a brief reconsideration of the augury he headed away,
towards the mountains. He could, hopefully, at least work out
if she had escaped the island—a faint hope—or if she was dead.
Destroying the merrows' treasure was a small task compared with
the need to take her, alive. The hierarchy of flames had plans.
Those involved the attempt to recreate this folly of a plane of
dragons—with all the attendant effects that it would have on the
rest of this interconnected ring of planes.

There were fewer limits on Haborym than on creatures of
flesh. Walls were no impediment—at least walls without protections against the nonmaterial. Roads too were more directional
indicators than surfaces upon which to walk. And he could move
as fast as a running man, without tiring the way a man would.
Of course moving used up energy, but not in the same way that
using a cloak of illusion did, or did other magical exercises. But
the darkness was an adequate shield, for now. By dawn he had
traveled many leagues. He did not like daylight, but the fear
drove him on . . . until he came to a landslip that had completely
blocked the road, and indeed, the river. It would have stopped

most men, and possibly anything except a dragon. But Haborym crossed the shifting, precarious loose rock and headed past the temporary dam it had created. There was a solitary sentry there. In the normal course of things there should have been a fair chance that he would have been aware of the fire-being and able to defend himself. But the Loftalfar blood ran thin in this one, and he did not expect Haborym, who overpowered him and put him to the question. Haborym knew that he would have to kill him afterwards and dispose of the body carefully. The alv knew it too, and resisted as best he could. It was a contest of will and of pain.

Finally the alv told him what he needed to know. "The last of the human thieves were driven into the high places. But the hunt was put to flight by the giant."

It was enough to startle Haborym into a moment's inattention. The little Huldralfar squirmed and broke free, and ran as only one of the alfar could, and donned a glamour among the wet trees.

Haborym did not try to catch him. He might have succeeded, and that would have been desirable, but he would probably fail. A sprite would have had the alv out of there in no time, but the dripping woods were no place for fire-beings. Not even to conflict with a badly injured alv. Instead he moved on with as much haste as he could muster, heading for the high peaks beyond their white city.

It was not somewhere you could follow a road to anymore. And soon, as he gained altitude, there was worse than the wetness. There was snow. Haborym kept going, although it took a great deal more energy than he liked.

If the alvar warrior lived, they'd be hunting his kind and barring them from entry into various places. He doubted that the alvar still had the strength or the allies to set a spell that would bar his kind from the whole island again. In the meanwhile . . . it was possible that the accursed little human quarry had fled from this plane entirely. His only satisfaction to that was that it would appear that somehow, the human magic worker had fallen in with his thieves, and they'd taken the merrows' treasure with them. The merrows' oceans would die without it. And with that would go this frozen wet stuff. The place would warm to a habitat suited to his kind.

— Chapter 28 —

MEB REMEMBERED THE FOOD WELL ENOUGH, EVEN IF THE REST WAS a little vague. A huge hot crusty loaf, big enough for fifty . . . or Groblek and them. Thin slivers of a salted meat. Some fresh curd cheese. Bilberry preserve. She'd loved that.

"It's good, eh?" said their host, when she asked.

"It is just the best thing I have ever eaten," said Meb.

Groblek beamed. "Little berries. About the size of your little finger's first joint, where I gather them. And they don't grow in bunches, but in ones and twos on a stalk. A lot of work, but they go well with the cheese."

Meb had to wonder how his great big fingers could ever handle such tiny berries.

And of course, there was beer. Meb drank cautiously. Nearly as cautiously as the merrow ate.

"Don't you like my food, little fish-man?" asked Groblek.

"It's of the unfamiliar kind," said the merrow. "I'm more used to fish, if you take my meaning. So far I'm liking it, especially the red salty stuff, but I've a feeling that I would prefer not to know what it was. It's a little like marlin, a little like mako, except that something's lacking and different."

"It doesn't taste of fish," said Meb, nodding.

"That's a bit unnatural, to my way of thinking," said the merrow, seriously. "But understandable up here."

That amused Groblek, rather than offended him. "I get salmon and trout and some eels. But I am more familiar with the harvest of the high places than the sea. But if you have had enough I'd not say no to some more music. Without quite so much dance to it."

The merrow scowled. "I can't but play the dance with the music. I've tried, to be sure. But it is as much part of me as the playing is."

"Magic, strong magic, but intrinsic and uncontrolled," said Finn.

"That's the way of it with us," said the merrow. "Mostly anyway. Wild magic."

"Well, you could play us something quiet then," said Groblek. "And get the dvergar to teach you. They're of the opposite ilk. Form and discipline make their magics."

"Part of the balance of all things," said Finn, lazily, lifting his leather tankard. He was enjoying the food and the beer, without any appearance of caution to the consumption of either.

Groblek nodded. "Play, fish-man. I enjoyed the earlier tune."

So he did.

Later Meb juggled some more—and Finn talked to the giant. It was a very odd conversation that she quietly listened in on. Almost as if everything they said had more than one meaning, and the second meaning was just beyond her. It was like hearing Wulfstan and Hrolf discuss whether they'd get sprats or mackerel today without knowing that the mackerel chased the sprats inshore, and that they were very seasonal. "There are cracks in the mountains, Groblek."

"There have always been cracks in the mountains, Fionn."

"Well, there are cracks in the sea."

"I'll have nothing to do with the sea. Unfathomable stuff. And powerfully wet too," said Groblek.

"Full of salt, too."

"Salt as tears. I'll have no more of it."

"Without it there would be no rain and no snow for the mountains."

"You make a good case, Fionn," said Groblek heavily. "But no."

"Do you know what they're talking about?" whispered Meb to the merrow.

The merrow nodded. "I grasp some of it anyway. The Lord of the Mountains is in love with the Sea. But she cannot not live in the mountains and he cannot live by the sea. It's an old, old story. I'd thought it just a story."

'Brys cleared his throat. "I'd be owing you an apology, human."

"It's all right," she said awkwardly. "It all worked out. I mean if you hadn't cut my hair and taken my clothes, I would, um, probably have been just in time to get killed. And Finn wouldn't have taken me on as his apprentice if he'd known I was a woman. You're not going to tell him, are you?"

"Ach, you must be the worst bargainer in the world," said the merrow with a fine imitation of disgust. "I'll not do so, but it was ever so reluctantly I was going to let you persuade me, in payment for throwing a soul-net of your hair at you. You take all the fun out of it."

Meb shook her head at him. "You're impossible."

"Never. It's just improbable that I am. But the truth be told you are still wearing the Angmarad, and you have my cloak of red sealskin. I can't return to my kind without it, or leave the diadem of the sea."

She touched the piece of twisted bladderwrack. "Finn said I must keep it on my head."

The merrow smiled wryly. "And I wouldn't be quick to disagree with him. He's a power, that one. I was just a bit slow in recognizing it. It's something I'd not have Margetha told, if you've a wish to have the balance of the bargain with me."

She understood that this too was a gesture of good faith. She nodded. "Fair enough."

"Well," said Groblek. "I've tasks for the morning. Play us a last tune, merrow. Something soft and restful."

What he did play was sad enough to make Meb weep. At the end of it Groblek got up and walked away into the shadows without saying a word.

"You took a chance," said Finn.

"'Tis my nature to do so," said the merrow, shrugging.

Meb realized she was missing something. "What was that? It was so sad."

"It's a lament. The lady of the water longing for the tumult of the waves and the sound of the gulls and the Lord of Mountains wanting his majestic silences, and the distant spiral of eagles," explained Finn.

Taking on board what the merrow had said earlier, it made a kind of sense. A love that was doomed . . . The practical voice in Meb's head said *Huh. They're both too used to having things their own way.* But the song was so full of the tragic longing that Meb studiously ignored the practical part of her mind.

Finn stood up and stretched his long limbs. "You two stay here at the fire while I go and look around. It's possible that the music has distracted our host from closing all his doors and windows. And who knows what else I might find. I'll be back."

He was, eventually. Meb was desperately fighting sleep, and the merrow had long since lost the struggle.

"It hasn't got any smaller and less complicated since last time I was here," said Finn suddenly from behind her. He really could move as silently as a cat.

The fright did much to dispel the cobwebs of sleep, but in her tiredness, it did nothing to reset the bounds she normally restrained her questions to. This one had bothered for some time. "Master, why does he call you 'Fionn'? The dvergar did too."

He shrugged. "It's an old name. Something of a joke which has lost its meaning these days. You know how very short men are sometimes called 'Lofty.' In the old tongue it means 'fair,' which I'm not. Over time it's become Finn among humans. The dvergar have long memories."

Various things began to fit together in Meb's head. "How old are you, master?"

"As old as my eyes and slightly older than my teeth," he said with an easy grin, showing those same teeth. "And it is about time you stopped calling me 'master.' It might go to my head if I believed it."

Meb shook her head. Her throat was tight. "No. You are my master. I would have died if you had not rescued me."

He snorted. "I knocked you into the water in the first place."

"That is not what I meant, master. I was a g—boy alone and I would not have lived to winter if I had not found a master. I am yours to command, master."

"Then I command you to stop calling me 'master.' I'm a poor hand at it, as I must have nearly got you killed you a good half a dozen times since then, and I'm not done yet. So stop calling me 'master.' Finn will do. And while you are at it, think of a way to get out of here. Time is passing."

Meb didn't like it. But it was an order. She considered the other order. "But it's only been a few hours, m . . . Finn."

"It's been about two days back on Yenfar," said Finn. "Time

does not run here as it does elsewhere. The last time I was here for a month or so, but missing in Tasmarin for twenty years. It's one of the things I'd love to understand. All he will say is that space and time are somewhat rotated."

"I've felt a bit turned around ever since I got here," said Meb, nodding. "Nothing is quite what it seems to be here, is it, m . . . Finn?"

"Hmm. You are right. But just what do you mean by it?"

Meb thought. "Uh, well nothing is the right size. And things are bigger . . . and sometimes smaller. They change."

"I do believe," said Finn, thoughtfully, "that size may offer us a way out. It's that or stay here forever."

On that disquieting note he lay down and seemed to drop off to sleep instantly, having thoroughly woken her up.

In fact she was not the only one not asleep, as she established when she got up a little later. Groblek was watching from the shadows, a thoughtful expression on his face.

"What do you want?" she asked nervous at suddenly seeing him.

"Many things. But what I can have, and what I am going to get are another matter," said Groblek. "I noticed the crown, little human. Will you take the Lady Skay a message from me?"

"Um. If I can." Meb did not pretend that she didn't understand. Although she was not at all sure how you talked to the sea. She could ask the merrow.

"Tell her I miss her. That's all. I actually let you in because I recognized her symbol. It's a bit dried up, mind you. I try to avoid thinking about her, but that symbol, Fionn, and the merrow's song . . ."

"Will you let us out?" asked Meb, taking her courage in both hands.

His eyes twinkled. "Of course. But you'll have to think of how. And of course when and where are also different matters."

And with that Meb had to be content because he faded away like shadows when a cloud hides the sun.

"You're a different size this morning, Groblek," said Finn.

"I change. Most things do."

"Even rocks or mountains?" said Finn, dryly.

"Even rocks and mountains," said Groblek. "A rock is a little larger when the sun bakes it. A mountain can wash away to the sea or grow with fires of the earth in it."

"Well, I've seen you small, and reaching to places far beyond. But some places are proof against you."

"Not really. I don't like the heat in the lowlands."

"In Yenfar the alvar plan to stop you. They've no liking for the way you let us get away from them. They've worked magic against things of great size. They'll block you."

"First they would have to understand me," said Groblek. "I am merely big footprints in the snow and lost travelers and occasional strange tales to them."

"You don't understand alvar magic," said Finn dismissively. "Anyway, what about some breakfast, good host?"

"You do understand alvar magics?" said Groblek, his eyes lazily half-lidded. It didn't fool Meb.

"Yes, to some extent. Better than I understand you, to be honest," said Finn. "Now about breakfast . . ."

"It is often the very simple concept that's hardest to understand. They cannot stop me. Neither can anything else. The harder they try the easier it is."

"Ha," said the merrow. "Show us then. I'd be wagering they'd stop you."

"Ach. He can change sizes. He'll just go as a small thing," said Finn, shrugging. "We were talking about food."

"Only you were," said Groblek. "How much do you want to wager, little fish-man? Or man-fish."

The merrow dug in his pouch. Pulled out a coin. Looked at it. Put it down. "Old silver."

"Not of much worth to me. I've plenty of that in the bones of the mountains."

"And gold?" asked Finn, eyes sharp.

"Ah," said Groblek, grinning. "You'd like to know that, wouldn't you? There are spider-web veins of it still underground. That which hasn't found its way into the hoards of dragons or to the sea. Most of it gathers there eventually, before it'll come back to me. So what do you have to wager, musician?"

"What a musician always has, that others want, I suppose. Music. Your choice of piece."

"Now that is not without value," conceded Groblek.

"Against that you could not do it without being made to let us go."

"I am not usually made to do anything."

"Then it is no risk, is it? So show us then. A mountain from here to Yenfar."

Groblek grew and changed as they watched. And Meb felt Finn take a firm hold of her arm. He gripped the merrow with his other hand. "When I say so, jump with me," he said in an undervoice. "And grab hold of any part of him."

Groblek was no longer a giant. Where he had been was the foot of something so vast Meb could not see the top of it. A thing of stone and ice.

Finn's grip tightened. "NOW!" He yelled and jumped—onto Groblek.

They were actually on the mountain, grabbing rock . . . and the snow began to fall on them.

Finn hauled them again, sending them falling, rolling down the slope.

Then he stood up. Dusted the snow off himself. "It would appear I understand your nature better than I thought, Groblek," he said with a bow toward the mountain, shrouded in the storm. "I win my wager, and the merrow owes you a song, sometime."

"In a manner of speaking," said the huge voice of Groblek, "he wins too. I am here. I cannot be kept away from somewhere I already am. But it was a good wager. Neatly done, Fionn. Look after the little ones."

"He liked you two," said Finn. "There is no accounting for tastes. Come on, let's get moving. There'll be less snow, lower down the mountain."

Meb realized that when they'd fled up the strange stair to Groblek's castle, there had merely been patches of snow next to rocks and in the gullies. Now it lay thick over everything. It was a few finger widths short of the tops of her boots—and it was still drifting down. The sky was heavy with clouds, and it was hard to tell if it was morning or afternoon.

"The good part is it'll be hard for Zuamar to fly, let alone see us in this," said Finn, leading off, downslope. "The bad part is that anything that's not white and still does stand out. And from experience, walking under the trees will get abrupt loads of this stuff to fall down the back of my neck. I see that our friend has left us a trail to follow." He pointed to the big footprints. "He liked the Scrap, so let's hope he is being nice to us."

The footprints led down and then over a ridge—and it was immediately apparent that this was a good place to head for, as it was a bit of a snow-shadow. Walking was easier, and they were soon able to find a trail of sorts. There was no sign of it having been used since the latest snow started. Finn was wary about it, but it was a great help. Meb found it less exhausting as she didn't have to lift her feet so high to follow Finn. At last, she had enough breath to ask questions. Meb thought it was about time she understood a little more of what she was dealing with, especially as the merrow, Groblek and the dvergar had all given her clues that Finn was no ordinary human. Meb had decided that he must be some kind of magician. That was very rare among humans. She—and every other human being on the whole of Tasmarin—knew dragons didn't approve of magic-working humans. Of course, she was now intensely curious about what he was actually up to. But if she had to be honest with herself, she'd spent most of her life being intensely curious about far too many things. Hallgerd had always said that it was a fault in a young woman. "Ma . . . Finn, what exactly is Groblek?"

"I thought I told you as much as I knew," he said with a disarming grin. "He is a mountain here, among other things. Humans are seldom just one thing, so why should mountains be?"

"I'd be thinking it'd be less confusing if they were," grumbled the merrow. "It's far too complicated out here, away from the sea."

Finn laughed. "There is more to the universe than most people guess. Or maybe it is caused by most people guessing. And we'd better get a move on before we freeze."

═ Chapter 29 ═

"YOU TOLD ME THAT YOUR KIND COULD NOT ENTER YENFAR," said the Lyr.

For a brief moment Haborym considered using his energies to turn the tree-woman into a blazing, bubbling torch, turning the very sap in her to boiling steam. But, satisfying though it might be, he'd have to get what information she had out of her first. "We were prevented from doing so by the spells woven into the protection of the Angmarad. The treasure of the merrows."

"Ah. Your thieves have stolen that," said the Lyr.

"And the thieves have been followed into the high mountains where the pursuit was put to flight by a giant."

"You are incorrect. Not a giant. A dragon. He has been setting the forest alight. There will be a reckoning," said the sprite with the implacable grimness of her kind. "They will have to be eliminated, along with the rest of the animal things."

The sprites held the belief that as they and the fire-beings were the only non-animal intelligences, they had a bond. The creatures of smokeless flame were happy to allow them their delusions. Haborym was less than sure that the alvar would not know the difference between a dragon and a giant. He had no doubt there had been a dragon, and burning woods, but whether that had anything to do with it was another matter. "My techniques tell me that the treasure of the merrows is no longer on this island. I am having similar problems locating the human mage. What news do you have for me there? You've had your acolytes out searching for her."

"We've come close," said the sprite. "But it would seem that she's an adept. She vanished thrice, when we were on her heels."

Haborym tried to contain his irritation. "Impossible. There is no one to teach her. Raw talent she may have, but nothing more than that. Where was this?"

"In Tarport. I have many followers there. And then in the country near Twowaters, and later in the Albar-slum. Some four days ago."

A horrible conurbation of events began to reveal itself to Haborym.

She'd disappeared. So had the Angmarad.

And a dragon had been setting fire to the woods.

"Take me to the place where these fires occurred." Within him he was aware that his own flames burned cold. There might be another human mage one day. But they'd waited long enough for this one.

She looked at him coolly. The sprites did not like anything that might just possibly be an order. "We will get one of the acolytes to lead you up there."

"That would be appreciated. However, you had better come with me. Our magical skills are complimentary." He might as well flatter her. They'd still need the sprites for some time to come.

She stared at him for some time in the unblinking way of her kind. Fire can burn steadily too, so he stared back. Eventually she nodded. Nonetheless she got one of her pet humans to lead them.

He took them to an area of charred stumps and scattered patches of snow on the mountainside. It was plain that the damage caused her some distress. There was still some warmth from the fire in places. Haborym liked the ash and heat more than the snowy wet forest.

Fire-creatures were, naturally, good at identifying sources of energy. Dragonfire left clear traces. The sprite was quite right about the source of the fire. And yet . . . had the Angmarad been destroyed, that too would have left a sign. It was perfectly possible to destroy it, but it would have a marked effect on water. It might . . . well, cause snowstorms.

So might winter.

Waterspouts or a rain of fish would be more indicative. Haborym looked at the sprite's faithful human. He still wore the finder charm

Haborym had made. Well, human blood made a good magical indicator. It was the iron. "I need a sacrifice . . . ."

As he said that Haborym was instantly aware of the return of the Angmarad to Yenfar.

From this close it was like being stabbed in the gut might be, to the sort of lifeform that had a gut. All Haborym wanted to do was to flee. But he was dimly aware, through his pain, that the human was pointing excitedly at the finder-charm.

The mage must have the accursed thing. And they were close. How long could he endure this for?

And then abruptly, the pain lessened. He could still feel energy draining away from him, but at least it didn't hurt. "We have bespelled you," said the sprite. "Now let us see if we can capture her."

"Quickly, though," agreed Haborym. He had not realized that sprite magics could affect his kind. He wasn't sure he liked that fact. It was the strangest feeling—this must be how other species felt when they were drugged by a powerful opiate. The sprites were able to do that, he recalled in this strange wooly-headed region of clouded thought he now occupied. They could even—with the help of another species, affect dragonkind. Knock them out. Haborym was faintly aware of the danger of this strange state of mind he was in. He did like the surcease of pain . . . and if they could capture the human mage and get her away from here, his work would be nearly all done. Victory would be in his grasp.

They followed the human acolyte up the slope and across a ridge. There they cut a trail. One that had been trodden, recently. A little further on Haborym, looking down, could see that the trail switch-backed and there, some distance below, he could see three figures. To Haborym their different body-heats made it very obvious they were three different species. He could see his target now and set a compulsion on her. She would turn and come up to him. Now!

Meb was beginning to tire, and, even walking hard and wrapped in her cloak, the cold wind was biting at her. She wanted, firstly, to rest somewhere out of the wind, and to eat. And then, suddenly, she wanted to go back up the trail. NOW. She turned and pushed past the startled merrow and was running up the snowy slope—never mind the trail or the snow that was over the tops of her boots.

It was that snow and an unseen gully, just short of her goal, that betrayed her. She stepped forward . . . and just kept going straight down and then sprawled on her face into the snow—vaguely hearing Finn's shout. Looking up she saw that her goal was coming down the slope with his companions. He was tall and wrapped in a long black cloak. His face was inhumanly handsome, and he seemed to glide across the snow. The tall, slim woman with the greenish-white skin next to him struggled through the snow. The third man was floundering through it. But not the wondrous, handsome desirable man. He floated above it. She wanted to reach him desperately.

The first Fionn knew of it was when he heard the merrow's surprised yell. Scrap was running up the slope as if the fire-beings were on her heels. And then he realized, looking up, that she was running straight to the creature of smokeless flame. His first instinct was to run straight after her. The merrow was already doing that. Only it must be a truly powerful fire-being and a powerful calling spell. Because the Scrap was going to beat him to it. That was impossible. He could outrun any human—and then he realized what was happening. The sprite that was with the fire-being was bespelling the bracken under the snow. It was twining frantically around their legs.

The merrow too had fallen and the fire-being had almost reached the Scrap. But the shape it had assumed wavered and for a brief instant revealed the flame-being there.

Fionn had seen fire-beings before. Only . . . this one was not well. There was no searing heart of dancing white heat surrounded by reds and oranges. It was only a pallid yellow flame, which faded to a green and then violet . . . and then black. It crumpled, the black hooded cloak falling to the snow, empty.

The Angmarad! She was still wearing the diadem of the sea under the hood of her cloak. It had been wrapped in protections against his kind, Fionn knew. And besides—when the flame met the sea, the sea always won. But there was still the sprite—she had stopped in horror, but now she was coming forward. Fionn began to change. Tree-people were no match for a dragon. The merrow meanwhile had flung that trident of his. He pronged her neatly. It would not stop the tree-woman but it did have an unexpected effect. The human with her gave a distraught cry and tried to wrench it out. He pulled her off her feet, and the Scrap hauled herself out of the gully and half-rolled, half-fell back down the slope toward Finn. The sprite tossed her loyalist into a snowdrift—with a casual inhuman strength—and ran after the Scrap.

Changing took time and Fionn realized that he didn't have enough. On the other hand the tree-woman, once he was close enough, he could deal with in any form. He surged back up tearing bracken out by the roots. He grabbed the sprite just as she reached for Scrap. The trident made a good lever, and he rolled her into the snow. What he was unprepared for was Scrap—instead of sensibly running off—attacking the tree-woman like a wildcat herself.

And she fought like a wildcat who was determined to disembowel her attacker. Sprites were creatures of strong magics, but that magic is almost totally ineffectual against humans or dvergar. Humans can, on the other hand, inflict magical damage on the tree people, nearly as effectively as the dvergar can. And the Scrap was putting out raw furious magics, amplified through a dvergar magical artifact. The tree-woman went from a determined attack, to trying to get away in a few heartbeats. Fionn realized why, as he pulled himself free from a stony arm. The sprite was petrifying wherever the Scrap had struck—and the stone was spreading.

In the meanwhile, the merrow had broken free of the bracken and was fighting with the human follower. The merrow was larger and stronger, and a hunter too. But the scrawny human fought with hysterical strength. Fionn was obliged to haul him off the merrow and hold him up by the scruff of his neck, to kick and squirm in mid-air. His little human mage had realized that Fionn no longer needed rescuing and had backed off herself. But it was too late for the sprite. She'd managed to get to her feet, but did not get any further. The petrification continued to spread. Her face and arms were already stone and her human companion screamed in horror as she became a sprite statue.

Fionn tossed him face-first into the snow. "Cool off," he said sternly. "Are you all right, Scrap?"

She nodded, panting and wide-eyed. "Wha . . . what happened?"

"I'd guess you met your first creature of smokeless flame." The sprite's follower was kneeling in the snow, sobbing. Fionn watched him, carefully, as the merrow tried to pull his trident out of the stone sprite. "Now how am I supposed to be getting this thing back," he said grumpily. "You're expensive on tridents, Mage. You know that?"

The sprite's companion chose that moment to launch himself at the Scrap. Fionn had been expecting it, so he stuck a foot out and the man landed on his face in the snow. Fionn stepped over and put a foot on his back to keep him there. "Come and sit on this one and I'll take it out. Or at least have a try."

So the merrow did. He removed a knife from the man's belt too, as Finn tugged at the trident. "Here, Scrap. Come help pull." The little human did. "We want to give it back, to get it out," said Fionn. "Our merrow friend is probably lost without it."

It suddenly came loose and they both fell over in the snow—but they had the trident.

"What are we going to do with this?" asked the trident's owner, prodding the man he was sitting on.

"Hmm." Fionn pulled a glowing amulet from the fellow's wrist. He saw that the Scrap was starting to shake. Well, she'd be unused to fighting. He'd seen humans who had been as brave as young lions fall apart afterwards before. Best to try and make her laugh. "I suppose we could use him as a sled. Take turns sitting on him while the others pulled. Or we could let him go and deliver a message back to the sprites to leave us alone."

"I'm in favor of the sled idea," said the merrow.

"Yes, but I don't think he'd slide too well. He's not the right shape."

"We could take his clothes off and freeze him first. Into the right shape. What do you think, Scrap?"

The man moaned. "The Goddess of the forest's curses on you."

"Let him up," said the Scrap imperiously, still holding the trident. She poked him with it as he sat up. "You understand this," she said grimly. "You leave my master alone or I'll push this trident so far up your behind that it'll come out of your mouth."

"She is a goddess..."

"She's a statue," said Fionn. "Remember that too. Now get going. If we see you again, we'll come and turn the rest of the sprites into the same thing. Go."

And staggering to his feet, the man went.

"Come on," said Fionn. "Here. Take my arm, Scrap. Hrodenyn-brys, you take the other side. There's a shepherd's hut relatively close by. It's about time we took a rest, anyway." It had not been his plan, but the little scrap of humanity was ready to fall over on them. And she'd done well. He was still a little taken aback by her attack on the sprite. So plainly, was she. "I thought she was going to hurt you, master."

"I'm fairly tough, Scrap. I don't hurt easily. And now I need to find some way to proof you against the call of the creatures of the smokeless flame."

"I'm sorry, master."

Fionn decided to ignore the "master" this time.

The rough-stone hut was fortunately supplied with wood and was reasonably weather-tight. It was, of course, very cold, but Fionn had a fire going soon enough. It would be dark soon, and it was snowing again. They should be safe enough for now, no matter if the sprite's worshiper called out all his friends and all the alvar too.

Fionn was a little worried about the Scrap. She'd fallen asleep just as the fire was getting going. He knew that humans could burn themselves out with magic-use. Too stupid to know their own limits, he supposed. That was what he liked about them.

═ Chapter 30 ═

HRODENYNBRYS TENDED THE FIRE. THE HUMAN MAGE WAS FAST
asleep. Finn had gone back out into the snowy twilight. 'Brys
was sure, by now, he was not human. He wasn't too sure exactly
what he was, except dangerous to anger, and wily as a big old
sea-pike and just as fast. 'Brys had to admit that for chance-met
companions who constrained him to accompany them, he could
have done worse. He had always known his power with music set
him apart. All merrows had some magical skills, but they tended
to be fairly minor manifestations of it. It was . . . refreshing to be
in company of those similarly blessed, or cursed, depending on
how you looked at it.

Finn came back with a large, dead animal, already flensed. "I
bought it, believe it or not. The Scrap would be proud of me."

"What is it?" asked Hrodenynbrys.

"A sheep. I found the owner flensing those he'd had to kill or
that had died when Zuamar burned a piece of mountainside," said
Finn with a scowl. "He was a ruined shepherd. Now he's got some
silver and a fine ruby that'll buy him a bigger flock, if he has
the patience. Right, let's hack some bits off this carcass and cook
them. They'll be tough as old dragonhide, but it'll be food."

"Is dragonhide something you'd be making a habit of eating,
then?" 'Brys asked, taking out his knife.

Finn grinned wryly. "It's come my way before. Trust me, you
haven't missed anything. Too full of metals to be good for you
anyway. Slice some collops off that leg. There is a bit of fat there,

and in the cold humans need the energy from it. Our little mage needs feeding up."

"And you, lord?"

Finn rolled his eyes. "What with her 'master' and you calling me 'lord' it's a wonder I don't get too self-important for my own good. Call me Finn. I like a bit of mutton, but this weather is not really cold for my kind." He threaded lumps of meat onto a long stick he'd sharpened, and held them into the flames. They began to smoke and fizzle on the edges. "You hold this—I'll get out some salt."

'Brys did as he was bade, although the heat was fierce. "So . . . Finn. What kind are you that would not be feeling the cold? Or," he looked at the fire, "the heat."

Finn shrugged. "You're burning them. Turn them. Here, let me put some salt on first. I am what I am, for me to know and you to keep your mouth shut about if you do work it out." He jerked a thumb at the sleeping woman. "Scrap has delusions. I'd prefer for her to keep them for now."

"Consider me silent," said Hrodenynbrys. "Is this meat done? I have never cooked meat before."

"That's obvious," said Finn examining the sizzling meat with its one blackened side, critically. "Let me wake the Scrap and we can eat this lot before we try and do better with the next attempt. It's all supposed to be more-or-less this color,"—he prodded a part of the meat—"not alternating black and red."

— Chapter 31 —

MEB AWOKE TO FINN'S IDEA OF A GENTLE SHAKE—AND SAT UP before her head came off her shoulders. "We have some wonderfully burned mutton ready. Or as ready as it'll ever be."

Meb was far less of an experienced epicure than her master. All she knew was that her stomach was sure that her throat had been cut. She ate ravenously. So did the merrow. "It's not that bad," he said. "Indeed, the texture is rather like abalone. Gives one something to chew on."

"Fine exercise for the jaw," agreed Finn. "And the burned bits add something special to it."

"You can be cooking the next lot yourself," said the merrow. "I'm still not sure that it's natural to be eating something that has no fish in it."

"I will," said Finn. "You can cut me some more pieces and thread them."

Meb, warm, rested, with some good chewing on the food she'd been offered, finally had some time to think.

She'd seen death before, of course. A poor fishing village had more than its share. But it wasn't a violent place, any more than it was a place where literacy blossomed. But she'd seen two living things die today. Die strangely, full of passion and fear. She'd almost been willing to kill the second one herself when Finn had come to her rescue. Still, there was a difference between being willing and actually having it happen. The spell that Finn must have used frightened her. Magic was the stuff of fear to that increasingly distant person, Meb the fishing village girl. But even sensible Meb and the fanciful daydreamer Meb had trouble with a beautiful-but-terrible sprite turning into stone. That was powerful magic, moreover, typical earth magic, that for which human mages were once supposed to be famous. So: her master was a human mage. No wonder he had so little love for dragons.

"Master. Um. Finn. That handsome man . . . the one that shriveled and vanished away when he got close to me. What did you do to him?"

"Nothing, Scrap. He did it to himself trying to reach you while you were wearing the Angmarad. It was seeming he wore—trust me, he really was not a man at all. I've changed my mind about you again, Hrodenynbrys. I'd prefer to take the Angmarad to the cauldron of the waters myself, but if things fall apart, and there is water near, well, Scrap, give him that cloak of his. He can turn back to his water-form self and take the Angmarad. I'm beginning to think he'd honor a bargain."

Meb nodded earnestly. "He would. But he drives hard bargains. And you have to watch him." She suddenly realized that the merrow was listening too, and colored. "Not that I think you're dishonest . . ."

"Just a little sharp," said Hrodenynbrys, grinning. "I'll be glad to have my cloak of red sealskin back though."

"It matches your nose." said Finn. "Now let us cook up the rest of that sheep. We may as well eat as much as we can and take a few cooked joints with us, because I don't think we're going to go from hamlet to hamlet, village to village, entertaining on our way to the sea. And we must have a good ten leagues to travel."

"There's nothing good about a league if it is on the land," said the merrow, taking his cloak from Meb, bowing his head at her and smiling.

"And this is steep, folded country, to make it even sweeter for you," said Finn cheerfully. "Not to mention the snow as an extra reason for enjoying the countryside. I've no idea why people don't just leave it and move into the water like lemmings do."

"Ach. They do," said the merrow waving a hand majestically. "Everything comes to the sea in time."

"Even sheep droppings," said Finn. "Now, what do you think will be the best way to roast this without it turning out like your earlier cooking?"

✧ ✧ ✧

It was still dark when they got on the trail the next day. However, the snow had turned to rain, turning the snow to slush and mud. "At least it is wet," said the merrow.

"If it was any wetter, you'd sprout fins on us," said Finn. "Now there is, by my reckoning, a nasty deep gorge over there, with a bridge over it in that notch in the hill." He pointed.

"Why aren't we going that way then?" asked Meb, as he'd promptly turned from the muddy track onto a ghost of a trail overhung by wet, dripping bushes.

He shook his head sadly. "They always put up checkpoints at bridges, Scrap. You have so much to learn about the life of a rogue."

She had feeling she was being teased. "I think they should make rogue-masters tell those who want to be apprentices just how much time they will spend being cold and wet," she said.

"And the number of hours they may spend being hunted by those who want, at best, just to kill them," said Finn. "Most of the stream in the gorge's catchment is higher up, full of snow, not rain, so with luck it won't be in flood yet."

They made their way down steep snowy banks and eventually to the stream. It was knee-high, brown with earth and ribbed with drifting rafts of sticks and fallen leaves.

"Coming up fast," observed Finn with some satisfaction after they'd crossed. "Let's give it some help." He took out a handful of the rubies they'd taken from the alvar treasure-house and dropped them into the rushing, dirty water, one by one. "That should do nicely," he said, as Meb gaped.

They made their laborious, slippery, muddy way out of the gorge, keeping under the dripping trees. "It's a bad day for a dragon to be doing aerial reconnaissance, but there is no sense in tempting fate just to keep our necks dry, especially as they're already wet. Besides, it is cheering Hrodenynbrys up as much as it is making you miserable," said Finn, when she suggested they might walk in the mountain meadow up slope from them. So they soldiered on. And then Finn stopped. Sniffed.

Meb did too, trying to smell anything but wet woods. There might have been a hint of smoke on the air.

"Dragonfire," said Finn, grimly. "We need to go back and find another way."

They did. A little later they came to a stony knoll where the trees were a little more scattered. Off to the right, through the trees Meb could see a burning hamlet amid a patchwork of stone walls and winter fields.

"It was a good little spot, said Finn, crossly. "Well aligned."

Meb was not sure what aligned meant, but it scraped raw memories of her own village and the huts burning. "Can we do anything to help?"

"Right now, probably not," said Finn. "But we can go and see what we can do. Zuamar is not likely to come back. It's not in his mind set."

The practical part of Meb wondered how anyone knew what dragons thought. On the other hand he did seem to know nearly everything, especially about trouble and how to get out of it.

They walked to the handful of burning crofts. And Meb realized very soon that there was going to be no one to help. It had been a cold, wet, raw day with, by the looks of it, everyone indoors when the dragon had struck. And Zuamar had been brutally efficient about it. As they'd fled the burning houses—he'd burned or disemboweled the peasants. Even the babes in arms had been roasted, skin-split and dead. The little village turned into a horror of a reeking charnel house in which nothing lived. Even the milk cows had been killed in their stalls.

"Why?!" Meb, tears streaming down her face shook her fist in rage.

"He doesn't need a reason," said Finn, his tone carefully detached. "Power needs limits, and here he has none. He could also be looking for us. Let's go. The best we can do now is to frustrate that ambition of his. He'll be dealt with in time."

The merrow too was subdued by the slaughter. "I've seen fish go kill crazy. Orca too. But not like this. This is a kind of senseless brutality that took a great deal of intelligence. It's a dangerous thing."

"I think we should go," said Finn, firmly, turning Meb by the shoulder. They walked away, not looking back . . . and then something touched Meb's calf. She jumped and turned.

The black-and-white pup backed away, nervously. Looked at her with frightened eyes—one blue, one ale-brown. It gave a quiet little whimper.

Meb fell to her knees and gathered it up into her arms. It shivered slightly. Then sniffed at her neck and snuggled into her.

"I have to take her. I can't just leave her here, master. She'll starve. It's . . . it's like when you took me in. My village was burned too."

Finn shrugged. "Black dog with white ears. Good demon dog in those colors. But I suspect that he's a sheepdog rather than one of the pack of the wild hunt. Well, we'll find people for him. It's a him, Scrap, not a lady-dog. Scrap of a dog for a scrap of an apprentice," he said with a wry smile. "Dogs don't like me much, I am afraid. Let's get away from this place. There doesn't seem to be another living thing here."

They walked, Meb carrying the puppy. It seemed, at this stage, utterly content to be carried, to be warm and with a human. There wasn't much to it but loose skin, fur and bony elbows, and it didn't weigh that much. Besides, no matter what it weighed, she'd have managed to carry it, somehow.

They walked for some hours, taking cover from patrolling troops of mounted alvar, and the dragon a mile or two away off to the south. Meb had to marvel how Finn knew just where the searchers were. He was plainly keener of hearing and, it would seem, smell. Maybe, thought Meb, sniffing, she still had to learn. Perhaps she could teach her dog. Dogs had keen noses.

When they sat down to rest, the pup got a mutton bone, and if it had been traumatized earlier, it forgot all the day's disasters in this vast treat. He lay with his back against her and chewed to the limits of those white sharp puppy teeth. He was not in the least worried by the quality of the cooking. He was keen to lick her face to show appreciation though. He put up with having to drink water from a tiny brook, even if it was not mother's milk.

He was slightly heavier when she had to pick him up and carry him later—but even more content. He was warm and soft and smelled of puppy-fur and mutton-bone. And he radiated complete adoration and trust. Meb was already trying to think of good reasons not to leave him with the people at the next settlement they came to. After all, if the dragon was marauding, far away from here was the best place for him. And her, for that matter. When he awoke from his little nap in her arms he showed that he was keen on nibbling things too. She removed her cloak's toggle from his mouth and gave him a finger. He preferred to lick that.

They found shelter in a half-tumbled down barn that night.
'Brys was all for pressing on. "I can smell the sea," he said, his
voice full of longing.

"You're also tripping over your own feet from tiredness," said
Finn. "We stop now."

When he gave orders, it was hard to even consider arguing.
Besides, Meb's feet were desperate for a rest. It was still cold for
sleeping rough, and the barn barely kept the rain off them. The
pup was keen to play. And to eat. But at least he was warming,
snuggled inside her cloak that night.

Fionn waited until they were both asleep to slip out. He'd done
his best to ward the place against scrying or prying eyes. But he
needed to fly upwards. He needed to be in the presence of lots
of gold for a few hours.

Soon he was above the cloaking cloud that hung over Yenfar,
and beating his way upwards to the moon that hung so close.
It was a total conceit and a waste of magic to have it there—to
say nothing of an ever-present danger to the people below. Of
course it wasn't the size of a moon obeying the more natural laws
of physics, but it was still enough to destroy life on Tasmarin if
it were to fall. And it would destroy his gold too. One had to
consider the seriousness of things like this when dealing with
such folly, even if it was amusing.

After spending some time being bathed in the revitalizing effect
of lying on gold—something Fionn realized only a dragon could
consider remotely endurable, let alone comfortable and soothing—Fionn took himself to the conclave.

Things were noisy in there. No one seemed particularly interested
in talking to him, so Fionn set about his usual information-glean-
ing. It was mostly the younger and smaller ones in here tonight,
and a frightened lot they were. Rumor was having a field day.

"... traces of dragonfire on it ..."

"... the alvar are arming ..."

They would be, thought Fionn. He wondered where the great
ones were. Zuamar was probably still angrily scouring and burning.
Or sleeping off having done so, most likely. Vorlian, Chandagar,
Jennar, even that tail-vent Myrcupa, to name a few, were all out
and about. That should be worrying too.

✧   ✧   ✧

Vorlian contemplated his gold. There was a lot of it. His island was a rich one, fertile, if not as large as, say, Lord Zuamar's holding. The big old dragons had originally taken the largest territories, with no thought as to the nature of those territories. Ones with cliffs and mountains were good for eyries and take-offs. They were often less than agriculturally ideal, Vorlian had concluded. Agriculture hadn't been a factor dragons considered . . . but here on Tasmarin it had become fairly apparent that growth among dragonkind related to hoard-size.

And that, Vorlian had come to realize, related to the other species. Someone had to dig the gold up, and that one wasn't a dragon. Fertile fields and trade brought gold, even if no human or dvergar miners did.

And for that, Vorlian knew he needed humans. They were annoying, smelly, prolific creatures. But dragons needed them. There was a difference between eating one, once in a while, and embarking on a wholesale slaughter—as Zuamar was now calling on all of dragonkind to do.

Vorlian had the feeling that it was at least in part his fault. His island, Starsey, was far too geographically close to Yenfar. Vorlian had already made up his mind that he would defend its population.

But could he, if Zuamar came with the sort of support he seemed to be gathering? One-on-one they were not too unevenly matched. But no dragon could stand even against three. That was how the conclave kept the peace.

Meb awoke to a throbbing growl in her ear. There was a dark shape over at the rotting arch that was all that was left of the doorway. And the pup was letting her know that he found it alarming. Meb stuck out a hand to wake Finn—only he wasn't there.

"I see we have a guard dog," said Finn's voice from the dark shape. "More use than a chewer of mutton bones, even if it still has to learn who its enemies are."

"I think he thought you were the dragon again. He's shivering."

"The Scrap should tell her scrap that it's only me. We want to get moving before dawn. We've got an hour or two's walk to the cliffs, and there is not much cover close to the sea."

They got up and left. Meb felt that cold mutton was less of a breakfast than she'd hoped for, but it was food, and they could both eat and walk.

It was predawn gray when she first heard the distant rhythmic sound of the waves carried on a salt-laden breeze. She hadn't realized just how much that sound and smell were part of her, or how much she'd missed it, until that moment.

"Will the two of you stop standing stock still and get a move on," said Finn. "You'll hear it better from closer."

So they walked on. It was an effort to keep up with the merrow. They made their way down a section of crumbly, broken cliff and to a small bay of shifting grumbling cobbles. The sun was just coming up. The merrow rushed down to meet the foam-line of the wave. He grabbed water and splashed himself. He thrust his arms out and stretched, as they watched. The pup, put down on the stones, looked warily at the water. The foam rushed up at them, sending cobbles clacking. The pup pressed against Meb's leg and barked at it.

"I didn't realize what a lot I had in common with your brave hound, Scrap," said Finn, grinning. "There should be some caves for us to rest up in. We'll need to find a boat, unlike you, Hrod-enynbrys. I can see no reason why you can't swim away and tell Margetha that Fionn is coming to collect the hammer."

The merrow looked torn. "I should stay and guard the Ang-marad."

Finn shrugged. "If the worst comes to the worst we'll just toss it in the water. We're not going to be more than a few feet away from the sea until we get there, with luck. We'll go hunting a fishing boat after dark."

'Brys bit a long fore-finger, and then nodded. "I'll find some-one to take word, and will be back. But . . . could I ask you to do one thing for it? Let the water touch it. It needs the sea and the sea needs it. Please."

He seemed as earnest as the merrow ever got. Meb looked at Finn. He nodded. "Just hold onto it."

═ Chapter 32 ═

MEB LIFTED THE TWISTED CIRCLET OF BLADDER-WRACK OFF HER head and stepped down the sloping beach to the foam-laced top of the surge. The sea was still gray in the new light of morning. The sun, still a half red orb on the eastern horizon, hazed by the wind-whipped sea-spray that trailed the breakers, gave everything curiously sharp outlines, even the flight of curlews moving in a ragged vee above the water. A wave came rushing up the stones, sending the cobbles hissing and clattering. Meb put the circlet into the water, and realized that she'd misjudged the strength of the wave. The water came half way up her boots. From being icy cold when she touched it, it was suddenly as warm as blood, and tingling. Meb was aware of a curious whistling and ringing in her ears, like the sound of the sea being somehow echoed through a thousand distant bells. Just for a moment she felt the race of the tide, the swirl of the water and the heartbeat of the waves, as if the sea were part of her and she, part of it.

"Groblek said to say he misses you," said Meb, feeling mildly foolish.

Beside her the pup sneezed. Snorted salt water. That didn't stop him biting the wave that was attacking her feet again. A dog couldn't be tolerating this stuff even if it was excessively salty! He'd teach it a lesson!

It did make her laugh and break the spell. The sun had risen just a fraction more, and the sea was bright with it. Or bright with something. It seemed bigger and wilder somehow.

The merrow did too. He was changing back into the blue-skinned tassel-finned creature she'd first met. He bowed respectfully. "For that, the thanks of all of the waters and all that live in them. I'll bid you farewell, for now."

And he slipped effortlessly away beneath the tumble of foam of an incoming wave.

Meb looked at the circlet of dried seaweed. It wasn't so well-dried any more. But it still looked pretty much like any other piece of seaweed that might have been washed up after a winter storm.

"Well," said Finn. "Unless you want to keep getting your feet wet and make your scrap of a dog even wetter, and swallow half the sea, maybe you'd better come back up to the caves. There is bit of driftwood there and what with the spray blowing up the cliff the smoke will be lost. And after that," he pointed at the dripping loop of seaweed, "there are going to be magic workers from here to far Prettisy Island wondering what is going on, anyway."

So Meb came away from the sea, away from the oneness and the power and deep currents of it, and was showered by the pup, who celebrated her return to common sense by dancing around her and shaking.

Finn was a wizard when it came to getting even an unpromising damp salt-encrusted pile of debris and flotsam to burn. He yawned. It was the first time Meb had seen him so obviously tired. "Tide's coming in, and this beach will be covered. But the top end of the cave stays dry, or not more than spray-damp. Sorry, Scrap. I need a rest. Then we need a boat."

Meb had noticed that there was not a sail to be seen. That was unusual unless it was stormy. Yet it seemed a good brisk fishing day to her.

The Lyr had been aware, at some basic level, that something had happened to one of itself. When news came, via the shocked priest of the Hamarbarit grove, that not only was the sister-Lyr that he had been with destroyed, but that Haborym had been destroyed too, Lyr knew fear. And, as near a plant-lifeform could rage—a sort of cold, bitter anger. They needed the human mage. But the plant-lifeform feared humans as well. She had every intent of seeing the human destroyed the moment that their work was done. Humans were near defenseless against the fire-being kind, and this had been part of the great agreement reached between them.

Still, human reportage could not be trusted. A Lyr was dispatched from her grove to go and see how much of the story was mere human exaggeration. They were very prone to that.

What came back frightened the Lyr even more.

Emissaries were hastily sent out.

"The alvar ships certainly always made other vessels look clumsy and slow," said Cyllarus to Ixion, his companion of the day, as they paced the low dock of Port Lapith.

"They're elegant enough." Even in today's light breeze the long hulled alvar vessel glided across the water. It was not by chance, naturally, that two of the centaurs-folk's leading generals were on the quay-side. Yesterday had been wind-still. They knew what the swan-ship carried.

They waited as ropes were cast ashore and the vessel was secured. Soon the gangplank was lowered and that in turn was used to put a horse-ramp in place. Soon an alvar prince, resplendent in sky blue silk hose, a delicately engraved silver mail-shirt, with a midnight blue surcoat embroidered in silver over that, rode out on a spirited gray horse, with silver bosses on her fine tack . . . And nearly fell off, as the fine mare found the half-horses very much outside of her experience.

"Prince Gywndar," said Ixion in greeting, as the alvar tried to keep the last shred of his dignity intact by at least staying in the saddle.

The use of his name was almost the last distracting straw, and Gywndar had to grab the saddle to stop his suitably grandiose arrival in the lands of the centaurs from ending with a splash in the harbor. But, like all of the alvar he was good with horses and did eventually calm his steed. "Greetings," he said. "I seek urgent counsel with the leaders of the centaur peoples, our ancient friends."

"Speak, Prince." It was true enough that the alvar had always avoided conflict with the centaurs. Although to call them ancient friends was a little disingenuous.

"Take me to your leaders. I must speak with them," said Gywndar, tilting his head back and trying—and failing—to look down on them a little. They were taller than he was.

"We do not have hierarchical ranks as you do, Prince. In the herds Cyllarus and I are counted as the leaders of Phalanxes. I think it is us that you wish to speak to. That is why we are here."

The alvar prince looked at the two big centaurs facing him. Ixion had made a study of alvar kind. If the centaurs had been setting out to make things easy, they could have worn some kind of insignia or symbol of rank. Faced with two bronzed torsos, and no clothing at all, unless you counted the utilitarian weapons of war they carried, how was the alvar to have guessed? After a few seconds of looking into their faces he looked around and said awkwardly. "Um. Here? On the dockside? There are humans unloading loading crates of fish over there."

Cyllarus nodded. "We do not have palaces as you alvar do. We speak where we meet, Prince. What is it that you wish to talk to us about?"

Gywndar was by now thoroughly off his stride, and discomforted. Which, if he had been a centaur . . . or even a fire-being or a dragon, he would have realized was the purpose of their actions. But the alvar had fixed ideas about protocols, and had become very set in their ways. "Erm. Well, I come as an emissary. Can I present my credentials to someone?"

"We know who you are, Prince Gywndar," said Ixion. "Your coming was foretold."

"One forgets that the centaurs are so adept at reading the future," said Gywndar, favoring them with his best smile.

"We have not forgotten that the alvar are so silver-tongued. We are here to listen," said Cyllarus—which was true. They were.

"I've come to tell you of portentous and tragic happenings and to beg for your aid. I am the prince of Yenfar. We are the guardians of an ancient treasure . . ."

"The Angmarad of the merrows," said Ixion.

"Er. Yes. Anyway, there has been some kind of vile conspiracy. A conspiracy between some humans, the merrow, and, we are sad to say, a renegade dragon, to steal this sacred trust."

"They have returned it to the water. The shock of it, and the renewal of the sea, was felt everywhere," Cyllarus said.

"No, we recovered it. A large group of the thieves were caught with it in their possession. Nonetheless it was a breach of trust. A breach of the ancient compact. They must be dealt with before they try again. This means war!"

"Why?" asked the two centaurs, together after a moment of silence.

The alvar princeling opened and closed his mouth at them,

like a fish out of water. "The balance of powers, the merrow and, and, and a human!" he squeaked eventually.

"Not to mention a dragon," said Ixion, controlling a desire to laugh.

Gywndar drew himself up. "The dragons rally behind us to show that this was just one renegade. They are our staunch allies. We are now gathering all the peoples to deal with them."

"All of them?"

"Yes," said Gywndar firmly. "Well, some of them. We're sending emissaries to the merrows to demand that they turn over the thieves for justice. And we'll give them a good lesson."

"I meant all of the dragons. Our scrying of the dark glass of the future shows dragon fighting dragon, and the lands of Tasmarin aflame."

"Lord Zuamar gathers the great ones to him. We'll soon weed out the handful of traitors. They and the merrows and their human allies will be eliminated. Will you join us?" demanded Gywndar.

Ixion tried reason, although he was sure that it would fail. "The merrows' sea does not threaten your forest and mountain home, nor our high grasslands. The war we see coming is an evil and ugly one, where friend will slay friend, and brother will turn on brother."

Gywndar lifted a face set in flinty determination. "We have no choice. I had not wished to tell you this, but the human thief is also a worker of magic. That must be dealt with. The dragons will give no respite until that is done. At this stage we hold them in check, barely. But they will destroy every human and every human holding until they find them. They will not spare the centaurs."

Cyllarus turned to Ixion. They looked at each other in silence remembering what they had seen in the dark pool. Then they turned to Gywndar. "We will gird for war. But we are a peaceful species. It will take us a great deal of time. We beg you to hold the dragons and your fellow alvar in check for as long as possible."

Gywndar looked at the two centaurs. "Shall we sign a treaty? Agree to timeframes?"

"No," said Cyllarus. "And in the end we foresee it being to no avail. The black dragon continues to work his destruction. We can see nearly all of it."

"What black dragon?" asked Gywndar.

"The one who is entwined in all the fate-lines. Can we help you to your ship?" asked Ixion, meaningfully. He wished again that his brother Actaeon might have been here to deal with the alvar. He had been better at it, which was why he was now in exile. For a centaur, death was easier than being apart from the herd.

The conspirators met at a request from the sprites. It was in a neutral spot here on Vorlian's Starsey, not far from one of the sprites' great dancing-glades. The centaur had to make do with a hand-mirror. He lived, Vorlian gathered, a very lonely existence in the meadows in the rocky north of the island. Lord Rennalinn had come across from the nearby Maygn isle—Vorlian wondered what his dragon overlord, or, for that matter, the alvar prince to whom Rennalinn gave fealty, would feel about this meeting. The alvar of Starsey were few in number, and, Vorlian gathered, not of a particularly noble lineage. Their duke was a bluff fellow of no particular intellect, who did his work for Vorlian well. Vorlian wondered why he'd never considered him for this role instead of the pretentious Rennalinn. As far as he could remember, he'd been introduced to this alvar by the sprites, when the panic about the collapse of the first tower was still raw.

There was a new visitor. Haborym had always seemed—and the dragon was aware that it was probably nothing more than a seeming—tall and affable.

This was one of the energy creatures, but it was not Haborym.

He was taller, and it would seem that his flames burned even hotter.

"Who is this?" asked Vorlian, his voice neutral. It was said that, yes, in open conflict, dragonfire, with the liberation of energy from any form of matter, was the one thing creatures of smokeless flame struggled to endure, besides immersion in water. The alvar were generally quite at good magical repulsion of the creatures of heat too, although Vorlian was not sure how they did it. But fire-beings were even more strict of rank and hierarchy than alvar, so it was unlikely that Haborym's master would not know of this.

"This is Belet," explained the sprite. "Haborym has become discorporate."

"What?"

"His energies have dissipated. You would say that he is dead," said Belet. "I have been sent to replace him. To see that the great goal is pushed towards its desired conclusion."

"The human mage killed him. She destroyed one of the parts of us too. She has allied herself with the water-people. And, also, we believe, with a dragon, although our acolyte says he saw a tall human with her as well. And there were traces of dvergar magics on the sister they killed. It seems she has been found by, and co-opted to, the cause of those who oppose us," said the sprite.

Vorlian sighed. "And to make matters more complicated there are several dragons now calling for the destruction of all humans, and also any dragons or others who try to stop them. Have our plans gone awry in any other ways?"

The sprite nodded. "Yes, Haborym's thieves succeeded in getting the merrow treasure. Unfortunately the alvar have recovered the treasure. They gear for war with the merrows."

"Awkward," said the centaur, admiring himself. "Merrow magic is effective on alvar, but not the other way around. The merrows are not going to be impressed, I think. But the sprites can deal with that, eh?"

"If we choose," said the sprite.

"And do you?" asked Vorlian.

"There is a price to all things," said the sprite.

"And the question of the dvergar, who in turn are beholden to the merrows to keep the dvergar hammer safe. It's all very beautifully balanced," said the centaur Actaeon.

"Perhaps you need to think about that bag of yours," said Duke Belet. "Now, Lord Vorlian, they're gathering their forces. Obviously they cannot be allowed to destroy our human quarry until we have done with her. In the interests of peace and security can we rely on you to raise some delays? We have some forces of our own. Besides those of our kind we have armies at our disposal who can fight delaying actions if need be."

"Do you propose to let me lead our world into war?" asked Vorlian dryly. He'd planned to defend his own. But . . . what other forces? Armies were not raised and trained overnight. Armies of which species? This smelled. And not of anything wholesome. And yet . . . what other way forward was there?

"Surely it won't come to that," said Belet. "Once they realize the weight of forces arrayed against them, they'll back down."

Vorlian suspected that Zuamar had no idea what the words "back down" meant. But . . .

"I'll look into it," he said.

"We arm our worshipers," said the sprite. "And the alvar have come calling on the Mother grove. Some, like Prince Gywndar, call for war, a war of punishment against the merrows. Other alvar beg us to hold back. We have told both sides that we favor them."

So much for the deep trustworthiness of the sprites, thought Vorlian. The alvar seemed predisposed to believe whatever the sprites told them, but he didn't. Still, he had a goal, and he needed the sprites.

= Chapter 33 =

FIONN WONDERED IF THE MERROW HAD HAD ANY IDEA HOW complex the process of leading him—and of course the rest of them—safely to the sea had been. The black dragon's knowledge of Tasmarin was encyclopedic—the charts were merely a way of helping to work out the enormously complex relationships between the energies when he wasn't precisely on site to feel or see the effects. He could see deep into the infrared, so, circling in, he'd pinpointed the checkpoints.

That had been all very well but there were still patrols to be avoided. He could smell and hear and sense the moving mass of metals—they caused tiny gravitational changes. It had still been difficult and stressful getting them to this hidey-hole, and down the cliff. That had been unstable and therefore even the local cockle-pickers avoided the place. Fionn had had to resort to unnatural means to get them down in one piece. If anyone else tried it they'd not be so lucky.

The tricky part was going to be getting a boat away from the island. Normally this bay was popular with little fishing cobles, with men working handlines for reef-fish, and Fionn had thought they'd hail one, and get it to take them to something larger, for a suitable bribe.

Only there seemed to be no fishing boats about. Fionn could think of only one reason, and that was that they were being stopped from putting out to sea. The artisanal fishermen who scraped a living from the sea couldn't afford to do that for very long. But then, Zuamar didn't really care if they starved to death. The alvar were less merciless, but also somewhat distant from the suffering of the peasantry. Fionn suspected that many of them were rather enjoying galloping about the countryside, making a pain in the nether end of themselves. It made them feel important or something. That was a need Fionn had never felt.

On the other hand the conjugation of events and forces said that, pleasant as the damp seaweed-reeking cave might be, it was time to move along to see to those forces. Besides, he couldn't leave the Scrap and her puppy here. The pup was an odd thing. Dogs instinctively shied away from Fionn, along with horses. But, because the small dog's god did not run away from the dragon smell, and Fionn still had some cold mutton . . . the little beast was wagging its disreputable feather of a tail at him, and looking at him and edging forward tentatively. It was—despite being a victim, something of a rogue, and probably going to prove more trouble than it was worth. But he still fed it.

"Come dusk we're going to have to go and look for a boat," he said to Meb, who was hypnotizing the dog with her juggling. The dog might just unscrew its own head if it kept following the balls like that.

"Yes, Finn." She paused. And then thought better of whatever she'd been about to say, and started to turn away.

"Spit it out," he said.

"It's just . . . we can't be more than a few miles from Cliff Cove. They . . . the raiders, wrecked all the boats. And most likely they'll have taken all the small-craft away. So not much use going back there," she said.

"Are there other boats likely to be on fishing grounds between here and there?" asked Fionn. Fishing boats were not rocks or features of geography. Those he knew intimately.

She shrugged. "Don't know, Finn. We had good banks. I think the men used to fish here too, by the way they talked about it. I'm sure they mentioned that double-spike rock on the point . . . There was another place further along the coast from here going west. I never went to sea with them of course. And then there's Tarport's fishermen. They'd come this far if there were no fish closer. It's far enough overland, but not so bad with a good following breeze."

"Well, we'll be going toward Tarport. So you might get to see your old village—in the dark. There is probably nothing much left, Scrap."

She nodded. "There wasn't much left by the time they'd finished with it. And people took what they could, I suppose. It was nothing like as bad as my scrap's"—she patted the dog—"home. Only a few people died."

There was something about the way she said it that told Fionn that those few people had still been far too many.

They made their way up the treacherous cliff again that evening just after dark. The cloud had broken up enough to allow them shreds of moonlight. It was still tricky. And made trickier by a guard on the headland. It would have been worse if he had been watching the sea instead of the land. It could have been better if Finn had been leading the way. The startled guard tried to draw his sword from under his cloak. Meb simply dropped her head and cannoned into his stomach. They fell in a scuffle of two and a puppy.

Finn rapped the alvar warrior on the head, and hauled him off the two of them. "You really have to stop fighting with everyone you meet, Scrap," he said with mock severity. "Now we'd better tie this fellow up and leave him somewhere. It does mean that we only have tonight to get away."

They bound and gagged the guard and Finn hoisted him onto his shoulder, and carried him inland to behind a little hummock and dumped him into the gorse bushes.

"Well, let's walk. Hope there are not too many of those. Eventually something will go wrong."

They walked on through the dark for a good hour. Meb was glad to quietly take hold of Finn's cloak again, as he did not stop or slow down when the moon was hidden by the clouds.

"Looks like your little village has people in it, Scrap."

Meb had not even known that they'd arrived there. But now she could see a thread of light through a crack.

"Let's walk a little closer. It sounds like a few fishermen," said Finn.

"How do you know?" she asked.

"Not many other people talk of salt cod with enthusiasm," he said dryly.

They walked closer. Meb realized that she too knew that they were fishermen—because she knew exactly who they were, and not just because they were arguing about which bank to fish in this weather. Her step-brothers had mostly been carelessly kind to her.

"Er. I think I know them," said Meb wondering how she was going to explain her appearance to them. They'd surely recognize her and give her away.

"Good." Finn pulled out a handful of silver. "You go in there and talk them into taking us to Starsey. Or Pallin. We'll pay them that much again when we get there."

Meb felt the weight of the silver in her hand. "We want them to take us there. Not buy their boat!"

"I'll leave you to bargain. But don't be mean. It'll mean putting to sea tonight, and maybe staying away for a while. I'm going to check on the headland. There was something moving there. If you have a problem, yell. I'll hear."

Swallowing, Meb walked toward the little bit of light. Knocked on the door.

There was a sudden silence from within. "Who is there?" asked Mikka nervously from within.

"It's just me," said Meb.

"Meb?" said Hrolf incredulously. He pulled open the door. "Come in. Come in! There's supposed to be a curfew, idiot. Where have you been? We thought you had been killed or captured!"

"Close to both," said Meb, going into the small croft. Half a dozen familiar young men's faces stared at her. Several had boar-spears at the ready. "Hush."

The sight of her and her puppy made the points drop.

The two of Hallgerd's older boys—men now, hugged her. She was surprised. Touched. "What happened to your hair!" demanded Hrolf, the older brother.

Meb realized she'd actually forgotten all about it. And giving it to a merrow would not impress them. They'd call her an idiot . . . "It's a long story. Have you got a boat?"

Hrolf nodded. "Not much of one. We pay the owner half the catch. But it was better than staying on in Tarport."

They all looked thin. And there were no women here, although at least two were married. Mikka bit his lip looking at her. "That's . . . a gleeman's cloak. Why are you wearing trousers?"

Meb hugged him . . . and whispered in his ear. "You just forget

I am Meb. I'll forget about telling Morin what you were up to with his wife on the dunes." Then louder, she said, "I'm an apprentice gleeman. I need you all to pretend that I am a boy to my master . . . or I will be out of a job."

Hrolf put his calloused hand on her shoulder. "We could feed you. The ban on putting to sea has made things tough. But you're my little sister."

Well, Finn had said that she could be generous. She put some silver on the table, more than most of them had likely seen in their lives. Fishermen earned coppers, not silver. "I need you to pretend that I'm not your sister, and I need a boat. Tonight."

They stared at the silver. That was a couple of years' worth of hard fishing on the table. Enough for a boat, probably. "We dare not. Lord Zuamar has stopped any vessels sailing. And not at night!" said weak-chinned Morin.

"So you'll just sit here and starve." She added some coins. "Count them. My master has offered the same again for him to be taken to Pallin. But we must sail tonight. They're looking for us. And they won't pay anything like this if you turn us over to them. More than likely they'll just kill you."

"They've been killing and burning already. Lord Zuamar's gone mad, I think," said Hrolf.

"Stark raving," said Mikka. He had started splitting the silver up into piles. "That's twenty-one marks each and the same for the boat."

Meb took out another few coins. "And the same for the skipper. I haven't got much more, here. But deliver us to Pallin Isle and we'll double it. Every man's share, and the boat and the skipper."

She was speaking their language—the shares by which the fishermen worked—one for the skipper, one for the boat, and one for you. A straight offer of money, they might have balked from. But not a fisherman's share. She was one of them.

"There's a good wind blowing. And the tide's near full, too," said Mikka.

"We could stay away a week or two," said another one of the men. "Let things blow over."

Morin shook his head. "It's not safe. Lord Zuamar has gone mad. He's burned whole villages for less."

"What's left here to burn?" asked Mikka. "That's enough money for a boat of our own and we can be a long way from the shore by dawn. Where is this master of yours, Meb? Or is he disguised as the dog?"

"Just here," said Finn from the doorway. "Come and look out there. I think you need to put to sea as fast as you can."

There was a fire on the distant hills.

"He's burning out a village up there, for no reason at all. Ask the Scrap. We've seen what is happening. He's killing everything alive."

Hrolf stood up. "Come, lads," he said. "Get your oilskins. There is rain on that wind. That'll make it hard for any dragon to see us, but it'll make it a wet, wild night out there." He scooped up his share of the silver, and another two shares.

Meb's eyes widened slightly. So he was the skipper now. The skipper saw to the finances of keeping the vessel intact and sea-worthy—hence he got the boat share too. And once the skipper had made up his mind, the rest of the boat crew would go along with him.

A few minutes later they were clambering on board a fish-reeking small two-masted vessel. Meb looked rather disdainfully at it. It might be better than being a crewman and living back in Tarport. Maybe. She could see that the fat-bottomed yawl—even in the broken moonlight—had plainly seen better days. On the other hand, it was quite adequate for taking them across to Pallin. "Look lively, lads, let's get her out of here, and into the open water," said Hrolf.

It was only when they were out, over the bar, that someone said, "Where's Morin?"

"Dunno. He went to pick up his sou'wester . . ."

Mikka spat. "He wasn't keen on this anyway. Likely he's taken your silver and run to tell the guard on long hill, gleeman."

"What can we do? We'll never catch him," said one of the fishermen in a panicky voice.

"And he won't find anyone sitting on long hill either," said Finn. "I . . . paid them a visit. It seemed they'd see the sail with you putting out to sea. They're tied up and not watching anything. So I'd say make sail. Let's run as fast as your noble vessel will manage."

Hrolf snorted. "Without half a gale to fill her sails, she's not much faster than a spavined donkey on a steep uphill. But there is no turning back, anyway."

They continued to draw away into the darkness, with only a betraying sparkle of phosphorescence in the fishing-boat's wake, and, when the cloud did not hide the moon, the darkness of the old patched sail against the sky.

The wind carried the sound of a horn from the shore.

"He's found someone," said Finn.

"Aye," said Hrolf from the tiller. "It's a question of if they can find us. I'm shifting course, gleeman. We'll make for Starsey. Morin knew were going to Pallin, and we can run more directly before the wind."

Meb knew her half-brother well enough to pick up the fear in his voice.

Fionn watched the sky. The alvar might have a few of their own vessels—much faster than this little scow—stationed at Tarport. But it would take them an hour's sailing just to get to Cliff Cove. Starsey, Pallin and Morth Islands lay on the edges of the huge ancient underwater caldera that he was heading toward. The shortest route was between the cliffs of Morth and the reef at Pallin—but there was a vicious tide-race with a maelstrom. So they'd have had to take the route around between Pallin and the lesser islands and Starsey. That was a good ten hours sail at the best speed the little yawl could manage. The alvar swan-ships were capable of twice that speed, but they'd have to put to sea and find them first, and rain-squalls and the false assumption that they'd headed for Pallin could make that a tight chase. But once Zuamar began the chase, it would be over all too quickly. There were times when Fionn could become severely irritated with the limitations he had to operate under. But they were as much part of him as his black scales.

Vorlian of Starsey—Fionn suspected—would not take kindly to Zuamar flying too close. Of the other two dragon-overlords he was less certain. If they got to land, well, Zuamar could ask for the fugitives to be returned to him. But to actually trespass would almost certainly lead to a fight.

So now it was down to a wet night and plowing steadily through the ocean's billows.

Meb and the pup sat against the tiller-house. It was there or in the crowded fo'c'sle, and this at least had fresh if wet air. She had time now to ask after the rest of the village, and just how they'd ended up back at Cliff Cove.

"It all came down to Wulfstan," said Hrolf. "You know he used to do the dickering for our fish?"

"Yes. He drove a hard bargain," said Meb, remembering the shouting and performance.

"Huh, hard bargain, my futtering left toe up a mackerel's arse. Turns out he and Roff had a scheme going. The buyer was Roff's cousin. Roff would go to Tarport and they'd agree a price. Then the buyer would show up and Wulfstan and him would put on a good show for us. And he'd get our fish at half the going rate. Wulfstan and Roff got a good cut. So when we went to town after the raid, Wulfstan got us sites on some boats and we were all going to stay together. Stick together in the big town, see. Most of us got a day's fishing as soon as we got there. Only Maric got hired to carry stockfish to the same dealer. And he saw what was being paid. You know Maric. Could never keep a still tongue in his head. He came back and told Wulfstan in front of everyone what an idiot he'd been. Of course Wulfstan held he'd been cheated by that rogue of a trader. Anyway, Roff was missing. Hadn't come to town. We didn't like the fellow much—but you were missing too. All the others were accounted for, either in Tarport or dead. So Mikka and me, we put two and two together. I'd had words with the bastard piece of shark-shit before about him pestering you, and we thought we'd go and have another look. Maric and Tam came along. We found him—and a sack of money. Not you."

He took a deep breath. "He'd been cut up real bad. Kept telling us he swore he didn't know where you'd gone. He didn't even know who we were. He was dying, see. Frightened us witless. Kept asking for his cousin—the fish dealer. And offering us the money to stop hurting him. We weren't doing anything to him. He was just delirious. But bits came out that didn't add up. We carted him back—and Wulfstan got the idea we'd done it to him. And then the entire mess came out—with half the village still standing by Wulfstan." He spat. "They were all for having us hanged. Except that someone pointed out that wounds don't turn pus-filled in one night, and Roff was going rotten already. The Tarport Councilors got one of the alvar involved, and they laid a truthspell on us, which worked out well for us. But Wulfstan and the fish-buyer got leaning on people, saying that they weren't to hire us." He grinned, teeth white in the darkness. "There wasn't much work there anyway, and the town was all in an uproar about the burning of the tax hall. Have you heard about that? My word, it had them behaving like mad hornets, and it was hard for everyone, especially newcomers. Lord Zuamar was even searching ships himself."

Meb blushed in the darkness. "Go on."

"Not much more to tell. See, we had Roff's bag of coins. We figured Wulfstan had the rest—so that might, fairly, be ours. This old tub was laid up, and even if we did not have enough money to buy her, we got a working share. We weren't much welcome in Tarport, so we came back here. It was good place for most of my life, until the raiders came. And we know the fishing banks here. Don't around Tarport. A few of the others came along later, because Tarport is no easy place to live. The fishing wasn't bad, and it beat paying to live in town, even if we do have to carry water."

═ Chapter 34 ═

DAWN SAW THE GREEN BULK OF STARSEY AHEAD WITH THE CLIFFS of Pallin point to starboard and the lookout keeping a very nervous watch for any smaller islands and rocks. It was a blustery cold morning—and they could see the white hope-sails of the alvar craft, not more—by Fionn's estimate—than two hours sail behind them.

It would take their yawl longer than that to gain the shore.

The fishermen could see that too, by their expressions. Fionn bit his knuckle and calculated. It was a complex equation of the current and the wind. It might not work. On the other hand he had no real use for the rubies anyway. He'd already returned some to the stream from whence they had come, and as long as the rest were scattered it would still achieve his purpose. "I need some net-floats," he said to Hrolf. "As many as you have. And if you have a pot of tar, make it hot. And take a bearing on the second peak of Starsey and steer towards that. The one to larboard."

"We'll lose a few points on the wind," said Hrolf.

"Hopefully cost us less time than what I will do will lose them," said Finn, jerking a thumb at the sails of the closer swan-ship.

Hrolf nodded. "Mikka—you and Peg get cutting the floats off the big net. There's a pot of tar in the for'ard hatch. The brazier's burning already."

Soon Fionn was sitting with a pile of red floats, and sticking rubies to each with a spot of tar. Mikka—once he'd worked out what was going on and stopped swearing in amazement—took a close look. "You're going to toss them overboard?"

"Yes. I'm hoping the alvar will choose to gather them rather than letting them scatter across the beaches of the islands."

"That'd be some find for a beachcomber!" He peered at the float. "I'll get you a bit of ballast-stone to shove in the top-line hole. It'll keep them the right way up."

Meb looked at the line of red floats drifting away in a line behind them. They seemed very small in wideness of the white-capped ocean. Surely the ships following would not see them? Or stop to find out what they were? She wished that the sun would come out and make those rubies sparkle like fire.

And behind them it seemed that the clouds were set to oblige her. It was amazing how the rubies did catch the sun.

Fionn felt the power of her enhancement. He said, "I still have at least thirty stones. You stick them on. Put a bit of thought into how brightly you want them to shine and how desirable they must be."

With someone of lesser power, doing that would have needed ritual and skill. With her . . . well, untrammeled power would do. Even the frightened fishermen were looking on with interest. Looking as if they might just dive in after the floats that she was tossing overboard. Fionn passed them each a stone. "Pop them in your pockets. If you get out of this you'll at least be wealthy enough. I'd take care about selling them, though."

Then it was back to the waiting game. And watching the sky.

The island of Starsey loomed far larger now, with its patchwork fields and stone walls. Meb thought it looked like a fertile place. Smaller than Yenfar, but more cultivated. And there were other ships to be seen on the sea.

"They've left one vessel to pick up the floats," said Hrolf. "The other one is coming on, under full sail. It held them up for a bit, but not for long enough. And we're losing the wind here."

Finn seemed not to have heard him. He was staring over the stern, squinting a little. He took a deep breath. "You may want to take the skiff and row toward those fishermen. That's Zuamar flying towards us."

The dragon must have been flying fast, because Meb could make out the batwing shape. Fear and anger surged in her. What had they done to him? Well, a few things, sensible Meb admitted. "You reckon it would work, gleeman?" asked Hrolf. "Just leave the tub to sail on, and they won't know we've gone until it is too late?"

Finn looked up again. "No. He's seen us."

"Hrolf! The sea is looking strange," said Mikka urgently. Meb looked at it. For a moment she did not know what he was talking about. Then it came to her. It was nearly still. Off in the distance there were whitecaps. But around their boat it was mill-pond calm. The one thing that was obvious was that the fishing smacks about a mile off were hauling up their sails, in what seemed like an enormous hurry.

"We're in the eye," said Finn. His eyes glittered.

Meb wondered for an instant if this was he meant. Or if this was some kind of magic he was working. He was the last human mage, she was sure now. He must have many a trick up his sleeve. The air felt . . . odd. She swallowed, and her ears popped. She noticed that her step-brothers were looking really afraid. The alvar swan-ship had been closing on them with some speed. Now Meb could see that the sailors were frantically working in the rigging.

Hrolf turned to his brother. "Get three reefs in that mainsail. Jump to it."

He started lashing the rudder.

Meb saw that the sky around them was changing color. Lord Zuamar was flying ever closer. And then, looking towards the land, she saw something else.

They were about to be attacked by another dragon. She yelled and pointed to it. She had to yell, because her ears were being assaulted by the roar of the water—there were three waterspouts rushing up at the tea-colored sky—and they were converging on the alvar ship as they raced across the water.

The attacking dragon coming from the land-side was beating his way up into the air. Zuamar was flying straight toward them— buffeted by the strange storm that raged around the yawl. Meb could hardly see the alvar swan-ship now, it was so obscured in the midst of a seethe of wild water. It appeared to have lost at least one mast.

"Looks like Vorlian is taking exception to Zuamar being too close to his lair," said Fionn in her ear. "And you'd better hold on tight, because those damned merrows have just no idea about how unseaworthy our little fishing-boat is." Meb realized that the shapes in the waves . . . were somewhat familiar.

Above them the two dragons met, and plummeted downward in a spiral of furious fire . . . and suddenly tumbled apart in a chaos of frantically flapping wings, as they were both blown wildly across the sky.

Finn shook his head. "Don't mothers teach these young 'uns of today anything about windshear?" he asked with mock sympathy. "Hold tight. Here it comes."

Meb clutched both the gunwale and her pup, as the rage of the wind suddenly hit them and the water picked up the fat slug of a fishing boat, and flung it about like a . . . well, like a small fishing boat in a hurricane.

Meb was not sure how they didn't sink. She was not too sure how long it went on for, even. It seemed interminable. The boat raced and bucketed, waves slopping over its decks, and the seamen frantically alternated between holding tight and bailing desperately. Meb got soaked to the skin. So did the shivering pup. Yet there was a curiously electrifying and almost joyful feeling to it all. Meb knew that she ought to be frightened for her life. But part of her wanted to shout with glee and laugh.

Eventually the wind slackened, and the battered little yawl sailed out of the cloak of rain and into a gentler ocean. The green bulk of Starsey was gone. Instead ahead lay towering gray cliffs.

"Where are we?" asked Meb.

"That's the back of Starsey," said Finn. "We're in the caldera bowl between Starsey, Pallin and Morth."

"In dead-man's sea," said Hrolf. "Well, we lived through the storm. Maybe we'll get out of this alive too." He didn't sound at all optimistic.

"Wh . . . why is it called that?" asked Meb.

"Because no living man comes back from fishing here," said Hrolf with morbid relish. "The merrows take you down and devour you."

"You'd be having that all wrong, as usual," said a voice from the water. "It's called that because we gather the souls of the dead here. And we're not after eating your kind. We know where you've been."

Wide-eyed fishermen grabbed for anything that could possibly be used as a weapon. Hrodenynbrys grinned toothily at them from the water. "And what do you think you'd be doing with those?

If we'd wanted to drown you, we'd not have brought you here."
He looked at Finn. "Couldn't you have found a better boat than
this ratty little tub with a crew of layabouts?"

"The famous gratitude and grace of the merrows," said Finn
sardonically. "Open that brazier, Hrolf. They don't want the piece
of flotsam we have worked so hard to bring them."

"Well, I wouldn't be putting it quite like that," said Hrodenynbrys. "No point in being hasty and nasty about it. It's just that a
fine vessel would have seemed more . . . appropriate."

"Unfortunately, all the swan-ships were going the other way,"
said Finn. "Now, having frightened both the Scrap and her pup
out of a year's growth, not to mention having got salt onto my
cloak, what are going to do about it?"

Hrodenynbrys looked sidelong at the crew. "Well, the Chieftainess Margetha has extended a welcome to all of you below.
But I'd be thinking that these fine fellows might be happier out
here in the sunlight."

The crew, like a row of puppets on a single string, nodded.

Hrodenynbrys nodded back. "So, we'll bring a bell up for you,
Fionn. I'm knowing that your apprentice does not like the swimming much. Near drowned me, she did."

The merrow disappeared beneath the waves with a flick of his tail.

The fishermen looked at the water, warily. "You're not going
down there, are you?" asked Mikka.

"Yes. You'd be amazed where gleemen get invited to go to,"
said Finn. "I'd say we ought to leave our boots behind, Scrap.
It's wet down there. And maybe leave the pup as well. We'll be
back soon, or not all."

Meb nodded, less frightened because Finn wasn't, and anyway,
she trusted 'Brys. You had to watch him, that was all.

A wood-framed bubble—well, that was what it looked like—
popped up to the surface of the water. Several merrows pushed it
up to the side of the fishing yawl, and flipped it onto its side.

Finn jumped down into it, showing that he was familiar with
the device.

"Can you hold my dog?" Meb asked Mikka.

He smiled for the first time since the merrows had appeared
and took the pup from her. "Are you sure that it's a dog? More
like a half-drowned rat, s— uh, gleeman."

"He's still growing. I shall bring him back in a year or two to bite you if you insult him," she said firmly, winking at her step-brother, and climbing down into the merrow device.

"Climb up here and sit on the pole," said Finn. "Hold tight onto the handle. They'll flip it in a moment. The first time I fell out into the water."

The strange bubble flipped and Meb nearly imitated Finn's first time, but stayed on the pole more by luck than good judgement.

The whole device began to descend into the depths, hauled down by thick ropes.

"It's not too deep, but they dribble air in as we go. Keep your feet up. The water rises."

"It leaks?" Meb looked out of the now transparent walls of the bubble between its thick wooden struts.

"No, it's the pressure. They're cautious about the time we spend down there and how long they take to bring us to the surface. I can only assume a number of humans died before they got it right. But by now they seem to have got it right."

"There are fish out there!" She ought to be terrified but instead found herself fascinated by it all.

A shoal of silver moved around them, flickering and changing with the light like some huge magical metallic ribbon. "Yes. It's one of the things about water. Fish live in it, in spite of the merrows. And they keep this caldera lagoon as one vast sanctuary, which is why we probably should have told your fishermen friends not to drop a line. Now, to warn you, when dealing with merrows, give as good as you get, Scrap. They respect that."

The bubble was being slowly towed towards tall and impossibly slim towers. Meb blinked. They swayed. She was sure that they did! She asked.

Finn nodded. "They move with the waves. They're not solid—more like an airtight fabric. Very strong."

They came down to the ocean floor, where Meb looked out onto a series of odd, shimmering structures set in a neat double rows in an avenue. "Soul nets," said Finn, "Made of the hair of drowned sailors."

Meb shuddered. "Why?"

"Ask Hrodenynbrys."

They passed down the avenue of soul nets, to a building—if you could call it that, with an enormous roof framework—made of the great timbers of lost ship keels. The bubble was pulled under the edge of a framework, and allowed to pop up into it. Merrows appeared to have been swimming down after them and they came and tipped the bubble on its side again. Meb did fall off the pole this time, but just onto the wall of the bubble. The air was thick and humid and redolent of salt and seaweed. The merrows towed them to a little dock, and helped them out. "Welcome to the place of the merrow, the land beneath the waves," said Hrodenynbrys somewhat formally. He led them up a short flight of stairs and along to a huge chamber. The transparent walls between the pillars gave a view out onto an underwater garden of seaweeds and corals. The light was a little muted by the depth, and the dancing effect of the sunlight on the waves made subtle changes in the varied hues outside. Of course it was a little odd that they were sloshing through knee-deep water. But it was quite warm—a lot warmer than the cold seas of Cliff Cove. "Why is it so warm? I thought it was cold under the sea?" she asked Finn.

"Geothermal vents," he answered. He took in her puzzled expression, and explained. "The inner fires of the world warm the place. Not the safest spot under the ocean to live, but merrows don't do 'safe' very well."

At the end of the room was a throne of pink coral, and in it lounged a woman. Well, her skin was—like Hrodenynbrys's—blue. And she too had tasseled fins. And she'd omitted to wear a blouse. But her chest was . . . uh . . . womanly. Meb understood why sailors were supposed to be distracted into jumping overboard by merwomen. There was quite a lot of exposed chest. Meb found it very embarrassing.

"Didn't I tell you slouching around in that seat would ruin your figure?" said Finn sternly. "You'll end up with a belly as broad as your behind!"

"Fionn! I'd have guessed it was you, if Hrodenynbrys had just said that you were so ugly only a mother could love you." She was smiling as she said it.

"As it was, he said that you were so ugly your mother ran away," said Hrodenynbrys with his usual toothy smile.

Meb found herself mildly offended. She'd never really thought how Finn looked. Just . . . like Finn.

"And this here is his apprentice. Scrap has a fine mouth," said 'Brys. "You know what Scrap told old Shellycoat to do?" And he proceeded to explain it to her in graphic detail, with embellishments.

"And if you'll look at what is on the youth's head, you'll know that old Shellycoat had a long, interesting, uncomfortable day," 'Brys snickered.

"I'd better watch my tongue then," said Margetha.

"If you do, you'll go squint," said Meb, determined to get at least one comment in.

"Ach, you'll do," said the bare-chested female merrow chieftainess, approvingly.

"Has this daft fool told you what he tried to do to us, Margetha?" said Finn, pointing to Hrodenynbrys. "You're likely to have a war with the alvar on your hands."

"Aye," said Margetha. "To be sure they're already demanding you be turned over to them for punishment. At least one prince with a face like a hake is. The description is a bit off though. They said a tall renegade alvar with a foxlike face, and a human mage. They made no mention of the Angmarad, though."

"You know," said Finn, thoughtfully, tugging his wispy beard, "bizarre though this is, they may not know that it is missing. It was not kept in any special place. And we relieved them of a large number of the rubies that Prince Gywndar obsesses about. There were too many of them in one place."

"You're still on about balance, Fionn. Well, can we redress that balance? We want the Angmarad. We should never have let them take it in the first place."

"We should never have even made it in the first place," growled Hrodenynbrys.

"Well, yes," said Finn. "But there is the matter of a hammer that you agreed on as price for it. I'd have been more trusting, but for him and his soul-net. So I thought it would be best if we exchanged the two, instead of me having to come asking, later."

Margetha scowled. "If I'd known what was going on, it would never have happened. 'Brys did as I told him. It was a mistake. We made our bargain, and we'll stand by it, even if we're reluctant, because the dvergar have dealt fairly enough with us, and we rely on them for much."

"A bargain is a bargain. When I said I'd get it for you, you agreed to the price," said Finn, his tone mild, but with a hint of steel behind it.

"That was near on ten years back," Margetha said. "We were thinking it was all just talk by now. But we'll hold by it."

"These things take time. There are portents and signs. And of course getting around to it," said Finn. "But we're here now. The Scrap has the Angmarad for you."

"And we have the hammer for you," said Margetha, picking up a silvery oblong box from next to her seat. "It needs to stay in the box to stay away from the moist air down here."

Finn took it. Cracked the seal around the edge. Took out a plain, unornamented hammer, with an odd-shaped head. It was made of a silvery-blue metal, but seemed quite un-special looking in any other respect. "And to stop curious merrows from playing about the hammer of artifice. It's an old thing. Been around since not long after the First. It doesn't rust."

"We did wonder what it could do," admitted Margetha. "What are you going to do with it?"

"Ah, now that's for me to know and you to find out," said Finn.

"It's a singly annoying fellow that you are," said Margetha irritably.

"It'd be likely that he'll give it back to the dvergar," said Hrodenynbrys.

"Then why would he not just say so?"

Hrodenynbrys shrugged. "It's that he likes being thought a rogue."

"And you never know. I might be one," said Finn. "Now I suppose we can be leaving."

Margetha cleared her throat. "There *is* the matter of returning the Angmarad."

"Of course," said Finn, airily. "Silly me. Scrap."

Meb reached for the twist of bladder-wrack on her head.

Margetha held up a hand. "It would probably be better if you just took it to the water for me, child. The temptation to hold onto it otherwise might be too much. Come, there is access to the open water from the antechamber."

So they went together. The transparent walls showed a view onto a seascape of delicate corals and fish feeding in bright twists of color and silver.

"If you reach under that rim," said the merrow-woman, pointing, "your hands will be out in the open water. Please, will you put it there." There was no jest in her voice now. It was a genuine plea, humble and faintly desperate. Meb looked at Finn. He made no sign at all. Well, thought Meb, she could live without a piece of old seaweed around her head. She'd only put it on—and kept it there—because he told her to. So she took it off her head and—even though it was going to mean getting wetter—knelt down and pushed the Angmarad through into the water outside. She could see the trailing fronds of the beer-brown seaweed swelling. Looking as if they were almost alive again. The coronet had a strange shivering feeling in her hands, almost like a live fish.

"Will you let it go for us, mage?"

Mage? They thought she was like Finn because she was his apprentice. Let it go? But it would just drift away. But if that was what they wanted . . .

So she did. And it did drift away. Although it seemed to be growing and spreading as it did, and there were shoals of fish darting through it.

Meb stood up again, aware that Hrodenynbrys was suddenly exhaling. And so was Finn. "It is back where it belongs. Thank you," said Margetha. "The people of land beneath the waves are forever in your debt. Call on us at need." She looked at Hrodenynbrys. "I would give you the gift of making you safe from drowning, but that is your birthright anyway. He owes you for the hair and the garment."

"Ach," said the merrow, "it'd be a small price to pay. I'll have it ready for your wedding, belike. And I wasn't to know what the future held."

Meb didn't feel she could say "Just what is going on?" but she wanted to.

"There'll be feasting, dancing, music, and probably a fair amount of fighting and wild lovemaking to follow this," said Hrodenynbrys cheerfully. "I'll be playing my pibgryn."

"Some other time," said Finn. "This is a party for merrows, this time, I think, besides, I have to move. Strange things are afoot, and great powers and magic wait not on partying."

"They should," said Margetha. "But we'll see you safe to your boat and safe over the rim-wall."

So they were escorted back to the bubble they'd come down in. Meb got to ask about the soul-nets finally. Hrodenynbrys blinked. "Because it's our duty, see. Otherwise the sea would be too haunted to swim in or sail on."

"Why?"

"Well, you have the spirits of the dead that are linked to the stuff of the body sometimes," said Hrodenynbrys seriously. "Hair's best, but the whole body is linked . . . that's why you have grave-yards being haunted. Only, as there no graveyards down here for sailors lost at sea—and the bodies break up, get eaten, rot and scatter, you end up with the souls following the water they died in. Some are right nasty about it. So we gather them in, and give them a place to rest with suitable respect."

"Oh." Meb swallowed. It was sometimes easier to think the worst of people than the truth revealed.

Meb and Finn got onto the pole and held onto the handle for it to be flipped upright, ready for the long slow ascent. Once they were sealed into the privacy of it Meb felt she could finally ask: "Just what was I doing? And did I do it right?"

Finn laughed so much she thought he might fall off the pole. When he eventually stopped he patted her on the back. "You did fine. And they did what I had been leaning on them to do. It was a big temptation, that piece of old seaweed. It was more powerful than most pieces of seaweed, but the merrows and the sea will be better off for it being let loose again. At least half the power and life of the sea was bound into it. You gave it up, willingly, freely. No chieftainess has been able to, before. Margetha wouldn't, if she'd touched it."

"Oh. Why me?"

"Someone had to do it," said Finn. "And you were quite used to the smell of seaweed."

She got the feeling that that wasn't the entire answer, but it appeared that was all the answer she was going to get. So she looked at the fish instead of talking.

The pup scrabbled from the arms of Hrolf and leapt into the bubble and bounced up on her, trying to lick her face and bark and wag his entire tail end, let alone his tail.

Mikka leaned over the gunwale. "Next time, think before you do these things. He's been crying fit to drive us all overboard. And we had to fish him out the drink with a dip-net, when I let go of him for the first time."

Meb found herself trying not to cry. He was only a dog. But . . . well, he made it plain that he was *her* dog. Meb had never really been on the receiving end of loyalty before. She could get to like it, but possibly with less licking.

=== Chapter 35 ===

"PRINCE GYWNDAR, THEY COULD NOT HAVE SURVIVED THAT STORM."
The former captain of the swanship *Melchior* was still, a day later,
a bedraggled and miserable alv. He, and most of his crew, had
been rescued by the local fishermen from where they clung to the
wreck before it went down. The other ship, which had been further
offshore, had not been found yet.

Prince Gywndar's always uncertain temper had not been helped
by the fact that floats with rubies attached had washed ashore
from the swanships. He slapped the captain. "It was plainly a
magical storm. Why would they make such weather if they could
not survive it? They're in alliance with the merrows. That was
water magic."

The captain, a minor alvar lordling himself, stared angrily back
at his prince. "Prince Gywndar, I know that it was a magical storm.
But that was not much of a vessel they were on. They'll have sunk
themselves. The people of Starsey say no others were cast ashore.
The *Melchior* was a powerful ship with a good, experienced crew.
That was why we nearly made it to land. And the Starsey fishermen say that the merrows gave them warning. They told them
the sea was going to boil with anger, and they must flee."

"Like my anger with you," shouted Gywndar. "Go. Before I
have you strung up."

Later, standing speaking to his dragon overlord on the outer
wall of Tarport, Gywndar slammed his fist into his palm. "The

merrows refuse to cooperate with us. We have asked them to surrender the fugitives or their corpses. They say they have neither.
They say we're welcome to come and look."

"Compel them," said Zuamar irritably. "You tolerate too much."

"We are fairly powerless—especially on the water—against the
magic of merrow-kind," said Gywndar. "That is why we have the
merrow treasure. At least we recovered that."

Zuamar spread his wings. "Use it then."

"But that would be against the compact!" exclaimed Gywndar.

"The compact is dead. And now I must go. I must evolve a
plan to deal with Vorlian. The more I think about it the more
logical it is that he must be the dragon that is involved in all of
this. Consorting with lesser species . . ." Zuamar snorted a great
gout of flame skyward.

Prince Gywndar stood for a long while after Zuamar left. Just
stood, staring out at nothing. Then he called for one of his generals.
"What more information do you have from the informant?"

"He died, Prince. He did tell us, repeatedly, that the woman's
name is Meb, and that she is the sister of two of the fishermen.
She was traveling with a gleeman. His description seems close
to that of the thief and hers—by the height and size, could be
the juggler-girl."

"I already knew that, fool." He took a deep breath. "I need a message carried to the merrows. You know the spells of calling."

The general nodded.

Gywndar continued. "Tell them we'll burn their precious Angmarad, bit by bit, starting tomorrow, unless we get the fugitives,
and recompense in full for our ships and treasure."

The general was too shocked for speech. But he nodded.

Gywndar walked back into the governor's palace in the stinking
sea-side town. He wondered if he'd already gone beyond what was
going to be acceptable to his fellow princes. They were already
less-than-supportive, some of them. But it wasn't their treasuries
that had been looted! And he was sure that he wouldn't actually
have to do it. And he had to do something. Zuamar was burning
his principality to ash in his quest for the human mage.

It was a day later that Gywndar got a reply—just after he
had heard that the second of his ships from the chase had been

wrecked on one of the smaller islands, and had broken up on the reef there. The general bowed nervously. "The message from the chieftainess is that they do not have your 'fugitives' but you are welcome to come and have a look, as you were told before. She's tired of repeating herself. And she sent you this." He produced a very ordinary cheap-looking flask.

"What is it?" asked Gywndar, his suspicions aroused by the general's behavior.

"Uh. Some kind of alcohol, sire. She said that even very dry seaweed doesn't burn very well. If you pour this onto it first it might help."

Gywndar ground his teeth. "Is she telling me that it doesn't matter, or daring me to do my worst?"

The general coughed. "They're . . . not very polite, sire. Um. I was told that you could use the contents of the flask to set fire to the Angmarad, or drink it, but that you'd plainly had enough already. And if you were asking for repayment for your ships, she says ships and sailors who venture onto the wide and wasteful ocean do so at their own risk, and you should pull your head out . . . out of somewhere."

That was the final insult. "Call the magicians. And have the merrows' piece of seaweed-trash brought to me. I'll get dragons to drop rocks on their precious city beneath the waves, if need be."

Vorlian ached. The sudden, strange storm had almost been the death of him. Some of his left wing-ligaments were damaged. Dragons healed fast, but that didn't mean that they didn't hurt. He could only hope that Zuamar had suffered as much. But one thing was for certain: the dragon ruler of Yenfar had to be dealt with, and the sooner the better.

In his eyrie, Zuamar contemplated his hoard and thought dark thoughts about that young upstart. He had almost had enough of Gywndar and his prevaricating and his avoidance of pogroms too. The alvar prince had been urging restraint with the systematic elimination of humans . . . Bah. It was quite probable that the quarry had been in the vessel that they'd chased. That storm had merrow-magic written all over it, but that simply made the human more dangerous. Zuamar shifted some of his painful muscles closer to his hoard. His eye lit on a coin tossed there, recently. A very old coin—with the crudely stylized face of a bearded human holding a book on one face. A ducat, one of the original ones. Now where had he got that from? Ah yes. The late unlamented Jakarin, whom he now suspected had merely been a red herring, a distraction. He picked up the coin. Smelled it. Gold, of course, has no scent. But magic clings to it like one.

This coin did not smell, much, of the fat-witted Jakarin. It smelled of dragon magic though. And he recognized the flavor of it: the same dragon that had crossed the lake with the human mage.

He ground his huge teeth. Now all he had to do was to find out where she'd got the coin from. Then his eyes narrowed. He was not particularly adept at such workings, but the laws of contagion worked well on gold and dragons. The coin could work in a tracking spell.

Meb and the others—with the exception of her dog, who after the stress of losing his mistress to the sea, and then recovering her, was now sleeping the sleep of the exhausted but happy small dog—looked on in some fear as the yawl moved steadily, without any sign of a wind or current to push the vessel along, toward a gap in the barrier islands. The gaps between them were a tangle of raging surf and cruel spikes of black rock.

They did not seem to be slowing down at all as they got closer and closer. "They're going to wreck us!" yelled one of the fishermen fearfully.

"Don't be daft. If they'd wanted to, they could've driven us into the cliff back there," said Finn. "Hold tight, though. They like nothing better than to frighten the trousers off you."

And indeed, although the little fishing boat was thrown and tossed about, and seemed in imminent danger of swamping a few times, they ended up outside the reef, being pushed out between a line of breakers and into deeper open water. Then their motion slowed and ceased, except for yawl's rolling on the swell.

Hrolf took a deep breath. "Let's get the sails up then, lads. You've a story to tell your grandchildren about Dead Man's Sea, not that they'll believe you."

"Where are we going?" asked Mikka.

Finn looked at the westering sun sinking into the tatters of cloud. "Sundown should see you off the coast of Starsey in this wind. You can drop us and we'll pay you and be on our way. My advice to you is to do a little quiet exploring of waters away from home for a few months. There are islands to the southeast. The smaller ones are underpopulated and could use some extra fishermen, with a seaworthy boat. And contrary to my first impression this vessel seems to be seaworthy."

"Aye. But it's not ours," said Hrolf with a show of Hallgerd's stubborn honesty. "We owe the owner his share."

"He'll be happy to get it at all, and his boat back too, if you wait a few months. Go back now and Zuamar and Gywndar will kill you and probably sink the boat. But if they're still around in a few months, you can slip back quietly," said Finn.

Hrolf looked mulish about it. Meb turned to her secret weapon. "You've a duty to Mikka. You promised mother you'd look after him."

"I promised I'd look after you, too," said Hrolf with a reluctant smile. "Only it was usually you looking out for us."

"That's exactly what I am doing this time too," said Meb sternly. "He's no ordinary gleeman, see. You must have realized that?"

"I am not sure just what he is," said Hrolf.

"Well," said Finn, "I am a gleeman. But a few other things too. And here's a suggestion. Put into one of the fishing ports on Starsey. Spend a week or two patching the vessel up, and keep your ear to the ground. Don't get drunk and robbed, just see what's afoot. Mark my words, it'll be safer for you and your families to be away from Yenfar for a few months. Zuamar is burning far too much. And Prince Gywndar is gearing for war. Gleemen get to hear things. Also they saw your yawl, and your friend that ran off will doubtless have told them who you are."

Hrolf spat overboard. "Morin. I'd forgotten him. Well, it's not easy advice to follow because it makes us look like thieves."

"A thief doesn't come back with a cargo of good stockfish. I know the cod will be running off Marslet and the catches will be poor off Tarport. If anyone is fishing out of Tarport."

Hrolf nodded. "True. I'd forgotten somehow that we weren't even being allowed to work our trade. It's our livelihood. We always paid tax on it too. That is their livelihood. What kind of madness is stopping it?"

"The madness of too much power," said Finn. "Who would stop them?"

"You've got a point there," conceded Hrolf. "Well, where do you want to be set ashore?"

"This side of Starsey is shallow-shelving. Try to land anywhere but the deep channels and you'll be grounded a long way from the shore until high tide. So I've a suggestion. Sell us the skiff—you can buy another, and we'll take ourselves in. You can then follow the leading lights into safe anchorage."

Mikka coughed. "Well, gleeman, there's the matter of your apprentice . . ."

"I'll take good care of the Scrap," said Finn. "I need a good juggler. And I always honor my bargains, gentlemen. The Scrap does not belong at sea on a fishing boat." Finn began counting out silver onto the fish-hatch. "That's what we owe you, and a fair payment for the skiff."

Mikka said nothing except a quiet "ah" of pain, because Meb had slipped behind him and taken his hand in the grip she'd learned from fighting with them, and was pushing his pinkie-finger in a direction it did not naturally go. "Shut up!" she said quietly in his ear. "Try and stop me and I'll jump overboard after him. I'm a gleeman now."

"Um." said Hrolf, looking at the silver. "Doesn't your apprentice want to stay with us? We're . . . er, kin."

"No," said Meb firmly. "But thank you." She was touched that they cared enough to have even tried. But now they should stop.

And they did. A little later, she, Finn and the pup were paddling away in the little skiff—barely big enough for three fishermen but roomy enough for a puppy, Finn and Meb, heading toward the dark mass of the shoreline, away from the yawl, which was picking its way slowly to the pinprick lights further along the coast.

That almost forgotten small fishing village girl part of Meb did give a small sniffle at leaving the last of her Yenfar roots behind. But then the half-grown puppy stuck its nose in her ear.

"Cheer up, Scrap," said Finn. "In an hour or two we'll be enjoying supper. I happen to know of a good inn built in a most auspicious spot.

"Auspicious spot?"

"Well, it will be lucky to have us anyway. Let's hope you and your faithful hound don't get us thrown out. Will you tell it to stop putting its nose into my neck while I row? And pull a bit harder on your side. We'll be heading out to sea again at this rate."

"Yes, Finn. Pup, come here. I think he's hungry."

"He's always hungry. And he needs a name. Something like Díleas."

"Díleas." She tasted the word. "Odd word. It . . . really fits him. Why call him that, Finn?"

"Because it means 'loyal' in an old tongue, and because that is his name."

═ Chapter 36 ═

THE INN EXTENDED A WARM WELCOME TO THOSE WHO HAD SILVER. And Fionn was, here, making no pretense that he did not have that. It wasn't gold, so it was easier to part with. Yes, enough silver would buy gold. But it wasn't quite the same as handing out gold.

He hadn't been joking when he said that the inn was in an auspicious place, although there were many who might have been a little puzzled by what he meant, including the innkeeper. They were less aware of the great dyke of ironstone that ran behind it to the sea, that drew lightning and even lodestones. It was a place, Fionn knew, that played hob with many forms of divination and augury, where the forces of nature put out signs which could be confused with powerful magic. He would put what protections he could around her, but the Scrap was radiating magical force in such a way as to make her too easy to trace. Her brush with the Angmarad had left her even more charged with potential. He was going to have to explain this to her sometime. And possibly explain who was hunting her, and why. But first, tonight hopefully, Fionn needed some time with his gold.

They ate—the innkeeper soothed about having a scruffy young dog called Díleas in his inn, watching them at table, by the passing of some silver. After the innkeeper's pretty young daughter had served a good meal of rabbit and pearl onions cooked in cider, with a rhubarb tart with egg custard for afters, Fionn pushed his chair back. "Baths and bed, Scrap. We'll worry about tomorrow, tomorrow."

✧   ✧   ✧

Washing all over in hot water was something that hadn't come
Meb's way much before. Not that they hadn't washed in the village
at least every year . . . but all that water, hot, all to herself? The
problem, the innkeeper's daughter assured her, was cold water.
There was a hot spring—one of many, just up the slope from the
inn. Hot water was piped from there.

Díleas regarded it with extreme suspicion too—as well he
might, because Meb decided that if she was going to wash he
could be washed too. She discovered that it was a wonderful,
relaxing luxury.

He did not.

Sleep, warm, dry and comfortable with Díleas looking like a
black and white fluff-ball with sharp-pointed ears next to her,
was like a deep well that swallowed her down into its stillness.
Somewhere in its depths she dreamed of dragons.

Fionn had no time for dreaming. Instead he'd slipped away up
the hill across frost-hard fields to change into his true form and
launch across the ironstone. Here the warmth that the dark rock
had absorbed during the day lent lift to his wings as he beat his
way upward toward the sliver of moon sailing in the dark sky. He
took the hammer with him. Tonight was no time for the conclave.
Instead he headed to his gold-store and lay for as long as he felt he
could afford to, before launching down toward Yenfar. Things were
considerably simpler without a human in tow. He worried about her,
naturally. He'd taken what precautions he could, and laid protections
about her. And even on the dog. He was beginning to wonder if
it would be worth getting her to raise a horse from a foal . . . but
there probably wouldn't be the time, let alone a place.

He'd become fond of Díleas, he had to admit. The young
animal's trust was disarming. And dogs were peculiarly sensitive
to creatures of energy. He'd serve as a warning for the creatures
of smokeless flame. The pup had of course been shaped by her
and that dratted dvergar device, becoming what she wanted him
to be—yet remaining himself. She had good material to work on.
Sheepdogs were known to be smart.

A little later, refreshed, he set off for Yenfar, heading for a
stream from which a dverg artificer had just taken a fish. Breshy-
Dvalinn was so absorbed in it that he did not notice a dragon.
Fionn decided he'd better have words with Motsognir about that, so

they'd at least send a minder out with him. The tweak her magical interference had made in the place was a minor one. Adjusting the water energies of it—he could no more pass it by than he could do without gold—took a few moments. It was fortunate that many things simply re-aligned themselves, or it would take him months to cover a hundred yards, he thought.

He waited until the black-haired dverg had his salmon safe in the coracle before he called out. The dverg-artificer was undoubtably a genius with metalwork but he was also quite simple-minded in other respects. It sometimes seemed to be like that with the greatest. He could get very upset if he lost his fish. Upset enough to refuse to help, even if it was in his best interest. "A splendid fish," said Finn, as the dverg admired it.

"You nearly made me drop it!" he said fiercely. "Oh. It's you again. What do you want this time? How is the human-girl?"

"I've come to return some property," said Fionn. "And she's still pretending to be a boy. Quite successfully, thanks to you. I wasn't really prepared for some of the side-effects of such a powerful piece of magery, though."

"It was a good piece of work, wasn't it," Breshy said, pleased. "And she's given me great pleasure with the gift of the fish. So what did you steal that you're bringing back to us this time? We did an inventory after you left. Didn't notice anything gone."

Fionn smiled. "A hammer. I didn't personally relieve the dvergar of it."

The dverg exhaled slowly, his breath whistling between his teeth as he nodded. Then he said: "Well, you'd better come and see Motsognir. I'll take you down. It was his before it passed into my use. We've made others, you know."

"I thought as much," said Fionn as they slipped under the lip.

"It is still nice to have it back. The merrow were good custodians, though. We ended up doing a lot of business with them."

"A situation they'd prefer to see continue. They weren't too happy to give it up, but they needed the Angmarad."

"Ah. They have that back?" They walked on, down tunnels that Fionn had not even known existed. He was able to sense tunnels from above . . . but these must be very deep. They were warm enough. And with dvergar, you never knew quite what they hid. They were clever enough and understood enough to hide even from him.

Fionn shook his head. "They wisely let it go. It has returned to being part of the primal magic of the oceans. Theirs to draw on, but not to try to constrain."

"No wonder the alvar are spitting mad," said the dvergar.

"My heart pumps soggy curds for them," said Fionn as they reached a step and door, and he helped the dverg pull his fish up and through.

"Which heart? You have several," asked the dverg.

"You know too much," said Fionn with a wry grin.

"Yes. We do. Only the centaurs know more. The sea will be in their debt for returning its power."

"Indeed. But they didn't. The little human did," said Fionn, slyly. "So if there is a debt, that's where it lies."

"Your doing, Fionn? Clever," said his guide, as they came to huge chamber where many of the dvergar were happily at work—including their king.

"I have my moments. Ah, Motsognir."

The dvergar king looked up at him from the anvil. "And now?"

"Just this," said Fionn, producing the blueish silver hammer. It generated a suitable number of amazed comments and exclamations as he handed it to the dvergar king.

Motsognir held it. Felt its weight. Stood up and hefted it at the anvil—which broke in two. "To make sometimes you have to break," he said wryly. "It was never the easiest of tools, this one. But much thanks, Fionn. And to what do we owe its return? And what do we owe *for* its return?"

"The people beneath the waves have the Angmarad returned to the waters. It was not right that you should no longer have your treasure back."

"We've made several more, you know," said Motsognir, echoing his son's words.

"So I've just been told. But this is an old one."

Motsognir smiled. "Dragon logic. You like old things. We like to make things. We'll melt old things down to make new and better. Old things have worth only if the artifice of making them has been lost. We still know all of those arts. Still, it's a very rare alloy, and we appreciate the gesture. So what can we do for you?"

"There is the matter of the dragon treasure," said Fionn.

He was prepared to meet resistance. He was prepared to exercise his persuasiveness. The dvergar were intrinsically honorable, though . . . they'd agree in the end.

He wasn't prepared for the smirks and snickers that gave way to outright laughter.

"All right. What's the joke?" he asked, smiling back. There was no point in doing otherwise. Getting upset with dvergar was an exercise in futility.

Motsognir wiped his eyes. "What was the treasure of the dragons, Fionn?"

"A dragon. Made of gold."

"Very precise and lifelike it was," said Motsognir. "Who made it, with you dragons not being known for artifice?"

"The dvergar . . ." Fionn looked suspiciously at him. "Are you saying it was another of your tricks? You got every dragon in whole of the new Tasmarin to give gold and a small part of their magic to it. Even me."

"Their virtue went to the dragon statuette? The thing was not very large. Dragons hate giving away gold. You were one of the more generous, as I recall. A half-ducat."

"I've got rather a lot of those," Fionn admitted. "But I didn't want to draw attention to that fact. So I kept it small."

"It was all melted down, and blended together. Some of the gold went into stabilizing the plane. I believe you also had something to do with that," Motsognir said pointedly.

Fionn shrugged. "It's what I do. And seeing as I was stuck here, at first I thought it might be a good idea. I've changed my mind."

"So have we. But there was a very little gold left over. Enough for a hollow statuette."

"We all saw it."

"There was no virtue, no magic in the statuette."

"There was a great deal of magical power in it!" Fionn was starting to get a little irritated now. He remembered it perfectly, of course. He remembered everything.

"Oh yes. But the statuette was just a lost-wax casting. For pretty. We put no dvergar magic into it. The magic was in the gold itself, not the object."

Fionn blinked. He'd never fully understood dvergar magic, but it was in making of things, not just in the nature of the material.

The Angmarad . . . both the raw stuff and the structure of it, had been full of ocean magic. But the dvergar could take plain iron ore, and in their making, make it powerful. "So just what have you done with it?" he asked suspiciously as they watched and waited, with little twinkles showing in those dvergar eyes. They were enjoying every moment of this. And he'd hardly ever played any practical jokes on them!

"We gave it to you. Or at least we gave it to her. The little human mage you had in your care. It seemed right that humans had one of the great treasures."

Realization dawned on Fionn. "You reworked it?"

"Yes. We put a great deal of our own magic and some of hers into it this time. And the gold still has all its own magic. It is now a great deal more powerful than it was," said Dvalinn earnestly.

"You are a bunch of lunatics," said Fionn, as the entire shaggy black-haired bunch of reprobates laughed themselves into near apoplexy.

Eventually Motsognir had a coughing fit and managed to stop. "It serves our purpose. We think the towers need to come down. We wish it could be otherwise, Fionn."

"I think I'll have that drink you were about to offer me. You need one too, you devious old . . ."

"Friend, I think," said Motsognir. "Let's have some mead. What have you done with her, by the way? We liked her."

"She's on Starsey," said Fionn. "Safe, I hope. I put enough protection around her, and it's not an easy place to find. But I want to be back there by morning."

Motsognir handed him a tankard of mead. "Then you'd better drink up and get going. It is not long until the dawn."

═ Chapter 37 ═

VORLIAN HAD REACHED HIS DECISION. THE SKY HAD NOT EVEN begin to pale when he lumbered into flight. Taking the fight to another dragon was poor strategy, but he could see that he had little choice about it. Zuamar was a danger to them all. Besides he'd come here, into the territory Vorlian considered his own. The time had come to deal with him. Dragons were not early risers. They liked the heat of the sun to make flying easier. Vorlian hoped to be high up above his enemy's eyrie before then. Circling and waiting.

Zuamar had had traffic with creatures of smokeless flame before. He trusted them not at all, naturally. But they could make the kind of charm he needed, so he'd gone searching, and found them on a fumarole some seventy leagues away. They'd been cooperative. And he could spare a few hundred humans and some alvar to pay the debt. If they wanted slaves, they'd get them. He wanted to catch the guilty dragon. He was sure that it would turn out to be his neighbor, Vorlian. Upstart. This way he'd know for certain, *and* catch the human mage.

The amulet with the ducat in it pulled towards the dragon-magic that had flavored it.

Zuamar expected to fly to Starsey.

Instead he found himself drawn back towards Yenfar. It was a long flight through the night. Anger lent him strength. So the offspring of a diseased wyrm thought to raid Yenfar while its master was away? He doubted that the dragon would get through the booby traps that protected his hoard. But it still made him nervous. And very angry. Angrier than he had been in centuries.

Fionn hastened down the long passages of the dvergar's hidden kingdom, up to the water-door. He could only go as fast as the dverg guide, but he wanted to run. It was going to be awkward if he got back to the inn late, after they'd got up. Besides there were risks to flying over Zuamar's—and then Vorlian's—territory in daylight. A black dragon was hard to see at night, and all too easy in daylight. He did not wait for a coracle-lift out but simply dived into the icy water and swam out, and then on rocks at the far side of the long pool transformed himself and took flight into the predawn.

And that was when he realized that he was too late and in trouble. Because laboring in from the south was the bulk of another dragon. And far off, to the west . . . was yet another set of wings silhouetted against the sky.

Fionn used the fact that he was fresh and relatively rested to beat his way up into the sky. He pondered the idea of fleeing and hoping that he could simply outfly the closer dragon and that the second one was merely there in passing. But the nearer dragon—it looked like Zuamar now, was using all of his strength to close the distance. And even if Fionn outflew him . . . well, the second dragon was between him and Starsey. So Fionn kept gaining height. He had an advantage up there. Zuamar might possibly burst one of his hearts flying like that, which would solve some of Fionn's problems. Fionn could not kill him. It was imprinted into the very threads of Fionn's being. Zuamar had no such constraints in his make-up. Of course if old carrion breath would drop dead or fly into a cliff himself—well, that went beyond the caution laid on Fionn by the First.

Zuamar—by dint of super-dragon effort—had managed to gain enough height to try a rising blast of flame, trying to sear his quarry's wind tendrils and wing webs. He wasn't to know Fionn was more resistant to dragonfire than all the others.

Vorlian saw the start of the aerial duel from a distance, spotting the gout of dragonflame from Zuamar. The big old dragon had quite a range of flame-cast! The smaller dragon flew on however, seemingly unaffected. *It must be the distance, fooling my judgement,* thought Vorlian. *I'd swear he must have seared him.* Vorlian too began to put every last bit of strength into reaching the battle before it was over. If the other dragon had only waited . . . well, maybe it would hurt or weaken Zuamar.

The two were high enough now to gain the first sunlight. And Vorlian could see now that the dragon being chased was black. Black and a great deal smaller than Zuamar.

It ought to be a one-sided contest.

Looking south, Fionn saw that Vorlian was the second dragon he'd seen, and that he was now heading for the two of them. Fionn allowed himself a brief irritated snort of flame. So these two had now allied? Unless they were most conveniently planning to fight each other? Well, he'd have to deal with the situation . . . best to get Zuamar out of the way quickly then. He turned in a sudden sharp dive, neatly tearing Zuamar's left outer wing-web on the way into a steep bank and a corkscrew away from frantic talons, to snatch at Zuamar's tail as he went past and tumble the heavier dragon onto the torn wing. Zuamar tried to turn and flame—and managed to burn his own wing.

Fionn, smaller, faster and not dead tired from a long flight, streaked below him and twisted up overhead again, as Zuamar struggled with one burned wing and with a near useless wingtip, to cope with his smaller attacker—who had managed to get behind and above him again, and . . . when Zuamar tried desperately to turn and dive . . . did not come in for the coup de grace. Instead he side-slipped and ripped a talon through the opposite wing-web. As a parting blow he gave Zuamar a wallop with his tail that was hard enough to crack the diamond-hard scales, and send Zuamar reeling across the sky. The aerial duel raged on, with the smaller, faster, more agile opponent driving Zuamar towards death from exhaustion if nothing else.

Vorlian saw—as he flew closer, how the smaller black dragon—that he had now recognized as the impertinent Fionn—gave the far larger Zuamar a lesson in aerial combat. But Fionn was obviously unprepared for his successes—he'd missed two good opportunities for the kill, and he seemed very little affected by Zuamar's frantic blasts of dragon-fire. If anything Zuamar kept burning himself.

✧   ✧   ✧

Zuamar recognized his opponent. And knew fear. He knew
that Fionn was not just smaller. He'd also been there from the
very origins of this plane. Fionn had been the same size back
then, unlike other dragons that kept growing with age. Zuamar
suspected that he was not quite the same kind of dragon as the
others of Tasmarin. He'd . . . known too much. Always had a smart
answer. Zuamar had been a relatively young dragon then, but
the older ones, dead now, had been wary of him. Now Zuamar
knew why. Fionn was wholly unaffected by Zuamar's fire, and
far too fast for the talons or tail. Zuamar, burned by his own
fire, dazed, and now suddenly feeling the exhaustion and fear
that Jakarin must have felt, began to flee. It made him an easy
target, he knew. He tried to look back and defend himself as he
struggled to fly away.

Only the black dragon wasn't following. He was gaining height
again.

Zuamar could only think of one reason. The death dive. The
hard, neck-snapping strike. And the hard-bodied little dragon
was capable of that, if he got high enough. Zuamar flew, neck
turned to look back at the black nemesis . . . If he could sideslip
at the last minute . . .

It was only when he flew into a wash of dragon fire that Zuamar realized that he'd got the wrong reason entirely. And, seeing
Vorlian there, desperation led him into a last frantic effort. He
made no attempt to sheer off. Just collided mid-air with the other
dragon. They fell together in a rending tangle of tearing claws
and thrashing tails.

The hungry earth below reached for them both. At the last
minute both struggled free, flapping wildly.

But Zuamar, with torn wing webs, found that he could not
stop falling.

Then rock stopped him instead.

The last thing he knew was that he had failed: human mages
would not all be destroyed. Neither would the dragon that had
raided his territory.

Vorlian barely managed to spiral out of the tangle to catch air
in outspread, desperate wings. He had fallen too fast and too far!
There was no way he could remain airborne. The injury from the

storm was a screaming agony now, as he frantically air-braked. It was still never going to be enough. He landed hard.

With a muddy splash.

Zuamar had struck a rock-ridge. Vorlian had been luckier. He'd landed in a peat bog instead, and had struck it moving a great deal slower than Zuamar had.

He was in pain, covered in glutinous black mud, and his wing was injured.

But he was alive.

Zuamar was not. It took a great deal of force to sever a dragon head. The speed of the fall and impact with the rocks had provided that.

Vorlian tried to move. Winced. He was a sitting duck like this. He struggled to pull free of the bog.

Fionn glided in to a perfect four point landing on a rock spike—out of easy flaming range. But then he hadn't taken advantage of Zuamar's incapacity either. Maybe he didn't want to flame Vorlian? The black dragon appeared completely uninjured, and perfectly capable of killing a trapped dragon.

"Just what, in the name of the seven hot places, are you doing here, Vorlian?" the smaller dragon asked. Fionn's voice was tinged with irritation, but he did not sound particularly aggressive about his questioning.

Vorlian was too sore for sophistry. "I came over here to fight Zuamar. He's been tresspassing in my air-space. Threatening my kine with elimination."

Fionn snorted. "He was one of the old ones, Vorlian. He's had more dragon fights than you've had sheep for breakfast. I always thought you were one of those who could rise above this. Anyway, I have things to do, and you appear not too badly hurt. Are you going to live without my help? Because I'm running late. Got Tasmarin to destroy, and time and arcane forces wait for no dragon."

He always made those inane comments—but he did not seem to have any interest in taking advantage of the situation Vorlian found himself in. "I've hurt a wing. I don't think I can fly for a few days. And I am stuck in this vile mud," said Vorlian.

Fionn chuckled. "The mud saved your life. So I'd be polite about it. Speaking from experience—you're sinking into it, and the more you struggle deeper you'll get. There is only one way

out. You need to transform yourself. You do still remember how?"
asked Fionn, sardonically.

"It is demeaning to take on any form but that of noblest of
creatures," Vorlian said, shocked despite the circumstances.

"I'm sure your mother said that to you," said Fionn. "But
right now you need to ask whether drowning in mud is any less
demeaning. A wyrm—one of the old forms—should get you out.
If it was good enough for your forefathers, it's good enough for
you. And don't go looking for Zuamar's hoard when you do get
out. He had some of the nastiest traps that you can imagine. Now,
I will leave you to decide whether you prefer being demeaned or
drowned. I've got work to do."

And he took off gracefully and flew away to the east. Toward
Starsey.

Vorlian had to wonder about his own hoard.

And then if he could still remember how to do what every
young dragon did . . . and was told off by its mother for doing.

Vorlian wondered just who Fionn was. And what his business
could be. Vorlian wasn't even sure which island he had his eyrie
on. He was always just around.

After one or two abortive attempts Vorlian found that cellular
memory still worked. He became a mighty wyrm and managed
to wriggle his way free of the bog. He could no longer see Fionn
in the sky, and in truth he was too sore and exhausted to care.
He dragged himself into the cover of a nearby pine-wood and
slept like the dead.

═ Chapter 38 ═

MEB'S MORNING BEGAN WITH A THUNDEROUS KNOCKING. SHE HAD barely sat up in bed when the scowling innkeeper burst in . . . with the daughter of the house who had waited on them and run Meb's bath. He appeared to be holding her by the ear. She was in tears.

Meb hadn't actually had enough experience of waking up in inns to be absolutely sure that this wasn't the normal way that for people to be roused. To her, "usual" was Finn waking her and having the two of them slip out in the darkness. That probably wasn't normal either. But it did seem odd.

Díleas—whose experience of beds, let alone inns, had to be less than hers, let her know that he also thought so. He growled, sounding, for a half-grown pup, quite alarming.

It wasn't enough to make an impression on the innkeeper. "Boy, where is your master?" he demanded.

She blinked. "In his bed, I should think."

"Ha! It's not been slept in!" said the innkeeper damningly.

Meb gaped at him, and piled out of bed herself, then pushed past him and ran to see, with Díleas at her heels, bouncing in delight.

The bed had plainly not even been sat on. And the window was open. It was bitterly cold in there. The larger of the bags he carried was still there, leaning against the wall. Looking at it, Meb found the only relief to be scavenged from the room with its neatly made and turned down bed.

"Where is he?" she demanded fiercely of the innkeeper. "What have you done with my master? Tell me!"

"Me?" The innkeeper was plainly rocked in his tracks by the savagery of her demand. "I've not seen him since last night. It's what you've done to my innocent young daughter, you serpent!"

"Your daughter! But . . . I've done nothing to your daughter." Behind her father's back the pretty apple-cheeked young woman looked at her imploringly.

The innkeeper sneered at her scornfully. "Oh yes you have, you vile deceiver. She's admitted the whole of it to me. Her mother and I found her bed with a bolster in it and we were waiting for her when she came sneaking in, just before dawn. She tried to put the blame on your master first to protect you! That's when we discovered that he was missing and the whole wicked truth came out. You seduced her with lies and promises when she took you up to your bath."

"What?!" Meb could scarcely believe that this was not just another strange dragon-dream.

"This wicked girl admits that she spent the night with you, and that you satisfied your carnal lusts on her, having beguiled her with your promises," said the innkeeper triumphantly. "You'll have to marry her and make an honest women of her now. You offered her that! I'll see that you make it good, you young limb."

"Marry? But, but. Uh . . ."

"You'll not weasel out of it, boy. My brother is the Mayton Lawman. Breach of promise will be enough to see you rot in jail or be sold. And you can't fool me. You're no traveling gleeman. Not with that kind of money!" There was a look of greed behind his righteous indignation. "Now, when will your master be back?"

Meb desperately wished that she had the least idea. Or even knew where he'd gone. He might have gone to the moon for all she knew. She was badly rattled by his sudden vanishing. Yes, he did strange, inexplicable things. Yes, he was no gleeman—although he was very good at being one. Yes, he seemed adept at getting out of tight spots. That didn't stop her worrying, did it? She was a lot more worried about him than the threat of being forcibly married to this silly girl. After all, she could just drop her trousers and prove her innocence. It wasn't something she was eager to do, but if Finn was not around . . . "He will be back when he's finished transacting his business," she said airily.

"Just what is your master's business?" asked the Innkeeper, suddenly suspicious.

"I'm really not supposed to say," said Meb, thinking desperately, as it also suddenly occurred to her that she had very little money.

The innkeeper, who was built like a side of pork, cracked his knuckles. "You'd better."

"Um. Well, we're traders."

"Where's your pack train? Your guards?" said the innkeeper, his face a fine example of what disbelief looked like.

"We, uh, trade in small valuable items. Pack trains get attacked and robbed. No one bothers gleemen." She hoped desperately that he would believe her.

"Oh. Jewels," he said knowingly.

"Possibly," said Meb, cautiously.

He seemed to take that as a "yes." And also that that was a good thing for his daughter. He made his best effort at an avuncular smile. "Well, boys and girls will be boys and girls, eh? She'll make you a very fine wife."

Meb tried to look as if the soft complexion, blue eyes and rosebud lips of the innkeeper's daughter, not to mention the generous curves that nature had not seen fit to give to Meb, were something she might find attractive. It wasn't easy. In the meanwhile she needed to find a way to get herself, Díleas and Finn's pack away from here. A fire or an earthquake or something.

Fionn was moderately tired by his brush with Zuamar. The constraint against killing generally lay within Fionn's natural bent anyway. He was involved in the manipulation of forces of vast power—he understood the need for such limitations. It was just a pain when it came to dealing with the likes of Zuamar. Still, things had worked out in the end. Yenfar would acquire another dragon ruler—probably not Vorlian—and the senseless killing would stop. And if all went to plan, it would stop mattering soon. Right now he had practical problems to deal with. A dragon, in daylight, was one of the most obviously visible things. It was just his ill-luck that right now it was a beautiful, clear, crisp, winter morning. Vorlian of course would not be on Starsey to challenge the interloper. But it did mean Fionn would have to land some distance from the inn and then walk back. Which all took time, and his human charge was accustomed to rising early.

He hoped that she would not panic if she found him missing.

Her power in a panic might have all sorts of undesirable consequences, not least that, in spite of the natural cover provided by that locale, she would show the searchers just exactly where she was. She was also all too good at getting herself into trouble without him.

"Why am I smelling smoke?" said Meb, sniffing.

This was not a faint scent of it in the distance either. A strong smell of burning was drifting up the stair. The innkeeper turned and ran. "The bread. I forgot the bread!"

It smelt like more than bread burning to Meb. But she wasn't going to look a gift fire in the mouth. She grabbed Finn's pack. Her own little bag of belongings—her juggling balls, and a few other pieces, was also was also packed, ready. She just had to grab it and run...

And then she realized that the stupid girl had not run after her father. "Go. Your inn is on fire!" Meb said.

"I'm coming with you. He'll kill me if you're gone," said the girl. "He beats me."

At least she wasn't trying to stop Meb. "I don't want to marry you," said Meb, having retreated to her room to pull her boots on. There was a yell to fetch water from downstairs.

"I just said that to stop him hitting me. If he knew I was really with Justin, he'd have killed me. He hates Justin. When I said it was your master... he was quite pleased. My father said that he must be a smuggler."

Meb opened her window. It was a long way down. "Is there any other way out of here?

The girl nodded. "There's a ladder from the loft. It's quite steep."

"Show me."

So the girl did. There was a narrow winding stair at the end of the passage that led into the loft. A little door led out and to a ladder stapled to the outer wall. Meb was alerted to the fact that dogs are not much good at ladders by Díleas's worried whine, when she began to climb down. She came up again and put him into the larger bag, slung it over her shoulder, tied hers to her waist and climbed down the ladder into the stableyard.

The girl climbed down halfway and then dropped. As, in terms of weight, she was bigger than Meb, they and Díleas ended up flat on the stable-yard floor. "You're supposed to catch me," said the girl. "Justin does."

"Well, stick to falling on top of him then," said Meb, standing up and dusting herself off. "We'd better leg it."

The inn was at a crossroads, with the main coast road that ran a mile or two inland of the sand-dunes, a track that ran to the beach and a little fishing harbor, and the road up the fertile valley between high ridges. The obvious start direction was up the coast road as the kitchen of the inn—and its fire—was around the back and the inn faced the coast road. The bulk of the building sheltered them from view . . . For the first few hundred yards. The truth was that Meb didn't want to go too far. She wanted to go up that steep slope behind the inn—and watch for Finn. And get rid of this annoying liar of a girl.

It soon appeared that that was not going to be so easy. For starters, although the girl couldn't climb, Meb, loaded down with her bag and with Finn's heavy pack, couldn't immediately outwalk her. No wonder Finn always seemed to have something for every emergency! This pack must weigh nearly as much as she did.

And the girl seemed determined to stick as close as glue. Meb felt faintly guilty about trying to get away, anyway. The girl had only lied because she was being beaten. And she gave Meb useful advice—first about the ladder and now a stile that would let them into a hedged field off to the left, which would allow them to circle back.

Meb soon realized that the lane led back to the small town that the inn was on the edge of, and that it hadn't been for Meb's benefit that she'd been led there by the girl. There was a large young man with a florid face in the roadway outside one of the cottages. "Justin!" panted the girl.

He looked, shouted "Keri!" and turned and ran up to them. Oh well, thought Meb, that's that problem solved. It was only when he knocked her down, that Meb realized that this was not the case.

"Steal my woman, would you, you little bas—" He reached down to grab Meb and Díleas jumped up and bit him on the cheek. The pup dropped back to earth and stood next to her growling like a full-grown wolf, not a puppy with very new teeth.

Meb, the initial shock now gone, did her best to swear louder than Díleas could growl. The young man probably hadn't grown up around fishing boats. He began pulling at the hedgerow for a stick, blood on his face and murder in his eye as the innkeeper's daughter clung ineffectually to his cloak.

Meb decided that if she was going to get beaten up or even killed she wasn't going to make it easy, not when he swung a heavy dead branch at Díleas. He dared try to hit her dog! She slipped her arms free of the pack, and struggled to her feet and ran at him, head down, fists flailing. He stepped aside almost contemptuously, lifting the branch . . . Only he'd miscalculated, quite seriously, on two things. One was the girl Keri clinging to him, which slowed him down, and the other was Díleas, whose teeth closed on his calf. Meb's head hit him in the solar plexus and he fell over Díleas. Then he caught a knee against his jaw as he fell, and a fist against his ear. He landed with a solid crack on the roadway, stunned, with the breath knocked out of him, and his tree-limb lost from his grasp.

Meb scrambled to her feet, grabbing the limb. Díleas danced around him, snarling and nipping. "You . . . you touch my dog, or me and I'll . . . I'll march your teeth out of your butt like parading soldiers," snarled Meb. "I've never touched this stupid girl of yours."

"There they are!" shouted the innkeeper. "It's that thieving scum Justin! He must have set fire to the kitchen for the little bastard."

There seemed to be quite a mob of people with him. "He's kidnapped my daughter and run off without paying the bill. Get them!"

Meb grabbed Finn's pack and bolted. She was aware that the man she'd fought, the girl and Díleas were running too. She was also aware of a big spiky dragon-shadow suddenly darkening the sky and terrified yells and screams. But mostly she was aware that it was time to run, and to keep running for as long as she could.

=== Chapter 39 ===

FIONN FEATHERED HIS WINGS TO ALLOW HIM TO STALL AND DROP just short of the ridge. Burning buildings, and a mob chasing her . . . It would seem that his Scrap was doing her usual best to raise chaos! And trust the dvergar to make his life complicated. He carefully scratched a set of symbols on the edge of the ridge. It would take a while for the spell to work, but such forces were intertwined. He'd laid the foundation for this spell on Morrisey Island years before.

He changed and trotted down through the coppiced woodland to the path that they had been running down. It would take the citizens of Vorlian's demesne some time to recover from having their hair frizzled by a breath of dragon-fire above them. Vorlian was, by dragon standards, a very enlightened overlord, who generally confined himself to consuming their taxes, occasional livestock and miscreants. A strange dragon was going to have the locals in fits and squalling for their protector—who was conveniently absent. If Fionn was any judge, he wouldn't be flying back for at least three or four days, by which time Fionn had every intention of being elsewhere.

He could hear them panting along so he sat down to wait.

Then there was excited flurry of barking and the black and white sheepdog pup ran up to him and danced gleefully around him. Fionn was rather surprised at the joyous reception he was getting.

✧　　✧　　✧

Díleas suddenly barked and ran ahead. Meb was barely staggering by now. But she looked up to see what form of trouble had
found them this time. The relief at seeing Finn standing there with
Díleas up on hind legs yipping excitedly was almost too much.
"Oh master! I thought you'd gone off without us," she panted out,
dropping his pack, and doing her best not to join Díleas.

"Now, Scrap. As if I'd do that," he said, cheerfully. "Anyway, it
seems that you have found help." He looked at the innkeeper's
daughter and her lover, who had panted to a halt. "And one who
has taken some blows for you, by the looks of it," he said, looking at the young man.

"Huh," said Meb. "She caused all this trouble telling her father
that first you . . . and then when you were away, that *I* was her
lover. And I had to hit him," Meb pointed, "because he tried to
hit Díleas."

Finn laughed. "Serves him right. And the fire?"

"I had nothing to do with it. Her father said he'd have me
locked up if I didn't marry his daughter. So when the kitchen
caught fire, I ran away."

Finn laughed some more, this time until tears ran down his
face. "I see the bride followed you, Scrap. She'd be well served,
and so would you, if I took you back and let them marry the
two of you off."

"I'd like to go back and explain," said Meb. "We still owe them
for the lodging. But I don't see why I should marry her." She
couldn't exactly point out that it would be a very disappointing
wedding night for both of them.

Finn shook his head. "No, we were well-enough overcharged
yesterday, and seeing as you brought my pack, I've no need to
go back. And explanations are so tedious. We have a ship to
catch, Scrap."

"Erm." The big fellow that had hit her cleared his throat.
"Masters," he said apologetically. "Um. Keri has just told me
what really happened. I must apologize, young master. I . . . I
thought . . . Anyway, is there any chance that you would need a
clerk? I can scribe and do numbers and . . . and if I go back there
old man Branna—the innkeeper, uh, Keri's father, will have me
locked up at best or gelded for rape at worst. I . . . we . . . want
to get away."

"The highway is all yours," said Finn.

"But, please, we have no money," said the girl, smiling at him in a way that would have had Meb's stepmother call her a trollop.

"A common problem . . ." Finn stopped. Sniffed. Looked at the young man, "I'll pay your passage to Lapithidia. A scribe should find work there."

Meb did not like that at all.

"But," said Finn, "I think we need to get off this track and walk across the fields for a while. They're going to be looking for you soon and we want to be in time to catch the tide."

"Not to mention the dragon," said Meb, shuddering.

Finn nodded. "I wouldn't mention that," he said with a foxy grin. "I don't want to catch it."

So they made their way across two sets of fields, and down to the track which led to the coast. After their rather unfortunate start the two newcomers were doing their best to ingratiate themselves with Finn and even Meb. Meb didn't really understand it too well. But she did know that it made her feel uncomfortable. If this Justin was a scribe—a man with a valuable profession—why then had Keri's father been happy to marry her off to an apprentice jewel-trader (or possibly a smuggler)? Why was Justin so happy to leave his home and all his possessions behind? Yes, there had been a mob—but surely he could have simply taken the innkeeper's daughter back and been the hero of the hour? Maybe even been accepted by the innkeeper?

It smelled like old fish. Meb set out to ferret it out of him. And just what had made Finn suddenly decide to help them? Thinking of smells, it was almost as if he'd scented something.

For a small price they got a fishing boat to give them a ride up the coast to a larger port. Meb found that with a little flattery Justin the scribe expanded like a flower in the sun. The poor man had been the victim of such jealous abuse, merely because he was handsome and skilled, she found out. Which was why he just at present was not working. They were complete falsehoods of course, merely because his employer had thought that he was being successful with a landlady that he'd fancied himself. "Meanwhile I was having it off with his wife *and* his daughter." As he was boasting to another, younger male, he felt no need to be shy about his conquests. "Girls can't resist me," Meb was informed. "And they can't get enough." He gestured.

Meb, who had grown up around fishermen, but under Mother

Hallgerd's eye, in an odd combination of coarse terminology, but actual prudery, found it hard to deal with.

"So, youngster...I bet even a pretty boy like you has had some good sluts in your travels," said Justin, now convinced that Meb was his best friend.

"Er." Meb was left literally wordless and blushing.

Justin grinned. Slapped him on the back. "You get some silver out of that old master of yours's strongbox. He must be rolling in it. Keri brought me some she'd prigged last night. He won't miss a bit. I'll lose Keri and we'll go for a night's whoring that you won't forget in a hurry."

Meb retreated in confusion. This was a long way from her romantic ideals. And as if she'd ever take Finn's silver! She had to talk to Finn. Soon.

Fionn had caught the scent of Lyr on the young bravo's clothing. Well, if matters came out as he planned he would need to get a message to the sprites. They were difficult to deal with, unpredictable, and entirely too prone to kill anything that wasn't Lyr. Humans, being humans, found them attractive. So did the alvar, but then the alvar were obsessed with beauty. And even Fionn had to admit that the Lyr were graceful and perfectly symmetrical. If that was what attracted them like moths to a flame, they deserved the Lyr. And splinters, which they'd get from loving plant-women. He looked at the Scrap, deep in conversation with the fellow while the other young woman sat on a coil of rope, combed her long blond hair and stuck her chest out. Fionn hoped that the Scrap wasn't taken with the young man's good looks. He knew the type. Still, they had about five days sailing to Port Lapith, and then they'd be rid of him, and the girl who was making calf-eyes at Fionn, and her lover, alternately. She'd be well served if Fionn took her along on his next little journey.

The magic Fionn had set at work on the ridge spread slowly, aligning particles of iron in the rock. Lines of force spread out from there, the sudden sharp magnetism affecting a sequence of other things. Deep within the earth a number of huge columnar structures—crystals of enormous size—gave out a low note that had dvergar across a thousand islands swearing. The crystals moved fractionally. A deep artesian spring stopped flowing.

Up on the high plains of Lapithidae the waters of the dark pool were still. The watchers watched, reading probable futures.

And then to their horror, the level of the water—constant for millennia—started to drop.

Nothing could have terrified them more.

═ Chapter 40 ═

VORLIAN FOUND THE FLIGHT BACK TO STARSEY QUITE THE HARDEST thing he'd undertaken. It took him three days to get ready to even try it. Lying in the forest, he had time to think a great deal. To watch as first alvar knights came galloping to the scene, and then somewhat later, curious human peasants. Fearful peasantry, but still overwhelmed by a desire to come and gawk. How very human that was! A patrol of alvar cavalry had spotted the trail out of the bog. Vorlian felt that eating two of them and a horse was fair recompense for being pestered with arrows. No more had come that way before he had made a short, labored flight to some nearby cliffs where he'd slept off the meal and begun to recover. It was only a stern sense of duty, and knowing he'd recover a lot faster if back with his gold, that persuaded him to try the flight back at all.

He'd wondered several times on the last section if he'd get there at all or simply fall into the sea. And . . . if he did that, could he transform into a sea-serpent and swim to shore? He'd never swum before.

He made it. Barely. Blown and sore, he landed on the shoreline. Dignity be blowed. He'd walk to the top of the nearest hill . . . when he had recovered his breath.

He was surprised to be approached by a delegation of humans—the dignitaries and Duke Ragath, his alvar princeling. They must have watched his flight. "Lord Vorlian," said the duke, bowing very low. "We are glad to have you back."

Vorlian was sore, tired, hungry . . . and quite surprised. The alvar might be glad, but the rest?

"News of your duel in Yenfar reached us yesterday. A trading ship took advantage of the chaos over there to slip her moorings after dark and come across."

"Zuamar trespassed in my territories. I could not allow that."

The duke looked uneasy. "Er. Another dragon has also done so while you were away."

Territorial anger lent Vorlian strength. "A black dragon?" he said, raising himself up.

"Er, yes," said Duke Ragath.

"I'll flush him out." The anger was just a little tempered by the memory of how Fionn had humbled Zuamar. But . . . Vorlian was a dragon. This was his island and his gold. "Has he been up to my eyrie?"

"Uh. No. Not that we know of. We haven't been up there ourselves," said the duke, wisely. "But I have had a sentry on every hilltop, keeping watch. We've had horsemen ready to warn the human citizenry."

"Is he ravaging the countryside?" asked Vorlian, just a little surprised. Fionn had never seemed the type to ravage anything.

The alvar duke who had plainly been quite proud of the steps he'd taken—and by the nods the civic leadership of the humans had been too—now looked embarrassed. "Um. No. He attacked and attempted to flame a group of people in Lenter-vale. They had a lucky escape, and there was only one injury—a broken arm. But he hasn't been seen since. We've been cautiously scouting, and we've had clear nights too to watch in. Not a dragon to be seen. He's either left, or is lying up somewhere, Lord Vorlian. But unless he walked—and we searched for tracks, he has gone nowhere near your lair."

Vorlian sighed smokily. "Someone get me a couple of sheep. And then leave me in peace. I'll look into it once I've got back to my eyrie and rested for a day or two."

But when, several hours later, he had managed the last few leagues to his eyrie, and had discovered his gold still apparently intact, there was still no rest for him. The creature of smokeless flame had plainly been waiting. There was an aura of power about Belet that made Haborym seem tame. "Congratulations on your defeat of the dragon Zuamar! There were those among us who thought he might be too much for you, but I knew you were made of sterner stuff!"

"Spare me the flattery," said Vorlian. He knew that if it hadn't been for Fionn, Zuamar might well have killed him.

"No flattery! Why, the story of your duel is all over Yenfar."

"And how would you know?" said Vorlian tersely. He was too tired for this.

"I was there. There are smuggling vessels that go to-and-fro all the time. Zuamar's tax collectors charge very high rates. They have the tar-business in a stranglehold."

The fire-being paused. "The alvar nobility over there are up in arms about it. Not directly of course, but I believe that they've sent out an appeal for another protector."

"I have no intention of being overlord there," said Vorlian, yawning. "You'd think they'd be glad to be rid of Zuamar. Who have I got for a new neighbor?"

"High-Lord Myrcupa."

"They may soon wish for Zuamar back again," said Vorlian. "Now, I need to rest. Have you anything else to say?"

"Just that we have these." The fire-being produced a little fire-proof box. Vorlian opened it. There were carefully painted pictures of three humans—a tall thin man with a foxy face, a beardless boy and a broad-shouldered fellow with a trident.

"The middle one is our quarry, disguised as a male. We believe that they fled Yenfar successfully. They were heading for your charming island. The one with the trident is a merrow. We have used the sprite's devotees to start a search—copies of these pictures were at every grove the night before your fight with Zuamar. But when I came here you had already left, Lord Vorlian."

Vorlian looked at the pictures. Thought of the organization on the part of the fire-beings which had gone into this quest and did not like it. "It has been four days. If you haven't found her by now, I doubt if a few hours will make any difference. I am going to rest on my gold, and then I'll see to it that Duke Ragath puts his soldiery to use looking for them. He likes to be busy. Now go away." Vorlian slumped back on his gold.

The next day, however, he was as good as his word. And he flew down to Lenter-vale and tried to get a scent of Fionn.

It was there that they brought him news that the fugitives he sought . . . were also being sought by the local law-guards. For a range of crimes . . . it would appear that the young fresh faced 'boy' was being accused of arson, rape and kidnaping, along with a local man of unsavory character. A petty thief, a ne'er-do-well, an informer. The human mage certainly picked her companions!

And the tall fellow . . . he'd last been seen the night before. They'd made their escape when the dragon had raided Lenter-vale. A little later word came in that the two, dressed as travel-ing gleemen, in the company of a young man and woman who did not appear to be compelled in any way, had taken a passage with a merchant vessel. The destination was unknown, but it had been sailing West.

Vorlian was not stupid. It seemed obvious that the human mage was somehow associated with the dragon Fionn. There were always dragon conspiracies . . . he was part of one, after all. It appeared that the human mage was part of another, with the small black dragon. And they were no longer on his territory. He sent messages to his fellow conspirators asking them to meet. He would also fly to the conclave . . . just as soon as his wings had recovered a little more.

Prince Gywndar of Yenfar looked uncomfortably at his new overlord. High-Lord Myrcupa had been invited to expel the tired and injured Vorlian. Myrcupa had, very conveniently for him, arrived some hours after Lord Vorlian had left. He had, however, wasted no time in stamping his authority on Yenfar. He'd made an example of two human villages. Unfortunately, one of them had been the settlement at Tarpit.

Gywndar was furious. The pit was still burning, sending its vile fumes wafting over the best hunting grounds on the island. Besides, the humans who had worked there were not easy to replace, especially now! Prince Gywndar had sent a respectful but firm message to High-Lord Myrcupa, asking him to come to the palace. Myrcupa had killed the alvar messenger's horse and eaten it. He had sent back a message that if Gywndar wanted to see him, he could come up to his overlord, not the other way around.

And when Gywndar had done so . . . "I want to make it clear to you, Princeling, that the tax revenues need to increase," Myr-cupa informed him.

"My Lord, we'll do our best, but you set fire to our main rev-enue earner," said Gywndar bravely.

A swipe of the dragon-tail knocked him out of the saddle. And then the dragon killed his horse with a backhand slash of one talon. "Are you questioning me?" hissed Myrcupa. "Undermining my authority? Let me make this clear. I will have no such thing and I will have at least one and a half times as much gold. Strike a bit of raw terror into the hearts of these humans. And we need to continue the search for the human mage among them."

Feeling his ribs, and seeing how his precious gray mare had been killed, Prince Gywndar nodded. He was too sore to speak, and he had a long walk back down the mountain.

He had to wonder about the motives of those of his friends among the alvar nobility who had suggested that Myrcupa would do nicely as a suitable old-fashioned dragon lord. It was Lord Rennalinn of Magyn who had been so effusive about how ideal he would be. Even better than Rennalinn's own Brennarn, Gywndar recalled.

"And you need have no fear of a return of Vorlian. I have formed a strategic alliance. Lords Chandagar, Lamdian, Brennarn and I are the largest of the dragonkind. Vorlian might have defeated Zuamar, but he can't deal with more than one of us."

That, somehow, did not make Prince Gywndar feel any better. He did not inform his new liege lord that Zuamar had actually been fleeing a smaller black dragon when he was killed by Vorlian, and that the black dragon had flown from the field of battle without any difficulty.

Nor did the news, later, that a large part of the fishing fleet and their families had fled Tarport during the night improve his temper. Humans!

He could send his swanships after them, but perhaps it would be better to wait until the merrows sued for peace. Gywndar's magicians had the merrows' precious relic and were working on it right now. He hadn't heard from them in some days. The incident with Zuamar's death and the unrest that had followed had kept him from following up on it.

On Cark Island the troops were being assembled. The fire-beings had bought slaves. They had no use for them as slaves, but they made good janissaries. They were completely expendable and in the long term valuable merely as a feint. A distraction. They'd been scattered across the island in many hidden camps. But the time for subterfuge was over. Now they were coming together in a huge, and ever-growing encampment.

The fire-beings were creatures of energy. The stresses and strains in the fabric of the plane that was Tasmarin where obvious to them. Were the place to break up . . . well, without magical protection many of the inhabitants would die. Not the people of smokeless flame. They had their own plans. The hellflame would be seized and safe if it came to that. When they'd discovered the existence of the human mage some two years back the conspiracies they ran as matter of normal business had become focussed on finding her, and using her for the "renewal."

The fire-beings were far more familiar with the energies in this artificial construct than any other species. The effect on the entire ring of conjoined planes from which the raw material of Tasmarin was drawn would be cataclysmic.

This plane might survive, but the others would return to primal fire.

It made for a great deal of new lebensraum, and got rid of a lot of the threats to the people of smokeless flame, not least of all, dragonkind. Dragon-gold—and part of their magical power—had gone into creating this place. Renewal would destroy that.

The planes of existence would be a hotter, better place without the dragons. No other species could survive the home territory of the people of smokeless flame except the dragons. And while alvar magics were effective at banishing fire-beings, dragonfire could consume them utterly—and yet the dragons were immune to the energies of all but the mightiest of the hierarchy of flame.

⸺ Chapter 41 ⸺

FIONN WAITED UNTIL THEY WERE FAR OUT TO SEA, AND WELL
into the second watch of the night, before slipping overboard and
changing his form. He really did not like doing that . . . especially
when after a hundred yards or so a merrow swam up next to
him.

"It's a poor imitation of an orca that you make, at least in your
ability to swim," said the merrow.

"I swim like a rock. I've not had much practice."

The merrow nodded. "That I can see. We had word from the
dvergar thanking us for returning their hammer."

"Umph. Thanking you."

"You could have told us," said the merrow.

"What, and spoil my fun? Besides, 'Brys guessed. Now if you
could do me a small favor I'd be somewhat in your debt. That
vessel over there has the human mage that returned the Angmarad
to the merrow. I've got business to transact elsewhere for a few
hours. Could you keep a watch on it?"

The merrow grinned. "She is as safe with us as it is possible to
be. We knew from the moment she went onto the water. That's
why I am here. There is a debt and we honor those."

"Good, because I have to go and visit the fire-beings."

"They're not overly welcoming," said the merrow.

"I wasn't planning to tell them I was there," said Fionn.

There was a small rocky islet ahead—barely a giant's handful
of boulders sticking out of the sea. Fionn got as close as possible,

transformed himself, and swam ashore. A little later the dragon took to the air, flying towards several fumaroles which smoked and steamed among the ash and pumice of a volcanic vent. He had to land some distance away and swim once again, as darkness and the sulphurous fog were no impediment to the vision of the fire-beings.

But the creatures of energy liked water even less than Fionn did. He swam up a lava tunnel and into caves they were unaware of. From here . . . well, he had to break down a wall, and then walk down several more lava tunnels to the place where the creatures of smokeless flame kept their stock of loot for use on other species. They had no real use for it themselves. The black lava-glass of the tunnels with its clinkery razor edges made for a good defense for the place . . . from anything less tough than a dragon. Fionn had to wait for several of the creatures to pass. It would have been so much simpler to help the flame beings to burn up, but they were still life of a sort. And therefore sacrosanct, at least from direct intervention by him.

Their treasure room had a door—but it was really just to keep the heat out. Its defense was a wall of seething, crackling energy, that would kill energy creatures and almost anything else that lived.

To a dragon it was like a gentle massage. Fionn ignored (not without difficulty) the gold and helped himself to the items he'd come to fetch, and then left. It was hard not to re-organize things or to start some trouble. But under the circumstances it seemed the wisest course, and even if the wisest was not usually his first choice, Fionn simply left.

A little later he was involved in the complicated task of getting back on board a vessel without being seen.

He was helped by the yelling.

The captain, who was trying to keep the shouting protagonists apart, was relieved to see Fionn. Too relieved to worry about the fact that his black hair was still streaming water, and that his clothes had been pulled on in haste.

"Just what is going on here?" boomed Fionn, quelling the riot by sheer volume.

"He hit me!" said Keri.

"I slapped you," said the Scrap. "Because you're a slut and . . ."

"I refused him and he tried to force me," said Keri.

Fionn laughed. He laughed so much he had to hold onto the

rail. "I think it's the sheer inventiveness of your kind that terrifies even the dragons," he said to her.

"You think just because he's your boy-lover he'd never look at a girl? He was being unfaithful to you!" hissed Keri, furiously.

That made Fionn laugh all the more. And the Scrap slapped her again.

Justin surged forward.

Fionn picked him up by the shirt front and deposited him, hard, on his butt on the deck. "Now, let's not have any more of this silliness," he said, firmly. "All of you go back to bed. Your own beds. Young woman," he said to Keri, "you should at least learn to lie a bit better. My apprentice never made any passes at anyone. She has no interest in women, not even ones of negotiable virtue."

Meb gaped at him, at a loss for words.

"Are you saying that he's a girl?" demanded the bravo, rubbing his hind end.

"Yes," said Fionn.

"But . . . he is wearing trousers," said Keri, the boundaries of her world challenged.

"It is possible for females to do so," said Finn. "As the Scrap has lived a rather sheltered life in some ways, I won't ask her to show you. Now be off with you. I paid your passage on this ship. I think the captain will be happy, after this little fracas, to put you off on the first rock we pass if I ask him to. Go. Now."

And they went. So did the crew. Fionn could, at need, command. That left the Scrap standing there, Díleas pressing against her leg. Tears were quietly streaming down her face.

"What is wrong?" asked Fionn gently. Partly he was soothing her because she was possessed of enormous talent, and a dvergar artifact of great power, and if upset, could do anything. Partly he was gentle because . . . well, he was fond of her. He hadn't ever allowed himself to get this close to any other living thing, for this long, in many, many eons.

She sniffed. "I"—she swallowed—"I can't be your apprentice, now that you've found out. I didn't mean to deceive you, Finn! I would never! It just . . . happened."

He fished out a handkerchief from a pocket. He'd left his clothes behind on the boat, and was glad the crew and the combatants hadn't seen him, wet, naked and assisted by a merrow, return to them.

"Wipe away your tears and blow your nose, then. I have always known exactly who and what you are. And I am not precisely an ordinary gleeman, as I think you've realized, Scrap. You must have realized that by now. My . . . trade hasn't had an apprentice for a long time. It was about time that I trained someone."

"You're . . . you're not just going to send me away?" she said in a voice full of both doubt and hope.

"Where do you get these odd ideas from?" asked Fionn.

Her little face lit up. "Thank you. Oh, thank you, master."

He had meant it as a comforting hug. She clung to him as if she was drowning. She lifted her face to be kissed. So he did.

Some long moments later, it occurred to him that when he next saw that black-hearted son of a ymir-maggot Motsognir, or Dvalinn for that matter, he was going to do something particularly fiendishly nasty to them. Steal all their treasures or something. The artifact they'd given her was thick with dragon magic, dvergar magic and of course her own. It would help her to become what she wished to be—which right now, was to be his lover. He pushed her away, but gently.

Instantly she was contrite, making him feel considerably worse about it. "I'm sorry, master, uh, Finn. I . . . I didn't mean to . . ."

He lifted her downcast chin. "But you did want to."

She nodded.

Finn sighed. "I wanted to, too." He did not explain why, or that love among his kind was brief. "But it cannot be, Anghared."

"My name is Meb."

Fionn smiled to hide his sadness. "It is given to me that I should know the names of all things. There are fewer names than you would think. They tend to get re-used . . . but I know all of them. That was your birth name. 'Meb' was merely what your stepmother called you. But that is why I cannot be what you wish me to be. I am not your of kind, my small scrap of humanity."

"I know. You're a mage. I know the dragons want to kill you, Finn. They kill all human magic workers. But you're cleverer than they are. And Díleas and I will keep watch for you." She patted the pup.

Fionn rubbed his face. "I think it is time I corrected a few of your misapprehensions. Scrap, it is not me that the dragons want to kill. It's you."

"Me? Why?" Her eyes twinkled with the audacity that she'd been learning, slowly. She cheerfully contradicted him now. It would have been hard to imagine once. "No, Finn. Sorry, but you have it wrong. I know that it's you. I'd never betray you, though. It is . . . too important to me."

Humans, thought Fionn, were rather like dogs. He'd got very used to having this one around him. It was not pleasant to hurt her. But it had to be said. "There are reasons why it cannot be me, just as there are reasons why you could not have impregnated that young woman, Scrap. You see, I am not human, whereas you are. I am the thing you fear and hate most. I am a dragon."

"You . . . look very human, Finn," she said, failing to restrain the dimple in her cheek.

This was not going quite as he had foreseen. "Dragons can take on a number of other forms, Scrap. I am . . . unusual, even among them. You are even more unusual. You do not belong here. My work—to put it in simple terms—is to put everything in the right places so that energies may balance. I know these things, just as I know where the trees and rocks belong. Do you remember the milestone we moved?"

"Yes. It was quite heavy." She reached out and put her hand on his arm. "It doesn't matter. I won't trouble you if . . . if you don't want me. I am happy just to be your apprentice. For always and always."

Her power was quite terrifying and she did not even know she was doing it. "Scrap . . ."

She continued, a look of trust in her eyes, that serious intent expression on her face that she got when she focussed her attention on anything—which was when she worked her magics best. "And it wouldn't matter to me if you were a dragon. Or an alvar with glamor to fool me with appearances, Finn. You are just Finn. Just like the mountain looked like all sorts of things but it was always Groblek. The world is a strange place, full of stranger things than I could have imagined once. I'm just a poor girl from a small fishing village. I don't know very much, or understand what you're doing. But I've seen enough to trust you. That is all."

Fionn sighed. "And you are probably going to drive me mad, Scrap. It's time you got some rest. I've still got other work to do." He dug out his charts and spread them close to the deck-lamp. He didn't actually need the light any more than he actually needed the charts.

✧   ✧   ✧

Sleep was very far from Meb as she obediently lay down on the plaited straw pallet on the deck and pulled both her cloak and the blanket tight around her—and then opened it up again to let Díleas in. She needed her dog's simple unquestioning love now more badly than ever. Her thoughts and emotions were in a turmoil, one that followed her even into a confused, restless sleep. The small-village Meb told her that she was a brazen hussy. The practical Meb told it to shut up. That he didn't actually like her and was being kind. She wasn't beautiful or curvaceous. And the dreamer Meb wondered about moving rocks and the love between Groblek and the sea. It was all very complicated, hard even to start to understand, like just what Finn actually did. That wasn't being a gleeman or even a thief. Well, he'd said he'd keep her as his apprentice. She'd learn. She peeped at him from under lidded eyes. His black hair was still dripping-wet. It was cold out. He ought to dry it. Odd. It was a clear winter night with no sign of rain to have wet it.

The next day brought Justin seeking to mend some bridges, exerting himself to be charming. Meb was not that easily misled. But he did have a skill she wanted to learn, and juggling on the rolling ship was not easy. "Will you teach me how to read and write?" she asked.

He laughed lightly. "Women don't do that."

"They don't wear trousers and juggle either," said Meb, tartly. "Show me how it works."

"Very well. It's not easy."

Meb did not find it as difficult as he seemed to think it should be. It was quite logical when it was explained. She rapidly got to spelling out and sounding the words, and working out what they were. Keri did not approve of her lover's spending time with a woman who wore trousers, and kept coming over to distract him, while studiously ignoring Meb.

The latter part suited Meb fine.

═ Chapter 42 ═

VORLIAN FOUND THAT HE HAD ONLY ONE ANSWER TO HIS SUMMONS. The centaur Actaeon. The centaur's eyes were a little wild, Vorlian thought. Perhaps it was finding himself here in the dragon's lair, alone.

Or perhaps it was something else. Vorlian was not sure what this centaur had done to be sent into exile. There were others of course, scattered about the islands. But Vorlian knew that it was considered a terrible punishment. He wondered if the ambition of renewing the plane that was Tasmarin, with a flawed reed, was such a good idea. But they'd needed a centaur. Well, even if the others were not here, he might as well tell the centaur. "You've seen these pictures of our human mage?"

"No," said the centaur, his skin twitching. "But I know what she looks like. I did not realize that she was dressed as a boy. The merrow on the right is Hrodenynbrys, the consort of their Chieftainess Margetha. Hrodenynbrys is possessed of very powerful magical gifts."

"Well, I have established that they are indeed in cahoots with a dragon too. They set sail a few days ago, having been rescued by the dragon."

"He could be compelled. Any two of the species, acting in concert can compel one of the dragons," said Actaeon.

"That's not what Rennalinn said," said Vorlian, digesting this. "He said that it had to be a human mage . . . which she is, but surely unskilled."

"Oh no. Any two of the species. We keep the record," said Actaeon earnestly. "Do you know which dragon, Lord Vorlian?"

"One called Fionn. Quite small. Black. I can't think of another black . . ."

Vorlian noticed that the centaur appeared to be having a minor fit, sweating and shivering with his head jerking forward.

"What is wrong with you?"

The centaur wiped his brow with a shaking hand. "Their fate lines cross, often, in many possible ways. The black dragon comes to destroy Tasmarin."

"Fionn?" asked Vorlian incredulously. "He's a joker, Actaeon. You shouldn't take his silly statements seriously. I've even heard him say he's busy destroying the world myself. We regard him as humans would a village idiot. A minor annoyance, that is all. I will admit that he's clever, fast and agile and he has a nasty tongue in his head, but he's harmless. I'm sorry, I could have reassured you earlier. He'll just be involved in this to annoy the senior dragons. You'll have overheard his nonsense, but it is just a joke."

"It is no joke. We have not overheard anything. We have seen him in the dark pool of foretelling. Often. Almost all the fate lines lead with a grim certainty to him bringing down the second tower too. And then the others will fail. Tasmarin will break up."

Vorlian stared at the half-horse. "What? What do you mean?"

"He is the oldest and the most powerful of your kind. Like, but not like, the rest in many ways. A worker with the great forces and powers that hold the world together. He works now to destroy this place. He is often seen in the dark pool. His ways are mysterious but his purpose is clear," said the centaur, his voice quavering a little.

"But he's just a troublemaker!" exclaimed Vorlian. "He couldn't have brought the tower down! We can't even touch the surface of them. It's just a symptom of the breakdown of Tasmarin. That is why we need a renewal of the old spells! That's why we need the human mage."

"And that is why he needs her too," nodded Actaeon. "To keep her, and you, from undoing his work of generations."

Vorlian thought about all this. There was one flaw in it all, besides the fact that he struggled to believe it of the sharp-tongued Fionn. Fionn had a nasty mouth, but he didn't seem pent on utter destruction. In fact he hadn't even killed Zuamar—and he could easily have done so. And he'd been seemingly genuine in his offer to help Vorlian. In his usual snide way of course ... but it was still not the behavior of a megalomaniac that sought the destruction of everything. "But ... why shouldn't he just kill the human mage?"

"It does seem odd. But much of what he does is inscrutable to us. May I use your mirror, Lord Vorlian?" Actaeon asked. "This will not wait."

"Mirror? Yes. Although this doesn't seem like a time for vanity."

"Vanity is emptiness," said Actaeon. "Which is what time away from the herds of my people is."

"And what is the mirror gazing for, if not for vanity?" Vorlian said, snidely.

"It allows me to speak with them. Any reflecting surface is captured somewhere in the dark pool of the Children of Chiron. The sages there can hear and see me, if it is a windless day. Otherwise, they will see it later, when the wind is still."

Vorlian suddenly recalled the centaur's endless posing in front of the mirror during their meetings. So much for secrecy!

The dragon led him to the gold-framed mirror. Actaeon stood in front of it, and Vorlian stared and listened. The centaur's chant was low and rhythmic ...

Not something that should crack the mirror-glass from side to side, and then shatter it into glass shards that reflected nothing.

The centaur turned and galloped out, without as much as a word of farewell.

Vorlian went back to his gold and lay down, deep in thought. So ... either the alvar had lied to him deliberately, or he hadn't known about dragonish compulsion. Vorlian was going have to fly up to the conclave tonight, no matter how tired he was, and talk to the others, and also—if he was there, and he was quite often—corner a small black dragon and ask him some hard questions, with no space for clever-mouthed evasions.

That evening he took to the wing, early, to take best advantage of what help he could get from the thermals. Magic would have to do the rest, but it was a saving in effort. And besides he needed to talk to a lot of dragons. Some of them might be a little irritated, but he was one of the largest, and his recent conquest of one of the oldest and biggest dragons would influence the others.

He alighted at the cavern-mouth where the treasure of the

creatures of smokeless flame still burned in its globe. He must have a closer look sometime. It looked rather like burning gas. But now to business . . .

"Vorlian."

He found himself faced by four large dragons, Chandagar, Lamdian, Myrcupa and Brennarn, backed up by several dozen smaller hangers-on. They blocked the entry to the conclave caverns. Chandagar and Brennarn had been on good terms with Zuamar. But Myrcupa had not been. Vorlian cleared his throat. "I have matters to address the conclave about. Things I have discover—"

"You have been banished from the conclave," said Myrcupa. "Go. Go or we will kill you."

"What! What for? Don't be ridicul—"

They answered him with a gout of flame. Fortune favored Vorlian—that and the fact that he was still outside the portal to the cave. The air was very thin making the flame far less effective. And Vorlian's reactions were fast. The sideways dive behind a projecting rock saved him from more than a tendril searing. But he did not wait to see if he could survive it twice. He was not that stupid. He retreated and dived out and down into the cloudy atmosphere again.

His mind roiled with fury and turmoil as headed back toward Starsey.

Fionn's Scrap was thoroughly asleep, having absorbed a far larger amount of knowledge in one day than was normal for her kind. As with her juggling, she did not know the limitations and thus, magically aided, was able to ignore them. Fionn had, by quietly listening in, made sure that the young Lyr-worshiping bravo didn't misteach, and that he also kept his distance. The man had delusions about being a great womanizer and being too handsome to resist. He was aware that Fionn watched, anyway. It had left the Scrap tired, as such magic use will. Fionn had taken the extra precaution of putting a simple sleep spell on the innkeeper's daughter and her swain. A little distraction, and he was able to slip overboard again. He needed time with his gold, and he needed to find out what else was afoot. And he needed to fly all the way to a cottage in the mountains on Yenfar to leave a silver harp with two Loftalvar women.

Once that was done he flew up to the conclave and sniggered at the flame in the orb at the entrance to the cavern. It never failed to make him feel good to see that. In the very early days dragons had only come up here rarely. It had been the simplest thing to replace it with a very ordinary globe which burned methane.

The caverns were quite full tonight, and definitely abuzz. He made his way to the back to the hot vents. The place had its attractions, as did the dream of a plane of dragons. But it too was dying.

He stood and listened in quietly, and warmed himself. It was both amazing and particularly foolish. Vorlian? Vorlian of all dragons. The only thing that was funnier was the idea that they'd somehow acquired, that a dragon did not invade the territory of another and kill it. Next they'd conclude that the hoard of the dead dragon—if you could survive the booby traps—did not belong to the victor.

"You always seem to find something funny, runt," said Myrcupa.

"Yes," said Fionn cheerfully, aware of the sudden silence. "It's all nearly as funny as you are."

Myrcupa raised himself up. "We've changed the rules here, you little black worm. We're in charge now. You owe me an apology." The place was utterly silent, as everyone listened.

Fionn chuckled. "What for? But I'll happily owe it to you. For as long as you live."

For a moment Myrcupa allowed a self-satisfied curl of the lip, and then he said: "What do you mean, 'as long as I live'?"

"Well, if you're dead I can't see any point in going on owing it to you. It's just like if I actually gave you an apology, I would no longer owe it to you."

"What?"

"Semantics. I can't owe it to you, if I have already given it to you. So I'll restrain myself from apologizing, until you're dead. And I see no point in owing or even apologizing to a corpse," said Fionn.

"Are you saying you're not going to apologize?" demanded Myrcupa, his forehead wrinkling at the mental demand, and signs of rage starting to show.

"I think you have finally got it," said Fionn, in mocking congratulation. "What do you think, my fellow dragons? Has he grasped it?"

There were a number of muffled sniggers, hastily hushed, as

Myrcupa looked around for backup. "I am now High-Lord of Marchpane and also of Yenfar," Myrcupa announced.

Fionn raised his brows. "By conquest? You defeated the great Zuamar? I am impressed. He was one of the old ones, but wily and tough. And large. I wouldn't dream of offering disrespect to the kind of dragon that could do that. Why, a few days back I saw Zuamar invade Vorlian's territory. Vorlian is bigger than you, and he struggled to see Zuamar off."

Myrcupa was left wordless . . . so Fionn continued a little louder above the rising hubbub. "All hail the conqueror of Zuamar, who was turning into a danger to us all."

Myrcupa turned and stalked off. Fionn grinned and winked at several of the dragons staring at him. "Now, do you think I have offended him? Poor fellow."

One of the watchers shook his head. "I think you've made an enemy for life."

Fionn laughed. "Well, that won't be for too long. Anyway, I must be going. Things to do, centaurs to tease, Tasmarin to destroy. That sort of thing. If I were you I'd drop a message with Vorlian sometime soon that it was all a terrible mistake, by the way. He's a lot cleverer and more dangerous than that tailvent."

Fionn was up and out of the portal before Myrcupa's little posse could gather. It would seem that quite a lot of the dragons got in his way as the new Lord of Yenfar chased after him.

From the shadow of the crater Fionn watched him dive out and down toward Tasmarin. He sighed to himself and set out for his hoard. He really didn't know why he bothered to fix their problems. He would enjoy lying on his gold and looking at the beauty of it in the light of the hell-flame.

But while the gold comforted him, he was still restless. The dvergar had done their best to give his little scrap of humanity protection, with, it was to be admitted, awkward side-effects. But she was still at risk from the species which had greatest power over humans. The magic of the creatures of smokeless flame was singly effective on both humans and—to a slightly lesser extent, dvergar. Their magic was in turn ineffectual against the fire-beings. If the fire creatures could find her when Fionn was not on hand to defend her, she could be compelled to do whatever they wanted her to do. And he was not always able to be with her.

Most dragons scarcely bothered with treasures that were not at least partially gold. Fionn was not that different from any other in that respect. But he did have a few bits of junk he had never got around to throwing out . . . alvar stuff. Silvery metals. Alvar magic was very effective at repelling and unmasking fire-beings. Perhaps there might be something there. He got up and went to have a look. Eventually he found something full of magic to repel fire-beings—a belt woven of silvery metal threads.

There was only one minor flaw in the whole idea. It had obviously been made for a child. A small child. It wouldn't fit around her waist. It probably wouldn't even fit around her neck. He looked at it for a while. By dvergar standards he was barely an artificer. By dragon standards he was nearly as good as a good human craftsman. But that was still not good enough to make this into a human-size belt. And even on the slimmest neck it would barely make a dog-collar. A dog collar . . . it would fit Díleas. Hmm. Finn rooted about. Found a pair of thumbnail sized hollow crystal orbs, which he'd kept because they had a gold loop on them. They were intended to hang on a chain, and could be bespelled to hold light. He took them back to the hell-flame, and read deep into the ancient energies that danced there. It was not hard to take a tiny piece of that and put it into the little orbs. It lacked the finesse of dvergar work, but it would have to do. He bent open the gold loop on one and threaded it through the silvery fibers. The other . . . he found a long chain, also in among the alvar stuff. It would do for a belt, or she could attach Díleas to it.

"Prince Gywndar. The dragon Myrcupa is on the outer wall calling for you."

Gywndar went in haste.

Myrcupa was busy eating someone. "Gather your troops. Embark them on your ships. You sail for Cark tonight."

By now Gywndar knew better than to question the order.

Not even the news, finally broken to him by his mages, that the object he had assumed was the Angmarad was nothing more than old seaweed could stop him from obeying.

On Lapithidia, less than sixteen leagues from Cark, the Children of Chiron—from a centaur nation preparing for war, had been turned into a nation in panic. The dark pool which had showed them probable futures ... was dry. This was a cataclysm for a people who used it for guidance in so many matters. They'd prepared for other cataclysms. Prepared for bloody war. Looked for answers far and wide.

No one had thought to look at the future of their pool.

That had always just been, and would always be.

Except that it wasn't.

═ Chapter 43 ═

MEB LOOKED UP FROM SHAPING AND SOUNDING OUT THE WORDS in the book Fionn had given her, to see the looming cliffs of Lapithidia. She stared at the sudden size of them, not having realized that she'd read for so long. The last time she'd looked up it had been a mere bump on the horizon. "Lapithidia," said Finn, lazily.

"The cliffs make Yenfar's cliffs look so small."

"Yes, but it's actually not as high in the middle as Yenfar. And relatively flat," said Finn. "Mostly rolling grassland. That suits them. They're obsessed with two things: soothsaying and story-telling. Don't look so eager. The stories are often dull and very full of details that most good story tellers would have very happily left out. They've got a very high opinion of themselves and skills at both, but there are limits on those skills."

That sounded like something that a good apprentice to whatever Finn's mysterious trade was, ought to know. So she asked: "How so?"

"Their histories are told from their point of view—and reality mostly has at least two if not more points of view—and their foretelling is the foretelling of the probable. I've found the improbable happens more often. Also they see true form. So glamor and shape-shift do not show. This can be very difficult for them. You're a woman in their scrying. I am a dragon. Which poses some difficulty for them, as we appear to be neither to ordinary sight."

"Um, Finn." The part about being a dragon was niggling at her.

281

She'd been thinking how the guards on Gywndar's treasury had not believed him when he had told the truth. And she'd seen how the merrow changed form. It couldn't be true, could it? But he was still Finn . . . not a dragon, surely. She knew from childhood stories—and actually seeing Zuamar's slaughter, that they killed without compunction. Finn went out of his way not to kill things. Well, the tree-woman he turned into stone, but otherwise . . . "Are dragons evil? I mean, I always thought they were."

Finn considered this with a wicked look in his eye. "Depends on what you consider evil. Some are. Some aren't. Dragons come in all kinds, good, bad and indifferent. Of course here, on Tasmarin, they've had too much untrammeled power. That's not good for anyone. But they are no different than humans . . . or alvar or merrows. It depends on the individual. I've known a few dragons who fit just about any human category, from saint to thief. They're more solitary than humans and more predictable, generally. Size matters far more among dragons than it does among humans. I am rather small."

Meb look up at him. "No, you're not," she said defensively.

"For a dragon. I am tall and very heavy compared to humans. I change my form. Not my mass. Dragons are very light bodied, really. They have to be. By the way, I was looking through my possessions last night and found a suitable collar and lead for Díleas. Centaurs tend to kick dogs." He patted the young black and white dog who had come nosing him at hearing his name. Díleas was a little less certain that he wanted to wear a collar, even one with a tiny red bauble with a faint glow to it. "It would be useful if he got lost in the dark," said Finn.

"It's very smart! No, Díleas, it's not too tight. I can get two fingers under it. It looks beautiful on you, boy," she cooed and cuddled him.

"Good. And here is a chain that'll do for a leash. Use it as a belt in the meantime. It's got one of those glow-baubles on it too, to match."

"Thank you, Finn." She beamed and glowed more brightly than the microscopic pieces of hell-flame.

"It's time, however, for us to put aside our gleeman motley, Anghared," he said. "Before you panic, you are still my apprentice, and still to dress as a boy. Just to follow a slightly different trade for now."

She smiled. "I've been a gleeman, a honey-bucketer on a night-soil cart, an arsonist's assistant, and even a thief. I am getting used to changes and strangeness, Finn. Just not to my name. I am your Scrap."

"I shall do my best, Scrap," he said seriously, and then his quizzical self reasserted itself. "Strictly speaking is theft from a thief theft? And too often taxation is little more than theft and extortion with menaces. But anyway, the centaurs are altogether too serious for gleemen. However, right now they are in dire need of water. We're water diviners. I have suitable garments in my pack."

"No wonder it weighed so much!" said Meb.

"That was the cast-iron skillet. But nothing else cooks mushrooms quite as well."

"I'd like to do that again one day," she said, her face intent. "With Díleas. I am sure he'd make a champion mushroom finder."

"For heaven's sake don't daydream about it. Your magic works best then. Anyway, it is winter now. Not mushroom time," said Finn.

"My magic?"

"Yes," said Finn, looking at her with a half-smile. "It must have occurred to you by now, Scrap, that you cause some completely unnatural things to happen. I have to start teaching you, but I am not sure how human magic works."

She snorted. "I'm as magical as Díleas, Finn."

Fionn had been working on the best way to teach her for a while, and had come no closer. Suddenly he was struck by a moment of pure genius. He could use the gift of the dvergar to his advantage. "That's a pity," he said. "It's a much needed skill in my apprentice. Something they must be good at and careful with too."

She wanted that. "But . . . but humans can't do magic," she said, doubtfully.

"Not humans from Tasmarin, no. The ability is in the blood and rare at that normally. The dragons here made sure that they could not be challenged by it. But as I have said, you came from further afield. I am just not sure where or how. But if you try, you will find that you can work magics," said Fionn, using his most matter-of-fact tone to keep her calm and collected.

"I was cast ashore on the beach as a baby. So in one way I don't know where I came from, Finn. But it can't be that far.

Babies die quite easily if they're cold. I saw a dead baby . . ." She
swallowed. "He was very small. And even I nearly died in the
sea, grown up."

In the complex mechanisms of Fionn's mind several pieces of
the mystery of just where she'd come from became clearer. The
merrows said that she could not drown. They would know. He'd
wager a large sum of his own gold that she had arrived here
almost exactly when the first tower had fallen. There would have
been a little balancing of power and energy then, and one of the
imbalances was in the earth-magics.

Meb found the idea of working magic terrifying . . . and com-
pellingly fascinating. And, well, she had been cast up on the
beach as a baby. Maybe from some place where magic was still
common among humans? Her life had got stranger and stranger,
ever since she'd met Finn. But surely that was because he was
strange? "Um. What should I try?"

"Make a coin appear," said Fionn.

She shrugged. Clapped her hands together. Held out a copper
penny. "I can already make coins appear. But that's not magic.
It's just a gleeman thing. They do that."

"Yes. But in the case of most gleemen, they actually have the
coin first. They don't just make it appear."

"Oh. I thought . . . well, I suppose I never did think. I just saw
you do it. So I tried it and it worked."

Fionn took the coin from her. Somewhere a dead man's eye
was missing a penny . . . He made it vanish.

"Is that magic?" he asked.

She nodded. "I think so."

He clapped his hands and made it appear again. "Now you
do it."

She did.

"Where is it?"

"I don't know. Gone."

"When I made it look like it disappeared it was in my sleeve.
It's a trick. A sleight of the hand." He grinned. "Except for you
it wasn't. If ordinary gleemen could make coins appear from
nowhere I don't think that they'd work, walking from place to
place, sleeping rough, and entertaining for pennies."

Meb blinked. "I feel very stupid now. I thought they did it

because they loved it. I did. I did think about the money, and maybe wonder . . . but, well, I was concentrating on juggling. You always had money. So, I thought that was maybe where it came from."

"That comes from my hoard. I have accumulated a bit over the years. At times I have to spend some. Just not gold, if I can help it."

"Oh. So . . . what else can I do, Finn?"

He shrugged. "I don't know. You seem adept at summonsing things. But humans are generally strong with earth magics. Rather different from dragons like me. Humans are good at making things grow. The trick is to always remember that you can do too much. That will kill you. But right now you need to be adept at changing your clothes, because Port Lapith is close."

He was so . . . matter-of-fact about being a dragon. Sensible Meb knew it was silly. People were not dragons. Sensible Meb that knew all the other things didn't happen either. The other dreamer Meb in her head said, "You were there. The magic works. You've talked to mountains. Why not the rest?"

And a little part of her still said, "Why me?" and was very afraid.

Meb felt that she was becoming quite a seasoned traveler with a knowledge of ports by now. This was her third, after all. It was also the most chaotic. There were armed centaurs running about everywhere—without, it appeared, any logical reason for doing so. The captain was not prepared to let the passengers disembark until the centaurs had given permission, and this took a long time. Eventually a centaur trotted up to the gangplank. "You can put to sea again, captain. The berths are needed. Or we will buy your ship. We want transports."

"Excuse me," said Finn. "Can we disembark? I believe you want us, more than transports."

"Why would we want you?" asked the centaur, looking down his nose at them.

"Because we're water diviners," said Finn. "And it was foretold that you'd need us."

The centaur stood stock still for a moment. And then took a deep breath. "Foretold? Come with me."

He set off at a hasty canter. Finn put a hand on Meb's shoulder. "Walk. He'll be back."

He was, with three others a few moments later. "We're not as fleet of foot as centaurs, friends," said Finn calmly.

One of the accompanying centaurs asked: "Who foretold that you would be needed?"

Finn smiled up at him. "A black dragon."

It is not really possible for the man-half of a centaur to fall off the horse-half's back. But the centaurs tried. Eventually one of the centaurs spoke. "What did he say?"

"He said that predictions are usually wrong, unless your understanding is complete. And he said that I was to give you something. This bag." He hauled a leather bladder out of his pack. "He says you could either play games with it, or let the contents loose. Doing the latter was his advice. And I was to ask you for a piece of stick, because that was what my assistant and I will need to find your water."

It was like tossing a deadly sea-snake out of a basket of fish onto the gutting table. Half-horses exploded away from them yelling, calling. Others came galloping, crowding around them. Shouting. Asking questions. Eventually a centaur with gray touches to his beard restored it all to some semblance of order. "I am Ixion," he said in a deep carrying voice. "I command the battle phalanxes. Tell me who you are and why you are here." He looked at the old leather bag in Finn's hand. "And what you are doing with our ancient treasure."

"Bringing it back to you. I thought that was quite obvious," said Finn. "Here. Catch." And he tossed the bladder to Ixion.

"It is a holy object! It should be treated with great respect. Not flung!" said the catcher in a choked voice, holding it as if it were very fragile.

"Chuck it back to me and I'll try again," said Finn, sardonically. "Now we're here to deal with your water problem. Can we get on with it? We have other work to do."

It was obvious that this Ixion too just had no idea what to do in the circumstances. "I . . . I will have to consult with the others."

"Go ahead. But it's a long way inland. And uphill. And we're in a hurry and so are you. Mind if we start walking?"

Ixion took a deep breath. Nodded. "Abraxis. Will you see that they are suitably escorted? I must take this to the high plains." He held the old leather bag aloft.

So, surrounded by a phalanx of centaurs, Finn, Meb and Díleas started walking. It was a long, steep, winding trail up to the escarpment, so Meb was very relieved when some more centaurs led a horse-drawn cart up to them. The horses seemed less pleased than she was.

The cart reached the top eventually, and the horses were unhitched, while more were led up. Along with them came a delegation of older centaurs. They were respectful, but wary. "Stranger. You say you come from the black dragon, the destroyer."

"Sometimes in order to fix things, you have to break them," said Finn, cheerfully. "What have you done with the leather bladder I brought you? The black dragon thought it would be a good idea if you opened it and let the contents go. Good for the centaur people in the troubled times that lie ahead."

"Can we consult with the black dragon?" asked one of the elders timorously.

"He's not where I last saw him anymore," said Finn. "He was just passing through, and he gave me this job to do, and paid me well for doing it too. Now, he said we were to ask you for a special piece of stick. We use them for divining, you know."

It was plain the centaur knew exactly what he meant—and was terribly shocked at the suggestion. "But . . . we hold it in sacred trust."

"It's a stick. I'll probably give it back to the owners, when we're done," said Finn. "If you want your water, that is?"

There was much stamping and muttering.

"How do we know you'll give it back to them?" asked the elderly centaur doubtfully.

"You don't. Or you can fill your pool with buckets and try to see."

Chapter 44

VORLIAN LAY ON HIS GOLD AND BROODED AND HEALED. HE LOOKED out of the cavern mouth of his eyrie across Starsey and to the purple bulk of Yenfar across the ocean. A visit from Belet was the only thing to interrupt his dark thoughts.

The fire-being was of course his usual apparently respectful self. Vorlian right now felt that he could use some respect, but that of the demon was . . . wanting. "Greetings, great Lord Vorlian."

"Spare me the flattery. What do you want?"

"Merely that you had sent a message to say that you had found out more about our fugitive human. We are finding her very hard to track down. She vanishes in our auguries."

"She's sailed from here, going West. She is in the company of a black dragon called Fionn. There are two other humans with her. An innkeeper's daughter called Keri and a man called Justin—he's a petty criminal and informer."

"West. I will alert our contacts," said the fire-being.

"Do that," said Vorlian, tersely. "Tell the tree-women too. I told the centaur. He broke my mirror."

"One of my informants tells me he has sailed for Lapithidia. I thought that he was in exile," said Belet.

"Umph," said Vorlian, deciding for now to keep his council about the centaur and the mirror. "Well, now we need a centaur and the human mage, and of course the merrow and the dvergar."

"The sprites can always constrain the merrows and we can deal with the dvergar."

The fire-being took his leave, and Vorlian continued his dark thoughts about Myrcupa and even the doings of that rogue Fionn. Then he spotted a dragon. Far off-shore, making no attempt to come closer. But plainly intending to be seen.

Fury roused Vorlian and, despite still being in some pain, he flew out. However, distance cooled his temper, added caution. What if it was a trap? The other dragon was not attempting to gain altitude and in the clear sky Vorlian could see no other dragons. He flapped slowly out. The other dragon was considerably smaller, but not black. He placed her. Tessara. He had nothing against her, and he would have thought she had nothing against him. They had mated once.

"What do you want?" he asked from a safe distance, still keeping a weather eye out for other dragons.

"To talk," she said. "Some of the others sent me. We're worried."

"Having chased me out of the conclave, why would you want to talk to me?"

"That was before Fionn came and set things straight. Anyway, that was all Myrcupa and his gang of friends. Nothing to do with me," said Tessara.

Vorlian absorbed this. "My wings are sore and I am still a little burned," he said in a more reasonable tone. "Let us fly to those hills over there and we can talk."

"Awkward not to have the conclave as a neutral meeting ground. I was ready to flee," said Tessara, turning to follow.

Soon they'd settled on the high, sunbaked rocks of the ridge. "So, just what did Fionn say?" asked Vorlian.

"He made us laugh as usual," said Tessara. "And he took a great deal of risk in irking Myrcupa to tell us that Zuamar had been in your territory in the last week or so."

Vorlian blinked. "Yes. But what does that have to do with it?"

"Well, it does make your ambush and the murder of Zuamar more understandable. I mean, we knew that he'd killed Jakarin. We can understand you felt threatened. Perhaps it is best that he's dead. And if you were injured, it made sense not to fight Myrcupa. You didn't just run away."

Vorlian opened and shut his mouth like a beached fish. Then asked in a dangerous voice. "Did Fionn tell you this?"

"No. Myrcupa told us about the ambush and you running away from the scene of the murder, and then him . . . I found that hard to believe. Fionn just made a fool of him and said you'd defeated Zuamar and that we should all be grateful. Myrcupa was all set to kill him, but he slipped away."

"Fionn would kill him, rather than the other way around," said Vorlian. "He was the one who defeated Zuamar. Not me."

"But . . . but everyone, even Fionn, says that you killed Zuamar," said Tessara.

Vorlian nodded. "He defeated him and let him go. I merely killed Zuamar afterward, but in a fair midair fight. Half of Yenfar must have seen it. And I'll fight Myrcupa, injured or not. I'll fly over there now and deal with him. He couldn't drive me to flee if I was on death's door, Tessara. I have my sources. He's there by invitation. By invitation from the alvar! They sought protection from me, alvar alone know why. In fact I think I will fly over and devour the liar! And those alvar."

Tessara shook her head. "They are flying in pairs, expecting you, Vorlian. It's not natural. And they're changing things in conclave. They attacked Marcellus there. Inside the caverns. There was almost a riot. But not quite. They're the largest, and are sticking together. They say we need to start a program to exterminate humans."

Vorlian took a deep breath. "Then maybe we need to come together too. In times of crisis, dragons have allied before. We allied to create this refuge." He looked around. "What I really need to do is something I thought I would never admit to wanting to do. I want to talk to Fionn. I'm not sure what his game is but I think it is time that I found out."

Tessara shook her wings out. "I will talk to the others. Among the females we have our own . . . arrangement. There are those who have contacts among the lesser species. They will tell us what happened on Yenfar."

"I will lie on my gold and recover for a while. But if you hear of any sightings of Fionn, will you let me know? I need to talk to that black smart-mouth." He sighed. "I ought to have before."

"No one takes him seriously," said Tessara.

"Maybe that was a mistake," said Vorlian.

"That is the strangest thing I've ever heard a dragon say, let alone you," said Tessara dryly. "You never admit to mistakes. Dragons don't." And she flew off, leaving Vorlian to his thoughts again. They were as confused but less dark. Where did Fionn disappear to?

The answer, when he thought about it, was painfully obvious. It was just so undragonish . . .

Fionn had no qualms about assuming other shapes.

He was the tall, foxy-faced human.

= Chapter 45 =

JUSTIN HAD RECOGNIZED THE TWO OF THEM THE MOMENT HE'D seen them together. The high priest of the lady of the forest's grove had showed them all the picture the day before.

Justin, scribe, petty thief, professional informer and would-be gigolo had joined the Lyr worshipers as a potential source of income, either from informing or from blackmail. It had been a good source of income and protection—his fellow devotees were, some of them, influential men. But this—this looked like the big pay-off. He'd originally had hopes of getting Keri pregnant and getting his way into the inn that way, but her father had made it clear that he'd rather see her dead in a ditch than married to Justin. The girl had the intellect and morals of a rabbit, and had been keeping herself occupied and miraculously un-pregnant with passing travelers for some years. Justin did consider that she was worth keeping as the first of his stable, because she'd sleep with whoever he told her to and bring him the money. Although he'd have to watch her. She stole! Now, he'd have the funds to set up in style. He'd caught up with two of the three that the Lady of the Forests wanted. There was no way off Lapithidia except via Port Lapith. And the sprites had a small grove on the island, just outside the port. Their sacred island of Arcady was close by.

The chaos generated by Finn and the girl's leaving made it a simple matter to hop off the ship without any centaur being the wiser. To his irritation Keri followed him.

"Go back," he ordered.

"No. You're up to something. Probably with that tramp in trousers."

It was a case of beat her there on the quayside, or put up with her. And there were any number of stevedores and other people about who would probably interfere in his business. So he merely shrugged. Let her tag along.

She complained about it being too cold to strip off once they got to the trees. Well, that was up to her. He'd seen what got done to those who broke the rules. He walked on, naked as the day he was born, while she carped at him. "Shut up or I'll beat you black and blue, bitch. Do as you're told."

"I only do as I wish," said the tree-woman suddenly. "Have you come to die?"

Keri screamed. Justin bowed. "I have found your quarry, Lady of the Forest. I have brought you the ones you seek."

This sprite looked identical to the one back on Starsey. "Explain," she said, as cool as ever.

For the first time doubt that he might get a reward crept into Justin's mind. But he could play hard to get.

A little later he knew that he could not. And that his life would be a great reward. But the Lady of the Forest was not finished with him.

Belet arrived on Arcady at the same time as the ship with the hasty message from Lapithidia did. The sprites did not keep the message from him. And he in turn shared what he had with them.

"He has to be a dragon. A shape-shifted dragon, protecting her."

"A shape-shifted dragon," said Lyr. "It fits. Well, we can deal with that together."

Belet concurred. They had. Compulsion had now been set on no less than fourteen dragons, together. But that was a complex working, and shaped their inclinations.

"I think we should settle for merely stunning it. We can do that too, you know."

"Of course I know. The first Lyr knew. We all know. We have some gold for us to bespell."

"I will move in some troops from Cark. We can keep watch . . . it will take them as long to come down from the plateaux as for us to land in force. We can move over by night and wait in the lee of the cliff west of Port Lapith. One vessel at sea with a mirror can relay the message by day, and a phosphorus flare by night."

The Lyr nodded, a habit she had learned from her human devotees.

On the high plateaux, with a phalanx of centaurs acting as outriders and guides, Meb found that she was pleasantly alone with Finn. She hadn't realized how Justin and the innkeeper's daughter had irritated her just by being in their space so often. And, for once, Finn seemed quite disposed to talk. He pointed to a rocky tor. "I put those there. I do occasionally have to do some hard work."

Meb looked at the strange shaped spike of weathered stone. "Why, Finn?"

He shrugged. "Energy flow problem. Think of everything as flowing rivers of forces. Patterns of it. Sometimes something disrupts that pattern. Mostly things correct themselves. I mean, think of a stream. It can only do just what it is meant to do if it flows exactly down a certain path. A child puts some stones in the stream and it deviates . . . it either comes back to the path or, next time there is a storm the stones wash away. Occasionally someone will come along and jam the stones together so that they cannot wash away. Then I may have to adjust things—either to compensate with other forces or to undo the blockage or put another rock in higher up or lower down. That's what that tor is."

It was said so matter-of-factly that Meb had no doubt that he'd done it. And that he knew exactly what he was talking about. "What would happen if you didn't do it?"

"It gets very complicated. It can actually just destroy things. Or it can distort other areas. It can affect anything from how much rain a place gets to how prosperous a local farmer is. Mostly it is fairly stable. But the world is not entirely self-correcting. Eventually the errors and problems and pressures build up and then you get the energy-equivalent of a storm, which tries to wash away blockages. It is my job to see that it doesn't get to that point."

"You . . . fix Tasmarin?"

"Good gracious, no! Only the energy flows. But not only for this world. I had a ring of eighty or so I was responsible for. Planes."

"Planes?"

"Places like this. When you are a little more experienced I'll try to explain the maths to you. Think of them as many, many different worlds. I traveled around them keeping them stable, keeping them linked."

"You mean . . . there are many worlds?"

"Possibly an infinity of them. There are also some that are joined. It all comes down to the First."

"The first?"

"The First. Intelligent beings, rather like dvergar. And centaurs. And merrows and creatures of smokeless flame. The whole boiling lot of you except us dragons. You are all in some way aspects of the First. I always have to laugh when one of the species—usually the alvar, tells me they are descended from the First. You all are."

"Except dragons," said Meb grinning at him. "They're entirely different."

He nodded. "Yes. The First made us, the way the dvergar make things of metal. We were to them something like what dogs are to people. I was one of the early ones, from just after they'd discovered how to make worlds link. Díleas was bred to herd sheep. I was made to fix energy imbalances in the great rings of worlds. See, there have always been multiple discrete planes of existence. Worlds . . . but really more than just worlds. Certain conditions cause them to form. That is intrinsic to existence. The First discovered this. They also discovered that, given certain stringent conditions, it was possible to cause planes to divide, but not to become discrete. To remain linked. Of course such a thing was not stable. In the beginning they could barely keep them mutually linked for the briefest of moments. But they found stable forms, shapes in multidimensional mathematics which could remain in that formation state—in which separate universes are linked—as long as they feed back into themselves. In other words: they created a ring of universes. Many strange and cataclysmic energies are required to remain in balance. That is my task. Energy is not destroyed or created, it merely changes states and places. It needs to move to prevent too much building or being lost from any one place. I was built in the beginning, to do this. There were . . . quite a few of us back then."

Meb thought she understood at least one word in ten of what

he'd said. But it seemed important to keep him talking. "And now?" she asked.

Fionn shrugged. "I may be the last. We never had much to do with each other. Saw each other in passing, occasionally. Anyway I have been stuck here on Tasmarin for a number of centuries. I've never been too sure whether the dragons were right, and that this was their escape . . . or whether it was merely human mages getting rid of more trouble than they were worth. Either way, both sides have been the loser. They may not have understood that."

"Now I am the one that really doesn't understand."

"Tasmarin—this world—is a made-up thing. Pulled together from the places that linked the ring of worlds. Think of that as a whole lot of ships anchored to each other, by their strongest and most magical of places—and that someone went and chopped out those pieces and made a new ship out of those pieces."

"That probably wouldn't be too good for the other ships."

"You grasp the problem. And they're not very well joined together any more either. That causes difficulties too. Makes them likely to sink each other. Of course the only way to fix it all up again is to give the pieces back. The people on the new ship need to be able to get back to the old ships in one piece. And that, you might say, is what I am trying to do now. Return the part that attached them to their place of origin. I have dealt with the Angmarad of the merrows, the hammer of the dvergar, and windsack of the centaurs. I'm on my way to do the next as soon as we get the staff of the sprites."

"They—the sprites—tried to catch us before."

Finn patted Díleas, who nuzzled up against him in response, and tried to eat the corner of his cloak. "It's a bit like being a sheepdog. There are some sheep who would prefer it if you left them alone. Others—the occasional ram—who will turn on you. Try to trample or to kill you. That doesn't mean that you don't still have to herd them along, without killing the awkward ones. Ah, we get closer to their puddle." He pointed.

There on the plain stood the remains of a marble column. In the distance stood another. And further over, a piece of what was left of a frieze still balanced on top of a column. "Needs work," said Finn with a grin. "Now unless I am mistaken they will expect us to walk. Try to stop Díleas from lifting his leg on the columns. They're quite touchy about them."

They walked between the columns, across manicured turf to the edge of . . . a hole. A big hole, but nothing more, surrounded by clipped grasses. Díleas sniffed at it.

"We need a divining rod," said Finn to their escort. "And only one will work."

"We have brought the staff of the sprites," said the elderly centaur, heavily. One of the others rode forward with an object in a long case. He opened it. Inside on the velvet lining lay . . . a stick. A dried out, ordinary stick, with the bark cracking away from the fork at the top and a few dead roots at the end.

Finn took it and handed it to Meb.

It was odd that a piece of wood could hold such despair.

"You can leave us to it now," said Finn commandingly.

The centaurs seemed totally taken aback at this, but did retreat back to among the columns.

"I have no experience of this," said Finn, which was just exactly what Meb did not want to hear. "You'll have to do it. I believe human workers of the earth-magics hold the two ends of the fork, and the shaft twitches down at the presence of water. Then they dig a well."

"What happened to the water that was here?" asked Meb.

"I knew I'd need a reason to come and collect the staff. When the first tower went down, I realized that to survive the destruction, the species needed their treasures returned—otherwise they'd be trapped, in part, with whoever held their people's treasure. So I set things in motion to stop the spring that seeps to this place. I was sure they'd give up the staff in exchange for that being fixed. The water came to it via the peat bog around this place. The water is still there. It's an artesian flow. I can feel it below us."

"Oh." Meb took hold of the fork. "And now?"

"Walk. Chant something for the audience. Then we'll tell them to get digging."

Meb began walking around the edges of the hole. It was possibly a hundred paces across and perfectly circular, except for one spike of rock sticking into it. She couldn't think of anything useful to chant so she hummed the last tune that 'Brys had played. The one about the love between the sea and the mountains. And when she reached the spike of rock the stick began pulling. Dragging at her hands.

"Aha," said Finn. The stick touched the rock. Meb noticed in the periphery of her vision that the centaurs had come galloping in. But she was focussed on the single drop of water that had formed on the end of the rock.

"Stop!" shouted the centaur, as Finn heaved at the rock. "It is a holy pool."

"It's a holy hole right now," grunted Finn, not stopping. "Give me a hand here. Your water is under that rock. Look. There are droplets forming already."

The centaur lowered his javelin and stared. A few more drops of water dripped down. Then a tiny trickle. "We need to move this rock," said Finn. "That is: If restoring this pool of yours is something that you want to do?"

Some thirty of the half-horses were now milling about. Peering down. Exclaiming. Someone produced a rope, and they hitched it to the end of the rock. The centaurs hauled. And hauled. The rope broke. The rock had moved a fraction more, and by now a cupful of water splashed down every few moments from the bottom edge of the rock. The hole was very deep and wasn't going to fill in a hurry from that.

"Let's have another couple of ropes," called Finn. "Come, Scrap. Tuck the stick in your bag, and let's give them a hand."

So they did. The rock cracked and popped out of the ground. And Finn and Meb got thoroughly soaked by the fountain.

"It'll take a day or two," said Finn, "but your pool will fill now. You may have to lead the excess water away, somehow. This area is mostly limestone except for that bit of granite we pulled away. This was the bottom of the sea once, you know. You're on the edge of the granite and limestone. That's why you suddenly got the hole. Sorry. The sacred pool."

"We owe you a great debt," said the old centaur.

"To my assistant," said Finn graciously. "But this is what we were sent to do. So if it is all the same to you, we'd like to be off your high plateau by dark. Because it is freezing up here."

"But will it still work, Asclepius?" asked one of the centaurs looking at the water pouring down. "It is . . . clear."

"Oh, it will still reflect," said Finn. "I believe that's what you find important? And it's the same water. It just hasn't flowed through a peat bog first."

"How do you know it is the same water?" asked the elderly centaur.

Finn waved his arms at the grassland. "What else can it be? If you want it dark you can throw some ink in it. Now can we go? I have to get along to Arcady. And you really don't want smelly humans peering into your magic pool."

The centaurs were, it seemed, not very sensitive to sarcasm. "A habitation will be provided, and viands will be brought for you."

They were. A tent. Straw pallets. Rugs. And a gamey stew that was long on boiled wheat kernels and garlic, but was still good eating. Díleas thought it very adequate, worth putting up with not being allowed to exercise his herding instinct on centaurs.

"Why are they keeping us here, Finn?"

He chuckled. "Because they want to see if their pool works. You see, the water used to seep along through the bog. It was acidic and the color of ale from the peat. The water now is as clear as centuries of rock-filtration can make it. It's also not acidic, so the pool won't grow bigger . . . But they used it for their scrying of futures. It's a fairly futile pastime, but they like it. So they want to see if it is going to work."

The next morning, at dawn, they walked back through the ruined columns and across the green turf. Dileas ran ahead and stopped at the edge of where the hole used to be. And drank.

"I think Díleas is giving our friend Asclepias the pool-watcher fits. No, Scrap. Let him drink. Fits are good for centaurs. They will make the Children of Chiron send us away. Because their pool is working."

Asclepias yelled, and other centaurs came running to peer into the water. "Acteaon on a ship!" "And a war-band . . ."

A breeze riffled the water.

For a moment Meb saw a black dragon.

Asclepias looked at the riffled water. Shook his head in amazement. "It . . . it works now without even the focus of will! It works better!" he said incredulously. He bowed to them. "Thank you. You have worked a great wonder for us."

"I think," said Finn, "that I ought to warn you, you will probably find it both clearer and . . . less clear. You'll see deeper and that can be confusing."

"You speak sooth for a water-diviner," said one of the centaurs.

"I've been around. Been told a thing or two. And now, seeing as your pond is full, and works and time and tide press on us, can we leave?"

Asclepias nodded. "Indeed. We will see you back to a ship with such rewards as we can provide."

"Breakfast?" asked Meb, hopefully.

Even the solemn centaurs laughed. And provided breakfast. It was oat porridge, and Díleas was less impressed than with the stew of the night before.

The centaurs escorted Finn, Meb and Díleas back to the cart, and back towards the only way down off the high plateaux. As they moved other centaurs came to hear the news. Their escort on the steep downhill pass to Port Lapith was a substantial one, and they all seemed happier now.

Which was more than Meb could say about the strange piece of stick. Just touching it felt . . . tragic. "Why is it so sad?" she asked Finn.

He sighed. "Because it is a sad thing, I suppose. When Tasmarin was cut off, there was only one sprite, and the sapling she was going to plant. When a token of trust was needed . . . well, it was all that Lyr had. And it was only going to be temporary, and the sapling wasn't due to be planted until spring . . . It's just a dead stick now. But that is why all the sprites are just one sprite. They are all grown from cuttings from the first one. She was a cold woman—not all tree-spirits are, in the wider planes. But it was still a bleak thing to have happen."

═ Chapter 46 ═

THEY WERE NEARLY AT THE BOTTOM OF THE WINDING PASS BY noon, when they were met by Justin standing waiting at the side of the trail. He waved at them to them to stop.

"I don't like him, Finn," said Meb, quietly.

"Neither do I, but we need him to take a message to the sprites. She . . . Lyr may remember me. We've crossed paths before and I left her with a grudge against me. Not entirely undeserved, I must admit. Besides, you turned one of them into stone."

"Me? That was you, Finn."

He shook his head. "Earth magic, Scrap."

They'd come to a halt next to Justin. "I have something for you," he said to Finn, and handed him a small bag cloth bag. Finn opened it and shook it out. A golden coin fell out onto his palm . . . And then Finn fell over like a mighty tree, onto Meb.

Justin leaped forward to grab her—to be kicked by a centaur as he did. That left Meb on the ground next to the cart, half-stunned by the fall. Finn was lying on the seat. Díleas had leaped after her . . . and there was a vast melee going on. Men and sprites had come running out of the trees. They were fighting with the centaurs.

"A rescue, a rescue!" shouted a centaur. The cart horses bolted with Finn, as Meb was trying desperately to struggle to her feet. Galleys were beaching, and hundreds of men, alvar and sprites were pouring towards them, outnumbering the centaurs.

There was the sound of distant horns.

✦ ✦ ✦

303

Ixion had watched from the head of the trail, watching as the glad cavalcade escorted the water diviners down, watching how the ships came and went. Watching one that did neither. He caught the sudden winking flash of a mirror. The windsack hung at his side—a heavy burden. As yet the council of elders had reached no decision as to what should be done with the breath of the nation. He had been given it, so he still carried it. Perhaps because he was thinking about that, he took an extra few moments to process the fact that the ship lying offshore was signaling to someone out of sight in the lea of the cliffs. On that flank it was only three or four hundred yards from the cliff-point to the shoreline just inside of the harbor. The harbor was not fortified. Why bother? The solitary narrow trail led to the high plains, and holding the harbor would not serve an enemy well. The centaurs could roll rocks down—right onto their ships and onto any who tried to come up the trail.

Now, too late, Ixion saw why defenses could have been valuable. He lifted his horn to his lips and called on his phalanx to gallop. But even as they plunged down the trail, Ixion knew that they could never be in time to save those who had restored the vision of the Children of Chiron. He saw how the few centaurs who were down there were being massacred. One of their guests was somehow behind the main fight, and there were some ten attackers closing on her and her dog.

Ixion knew he had but one choice.

Meb and Díleas ran desperately after the cart. Here she was again, running unarmed into a fight. She had to get to Finn . . . She wrenched the stick out of her pack. She'd give anyone who tried to stop her reason to be even sadder than the stick.

And then they confronted her. Díleas suddenly snarled in a way she'd never heard him do before. There was a hooded man—like the one who had called her before—and one of the tree-women and a group of men-soldiers. The hooded man called her . . . Only this time she was aware that he was trying to bespell her, and although she could do nothing—her arms were frozen—it had no effect on Díleas. Part of her mind screamed "no!" knowing that the sheepdog pup stood no chance. But Díleas—his hair standing out in a black and white mane—the silver collar shining, white teeth exposed, was not going to stop.

The fire-being reached out a casual hand, seething with fire . . . and then screamed like a woman, and turned and fled straight over one of the warriors who had a broad-bladed spear upraised to deal with Díleas. As the fire-being touched him he burned. Immediately the paralysis left Meb and she swung the stick at the sprite. It was a feeble stick, but it was if Meb had hit the tree-woman with a club. She fell onto her followers. It had a less traumatic effect on them than the fleeing fire-being. It was just a tumble. But it gave Meb a moment to call Díleas back, and to ready herself.

Dog and girl still faced seven men.

"We have to take her alive!" yelled one of the attackers.

She didn't feel the same about them.

Ixion ripped at the old thong that bound the windsack with his teeth as he rode. It broke . . . and he and the phalanx found themselves carried along on the gale, as it swirled in a fury down on the invaders. Some had run for their galleys already. The rest . . . the dry wind full of the dust of high plateaux hit them. And somehow it breathed new strength into the outnumbered centaurs too. Like the heroes of old they charged again out of the dust. Javelins, sabers and war axes came slashing down on the invaders.

Ixion rallied the centaurs, and, shortly, faced by the sudden berserker onslaught, their foes tried to flee. They'd left it too late. Centaurs swarmed the ships, burning, chopping and kicking holes in the planking.

Only two of the twenty-one galleys managed to get to sea, rowing as if their lives depended on it. They did. The centaurs, having faced no conflict for centuries, were giving no quarter now. An old battle rage filled them. Arrows followed the galleys, with centaurs actually running into the sea and swimming after them.

In the midst of the wind, and the chaos of battle, Ixion found the water-diviner's apprentice—a slight young human—walking into a gale that made armored men stagger. With the dog under one arm and a stick in the other hand, the young human walked forward, head bent against the wind. A small human, but a very determined one, Ixion realized. He stopped next to the apprentice. "Where is your master?" he called down above the gale.

"They took him. I couldn't get there in time. I think he may be dead." There was utter heartbreak in that voice.

It took a little time to return order from chaos, but it happened eventually. Ixion took the apprentice to a warehouse at the quay-side, and set a strong guard, and then began organizing a systematic search and capture operation. A force of some fifty were sent to search the grove that the centaurs had allowed the sprites to set up.

They found the human that one of the centaurs escorting the cart had seen precipitate the entire affair. He wasn't going to be telling them anything. Centaur hooves could make a terrible mess of a man's face and rib-cage. They found his leman too, tied up in the little patch of forest.

The woman was terrified when they released her. Cursing her lover. And then, as they walked out, went from fear and some relief, to anguish and rage, when they came across two of the other centaurs dragging his body to add to the rest.

Ixion—who had been told of the finding of the man's body—came on the scene at this point, with the woman screaming furious accusations, not at whoever had put their hooves down on his face and chest, but at the sprites and at some woman in trousers that she seemed to blame for all her misfortunes. "It's her! She did this. She killed Justin. She did this to me. She's ruined my life!" She clung to the body.

"Hysterical," said Hylonome.

"So it would seem. I am going down to the docks. The water diviner's apprentice is down there. Perhaps a human can comfort her."

The woman lifted her tear stained, fury and despair contorted face from the dead man's chest. "She isn't a water diviner's apprentice. She's a woman! She did this!" she spat out.

"But we saw her find the water," said Hylonome, slightly puzzled.

It came pouring out of the woman then like a lanced boil. Much was illogical . . . but it did mention the black dragon, and Starsey and, repeatedly, the fact that the water diviner's apprentice was a woman, who had tried to steal her man. A man who had promised her gold and jewels if she slept with the apprentice . . . And of how badly the sprite had treated her, when Justin had gone to tell her about the pair. The sprites had been looking for them. But they hadn't rewarded Justin after all . . .

"I understand now, why we find our scrying of human affairs so confusing," said Hylonome.

"I think we know now that this raid was simply to capture the water diviner and his apprentice. And that the sprites had a hand in it," said Ixion grimly. "I must treble the guard on her and move her up to the high plateau."

He galloped down to the warehouse, to find that she had other ideas.

Fionn awoke groggy and confused. And thoroughly tied up. Well, that was an interesting conceit. He cursed himself for a fool. Many the dragon had been taken that way, once, with a bait. And gold was so hard to resist and held magic so well.

He wondered just what had happened to Anghared and her dog. He was constrained against killing, but he could make the lives of the creatures of smokeless flame and sprites hardly worth living. He would think of something particularly cruel and unusual. It wouldn't be punishment if they didn't find it cruel. And expecting something made it possible to prepare. It would be exceptionally unusual. He felt the bonds. Gold thread in them, and some form of spell on that. They knew he was a dragon—well, that had been obvious from the trap. That might have worked for another dragon.

"It would seem that the prisoner is awake," said the sprite to her companions, one of the fire-beings named Belet, and an alvar called Rennalinn. Fionn understood the strength of the spell on the gold now. Three of the intelligent species had lent their magic to it.

They had tied his jaws, with a rope lashed repeatedly around his head. Tied him to a large slab of stone. He was outdoors but in the shade—under an overhanging lip of rock. A stream splashed into a cascade and a pool off to one side of him, to remind him of how thirsty he was. The place was slightly higher than the surrounding woodland, affording a fine view out over the treetops to sea, and, ironically, to Fionn's next target. The second tower. So: he was on Arcady.

"We have sent messages to the human mage that we hold you hostage. Our informant told us that she was infatuated with you," said the sprite.

"We need some answers from you as to how she was able

to fend us off," said the fire-being. "And by the way, there is a boulder above you, weighing many tons. We can't effectively bind you, but we can bind your bonds to it. Dragons are tough but you too can be crushed."

Fionn's relief at the fact that his Scrap of humanity was still free made any rock seem light. And now that the grogginess was gradually fading he could see the structure of the place and the force lines as well as the view.

"I don't think he can answer you," said Rennalinn. "His face is tied up."

"True. I will have to work out how to remove those bindings without bringing down the stone. In the meanwhile, we have work to do. A few things to prepare before Vorlian gets here," said the sprite.

"I have issued orders for the others too," said the fire-being. "The transports are leaving Cark. Let the war begin," said the demon.

"What about a centaur?" asked Rennalinn.

"We will ask for one of those too, along with her," said the sprite. "We will need the windsack as a bargaining chip."

"We agreed to provide that," said the demon, all too easily. "It shall be fetched."

Left to himself, bound and beneath an immense boulder, Finn looked about in the deeper spectra for signs of life-energy. He found some, soon enough. A lizard, slow and cold in the winter sun, basking on the rock. The reptile mind was small and simple. Quite easy to command. There were things about this island that the sprites did not know.

Vorlian stirred on his hoard. The healing had left him hungry. He began shaking out his wings, only to be aware that one of the creatures of smokeless flame—not Belet, but something far smaller, had entered his cave. He was going to have to remind the fire-beings just how close it was safe to come to a dragon's hoard, soon.

"I have a message from King Belet," it said. "You are to come to Arcady Island with all due speed. They have the dragon who is the human mage's companion captive and have sent for her. We must be ready to enact the rites of creation anew." It turned and left, as Vorlian stared.

Vorlian sat for a while in thought. He had to go, but . . . Then he reached his decision. He pulled himself out of the cave. Closed it with the sealing rock. Activated the traps. And then looked out to sea. There were some half a dozen dragons flying closer. He wondered, briefly, if he ought to open the cave and retreat into it. A dragon was safe like that. He could fill the tunnel with fire, and draw strength from his hoard.

Then he decided that if they wanted conflict, they could have it. But that looked very like Tessara, leading.

It was. "Vorlian. We need you," she called. "Strange and terrible things are happening."

She was in earnest, and it was, Vorlian discovered, good to be told that he was needed. Yet, strangely, he felt compelled to fly to Arcady. "What am I needed for?"

"We need you to lead us," said one of the others. "Brennarn, Myrcupa and some of the others have gone mad. They're attacking Malarset island at the head of an army of men and alvar and even fire-beings. They've killed Kyria."

In a way that made things simpler. Malarset was near to Arcady and Cark and Lapithidia. Which in itself made some kind of sense. Brennarn was the dragon-ruler of Cark. It was late afternoon already—a long flight to Malarset or Arcady. And then looking east, Vorlian saw the answer.

Moon-rise.

"We go to the conclave," he said. "It will transport us west, and give us a height advantage."

"And help us recruit!" said Tessara.

"Will I have trouble there?" asked Vorlian, beginning to beat his way upward.

Tessara shook her head. "The sisterhood of dragons did some investigating, Vorlian. They asked questions of fishermen. The humans bore out your version of events. And they have no reason to lie. Word has been going around about it. But we dragons do not unite and act together easily."

So they flew toward the conclave.

No trouble greeted Vorlian there.

No hellflame either.

The orb was gone from the entry. Just two sheared copper pipes dangled from the plinth.

Vorlian knew what that meant. The creatures of smokeless flame had their "treasure."

And some other dragon had taken it to them.

He was surprised to find himself given a hero's welcome inside.

The lesser fire-being on duty had not known quite what to make of the object that the dragon Myrcupa had deposited on the edge of the fumarole before taking off to complete his allotted work on Malarset. It took the orb down to deposit in the saferoom that the people of the smokeless flame used for objects that were of no use to them. In the process he discovered that two other objects, a bag and a harp, were missing.

The creatures of smokeless flame work according to a strict hierarchy, and many were away, busy with the great program. It took a little while for the news to be dispatched, by the fastest means practical, to King Belet.

— Chapter 47 —

"WE CANNOT LET YOU JUST GO OVER THERE," PROTESTED IXION. "They came purely with the intent of capturing you."

Meb had stopped shaking in reaction by now. The sweet wine she'd been given had helped. Now she was just bloody-mindedly determined. When Ixion had arrived she'd already bullied her way down to the quay and was attempting to bribe the captains of successive vessels to follow the galleys. Despite having offered a fairly large amount in gold, which she seemed to produce by clapping her hands, she hadn't yet had any takers. Then Ixion had told her what Keri had told them. Now she knew where she was going. And if she had to take a rowboat and paddle herself into the dusk across a wildly choppy sea, she'd get there.

Then a vessel had come in—flying a truce flag. It was allowed to approach—under the readied bows of a full phalanx. The bronzed, hard-bodied half-horse warriors were grim faced, unmoving, and apparently ready to kill.

The human messenger found it unnerving. "I come in peace," he said. "I am the high priest of the sacred grove of Arcady. I have a message for a human apprentice to one Finn. A person known as 'Scrap.' And I have a message for the Children of Chiron from the Lady of the Forest."

"Speak," grated Ixion.

The messenger gulped. The bows were still ready. "The Lady of the Forest says to tell the apprentice that we hold her master. If she will return to Isle of Arcady with me, he will be released

311

unharmed. She too will not be hurt. I have been instructed to say to the centaur people to send one representative of their kind along with her, and that the Lady holds the windsack of the centaurs. They will exchange it for the holy staff of Lyr."

Meb felt as if she was going to faint. Only a strong centaur arm prevented her from falling. She started forward. "Wait," said Ixion calmly. "Take back this message to the tree-woman. We will meet in council tonight. If this is agreed we will send a small vessel tomorrow with the dawn, to ascertain that the prisoner is safe and in good health. But tell your mistress to understand this: The act of aggression against us was an act of war."

"Uh . . ."

"Go," said Ixion firmly. "We have no further words to exchange with you."

The priest scrambled back onto the boat. Ixion kept a firm hold on Meb. "It will be all right," he said reassuringly. "This was foretold. We saw the possible battles. We just did not understand it. Now we do. And at least our course is one with honor. And the Lyr are treacherous to the core. Their assurances are worth nothing. But they will see him kept safe until the morrow."

"And then?" asked Meb.

"And then we go to war. We told the messenger that much, but I do not think he will understand it. They are liars—they do not have the windsack—and they attacked us without warning or mercy. We will sail tonight and pay them back in kind. Their magic is effective against the Children of Chiron, but we have their precious staff."

"No, you don't," said Meb firmly. "I do. And I can deal with them. Take me over there."

"You can deal with them?"

Meb put her hands on her hips and faced them. "You got the windsack back from Finn. We fixed your pool. If you want to go and fight with them, you go and fight with them. But me, and this stick, are going over there. I don't know if they'll honor their bargain, or if they lied to me. But I don't care. Finn gave me my life. If it costs me mine for his . . . that's the way it is going to be."

Her speech was slightly marred by the fact that at the end of it, the giddiness overwhelmed her, and she fell over.

She was surprised to see through blurry vision, the great

centaur nodding solemnly. "You are something of a lesson to us, little one. Loyalty to one's own and honor, they are what we are. And, true enough, the staff was given to you. We have no debt of honor to the tree-woman. In fact we owe them a punishment. We will help you in whatever way we can. But first—looking at you—you must rest and eat."

"I'm not going to be a lot of good if I keep passing out like this," admitted Meb. "And I really need a bath. No, Díleas, there is no need to look at me like that. You learn some words very quickly!"

"We'll feed you and provide a place to rest. Would a horse trough do for a bath? We will provide the vessel we promised. We will also ready our transports. We have been preparing for war for many years now. If they do not honor their bargain—we will land and do our best to avenge you and our dead. They can bespell us, but their forests burn," he said, in deadly earnest. "We are in debt to the two of you." He took a deep breath. "And though it was unthinkable before, possibly we are in debt to the black dragon. Not all foreseeing is clear. We saw war as something only to be feared. That we had grown past it, and that its return was an evil we were forced to contemplate. Now . . . yes, it can be. But there is need and honor too."

"I think your courage was in the windsack," said Meb, remembering the way that wild gale had felt.

He nodded. "You see very clearly, human. It was the breath of our nation."

Vorlian had not realized that he was good at giving orders. He also had not realized how good Tessara was at organizing. Vorlian retained a core of some thirty of the largest dragons. But the others were sent as messengers. Calling all to come to the conclave, or to fly toward Malarset. The moon moved westward, and soon they could see Malarset.

Burning. Vorlian knew Arcady would have to wait until morning, although he really felt he ought to get there. They flew out and downward, and, for the first time in hundreds of years, flew to war against other dragons.

In the small hours of the night, the in-coming dragons spotted Brennarn and her cronies feasting on the corpse of Kyria. Marsalet was an island of low, rolling hills, sparsely forested on its granite uplands. Those who had come to ravage the fertile little island had plainly driven its dragon-defender to the last high place, a rounded granite dome. Against the pale grey of the granite the dark spiky shapes of dragons could be seen from above, engaged in a gory noisy dismemberment of their victim. They plainly expected no further resistance to their conquest. Thoughts of being attacked themselves were far from them. The dragons high above looked down in horror and hot rage. Vorlian checked them before they could start to dive. "Hold," he hissed. "This we must deal with together. This we must obliterate. On my word we dive and flame. But you will watch each other. We must arrive together, or we will burn each other."

The dragons flying down on the renegades had never worked together, so it was perhaps less coordinated and effective than it could have been. But, suddenly blanketed in the concentrated dragonfire of at least thirty dragons, the feast became a funeral pyre.

As dragon combat went, it was clinical and quick, the worst damage being that some of Vorlian's allies got their wind tendrils scorched. The gout of flame was probably visible fifty leagues away.

That would have been enough for most of the dragons, but Vorlian marshalled them again. "The compact between the dragons on Tasmarin and the lesser people has been that we protect them. Brennarn, Myrcupa and their companions betrayed us. Now we must show that we honor that compact. There are other invaders. Let us harry them."

Even that might have gone over quite rapidly, had some of the creatures of smokeless flame, invested among the invaders, not tried to fight back. Dragonfire could consume them too. But it didn't end there. The invaders were crazed, it would seem. Alvar and human and sprites tried to take combat to the dragons. Arrows were fired. Ineffectual spells tried. Resistance wasn't something that had happened to the attacking dragons before, and by dawn, they'd made sure that it never would again. And more and more dragons kept coming to join in the fight. As the night wore on, some of the alvar began to surrender. Once again, Vorlian found himself needing to exercise control. The dragons were in no mood for accepting surrender. He had to force his will on them. But they listened. He did have a point. They needed survivors to make sure word got out about the folly of trying this. Some Alvar and humans were spared, thus. It was too late for Prince Gywndar, though. He and several of his nobles tried to flee with their troops, and found out that dragons fly faster than horses run.

By the dawn, though, Vorlian was once again feeling that he ought to fly on Arcady.

So he did.

Of course, a lot of the others followed him.

The mist clung, pinkly pearlescent, to the sea in the light of the new-risen sun, as they flew toward the green, forested island with its single peak that thrust up out of the cloud. Looking back, Vorlian could see the batwing silhouettes of hundreds of dragons against the still purple-dark sky. And on the far horizon stood the great tower, jutting out of the ravel of the sea, defending Tasmarin, anchoring the world. It thrust up dark and monolithic in the first rays of sunlight, windowless, impregnable and old and strong beyond all the fire and strength of dragonkind. It defended the anchor of elsewhere, keeping Tasmarin safe and isolated while it stood across the way to the other planes.

In the shrouding sea-mist Meb found herself on board a part of a mighty flotilla. It was frustratingly slow. To her surprise she'd actually slept like the dead after a good meal, and a much less-than-satisfying wash in a horse trough. The centaurs could be quite civilized in other ways, though. They were completely unworried by the fact that she was not a male, or that she wore trousers, for example. Male and female centaurs all got onto the transports to go to war together, and they were wearing nothing but battle-gear. The same battle gear.

The vessels had been rigged to allow them to row, which was just as well, as it was wind-still down in the cold, damp sea-mist. Meb sat on a small piece of decking near the prow with Díleas—quite the experienced sea-dog, provided he was a reasonable distance from the water—and looked at the black water parting in a slow curl around the bows.

"It would seem that you have a lot of company," said the merrow, surfing the bow-wave, turning to speak to her. "We and the sea are in your debt. Can we help you?"

"The sprites have got Finn as a captive on their island. They offered to free him in exchange for me."

"The sprites are not to be trusted," said the merrow shortly. "Wait. I go to call Hrodenynbrys."

A little later 'Brys put his head up. The familiar jesting tone was missing from his speech. "They'll kill him and you, girl, if they have the chance. It is weak we are against them, and strong that they are against us. Still, we'll stand by you."

Then Meb saw how the froth from the bow-wave curled and the phosphorescence shaped itself into a face. A woman's face, and it spoke with a woman's voice. "But she is not weak. Her magic is strong against them. And it is reinforced by the magic of the dvergar, who have great power over them, and the dragons whose fire they are powerless against. There is also the power of wood-stone about the opal, and water and light. You and the dog carry primal fire, and some of the breath of the centaurs, it would seem. And besides all of that, you gave me my own again. You can call on the water. I can bring a wave that will wash clean all but the mountain. I'll even bring that down in time," said the sea.

Meb had spoken to the mountain. So she was, after that initial moment, less taken aback than she would have been. She bowed politely. "Primal fire. I don't understand? And I'm not too sure about the rest either, really."

"The glowing jewels on your dog's collar, and on the chain around your waist. The dragon gave you a piece of primal fire each to protect you. It is both precious and powerful."

"He really is a dragon, then?"

The sea laughed. "Oh yes. One of the oldest and the first."

"I love him anyway."

The sea sighed. "It cannot always work . . ."

"That," said Meb firmly, "is because the two of you want your own way all the time. Find a mountain that comes down to the sea. Finn said that most islands are just mountains in the sea anyway. Now, tell me about the rest?"

There was a pause. "I see that the breath of the centaurs added still more to your courage. Tell him I will think about it. I need my freedom too."

"So does he," said Meb firmly. "Work around it. Finn says there is always more than one way of doing anything."

"And he should know," said the sea. "Well, as to the rest. You are a human mage, with the power of summonsing. You can command the powers of the earth, of stone, of fertility. The dvergar made that more powerful still by giving you a talisman of gold full of dragon-magic, and of course their own artifice. So you can command strength and fire and gold—the attributes of dragons. You are proofed against the rest to a greater or lesser degree."

"But how . . . I don't know any spells or anything?"

"Just tell them. That sort of power needs no aid. It will find its own way. And the land is close now. There is water there. I will be listening. Call on me in need."

"And you think about what I said," said Meb, gruffly. "Seeing as you're here, 'Brys, play her that last song you played for Groblek."

High up on the plains of Lapithidia, well above the mist, the centaurs that surrounded the foreseeing pool waited eagerly for the light. It was wind-still, and the surface of it was like polished sliver.

If they had looked far out towards the dawn they would have seen dragons tiny in the distance. Instead they focussed on the pool. Which showed them much the same as looking over their shoulders would have.

Except it also showed the black dragon. And for once, an unclouded view of the face of the mage.

They'd seen her before, and not in the pool. Standing next to it.

Actaeon, for so long a spy and exiled in the course of his stern duty to watch over the conspiracies between the creatures of smokeless flame, sprite, alvar and dragon, arrived at Port Lapith in the misty dawn. He'd had a mishap-ful journey, but he was home. He jumped from the ship to shore. Breathed the air of home. It was the same air he had been breathing from a few yards away, but it tasted better, made him feel stronger. He was greeted by a clattering-hoofed sentry patrolling the empty dock. "Hail!" he said. "I need to find my brother Ixion. And to carry word to the high plains. The black dragon is disguised as a human called Finn. He is actually the dragon Fionn. He's accompanied by a woman, a human mage."

"Hail Actaeon," said the sentry. "Ixion is away with the war fleet, bound for Arcady."

"What?"

The other centaur stopped. It was Cyllarus, with a bandaged shoulder. "We should have guessed she was a human mage. She restored the pool, she and the one we now know is the black dragon himself."

He paused. "We may have misunderstood our vision."

═ Chapter 48 ═

MEB, DÍLEAS AND IXION HAD BOARDED THE SMALL BOAT. MEB HAD to reflect, again, that centaurs ought to stay on land. They were ill-suited to ships, and even worse suited to small boats. Still, the water was quiet, and it was not too far to row.

Up on the bow as they came in sight of the mist-twined shore line Díleas growled. A deep angry burr that ought to come from the throat of a mountain-lion, not from a few pounds of young sheepdog. Meb took the chain that she had wrapped around her waist and threaded it through his collar.

They nudged into the shore with the keel crunching on the coarse sand. The water was virtually still, but a sudden wave pushed the boat up and broached it sideways. They stepped out into the wash. There, higher up the beach, stood ranks of sprites, and among them hooded and cloaked glowing creatures.

"I said that she would come," said one of the fire-beings.

"Seize them," said the sprite.

"Hold!" shouted Ixion in a voice that carried out into the mist like a clarion. It was enough to give pause even the sprites and fire-beings. "The centaurs lie offshore within earshot, many thousands strong." He held up his horn. "If I sound this, they will come. With fire and axe, they will come. We know your strengths, but still they will come. And the commanders watch an hourglass. If I do not sound the right call on the horn on the hour, they will come. We expected your treachery. We will bring down the wind on your demon allies. They are not proof against us."

319

"And if you think that's all," said Meb, her voice grim, "try me."
Finally, she'd had enough. "I can turn you to stone. Remember
that. You offered a deal. Now take us to Finn. Then I'll stay as
your captive or whatever. When you have let him go, safely. Not
before."

The breeze stirred the mist around the tall, pale, tree-women.
They stood still. Then one of the fire-beings—a taller, larger individual—said, "Let them have their way. For now."

Meb decided she'd trust him just as far as she could throw
Groblek. He was going to try some form of spell or trickery on
them. Well, she didn't know if it would work, but she tried to
think of a shield over her and Ixion.

The sprites and the fire-beings formed up in a mass around
them as they walked uphill.

"It appears that you have some of the very life stuff of smokeless fire about you," said the fire-being a little later.

"Oh yes," said Meb. They had lied to her, she'd lie straight
back. "One of your kind tried to make me come to him. That's
what could happen to you." The mist was thinning now and a
stiff breeze was blowing. They'd come to an enormous rock that
must have rolled down from the mountain eons ago. Just ahead
a stream splashed in the valley.

It had been getting lighter as mist burned off.

Now it got much darker. Something enormous flapped at the
last of mist. A dragon settled slowly down to land.

"Lord Vorlian. We are all gathered," said the demon. "Let us
call a merrow and one of the dvergar."

"I'd be thinking there is no need for that," said 'Brys from the
water. "And I'd guess the dvergar would be around here somewhere
too. They have tunnels everywhere."

Meb looked at the huge dragon. "Are you Finn?"

"Finn?" asked the dragon, looking at her.

"Uh. Fionn."

Vorlian shook his great head. "No. But you are his companion.
The one we seek to remake Tasmarin. Will you help us? Our world
breaks. Only with a human mage can we remake it."

The fire-being nodded his flame. "This is our quest. To save
the world. It is in great danger. One guardian tower has fallen.
The others show cracks. We must act now. As soon as possible.
With great urgency."

Meb had almost been swept up by the honest conviction in the dragon's voice until the fire-being spoke.

"There is the matter of the treasures," said the dragon.

"They can be restored as soon as it is done," said the fire-being. "There is no time. War, chaos and confusion spreads across the land." He pointed to a group of alvar standing under the trees—looking very much the worse for wear. "Here are alvar from Malarset. They brought word this morning of the blight that spreads. Let them tell you of the horror. It is a magical thing . . ."

"Show me Finn," said Meb interrupting.

"He is here. We had to ensure his cooperation . . ."

The fire-being had led her forward. There, under the edge of the rock was a stone slab. Some cords. A sleepy looking lizard, that scrambled away leaving only a twitching tail.

No Finn.

The sprites and the fire-beings were all as surprised as it was possible to be. More so than Meb, the truth be told.

Díleas barked. Jerked at the leash—one end of which slipped free. He ran through the sprites and up the edge of the earth-embedded side of the huge rock.

The rock grumbled and slowly sat down on the empty stone slab. The lizard scampered away.

Looking up, Meb saw her dog dancing around a black dragon, sitting next to an elderly black-haired dvergar. Motsognir.

"I smell right, I suppose," said the dragon in Finn's voice. "You should have known better than to leave me so close to a dvergar hole. And they too were watching this place."

Meb shrieked and ran, too. A sprite tried to stop her, only to get a slap that sent it, petrifying as it fell, to the ground. She hugged Finn's dragonish neck, tears running down her cheeks.

"Well," said the creature of smokeless flame. "How charming, if a little odd. Food that loves its devourer. Nonetheless, by agreement or by compulsion, the renewal must be done. We have the balance of power." He pointed upward. The last of the mist was burning off, and through it they could make out dragon shapes, circling. "And there is an emergency that must be dealt with. Malarset and many other lands are aflame."

"It was only Malarset," said Vorlian. "We could see most of Tasmarin from the conclave. It's a bunch of stupid and renegade dragons, humans, alvar and fire-beings. I'll want some explanation about that, Belet, because your kind will only act on orders. We've dealt with them. Fionn. You and I need to talk." He looked at the rest of the assembled species. "Although I have differences with some of my co-conspirators, I think we need to work together. Human mage, I beg your help. I never thought I would beg a human . . . but I love this place. It is a place of dragons . . . but we will change the way things are. And I will guarantee your safety and your freedom in exchange for your help."

"And he is an honorable dragon," said Fionn cheerfully. "And by the looks of it he has managed to unite most of dragonkind behind him."

Vorlian bowed his head slightly. "Thank you. I . . . was mistaken about you, Fionn. Misinformed."

"Indeed," said Fionn. "It's a pity that you are also misinformed about what the creatures of smokeless flame seek to do. The consequences of attempting to recreate the magics of this place without returning the tokens of trust—the treasures as you called them—to their own species—would be catastrophic for those species. Let me guess. You were at the conclave. Does the light at the entrance of the caverns still burn? The hellflame?"

"Uh. No. It is gone . . . I never had time to investigate," said Vorlian, taken aback.

"I would think that it has been transported to the fumaroles of the fire-beings," Finn sniggered. "And very happy they must be with it. Actually, Vorlian, that's what I've been up to the last while. You see, when I destroyed the first tower, I discovered that without those treasures the life forms and intelligent species of Tasmarin will die or be torn apart, and not return to their source. So my assistant and I have been working on returning them to their rightful owners. Speaking of which," he turned to Meb, "will you give the sprites back theirs? They're a painful and foolish bunch, but you have to save the bad with the good sometimes."

Meb nodded and took the stick out of her pack. A low moan went up from the sprites. She walked down from the rock with Finn. She reached out to hand it back to the nearest sprite. . . .

To have a fire-being seize it. The stick burst into flames. Meb nearly dropped it when a sudden spray of water from the stream put it out. It soaked her too, but that was the least of their problems. The sprites were shrieking in anguish.

"Treachery!" shouted Belet. "Quick, dragon. The human burned..." He was doused with a shower of water himself. He may have said some more, but it was lost in the steaming hiss.

It was not going to kill him, by the looks of it, but it certainly shut him up. "What nonsense you'd be speaking," said Hrodenyn-brys. "It was you yourself that set it afire. The human has given us the Angmarad. And they returned the hammer to the dvergar."

"And the windsack to us," said Ixion.

"I've even returned the harp to Loftalvar," said Fionn.

The only sound that came from the sprites was a low wailing.

Meb, still full of fear and anger at the act of treachery by the fire-being Belet, looked at the piece of charred stick that remained. And felt the agony of the sprite. Wished desperately that she could make it right.

She nearly dropped the burned stick as it began to writhe and expand in her hand. She grabbed it with both hands to stop doing so... It was a stick again... only it was a green stick. With swelling buds. Motsognir pushed past her. Hauled out a small spade and dug a hole. "You can rely on the dvergar for digging. I think you should plant it."

Finn nodded his dragonish head. "Good advice."

So Meb did. It was quite a relief. It was growing as she did it so. Sprouting leaves already and roots writhing into the earth as she pushed soil onto them. The sprites were weeping. Touching each other. Staring at the sapling as if it was their one hope and delight.

"We should never have given him up," said one of the tree-women tremulously. "We thought he was gone. Lost forever. All we could ever have was the token. The memory." She turned to face Meb, dragging her eyes from the still-growing sapling with obvious difficulty. "Lyr is forever in your debt. That was human magic. Earth magic."

"Learn, Lyr," said Finn. "They can cut down and burn. But they can also make grow. They are not for your casual killing, or they can take that back."

"Fionn," said Vorlian. "Can you and I not get the last of the treasures, and then," he bowed to Meb, "With your help, renew this place? I must do this. I must even if I must fight and force you. And I have all of dragonkind with me."

"Let me explain why it should not be done," said Finn.

"It *must* be done," said Vorlian. Meb saw him drawing breath to call the circling dragons.

She called instead to the sea, her last hope.

And got, in an outrush of air, two gigantic figures. Groblek, with his fingers entwined with those of a tall woman with long wavy hair.

Groblek put a huge finger on top of Vorlian. "Shall I crush you, little dragon?" he said in a voice of thunder.

"Vorlian, just stay very still and behave yourself," said Finn. "Not even dragonkind can fight either the mountains or the sea, let alone both of them. I'd say you labor under a very powerful compulsion, my dragon friend," said Finn. "It takes the First themselves to compel me. But any two of the species can set a compulsion on most dragons."

A frightened looking alv scuttled forward. "It's true, Lord. The creatures of smokeless flame and the Lyr set it on him."

"Rennalinn," said Finn. "Why am I not surprised. What did they promise you? Speak up, and for that confession, we'll let you survive."

"Rule over the alvar," said the sprite. "And we release you, Vorlian. Our will is no longer part of binding you."

"I think you can let him go now, Groblek," said Finn. "Having a mountain hold you down is hard even on a dragon." Vorlian straightened a little and looked nervously up at the giant . . . but made no other move.

Finn continued. "Vorlian, I've told you and the others many times, that I am going to destroy Tasmarin. I never said why. I am a planomancer. It is my purpose to fix energy flows to keep worlds whole. It is because the energy of many worlds—and that is part of the magic—is trapped here, depriving them of most of their magic, making them more fragile. The pieces that are Tasmarin need to go back. If we take more, to repair the damage here . . . we will break more of them. And here? Water will rush in here, and new mountains will rise with massive volcanoes. It's unlikely anything—bar the fire-beings and possibly the merrows—would live through it, especially without the treasures. That was why the creatures of smokeless flame wanted the merrow treasure, and obstructed any efforts to return the rest. And now it is the fire-people—and the dragons—who are the only ones left without them."

"We have ours. It was returned to us by our hirelings," said Belet sullenly. "You have no lever over us."

Finn chuckled. "Oh yes, I do. You see, you sent them to fetch the flame from outside the conclave."

"Yes," said Belet. "It is safe in our keeping."

"Actually, it isn't. You see, I removed the original and put it safe in *my* keeping some centuries back. The object they stole was a gas-light," said Finn with a nasty grin. "Ask Motsognir here. I bought it from him."

The dvergar nodded. "Maybe five hundred years back."

Belet hissed and spluttered.

"I would check," said Finn. "But I think you're in for a nasty surprise."

Vorlian cleared his throat. "I know I am in a poor position to speak for anyone. I . . . I even knew about the compulsion of dragons. I just . . . I should have worked out I was compelled, but . . ."

"It is very hard to make a compulsion work against your basic nature, Vorlian," said Finn. "You did want to preserve this place. That's why they didn't use you for their dirty work. The likes of Myrcupa and Brennarn had it come naturally to them—they were pushed in a direction they were willing to go. You're not a bad fellow for a dragon. A bit pompous, but it goes with having bad breath."

Vorlian swallowed. Realized he was being mocked—as usual. "Fionn. Can I make a public apology for being . . . pompous. I've been humbled, and I've learned. My breath is much like yours." He smiled, and bowed his head respectfully. "I think I have learned that only the truly powerful can afford to mock themselves."

"Good thinking, for a dragon," said Finn. "Now what did you want to say? Or was that too long ago to remember? Big dragons tend to become dim-witted."

Vorlian cleared his throat. "I wanted to make a plea for dragonkind. If the plane is going to break up, and the safety of the other species is assured by their treasures . . . I'd like that of the dragons to be returned to them. And . . . I feel responsible for this. I would give my hoard in exchange for it. And it would seem that the cauldron of humans must be in the sprites' possession. I think that they too should give it up."

"Lyr concurs," said one of the forest of sprites around the new tree. "Gladly!"

Finn looked slyly at Motsognir, and put a dragon-wing over

Meb, who had returned to having an arm around his neck. "I think," he said, "that the gold of the dragons will best stay where it is. You'd all better get used to treating humans a little better, because you owe a lot of your wellbeing to my Scrap of humanity. The rest is in the fabric of Tasmarin itself. It goes with you and you will scatter with it. Across the ring of worlds there will be dragons again. Being nice to humans, just in case."

A dragon circled in. "There are ships full of centaurs attempting to land. What do you want us to do, Vorlian?"

Ixion shook himself. "I will go and tell them all is well! Ah, the tale! And I was the one to hear it. I will tell it to the herds!" He shook himself again. "It is immortality of a kind. Will you wait until I return?" he pleaded.

"If you agree to tell it to a few other people beside centaurs," said Meb, going over and hugging him. "I could get to like you. Although you really need to learn about baths."

He bowed. "The matter of baths will be debated." And he left at a gallop.

Vorlian turned to the other dragon. "Fly up there, tell the others to settle. And whatever they do, not to eat any humans."

"They disagree with me anyway," said the smaller female dragon. "Hello, Fionn. Have you got yourself a pet human now?"

"I think she has me, Tessara," said Finn. "Now all that remains to be done is to settle matters with the creatures of smokeless flame. Unfortunately, I am supposed to keep you alive."

"Wait for the centaurs," said Motsognir. "They hate missing any part of the story."

So they did. The creatures of smokeless flame had gathered together in the meanwhile, standing a little apart from the rest. Finn looked at them, and looked at the tree-women adoring the fast growing sapling. "Well done there, little one," he said quietly. "They'll breed now."

"Won't that be worse?" said Meb, doubtfully.

"Some will be. Some will be better. At the moment they're all the same. But the offspring won't be."

A group of panting centaurs came galloping back, with Ixion at their head.

"So glad you could make it," said Finn.

"So are we," said the centaurs, entirely missing the sardonic tone.

"Well," said Fionn. "It's going to be an anticlimax for you.

We've given the rest back. Anghared will call the hell-flame here, smokeless flames. Maybe. If you ask her nicely. And remember that the dragons know where you live, and can fry you."

"Indeed," rumbled Vorlian. "Although, I am in favor of frying Belet as an example. And I am not happy with them compelling dragons."

"I think we will put a stop to that, yes," said Finn. "The rest of us can put a compulsion on them that will be hard to over-ride. We have representatives of all the intelligent species here—although I am reluctant to use Rennalinn . . ."

Meb didn't even know she was doing it. Leilin and her sister suddenly appeared next to Groblek and the Sea. Leilin's sister had a silver harp in her hand.

Finn looked at the two of them. Looked at Meb. "Whatever you do," he said quietly. "Don't let her play that thing with 'Brys. We don't want the world to end just yet."

One of the fire-beings spoke. "We do not like this. But we accept it because we have no choice. We have used what power we have to confirm that we do not have the hell-flame. So: we beg. Belet will be no more. There will be new kings, and a re-ordering of energies."

The situation was rapidly explained to the two startled-looking alvar.

"How do I do this?" Meb asked Finn quietly, still holding on to him.

"The little bauble on the end of your chain and on Díleas's collar has a fragment of the life-energy of their treasure in it. Concentrate on it and call the rest—over there, somewhere."

So she stared at the bauble. And the tiny glowing heart of it explained itself to her mind. And when she understood it, she understood the creatures of smokeless flame better. She didn't have to like them better.

It was a hot and nasty feeling.

While this was happening the others worked a slow steady chant, led by the centaurs around them. Meb walked closer with Finn, and of course Díleas to join in. Together, all the intelligent creatures leashed the creatures of smokeless flame. Meb felt strange intangible spiderwebs of demon magic snapping as they did so.

It was done, and it would be a slightly sweeter world. So she called their fire-ball to them.

But at the last minute she held it away. Kept it floating high above them. She'd learned a great deal, looking into it.

She hadn't realized that you could read things as well as books, and that energy was everything.

She had seen the destruction and scattering of all the parts that were Tasmarin.

She saw the fall of the next tower and the effect that would have on the remainder. It had taken Fionn fifty years to break the first. That had weakened the whole structure so that it would be mere months before the second one fell. The cascade of extra energies onto the next would make it fall in months, and then the next in days.

The place she called home was going to shred and scatter.

In her mind's eye she captured the view across Yenfar. The city beneath the waves . . . the pool of the centaurs amid the ruins.

And where they would go. And what would happen.

She pulled herself up straight and decided that it would not be so.

═ Chapter 49 ═

IN THE GLARE OF A BALL OF FIRE THAT HUNG IN THE AIR ABOVE them Meb stepped forward and raised her voice.

"My master has let many of you put yourselves in my debt. I have used my magic to help you. Now I am calling the debt I am owed due." She turned to Groblek and the Sea. "I am calling on the mountains and I call on the sea." She looked to the centaurs, and then as she called them, each of the other species. "I call to the wind and water, the earth, and metals under the earth, the light, the things that grow. Even the fire."

They all looked at her. Ixion, and another centaur that looked almost identical to him, put their heads back and nodded. They blew at her, and she felt the strength of that small magical gift, and continued. "I have given all of you your own. I have brought you together. Now, I remind you of what my Master has said to me: 'There is always another way.' Tasmarin does not have to be destroyed."

Finn shook his head. "It is a wondrous place, Anghared. But it must go. The towers are its anchors. They hold back the energies that hold Tasmarin together and isolate it. Those are energies that are needed in the greater ring of worlds."

She turned to Finn, using what she'd just learned. "You used to balance the great ring of worlds. You explained to me that the problem was that they cannot be isolated. That magic and many other energies are trapped here. Yet . . . the energy flowed between them when they were not isolated and they did not collapse. Can't we break down the towers, but keep Tasmarin? It is only the isolation that we cannot have."

Finn stood silent, calculating. Then he began to scratch formulae in the dirt.

"You will need to insert the iterative function there," said Groblek helpfully. "But it can be done. Just as neither the mountains nor the sea are limited to this place, but here you can talk to us. This plane too does not have to confined to any one place. It can be the linkage to many. Part of them and part of itself."

Finn snorted. "You tempt me to make you calculate it. It's doable . . . but Tasmarin will lose a little in the balancing. Gain a little too, of course. It won't be isolated. It won't be a place of dragons. It would be a way between the many planes of existence."

Vorlian cleared his throat. "Compared to the alternative, where we would have been destroyed, or even, Fionn, if you succeed—and there is nothing to stop you right now—scattered across the ring of planes from whence our ancestors came, that's a good option. We can stand together by choice too."

Fionn looked thoughtfully at him. "It'll need a lot more gold."

"Lots of gold always flows through a cross-roads. You'll recoup," said Motsognir. "We like the idea."

"It is what was foretold. The clouded mage with the black dragon, and nothing is certain. Every other path leads to destruction," said the centaur next to Ixion. "But this one is uncertain."

"It's a cheerful bunch you are," said 'Brys. "Uncertain is best!"

The fire-being who had spoken earlier asked. "Will we be able to return at will to the plane we were taken from?"

Finn nodded. "This place will be a transition between many planes."

"Then we will lend it our powers. We are tired of being cold."

The others reached agreement easily enough too.

Meb tugged at Fionn's wing. "Can we talk a little? Away from everyone?"

He smiled. "Of course. I am always yours. Although I am not sure Díleas is willing to let you out of his sight."

They walked off a little way to where they could look out over the ocean toward the tower.

"I looked too deep into the flame," said Meb. "It . . . showed me the breaking of everything . . . and the past and some pieces of future. It's . . . not all very nice."

"Could-be future," said Fionn. "It is energy and all things are that . . . the form the creatures of smokeless flame have taken, and aspects of the nature of the First, are not very attractive. But they are a part of all things too. I like the way you have solved it, though. Groblek says that it will work."

She put her arms around his neck. Squeezed exceptionally hard for a small human. "Finn. Always remember I love you." Then she bent down and cuddled Díleas so that he would not see her tears. But he did anyway. "Now let us do this thing," she said gruffly.

He wondered what was wrong. "I love you too, Anghared. I am not used to this. I have . . . distanced myself from it. And dragons do not mate for life."

"You are not 'a dragon.' You're Finn. And I am Scrap. Your Scrap. Not Anghared."

As was often the case with great and powerful magics, it was deceptively simple. It did involve the redistribution of a lot of dragon gold. And a willing binding of all of them into something that as a collective organism was not unlike the First, but more powerful, with the sharing of the power of the sea and the mountains too.

The towers, great, and near impregnable, crumbled . . . with the roaring of trumpets and the shivering of light . . . And a dance, carefully choreographed, of energy and gold leaped across the vast distances, which were also nothing at all.

And the shimmering dust of the towers reformed into bridges. Bridges of adamantine stone reaching out into elsewhere.

And when it was done . . .

Fionn felt the great flow of energies rushing back and flowing in. He looked at where the tower had stood, at the bridge from the island of Arcady to the distant forests, elsewhere. To rolling hills and limitless dusty plains, and towering mountains and seas that ranged from limpid blue to surging gray, and to dark places that rumbled with fire. To the great ring of worlds, plane linked to plane and linked to this magical place.

And then he realized that he was no longer holding her hand in his.

Groblek and the Sea stood next to him. There was sadness and understanding in their eyes.

"Where is she?" he demanded.

"She's been drawn back to where she came from, Fionn," said Groblek. "She was the one thing that was not of this place. She unbalanced it. She knew that would happen. And she knew the cost of her not going back."

"What . . . what could that be?" asked Fionn, his mouth dry.

"You," said the Sea. "This place must balance or you would die. She chose that that would not happen."

Díleas looked around at the emptiness where the heart of his world should be. He put his head back and howled.

Fionn felt like joining him.

Then the black-and-white sheepdog got up, and started walking towards the new bridge.

For a moment Fionn just looked at him. Then he picked up his bag and followed. "We'll find her, boy," said Fionn. "Somewhere, somehow, we'll find her. There is always a way."

Dog and dragon walked out together, into the endless ring of worlds.

= Glossary =

Alba	alvar capital on Yenfar.
Arcady	sprite's sacred island warmed by a warm ocean current.
Angmarad	treasure of merrows.
Cark	island used by fire-being to train troops of janissaries on.
Conclave	a meeting place for dragons on the artificially-near magically supported moon.
Cliff Cove	Meb's home village.
Dark pool	the foreseeing pool of the centaurs.
Malarset	island to the south west of Arcady.
Tarport	the main harbour of Yenfar.
Thessalia, Laconia and Lapithidia	island territory of the centaurs.
Starsey	the dragon Vorlian's demesnes.
Sea of the dead/ land beneath the waves	area within the underwater caldera with Starsey, Pallin and Morth forming the edges.

Soul traps   made of human hair with the souls of
                        drowned sailors inside.

Yenfar   large island ruled by Zuamar that Meb
                        lives on.

INTELLIGENT SPECIES (are magically effective against next
two, have power over various magics)

Fire-beings   fire, heat, energy.

Humans   earth magic.

Dvergar   metal, artifice.

Sprites/Lyr   land plants, trees.

Merrows   water, sea more than fresh water.

Centaurs   wind.

Alvar   light.

Dragons   are able to generate fire that will even
                        disassociate fire-beings.

TREASURES

Fire-beings   hell-flame (held by dragons).

Humans   copper bottomed cauldron of plenty (held
                        by sprites).

Dvergar   hammer of artifice (held by merrows).

Sprites/Lyr   staff (held by centaurs).

Merrows   Angmarad—a crown of dried bladder-
                        wrack and sea-jewels (held by alvar).

Centaurs   windsack—the breath of the nation (held
                        by fire-beings).

Alvar   silver harp of Tirithu (held by fire-
                        beings).

Dragons   golden dragon (held by dvergar).

About the Author

DAVE FREER IS AN ICHTHYOLOGIST TURNED AUTHOR BECAUSE he'd heard that the spelling requirements were simpler. They lied about that. He lives in a remote part of KwaZulu-Natal, South Africa, with his wife and chief proofreader, Barbara, four dogs and four cats, two sons (Paddy and James) and just at the moment no shrews, birds, bats or any other rescued wildlife. His first book—*The Forlorn* (Baen)—came out in 1999. Since then he has co-authored with Eric Flint (*Rats, Bats and Vats, The Rats, the Bats and the Ugly, Pyramid Scheme* and *Pyramid Power, The Sorceress of Karres*) and with Mercedes Lackey and Eric Flint (*The Shadow of the Lion, This Rough Magic, The Wizard of Karres*) as well as writing various shorter works. Besides working as a Fisheries Scientist for the Western Cape shark fishery, running a couple of fish farms, he has worked as a commercial diver and as a relief chef at several luxury game lodges. Yes: he can both cook and change diapers. (No man ever really gets tired of danger sports.) He spent two years as a conscripted soldier along the way, so he can iron too. His interests are rock climbing (he's still good at it), diving, flyfishing (he's still bad at it), fly-tying, wine-tasting and the preparation of food, especially by traditional means—smoking and salting, all the good unhealthy things.